Toward Home

MB PANICHI

Bella
BOOKS

2014

Bella Books, Inc.
P.O. Box 10543
Tallahassee, FL 32302

Printed in the United States of America on acid-free paper.

First Bella Books Edition 2014

Editor: Cath Walker
Cover Designer: KIARO Creative Ltd.

ISBN: 978-1-59493-400-1

Other Bella Books by MB Panichi

Saving Morgan

Acknowledgments

I want to thank my wife, April, for all her love and support and for having the patience to live with a distracted and preoccupied writer. Thank you, sweetie. I love you! Thanks to my family and friends for all their love and support as I follow this dream path, and to the BABA's for always being just an email or a phone call away! All of you rock!

Huge thanks go to my editor, Cath Walker, for her wisdom and guidance. Cath really helped tighten up the manuscript and make this book work. And always, thanks to Bella for continuing to take a chance on me!

About the Author

MB Panichi lives in Richfield, Minnesota in a little house on the corner with her wife and three dogs. *Running Toward Home* is her second published book and is the sequel to *Saving Morgan*. MB holds down a day job as a QA Analyst and Software Developer. She still obsesses about her drums and her old "heavy metal" band days. When she isn't watching the dogs she is either reading or writing or spending time with her wife.

Dedication

This book is dedicated to everyone who is a sucker for adventure, romance and a good story. This is for all of you, and I truly hope you enjoy the ride.

CHAPTER ONE

The candy-red MicroCruz Racer 3500 air car streaked through the summer sky, flying in the sky lanes over the plains of the North American Midwest. The car's sleek lines drew a thin, fast-moving shadow over the fields below.

Morgan Rahn leaned back in the leather passenger seat, legs stretched out under the brushed aluminum dashboard, one arm draped across the padded center console, her fingers entwined with her girlfriend's. The air vents feathered her dark hair off her face. She reveled in the feel of the outside air on her skin, even if it smelled vaguely of dust and the exhaust fumes of vehicles they passed. Morgan squinted against the light and smiled at the heat of the sun warming her skin through the car's moon roof.

She cast a glance at Shaine Wendt, who drove the souped-up air car with comfortable ease. Shaine nodded her head absently in time to the music playing on the sound system. Morgan appreciated the lines of Shaine's strong hand guiding the joystick with exacting control, long fingers wrapped around the silicone-coated chrome. Her rippling arm muscles slid beneath smooth skin as she shifted the controls.

Shaine was so beautiful, Morgan thought, all angular lines and strength. Her thick red hair was spiked barely an inch high and cut closely at her neck and over her ears. Broad shoulders stretched the tight black T-shirt she wore. Even sitting, she was tall. Morgan loved the stretch of her long legs in tight leather. Shaine still carried herself with the confidence of the military commando she'd been a decade ago. Morgan squeezed Shaine's hand, as always amazed at the warmth and comfort of her grip.

Shaine grinned. "Having fun?" she asked.

Morgan smiled. "Absolutely."

Shaine said, "If you think this is great, you oughta try a road-trip on an open-cockpit air bike."

Morgan shook her head. "No thanks. This is about as open-air as I plan on getting."

Shaine laughed.

Morgan turned back to the window, fascinated by the view. She was a spacer—born and raised on the Asteroid Belt's many mining facilities and on Moon Base. Like most true spacers, her skin was smooth and very pale because of the lack of exposure to true sunlight and weather. Her straight black hair fell just to her shoulders, feathered away from her face. Her bangs fell in wispy strands over wide gray eyes.

She couldn't wait to be able to sit in the sun. She wanted to feel the warmth of it on her skin and to experience what she'd only read about or seen in vids. This was only her third visit to Earth. She didn't really remember the first time—she'd been barely five years old. Her parents had taken her to the North American West Coast to visit her mother's relatives. Her father said she'd played in the ocean and loved it. She wished she could remember more than vague images of blue sky and water.

Her second visit had been a few years ago, with her ex-girlfriend Gina, and it was an experience she would rather forget. Gina took her to New York City, so Morgan could experience a "real" city. Morgan freaked out, overwhelmed by the press of people and the assault of unfamiliar smells and tastes and images. Instead of trying to help her adjust, Gina teased her and made her feel even worse.

Her third visit, only weeks ago, she had been running for her life with Shaine. There hadn't been time for sight-seeing or lying in the sun. This time, Shaine was taking her to a much quieter, less intense place—not an adventure and not an overwhelming experience.

They were headed to the organic farm Shaine's family owned, in the Territory of Iowa in the United Federation of the Americas. Shaine promised she would introduce Morgan to all the horses, cows, chickens and goats, but she wasn't sure she was quite ready for that.

In their short few weeks together, Shaine hadn't revealed much about her youth. She tended to talk more about her years in Earth Guard, and, occasionally, the time she worked for Mann-Maru Universal's corporate Security Department, though rarely about her time as an agent in Rogan's covert Security Group.

As they sped through the sky lanes toward the farm, Morgan found herself thinking about what it would have been like to grow up on Earth. She could hardly imagine living in a place where there was so much empty space or so much freedom to move around. She wondered how Shaine felt about her life here.

As the fields and farmland flew past, she turned her head to study Shaine's sharply-featured profile. Her expression was relaxed, with a hint of a smile on her lips. Shaine's hair had grown out over the last month. Morgan slipped her hand from Shaine's and ran her fingers through the thick strands.

Shaine sighed, leaning into the caress with a contented purr.

Morgan traced light patterns at the base of Shaine's neck, twisting lightly into the short hair. She asked, "Are you excited to see your family?"

Shaine glanced over briefly before returning her attention to the heads-up display of the sky lane projected in front of the driver's side windshield. There wasn't much traffic. In the last hour, they'd passed a handful of passenger cars and a single cargo transport.

Shaine nodded. "Yeah, I am." A wistful smile creased her lips. "It'll be good to have a chance to visit, to connect again. It's been too long."

"How long?"

Shaine sighed. "A little over three years," she admitted. "I was going to go back after I left Rogan's Security Group, before I settled on Moon Base, but things didn't work out. I think I avoided it because I didn't want to talk to my family about what I was doing in covert security. Mom would ask too many questions." She shrugged. "She probably still will."

Morgan processed that. "What about after you were discharged from the EG? You spent time here after that, didn't you?"

"While I was learning to walk again?"

Morgan heard the bitterness in Shaine's voice and noticed the tension as she adjusted her grip on the joystick.

"Yeah, I was here. I don't think I would have made it through all that physical therapy without their support. My nephew Toby was my little angel through it. He was the only one who could convince me it was going to be all right, that there was a reason to move ahead." She frowned, lost in memories. "It wasn't just losing my leg. It was losing my squad mates, and trying to accept that there wasn't anything I could have done to save them. It took a long time to be okay with the fact I was still alive."

Morgan's heart broke for Shaine, for the pain reflected in her eyes. She caught Shaine's hand and brought it to her lips, gently kissing her knuckles.

Shaine murmured, "I think I'm looking forward to seeing Toby the most." Abruptly, she shook off the darkness and a grin lit up her face. "He's gonna love you, Morg."

"I hope so. I hope they're okay with me being there."

Shaine laughed. "Oh, no worries about that. Mom and Leese will be absolutely out of their minds that I'm actually bringing someone home. They've been pissing at me about it for as long as I can remember. They'll probably make you as crazy as they make me."

Morgan raised a brow. "You never brought anyone home?"

Shaine shrugged. "Wasn't any reason to."

"I can't believe you didn't have dates falling at your feet."

"Who said I didn't?" Shaine grinned. "I just didn't have any reason to bring anyone home."

Morgan wrinkled her nose, knowing Shaine was tweaking her. Still, she wasn't entirely sure where their relationship stood.

Morgan turned back to the window. She felt like she and Shaine were more than just casual lovers. She felt a deeper connection to Shaine than anyone she'd ever been with. She trusted Shaine with her life, quite literally. More and more, she also trusted her with her heart. Was this what it meant to be in love? Did it mean anything special that Shaine was taking her home to meet her family? Did it mean that they were serious? That maybe they were forever?

Or was this just a convenient place to go to get away from the media hounds that had latched on to her since they discovered her hidden birthright?

Her birth father, Tarm Maruchek, was one of the most wealthy and politically connected men in the world. As founder and CEO of Mann-Maru Universal Industries, he had indirect control of millions of workers' lives. His corporation owned more asteroid mining facilities than any other. Mann-Maru ran Moon Base Security and Operations, as well as the space docks and the ships' maintenance crews at Moon Base, from which supplies were routed between Earth and the Asteroid Belt facilities.

Morgan worked for Mann-Maru as a Ships' Systems Mechanic for over a decade before her best friend, Digger, had become the victim of terrorists out to destroy Mann-Maru. Digger's death was the catalyst that caused her to learn the identity of her birth father and made her a target for her father's lifelong enemy. Shaine saved her life, but the sudden changes left her whole existence in flux.

Two months ago, she'd been an average worker on Moon Base. She spent time with her friends, worked and played rec league grav-ball. She was content with her life. It had been a very normal, ordinary existence. Vinn and Elise Rahn had adopted her as an infant when they couldn't have children of their own. Knowing she had been adopted, she'd grown up loved and cherished, even after Elise was killed when Morgan was twelve. She and her dad had grown closer, taking care of each other over the years. Now she knew that Vinn and Elise had known of her true parentage all along, but had never told her. The betrayal still hurt, but she understood why they decided to keep their secret.

So much change. So many lies to try to process.

On top of that, the tabloids had pounced on her, poking into her life, speculating about her relationship with Tarm Maruchek, speculating about her personality and her past. It was big news that Tarm Maruchek had an heir besides his son Garren, her older brother.

Everything about Tarm Maruchek was news. He was active in politics. Mann-Maru Universal Industries was one of the largest corporate entities in the solar system. Everything Tarm Maruchek did had an impact on the business world. Morgan hated that she had become part of it. She tried to ignore the press, but so far, that wasn't working so well. Reporters had been harassing her day and night on Moon Base, and she'd had enough.

Now they were escaping to Shaine's family farm.

Maybe it meant something more that Shaine was taking her home, and maybe it didn't. She frowned inwardly. Did she want forever with Shaine? She'd never needed it before. Before Shaine, she'd never considered love a forever thing. An obsessive, needy, desperate thing, sure. But she'd never had a relationship she could equate to the relationship her mom and dad had.

She and Shaine had settled into a comfortable togetherness. Morgan realized they'd been inseparable for the past month. They hadn't spent one night or day apart. *I don't want to be without her, or away from her, or separate from her.*

It was odd, really. She always had her own space and believed she needed it. Now it felt wrong to be alone.

It wasn't that she and Shaine talked constantly. A lot of nights they relaxed on the sofa with the vid screen on or reading. Usually Morgan lay across Shaine's lap, while Shaine's long legs stretched out on the ottoman. Or they curled up in bed, always touching in some way. It would be good, spending time with Shaine and her family. Morgan smiled to herself.

Shaine asked curiously, "What?"

"Nothing. Just thinking."

"About?"

Morgan grinned. "That I like being with you."

Shaine flipped her a surprised and very pleased expression. "I like being with you, too, baby." She captured Morgan's hand and held it on her lap. Morgan reveled in the warmth of Shaine's thumb rubbing lightly on her skin.

Shaine sped past a handful of farm and transport vehicles lumbering along at ground level. They passed a holographic mile marker, and Shaine grinned, pointing. "That's our marker. This is our farm. It's only another few kilometers to the house."

"I knew you were more excited than you let on," Morgan accused.

Shaine chuckled and pushed the joystick forward. The air-car surged ahead. Moments later, Shaine dropped out of the upper sky lane to hover just above the ground, slowing down to guide the Racer off the road and onto a long wide drive that ended at a clearing circled by a sprawling house, barn and sheds.

Shaine smiled, relieved to finally be home. The house seemed a little more weathered, the gray trim chipped and the redwood siding faded. The main part of the house was a traditional two-story farmhouse. Solar panels covered the south-facing roof. A two-story dome-home was added onto the east side, connected to the main house through a short, windowed breezeway. The barn and working sheds were set back on the opposite side of the clearing, facing the house.

Shaine noted several vehicles parked haphazardly on the gravel between the house and the sheds. She recognized the two well-used air trucks, one currently filled with a load of hay. She didn't know the multipassenger air car or the small red commuter car. Near the house, a shiny black air bike rested in the shade.

As Shaine eased the Racer closer to the house, a lanky, sun-bronzed teenager with long red hair came running from one of the sheds. A huge, shaggy, black dog romped at his heels. The teen waved as he sprinted toward the car. He was shirtless, wearing loose work pants and boots. He ran to the car as Shaine pulled to a stop, not even waiting until she'd shut down the engine before he opened her door.

"Shainey! You're home!" he yelled, pulling her out of the car and into a bear hug.

"Hey, Toby!" Laughing, Shaine lifted him up and twirled him around as though he were still six years old.

The dog pranced around them, barking incessantly, his tail practically wagging off his furry behind. Setting Toby on his feet, she shook her head. He was as tall as her. "Holy shit, T, you grew!"

"I know!" he responded, patting her on the head. They giggled like kids. He said, "Grandma's got dinner on. She's been going nuts. Mom's in the house too. She said she's gonna kick your ass for not coming home sooner. Dad and Gramps are in the field, they'll be back in a while. Who's your friend?"

Big George jumped up and planted his paws on Shaine's chest, pushing her back against the car with his bulk. She playfully rubbed the Newfoundland's massive furry head. "Hey, Big George, you remember me?"

The dog barked excitedly and licked her face. Shaine wiped off the slobber with the back of one hand, rubbing George's ears with the other. "Stupid dog," she cooed. "I missed you too, ya big softy."

"So who's your friend?" Toby asked again.

Shaine pushed the dog off her chest and draped an arm around Toby's shoulders. Morgan had come around to lean on the front fender, watching with a cautious smile. Shaine reached out, catching Morgan's hand and gently pulling her toward them. "Toby Martin, this is Morgan Rahn. Morgan, my nephew Toby."

Morgan smiled. Toby grinned and stuck out a hand, firmly shaking Morgan's.

"Hi, Morgan. Welcome to the farm!"

"Hi, Toby."

Big George lumbered up and stuck his big, wet nose into Morgan's stomach. Morgan immediately backed away, eyes wide.

"George, sit!" Shaine ordered sharply. The dog dropped his butt to the ground, looking anxiously between Shaine and Morgan.

She wrapped an arm around Morgan's waist. "It's okay, Morg."

Toby took hold of George's collar. "Don't be afraid of George. He's just big and harmless." He grinned. "You can pet him. He won't bite you or anything."

Morgan shot a worried glance at Shaine.

"Let him smell your hand first, like this." Shaine demonstrated, easing the back of her hand toward George's nose, letting him sniff her skin, then she petted his head and scratched behind his ears. "Go ahead."

Morgan tentatively put the back of her hand near Big George's damp black nose. He studied her with curious, gentle eyes, shook his head a little and sniffed, then happily slobbered her hand with a big pink tongue. Morgan jerked back with a choked yelp.

Toby exclaimed, "He likes you!"

Shaine said gently, "It's okay. It's his way of saying hello."

Morgan bit her lip and reached out again, touching the big dog's head. Carefully, she ran her fingers through his fur. Toby scratched George's other ear. The dog leaned into the scratching and gave a big, loud yawn of contentment.

Morgan shifted away again. George leaned forward and pushed his head under her hand.

Shaine grinned. "He wants you to keep petting him."

"You're sure he won't bite?"

Toby said, "He won't bite. He yawned because he's happy and excited."

Tentatively, Morgan copied Toby, scratching behind George's ears. She grinned after a moment and ran her fingers down George's thick neck, laughing when he leaned against her legs, his bulk pushing her backward.

Voices called across the clearing and two women hurried from the house. Shaine waved. "Mom! Leese!"

She grinned and slipped from Morgan's side to meet Jeannette Ichiro halfway. Her mom hadn't changed much. She had the same short, stout frame that Shaine remembered, though gray strands highlighted her red hair. Shaine wrapped the older woman in a bear hug, dwarfing her in her arms.

"Oh, Shaine, honey, it's good to see you!" Her mom hugged her tightly, laughing even as tears leaked from her eyes. "I've missed you so much!"

Shaine kissed the top of her mom's head. "I missed you too, Mom."

Her sister stretched her arms around both of them. Shaine laughed. "Hey, Leese."

"Shainey, it's been too damned long, sis."

Leese was small and compact like their mother. Her hair was dark auburn, falling in loose waves past her shoulders. She was rounded some, but not overly heavy, her eyes a pale hazel. Shaine released her mom and squeezed Leese. "Missed ya, Leese."

They all stepped back. Shaine watched as her mom looked past her to Morgan who still petted a very content Big George's head. Jeannette's eyes sparkled, her smile wide and welcoming. "And you must be Morgan."

"Mom, Leese, this is Morgan Rahn. Morgan, this is my mom, Jeannette Ichiro, and my younger sister Leese Martin. Toby's mom."

"Welcome, Morgan," Jeannette said happily. Morgan held her hand out, but Jeannette ignored it and wrapped her in a hug. Surprised, Morgan stiffened for a second before she relaxed and tentatively returned the hug.

"Thank you."

George barked, pushing his head between them, making everyone laugh. Leese said, "Welcome, Morgan. It's great to meet you. Come on, we've got lunch on. Toby, grab their bags and bring them up to Shaine's room."

The tall young man whined, "Geez, Mom, do I look like a butler?"

"And put a shirt on before you sit down at the table."

Shaine popped the rear cargo hatch on the Racer. "Thanks, T." She slapped his shoulder playfully, then put an arm around Morgan's waist and guided her toward the house.

Jeannette directed Shaine and Morgan to chairs in the bright, open dining room, refusing their offers to help in the kitchen. She and Leese bustled back and forth, carrying platters of sandwiches and raw vegetables to the table, along with vegetable dip, potato crisps and pitchers of iced tea.

Toby trundled back down the stairs and gave Shaine a dirty look. "What'd you have in that one bag? Weights? Geez."

Shaine smiled sweetly. "A gal's gotta stay in shape," she quipped. *And carry an assortment of weapons in locked cases*, she thought. She never traveled without being prepared. She hadn't since she left the EG.

He grabbed a glass and filled it with tea, then filled a plate for himself.

Shaine swallowed a mouthful of chips. "Hungry much?" she teased as he piled on a third sandwich.

"Hey, I'm a growing boy," he protested, dropping into a chair opposite Shaine and Morgan.

Leese commented wryly, "He's an endless stomach."

There was a commotion at the back of the kitchen—male voices talking and the screen door slapping open and shut.

Jeannette's voice directed, "Leave those dusty boots in the mudroom, or you'll be mopping after lunch!"

"Where's my girl?" a booming voice demanded. Two men came through the kitchen. Shaine stood to greet her stepfather and her brother-in-law. Kent Ichiro was a small, wiry man with dark eyes and straight black hair pulled into a tight braid at the nape of his neck. He crossed the room and wrapped Shaine in a bear hug. It didn't seem to matter that she was taller. With just the strength of his personality, he still seemed larger. Shaine hugged him hard, smelling dust from the fields, exhaust from the combines, and a hint of his favorite cologne. "Hi, Dad. I missed you too."

He slapped her on the back. "Damn, it's good to see you, Shaine. You're looking good, girl."

She playfully backhanded his stomach. "You too, Pop," she returned. She turned and gave her brother-in-law a hug. "Hey, Mike."

"Welcome home, Shaine." He returned the hug and ruffled her hair. Mike was even taller than Shaine, broad-shouldered and muscular from years of manual labor. His light brown hair was matted from the ball cap he'd been wearing, his skin deeply tanned.

"Dad, Mike, this is Morgan Rahn. Morgan, this is my dad and my favorite brother-in-law."

Greetings were exchanged as the men pulled up chairs. Lunch was a boisterous affair. Talk ranged from news on Moon Base to news on the farm, what everyone was doing with their lives, updates on family and friends, the weather and sports. Toby expounded excitedly and passionately about being involved in a series of protests against the reopening of a nearby nuclear power facility that had been empty for over a century.

Shaine was proud of him. He'd grown up so much. He was a university student now, a bright and intelligent young man. Both she and Morgan asked him questions about the power facility. He believed it all came down to corporate money and greed versus good sense. Shaine suspected her nephew was an idealist in the making. She was too jaded for idealism. She'd seen the results of corporate money and greed when she worked for Mann-Maru Corporate Security. On the upside, Mann-Maru hadn't always been the bad guy.

The one thing nobody brought up was why Shaine and Morgan were spending time at the farm, or the facts of Morgan's notable parentage. Shaine had given her mom a quick summary of the situation and warned her not to bother Morgan about the recent media harassment. She was relieved that her advice had been taken seriously.

Shaine relaxed into the familiarity of her family. Jeannette still directed everything. Leese teased her incessantly. Her father alternately treated her like his little girl and the soldier that she'd been. Toby still apparently worshipped the ground that she walked on, and seemed to be passing that worship on to

Morgan. Shaine slouched back in her chair, feeling comfortable and happy. Her stepdad and Toby peppered Morgan with questions about what it was like to live on Moon Base or in the 'Belt.

Morgan seemed to be handling the attention well. Jeannette caught Shaine's eye and winked. Shaine couldn't stop smiling.

After lunch, Shaine and Morgan helped Leese and Jeannette with cleanup, then Shaine brought Morgan up the back stairs to her bedroom at the top of the dome. Shaine opened the door into a room bright with summer sun. The top third of the domed ceiling was made of clear glass panels. Shaine looked up at a crystal blue summer sky. Her bedroom was neat and orderly but remained the room of a teenager with dreams. Colorful posters covered the concaved walls, EG recruiting posters, a favorite thrash band in concert, soccer and grav-ball action shots.

A double bed took up the middle of the wall opposite the door. The comforter was a solid navy blue. Several pillows in primary colors rested haphazardly against the headboard. There were built-in closets and a dresser to one side, a functional student desk against the wall on the other. Framed holos covered the top of the dresser. A shelf with a handful of knickknacks hung above the desk. Beside the desk sat a low bookcase overflowing with books and journals. An outdated computer terminal rested on top of the desk. A pair of speakers were mounted on the wall to either side of the shelf.

Shaine closed the door quietly behind her.

Morgan cocked her head as she looked around. "Strong and comfortable," she murmured, "like you."

Shaine raised a brow at the comment and moved behind Morgan. She slid her arms around Morgan's waist and nuzzled her neck. She breathed in Morgan's essence and tasted slightly salty skin, closing her eyes with a sigh. "Mmmm. Not how I would have described it," she murmured. "You know you're the only girl I've ever had up here."

Morgan twisted around in her arms. Shaine lost herself in Morgan's kisses. Morgan locked her arms around Shaine's neck. Shaine backed Morgan up until the backs of her knees hit the bed and tumbled both of them onto the soft mattress. She rested on her elbows over Morgan's body. Morgan grinned up at her.

"So," Morgan murmured, "are we going to christen your bed?"

Shaine captured Morgan's lips again, delving deeply, leaving no doubts as to her intentions.

CHAPTER TWO

"Up and at 'em, sleepyhead."

Morgan groaned and buried her face into her pillow, hiding from the bright sunlight dousing the room and rudely invading her comfortable sleep. She decided living on Moon Base with no windows wasn't such a bad thing.

The mattress shifted as Shaine sat down beside her, rubbing her back through the thick comforter. "Time's a-wasting," Shaine sing-songed, her breath warm as she breathed into Morgan's ear.

Morgan mumbled, "Are you sure it's morning?"

"Mmmmmhmmmm." Shaine's weight settled over her. Morgan felt hot breath at the nape of her neck as Shaine nuzzled her skin.

"Jesus." Well, now she was awake. At least, her libido was. Shaine teased her neck and shoulders with teeth and tongue, sending goose bumps down her skin and sending her blood flooding south.

Grinning, Morgan shifted, forcing Shaine to roll off her. She wriggled around until she faced Shaine on the bed, worked a hand up from under the quilt and slid it around Shaine's neck, pulling her in for a kiss.

"You're a tease," she accused against Shaine's lips.

Shaine chuckled, kissed her hard and rolled off the bed to her feet. "Yup, I am." She whipped the quilt off Morgan's body.

Morgan made a sleepy half-attempt to get the quilt back before falling back onto her pillow with a sigh.

Shaine tossed a sleep shirt and shorts onto her chest. "I even made coffee."

Morgan sighed and sat up, fumbling to pull the shirt over her head.

A few minutes later, she followed Shaine downstairs and into the kitchen. Shaine put a cup of hot coffee into her hands and Morgan sipped at it gratefully with her eyes still half-closed. With an indulgent grin, Shaine guided her to a stool at the breakfast bar between the kitchen and dining room, then turned to get her own coffee.

As Shaine sat down beside Morgan, Jeannette breezed into the kitchen with a cheerful good morning. Morgan raised her cup in silent greeting.

"Morning, Mom." Shaine gestured toward her partner. "Don't worry, she'll come to after a cup of coffee."

Jeannette chuckled as she got a mug from the cupboard. "Not a morning person, Morgan?"

Morgan squinted in the bright morning light. "Not so much," she mumbled. "I think it has something to do with the whole sun coming up thing. Don't have that so much, out-system." She rubbed her eyes with the back of one hand. "Too bright."

"What do you girls have planned for today?" Jeannette asked as she joined them at the breakfast bar.

Shaine said, "I thought I'd take Morgan around the farm, walk the perimeter, introduce her to the animals."

Morgan smiled doubtfully. Being outdoors was still somewhat odd for her—the hugeness of it—all that open sky without a dome. And animals. She wasn't so sure about animals. Other than Big George, the only animals she'd ever known were her grav-ball teammate Ally's two house cats. She liked them. They were soft and warm, and when she'd slept over at Ally's, they'd curled up around her, and it had been nice. She liked to feel them purring. Farm animals were another story. She hoped they could just look at them from a safe distance. Somehow, she had a feeling that Shaine was more the "up close and personal" type.

Jeannette said, "That sounds like a lovely morning."

Morgan watched Jeannette turn a mom-like look on Shaine. "I hope you're going to make Morgan some breakfast before you head out."

Shaine sighed heavily, reminding Morgan of a nagged teenager. "Of course I will. We were just doing coffee first."

Jeannette smiled approvingly. "I have to be in town for a book club meeting this morning, so lunch is on your own. There's fixings for sandwiches in the cooler."

"Thanks, Mom."

"Thanks, Mrs. Ichiro."

Jeannette raised a brow at Morgan.

Morgan felt her face flush. "Sorry. Jeannette."

Jeannette chuckled and patted Morgan's arm. "Thank you, dear. No formalities here." She finished her coffee and stood up. "Time for me to get going. You girls have fun today."

* * *

The morning sun beat down on Morgan's head and shoulders as she and Shaine toured the farm. She wore a pair of cut-off cargo work pants and a tank top. Shaine had methodically covered all her exposed skin with a strong sunblock. She wore her work boots as always and was glad for the extra support. It was disconcerting to walk on the uneven ground rather than smooth tarmac or flat artificial grassy areas.

Hand in hand, she and Shaine sauntered along beside the low fence bordering a paddock that held several cows and horses. Big George wandered with them, coming and going as he investigated smells and bounded heavily through the high grass, always circling back for a pat on the head and reassurance that she and Shaine were still with him.

Morgan marveled at the natural wonders surrounding her. A light breeze occasionally broke the humidity of the August morning. The air was thick with new and interesting odors. Shaine identified the pungent scent of cow and horse dung for her. The wind carried the faint taste of wood smoke and the sound of the cultivators working in the west field. Their footsteps on the narrow path brought up the dusty, sweet smell of grass.

They hiked up a small rise. Shaine boosted Morgan onto the rough wooden fence rail and sat beside her on the top rung. Morgan gazed around. The fields stretched to the horizon where gold and green melted into blue. A haze of dust hung in a thin line where the sky lane crossed the field. Morgan realized it was the sky lane they'd flown in on. The occasional cargo transport or air car passed in the distance with a flash of light reflecting on metal.

Morgan counted twenty cows and three horses grazing and snuffling in the hay. Shaine said there were more cows out in the north fields. Occasionally, Big George barked and rushed through the grass, flushing a handful of birds or sending small animals skittering through the underbrush. Crows cawed as they fought over some small rodent or another. Songbirds twittered from perches on the fences.

Beautiful, Morgan thought. Of all the things she'd read about or seen in vids, she never expected to be on a farm. Yet here she was, sitting on the edge of a field with her lover. Amazing.

Shaine caught Morgan's hand in her own. "I thought maybe we could saddle up a couple of the horses and go for a ride," she said.

"Ride? I don't know how to ride a horse!" Morgan protested. She watched the huge animals wandering around chewing grass and couldn't imagine actually sitting on one.

Shaine grinned. "No worries, Morg. It'll be fun. You can ride Hoss. He's gentle, and he'll follow my lead. You won't have to do anything but hang on."

Morgan nodded dubiously. *They're so big. And alive. And they can buck me off, like in the vids. What if Hoss doesn't want to let me ride on him?* Still, she could see that Shaine was excited, and Shaine wouldn't make her do something dangerous. Right?

Shaine put an arm around her shoulders and gave her a half-hug. "I promise I won't let anything happen to you."

Morgan managed an uneasy smile. "Okay. As long as you promise," she capitulated. Shaine hugged her again and vaulted off the fence, putting her hands around Morgan's waist and lifting her down as well.

"Come on, then."

* * *

True to Shaine's assurances, Hoss was a perfect gentleman. Morgan grinned from Hoss's western saddle. She wasn't sure if she was actually directing him, or if he was taking his cues from Shaine and her big black quarter horse named Drake. Either way, Morgan was having a blast. Loosely holding the reins in one hand the way Shaine had shown her, Morgan reached forward with her other hand and petted the thick, dark brown fur on Hoss's neck.

"Good boy, Hoss, good boy."

The big horse swung his head back, blinking a chocolate eye at her. Morgan would have sworn he smiled when he huffed in her general direction.

"You look like a pro, Morg." Shaine handled Drake with a casual confidence Morgan admired. "I told you you'd like it."

Morgan chuckled. "Thanks for talking me into it."

"So, race ya to the barn?"

"What? Shaine, I'm not—"

Shaine kneed Drake and shot ahead. Morgan squeaked and held on as Hoss tossed his head and took off after Drake. After her initial panic, Morgan laughed at the rush of speed and the wind blowing through her hair. Leaning forward, she kept hold of Hoss's reins with one hand and the saddle horn with the other, and tried to clamp on with her legs while trying to relax into his gait.

All too quickly, it was over. Hoss slowed with Drake to a gentle walk before they stopped at the gate of the corral attached to the barn. Morgan patted Hoss's neck. "Good boy."

Shaine swung off Drake and came to Morgan's left side, patting her leg. "Have fun?" she asked.

"Absolutely."

"Want a hand down?"

Morgan raised a challenging brow. Having watched Shaine dismount a few times, she decided she could do it too. Just like in the vids. She swung her leg over Hoss and dropped to the ground without help.

Shaine whooped and swung Morgan around in her arms, planting a solid kiss on her lips as she set her back on her feet. Laughing, she said, "Come on, let's get the tack off these two, brush them down, and give them a treat."

An hour later, Morgan and Shaine wandered back to the house. They climbed up onto the porch and through the kitchen door. Jeannette Ichiro sat at the breakfast bar, sipping a glass of iced tea and tapping something into her comp pad.

"Hey, Mom, how was book group?"

Shaine kicked her boots off at the door and headed to the cooler. Morgan leaned over to unclamp her boot buckles.

Jeannette looked up and smiled. "Book club was fine." She gave Morgan a quick once-over, then Shaine. She tilted her head, pointedly sniffed the air and asked, "How was the ride?"

Morgan stopped in her tracks, unsure how to read that comment.

Reaching into the cooler, Shaine snorted. "Nice, Mom. Real nice." She removed a sealed pitcher and closed the door. With a raised brow and a twinkle in her eye, she demanded, "You think we smell like horses?"

Jeannette chuckled. "Yes, I think you do," she agreed.

Shaine sniffed her underarms and shrugged. "Well, at least part of me doesn't smell like horse."

"Shaine!" Jeannette burst out laughing.

Morgan snickered. She liked Shaine's mom. A lot. Jeannette reminded her of her own mom—what little she remembered. Morgan walked the rest of the way into the kitchen and sat down on one of the low-backed stools across from Jeannette. She said, "It was a really nice ride."

Shaine put the pitcher and two glasses on the breakfast bar and filled them. She slid one in front of Morgan as she sat on the stool beside her. "I put Morgan on Hoss," she said. "She did great. Rides like a pro." She lifted her glass in salute.

Morgan clinked her glass against Shaine's. "I think Hoss did all the work. He just made me look good."

Jeannette set aside her pad and sipped her own tea. "I'm glad you had fun." She turned her attention to Morgan. "Are you adjusting to being on Earth?" she asked.

Morgan nodded. "I am, yes. It's a lot different than home."

Jeannette said, "I imagine it must be."

"I think the oddest thing for me is not worrying about going outside. I mean, even on Moon Base, you're always aware that as long you're in the dome, you're safe, but what's beyond the airlock can kill you. You don't consciously think about it. But it's always there, in the back of your head. One crack in the dome and it's all over, you know?"

Shaine nodded in agreement and covered Morgan's hand with her own. Morgan flashed her a glance, surprised at the show of affection in front of Jeannette. Shaine smiled and Morgan relaxed. She entwined their fingers on the counter, meeting Shaine's deep green gaze. She knew she was blushing, but didn't care.

She let the conversation between Shaine and Jeannette wash over her for a few moments, recognizing a sense of contentment and belonging, much like how she felt with her friends at home, or with her dad. Only, for some reason, this seemed more intense. Maybe it was because of Shaine. Maybe Shaine was becoming her home. Morgan felt the smile on her lips and the heat flushing her cheeks thinking of that. Interesting.

She forced herself to follow the conversation and realized that Jeannette was focused on her. Jeannette studied her for a moment before asking, "I don't mean to pry, Morgan, but curiosity is killing me. How much truth is there in all the media hype that's following you?"

Morgan blinked at the directness. She took the time to sip her tea and gather her thoughts. The question didn't upset her, and she sensed no animosity in it. Shaine glared at her mother. Morgan squeezed Shaine's hand reassuringly. She was okay with this. "I guess it kind of depends on what you've heard," she said. "It's true that Tarm Maruchek is my birth father. He hid the fact that I was saved when my mother, who was eight months pregnant with me, was shot and killed. The doctors managed to deliver me via C-section just before she died. Tarm thought it was too dangerous for me, that I would be a target for his enemies the same as my mother and my older brother had been, so they let it be known that I was killed with my mother. I was given to Vinn and Elise Rahn to raise. I knew I was adopted, but never knew the real story until just a few weeks ago."

Jeannette nodded, her expression concerned and serious. "That's a lot to deal with. You're very close to your adopted parents, aren't you?"

Morgan nodded. "I am. It's been just me and my dad since I was twelve, though. My mom was killed in a pirate attack at one of the mining facilities." She frowned. "I worry about leaving my dad on Moon Base while I'm here. I mean, I'm sure he's okay, but I still feel a little guilty for being so far away." She shook her head. Why in the hell was she telling Jeannette Ichiro all this?

Jeannette asked, "Did your parents know of your birthright?"

Morgan felt the rise of betrayal and pushed it down. She didn't want to feel angry toward her parents, but the knowledge that they'd never told her the truth still rankled. "They knew. My dad said they always meant to tell me, but it just didn't come up. Then it just seemed better to leave it be." She shrugged. "I guess if things had gone differently it would have been just as well."

"But now you know. Are you okay with that?"

"Mom—"

"I'm not sure." Morgan met Jeannette's gaze. The warmth and empathy in her eyes made Morgan want to continue the conversation and spill her guts just because Jeannette cared. In a way, it was a relief to tell someone who wasn't in the middle of the situation. "I guess I don't have much choice but to accept it."

"What is Tarm Maruchek really like?"

Morgan considered. She shot a look at Shaine, who shrugged. "It's hard to say," she hedged. "I don't know him very well."

Jeannette turned a sharp eye on her. "Does he treat you well?"

Morgan nodded quickly. "Yeah, actually. He really seems to try." She frowned thoughtfully into her tea. Scenes flashed through her head of the interactions she'd had with him. "I really believe he thought he was doing the right thing at the time, when he hid me away."

The words almost surprised her because she hadn't said them aloud before. She realized she truly believed it, and it felt right. She felt Shaine's eyes on her, supportive and encouraging. "It's hard though. I don't want to make my dad feel like he's going to be tossed aside. He's still my dad. And I don't want anything from Maruchek. I don't need the money or the fame. I was happy the way things were, you know? I had my friends and my dad. I spent my whole life being a mechanic, working for a living like my parents did. Honestly, I just want my old life back."

Jeannette observed gently, "That may not be possible."

"Yeah. I'm beginning to see that."

Morgan felt a somewhat resigned acceptance settle over her. Maybe having this distance from Moon Base was allowing her to process all the changes. Maybe having Shaine's mother tease it out of her was a good thing. *Maybe I just need a mom, because I really miss having one right now.*

Jeannette smiled. "I'm sure things will be a lot easier once the excitement has settled down a bit."

Morgan nodded, wondering how long she'd have to wait for that to happen.

* * *

While they chatted with her mom, Shaine caught her space-born companion struggling to hide her yawns. After lunch, Shaine convinced Morgan to go upstairs and take a nap. She figured the fresh air and slight uptick of gravity was taking its toll on her. Moon Base was technically at Earth-normal gravity inside the dome, but in reality, the artificial gravity generators didn't quite reach Earth-normal. It wasn't a big difference, but for someone who had never lived on Earth, it was enough to cause fatigue and aches until they acclimated. She was tired herself, but it didn't affect her nearly so much.

She brought Morgan up to her bedroom. They stripped down to T-shirts and undies and crawled into bed. Morgan stretched out on her stomach, her arms around the pillow. Shaine pulled a light blanket over them and lay on her side, watching contentedly as Morgan's breathing evened out. She stayed with Morgan until she knew her lover was asleep, then slipped out of bed, dressed and padded back downstairs.

She found her mother in the kitchen, taking vegetables and a package of fresh meat from the cooler.

Jeannette looked up as Shaine walked into the room. "Grab a knife. You can cut up these veggies and put them in the steamer."

Shaine raised a brow. "I walk in the room and I get KP duty?"

"Just for that, you're also peeling potatoes for au gratin."

Shaine sighed dramatically then hunted down a small knife, a peeler and a cutting board, which she set on the breakfast bar. Jeannette handed her a bowl of washed veggies and an empty bowl to hold the peeled ones before returning to the counter by the sink. Picking up a butcher knife, Jeannette looked over her shoulder at Shaine. "Stew or pot roast?" she asked.

Shaine licked her lips. "Pot roast," she said. "Definitely."

"Good, because I don't feel like cubing this meat."

Shaine smiled and watched her mother move efficiently around the kitchen, comforted by the familiar sounds and motions and memories of a routine she'd seen repeated hundreds of times. She knew chopping veggies and peeling potatoes was just an excuse for her mother to keep her in one place so that they could chat. She'd become so good at skirting around the details of her life that she had no idea where to begin the conversation, so she simply worked and waited.

Jeannette got the roast into the oven, poured herself a cup of coffee from the dispenser on the counter and sat down across from Shaine. "Morgan's a sweet girl," she commented.

Shaine blinked. Not the starter she'd expected. "Um, yes, she is. She's good people." *And I'm in love with her.*

"I'm glad you brought her home. It'll give both of you a chance to slow down and get to know each other better."

"That really isn't why we came here."

Her mom chuckled. "No, but it does work out rather neatly that way, doesn't it?"

Shaine started peeling another carrot. Orange streamers flew from the blade. "It's nice to actually have downtime," she admitted. "Been kind of crazy, lately."

"I get the impression there's a lot more behind the story of you and Morgan than you've let on."

Shaine puffed out a breath. It never took long for her mother to get to the point. She finished peeling the carrot, tossed it into the bowl and picked up another. She contemplated what to tell her mother about how she and Morgan got together. It surprised her that for the first time in a very long time, she actually wanted to tell all. It surprised her even more when the whole story tumbled out of her mouth. She didn't leave anything out, not her assassination of the man who'd been trying to kill Morgan, or the fact it wasn't the first time she'd been involved in that kind of death and destruction.

She even disclosed her covert employment with Mann-Maru and how she finally reached a point where she could no longer handle how the "security" jobs she took on tended to more and more violence. She related how she had stepped in when employees were suspected of selling trade secrets to competitors, how she physically intimidated them into silence. She'd caught infiltrators and corporate spies and sent them back to their respective bosses either beaten severely, or in one case, dead. She'd "encouraged" MMU employees not to leave because they had skills and knowledge that were too valuable to lose. At first, it had seemed like just an extension of the skills she'd learned as a Special Ops Commando. Then it became just routine. Rogan pushed her harder and harder. He tapped into her military training, manipulating her into being a dutiful soldier again. He exploited that coldly focused mindset which allowed her to do what was necessary without considering the morality of her actions. Finally, she realized that she could no longer justify any of it. She described how she'd essentially blackmailed Tarm Maruchek and his Head of Security, Duncan Rogan, into letting her move into a benign job as a mechanic.

It was cathartic, though she spoke without tears or much outward emotion. She hesitated sometimes, searching for words, but just kept talking. She didn't look up from her work. She didn't want to know what her mother would think of her now. Hell, she was disgusted with herself. She couldn't imagine how her mother would feel. *So, now you know*, she thought. *This is who I am, Mom, something between a monster and a psychopath. I'm sorry. Please don't hate me.*

For what felt like hours after she finished talking, Shaine waited, uncomfortably aware of her mother's eyes on her. When she finally looked up, the gaze she met was concerned and sad, but also sympathetic and compassionate. "Baby girl, that is a lot of guilt to bear," Jeannette said quietly.

Shaine said, "By rights I ought to be locked up somewhere. Hell, Rogan, and me and half a dozen others, Tarm Maruchek included."

"There is some truth in that," her mother conceded, then added, "seems to me, though, that in a lot of ways you were a pawn in a larger game. You had little choice in the matter, once things got out of hand."

"I could have walked away. I should have."

"Rogan would have killed you."

Shaine shrugged. "Sometimes I think I deserve that."

Jeannette reached across the space between them and took Shaine's hands in her own. "Perhaps it's because I'm your mother, but I can't say that I agree. You are not a bad person, Shaine. You may have gotten a bit lost, but I know if you had no heart, you wouldn't be here right now." She patted her daughter's hand. "To be truthful, I had a pretty fair idea of what you'd gotten yourself into. I've waited a long time for you to get yourself back out."

Shaine looked sharply at her.

Jeannette smiled. "Mothers are trained to read between the lines, dear. And after all these years, I've figured out how to read between yours. And I think that Morgan Rahn is going to be good for you."

Shaine shook her head and sighed. Relief washed over her, making her feel almost dizzy. "Thanks."

Jeannette patted her hand again. "No thanks needed. That's what mothers do. Now, get peeling, or we'll never have any veggies with our dinner."

CHAPTER THREE

Morgan jerked awake, choking on a scream. Gasping for breath, she lay on her back blinking into moonlight shining through the domed windows overhead. Sweat soaked the sheet beneath her. Her heart pounded frantically in her chest. *Christ, I hate this damn nightmare.*

The familiar scenes continued in her head. Floating in space, enveloped in empty blackness, helpless and unable to get to the people she loved, she watched her best friend Digger and her mother die. The pirate bomber swooped in from above, guns firing. Bright white laser beams ripped through her mother's vac suit, shredding the front. Then she saw the explosion that took Digger's life, heard his strangled cry in her helmet speakers as his helmet shattered and his arm was blown off. Screaming, she reached toward them, but their lifeless bodies floated just out of her grasp. Their empty, dead eyes stared at her through cracked, blood-spattered faceplates.

Morgan rubbed her hands over her face, trying to banish the images.

Curled up beside her, Shaine mumbled and shifted, reaching a long arm across Morgan's waist with a sigh. Morgan waited until Shaine settled again, then carefully extricated herself from Shaine's sleepy embrace.

She pulled on a T-shirt and boxers and slipped out of the bedroom and tiptoed down the carpeted stairs. Padding barefoot into the darkened kitchen, she took a bottle of juice from the refrigerator.

She leaned against the counter and stared out the window over the sink. The moon was high and nearly full, the stars bright against the night sky. In the distance, the faint glow of city lights spread a dull orange-yellow highlight along the edge of the horizon.

Morgan's thoughts floated restlessly. She mulled over her future, wondering what it might bring. She wanted to cling to the certainty of her old life, but she heard the echo of Jeannette's observation that afternoon. *"That may not be possible."* She recognized the truth in the statement, but had no idea what it meant in the long term. She knew she would never have the same life back. She was no longer an anonymous face in the crowd, no longer "just" a dockworker. She might be able to pretend nothing had changed, but her true parentage was always going to be an issue.

Sighing, she finished her juice and pushed away from the sink. She tossed the empty container into the trash on her way to the entertainment room. Grabbing a quilt from the folded pile on the floor, she dropped into one of the leather lounge chairs. She found the remote for the vid-center and turned it on, setting the volume almost to nothing as she scrolled through the channels. She saw a couple action vids she recognized, but kept scrolling.

As she surfed through the channels, she was startled and riveted by her own image in a collage behind a popular gossip commentator. She'd seen most of the photos shown on screen.

Maruchek's standard corporate headshot was positioned in the upper right corner, the official picture from her Mann-Maru personnel badge in the upper left. The rest were grainier shots, mostly of her with her friends and Shaine on Moon Base, in public venues like Club Tranquility or playing grav-ball.

There was an action shot of her and another guy in the null-g grav-ball court, fighting for the ball. Blood dripped down the side of her face. Below it was a posed photo of her and her parents. She'd probably been about eight years old when it was taken. She wondered where they'd found it.

At the center was an enhanced photo of her and Shaine in the null-g dance cube at Club Tranquility, lustfully wrapped around each other.

Closed-captioned words scrolled accusingly across the bottom of the screen, underscoring the barely audible voice of the anchorman. "Mann-Maru CEO Tarm Maruchek's mysteriously hidden and recently found daughter continues to elude media attempts at contact.

"Despite Rahn's reluctance to talk to the media, investigators have discovered that the woman may not be the daughter that Maruchek would have hoped for. Raised by working-class parents in the Asteroid Belt's many mining facilities and on Moon Base, Rahn, who was buried Torwen Arella Maruchek, has an apparent wild streak that we're sure Maruchek was hoping to hide.

"Sources on Moon Base describe a tough young woman who plays no-holds-barred grav-ball in one of the local amateur leagues. Opponent Charlie Heathe told this reporter that Rahn has, quote, *bloodied him*, unquote, more than once. Indeed, in some of the photos we were able to obtain, it appears that fighting on the court is something Rahn is not afraid of."

A series of grainy photos from different games scrolled horizontally across the screen, shots of Morgan engaged with Heathe and a couple of others. Morgan studied the images. The photos appeared to have been taken by friends of one or the other of the teams. Morgan wondered whom they'd paid for those photos, and hoped it wasn't anyone she considered a friend. She couldn't decide if she was angry or saddened. Maybe a little of both.

She remembered at least one of the fights depicted. She hadn't started the altercation, but she'd finished it. Charlie

Heathe had elbowed her in the face that night as she went for a point. She'd been amped up on adrenaline, pissed that he'd been harassing her all night. She remembered ignoring the pain and the blood trickling from her nose. She launched off her defenseman's hands and forced her way past Heathe to sink the ball into the goal hole, then spinning, she kicked away from the wall and slammed her fist into Heathe's face. They'd both been thrown out that night, and Heathe ended up with a broken nose. The photo showed blood droplets floating around them in the null gravity field and her fist connecting with his face. The blood in the photo had been hers. She didn't regret the fight. The bastard had deserved it, but the way it was depicted in the photo, she'd been the aggressor.

The commentary continued. Morgan wanted to turn it off, but found herself sickly fascinated with the description of her life. "Rahn has been seen often in the company of this woman, whom we've identified as Shaine Wendt."

The background screen flashed up a photo of Morgan and Shaine on Moon Base, leaving work together, walking near the tram that traveled to the dry docks and supply depot facilities near the spaceport. Morgan remembered that day, too, and the photographers that Shaine had threatened with bodily harm. Always her protector, Shaine. Morgan sighed. Would it always be like this? Would the press always be hovering, curious, demanding, prying? Would Shaine always be shielding her from the hounds?

"Identity searches on Wendt have come up curiously empty. She is currently employed as a mechanic for Mann-Maru Universal Industries, though there are records of her working as a midlevel Security Administrator at Mann-Maru Corporate, and having spent nearly ten years in Earth Guard, most of that as a Commando in the Special Operations Division. She got an honorable medical discharge and a purple cross commendation for her injuries in the line of duty. A great deal of her service record is classified, which is expected for a commando operative. Wendt's relationship with Morgan Rahn, however, has been well documented, as shown by the photos of the two of them at Club Tranquility on Moon Base."

Several more photos popped up on the screen. Morgan hadn't been aware of any of them being taken, though she remembered the night well. The photos were grainy personal holo reproductions, and it looked to her like most had been cropped and edited.

She looked tough and confident in cargo pants cut off at the knees, work boots and a cropped black T-shirt sporting the band's logo, the arms sheared off and the neck cut out. The vivid colors of her tattoos showed bright against her pale skin. In one photo she leaned against a high table with a beer in one hand, the other gesturing toward the stage. In another, she leaned against Shaine, the redhead's long arms wrapped loosely around her middle as she spoke intimately into Morgan's ear. Shaine wore faded combat fatigues and a tight black tank top that showed off her attributes quite nicely. In the club lighting, her hair seemed even redder than it was, standing up in short spikes.

Despite the invasion of her privacy, Morgan smiled at the photos. Anyone looking at the pictures could see what Morgan thought was obvious—two women who seemed to be very comfortable together and very much in love. *We look good together*, she thought. *God, I love her.*

The shot of her and Shaine in the null-g cube popped up again. Morgan felt a flush of heat at the memory of that night. Shaine had practically taken her right there in the cube. Neither of them had been particularly sober. She remembered the driving energy of the music and the slam patterns in the cube. The gang of regular dancers who controlled the slam sphere was wired up, the band screaming loud and the pace of the slam patterns had been bordering on out of control as they flipped each other around the null-g cube. She'd been so happy to be alive, so relieved that Shaine was all right and that her friends had accepted her newly revealed status as Maruchek's daughter. Joy had morphed into desperate, lusting need that exploded between her and Shaine.

"Neither Maruchek nor his organization have commented on whether Morgan Rahn will have a role at Mann-Maru other than her current job as an external ship systems mechanic.

Speculation is that there will be some kind of continuing relationship between Rahn and Maruchek, if the amount of security around the woman is any indication of Maruchek's intent. But obviously Rahn has neither been groomed nor educated for a high-ranking position in the corporation."

The reporter made a few more remarks before moving onto the next news story.

Morgan flipped back to one of the action vids, but her mind remained on what she'd just heard.

I am not the loser and the troublemaker they want me to be. I'm no angel, but I'm not a bad person.

She wanted to be angry, but she couldn't find the energy to be anything other than depressed. She didn't know what to do. She could go back to Moon Base, but nothing there would ever be the same. She had not asked for any of this.

She had no vision of her life other than what it had been. She'd never conceived of doing anything else. Technically, she could go anywhere and do mechanic work. But where? She didn't want to leave her dad on Moon Base. She had a life there, and friends who were more like family. How could she walk away from that?

Morgan sighed heavily and sank further into the chair, tucking the quilt up under her chin, pulling her feet up and curling onto her side. The screen flashed with explosions as the action vid played with the volume muted. She stared at the screen without really seeing it. After a while she finally slept.

CHAPTER FOUR

The early afternoon sun bathed the vegetable garden in bright heat. Shaine knelt in the dirt, weeding and pulling small seedlings to make room for stronger ones. She wore a sleeveless cut-off T-shirt and shorts and had kicked off her shoes, enjoying the feel of the earth on her bare feet. Her already tan skin picked up even more color in the sun, except where she'd managed to smear dirt on her face, arms and legs.

A couple of rows in front of her, Morgan also knelt in the soil. She'd opted to wear one of Jeannette's big-brimmed straw hats and a long-sleeved T-shirt to ward off sunburn on her pale skin. Shaine thought she looked adorable in a goofy kind of way. Morgan twisted around and sent Shaine a wide grin. "Hey, look!" She held up an angleworm as long as her hand.

Shaine laughed. "That's a good one."

"This is so wild! Everything is alive, and it moves!" She set the worm back in the dirt and watched as it wriggled away into the coolness.

"I'm really glad you're enjoying yourself. I was worried you'd freak out."

"It's just so amazing. I mean, if you go to the park in Moon Base, there are some insects. But here, it's just free and open and—" She shook her head. "Just different." She turned back to her weeding. "And there's something to be said for playing in the mud."

"Don't let my mom hear you say that, or she won't let you leave," Shaine teased.

Morgan smirked. "Who said I wanted to leave?"

Shaine raised a brow. "Oh? Hmmm. I'll keep that in mind."

"Good." Morgan held up a bit of green. "Is this a weed?"

"Uh, no, that's a baby tomato plant."

Morgan frowned. "Looks like a weed. Sorry."

"No worries. More where that one came from."

Morgan returned to her work and Shaine to hers in a comfortable silence. Shaine smiled. She enjoyed being mindlessly busy and reveled in the lack of stress. It felt good to share this with Morgan. She was happy. Content. Hell, practically joyful. It had been a long time since she'd felt this way.

Being home was a good thing. She had missed her family. But, more than that, she knew the happiness she was currently experiencing was all about Morgan. Just being near her was like a balm to Shaine's soul. Having Morgan be part of every day, every night, was wonderful. She'd never felt this way about anyone. She had never trusted anyone the way she trusted Morgan. Morgan was the only one she'd ever wanted to take home to her family, to share her safe space, to share her life.

Shaine blinked. *That's it, isn't it?* she thought. *I want to share my life with her.* She chuckled inwardly. *Well, hell. There's a revelation.* Then she frowned, wondering if Morgan felt the same way. Her stomach twisted at the thought that Morgan might not, and she quickly pushed that aside. *Not gonna go there,* she decided. *Not right now.*

She let her gaze travel over the small woman, so serious as she worked her way down the row, and Shaine couldn't stop the smile that formed. *Damn, I love you, Morgan Rahn.*

"Shaine!"

She turned at the sound of her mother calling her name and waved a hand in response. Jeannette stood on the back porch.

"Shaine, your com has been buzzing incessantly for the last half hour! Can you come and answer whomever is calling you?"

Morgan looked over as well, a question on her face. Shaine scowled. There was only one person she could think of who would be calling her. "Fuck. Gotta be fucking Rogan." She pushed to her feet and called back to her mother, "Yeah, I'm coming!"

Morgan got up as well. "Wonder what he wants now?" she muttered.

Shaine shook her head, wiping her hands on her shorts. She waited until Morgan was at her side and they headed toward the house. Jeannette stopped them on the porch and pointed at their feet—Shaine's bare and covered with dirt, Morgan wearing muddy boots. Jeannette handed Shaine two towels. "Rinse pail is over there."

"Thanks, Mom." She was all too familiar with the evil "rinse pail," with which she'd had a close relationship all her growing up years.

Morgan took off her borrowed straw hat, toed off her boots and peeled off her socks, leaving them on the porch steps. When they'd finished washing off the mud and drying their feet, they grinned sheepishly at Jeannette and filed past her. Shaine grabbed her com off the breakfast bar, and led Morgan back into the den.

Closing the door behind them, she jacked her phone into the vid screen and recalled the incoming number, which she recognized as that of her former Security Group boss. When the call went through, the screen cleared to show Duncan Rogan sitting stiffly behind his desk. His muscular bulk filled his chair. His unadorned black uniform was as stark as his office space. Dark eyes pierced Shaine and Morgan impatiently. Shaine ignored his obvious irritation, as she always did. She hated that her knowledge of Mann-Maru's corporate secrets tied her to him. She hated that he held her own actions over her head, as much as she did the same for him. She pushed her hands through her sweat-dampened hair. Morgan stood beside her and slipped an arm around Shaine's waist.

"What do you want?" she demanded.

Rogan lifted a brow. "Am I interrupting a mud fight?"

Shaine said flatly, "Actually, yes. And I was winning. What do you want?"

He crossed his arms over his chest. "I have a proposition for you, Wendt."

Morgan cocked her head and said to Shaine, "You'd have thought he'd know by now that you're taken."

Shaine chuckled, settling her arm around Morgan's shoulders. "So, what's on your mind, Rogan?"

"How do you feel about Mars?"

"Mars?"

He nodded.

Shaine frowned. "What's on Mars?"

"Mann-Maru finally got mining rights there, which means we have the go-ahead to develop a mining site. Development requires security. I want you heading that security detail."

Shaine schooled her expression into unimpressed boredom. "I am a mechanic. I don't do security work anymore."

"You are no more a mechanic than I'm a nice guy."

Morgan murmured, "Well, you're certainly not a nice guy."

Shaine held a finger over the disconnect button. "I am not having this conversation."

Rogan asked sharply, "Do you plan on hiding on your parents' farm forever?"

"Actually, we were thinking of moving in permanently," Shaine returned. "Talk to ya later, Rogan." She disconnected the call.

Morgan shook her head. "He's an idiot."

Shaine nodded. "Yeah. Come on, let's go finish up the garden."

"You think he was serious?"

"Sure he's serious. He enjoys having his claws in my skin. And he's too paranoid to trust outsiders with anything this big."

Morgan added thoughtfully, "He's right about us not being able to hide here forever, though."

"Why not? Don't you like it here?"

"Well, sure, I like it, but—"

Shaine grinned. "Relax, I'm kidding." She gave Morgan's narrow shoulders a squeeze. "And you're right. We can't hide forever. But I don't want to admit that to him."

Morgan returned the grin. "Okay. I can live with that."

"You ever been to Mars?"

"Considering a road trip?"

"When he calls back, we can see what else he's got to say."

"Seriously?"

Shaine shrugged as they exited the house, pausing on the porch for Morgan to put her socks and shoes back on. "Eh, maybe. Call me stupid, but I'm curious. Besides, going back to the way things were isn't going to work, at least for the immediate future. If we go back to Moon Base, it's just going to be more of the same press in your face and pissing us off."

Morgan said, "That's probably true. But he's just using you, Shaine."

"I know. That's not gonna change."

"It pisses me off."

"I don't like it either, but as long as there is Mann-Maru and me, he's going to try to use me. It's just the way he is. In a way, it's kind of a mutual blackmailing. I know things about Mann-Maru that would be damaging to them. They know things I've done that would be damaging to me. I've been thinking about that. Maybe I should quit being pissed and figure out how to take advantage of the situation."

Morgan nodded. "Yeah, I can see that. Use it to get what you want. But he still pisses me off."

"No doubt."

"So, do you really want to go to Mars?"

Shaine shrugged. "I don't know. Never been there. It might be interesting. But I'm not going to worry about it right now. We can talk about it, roll it around and see how it feels. In any case, I don't want to give in to Rogan without a fight. He can sit and stew for a while, wondering what I'm going to do."

Morgan smiled. "Works for me."

"Good." Shaine grinned. "Let's go kill some weeds."

CHAPTER FIVE

Morgan decided she liked loud, boisterous dinners. Leese, Mike and Toby had joined Morgan, Shaine and Shaine's parents for the world's absolute best pot roast with roasted potatoes and carrots. Morgan swore she'd never had food so wonderful in her life. There was so much flavor in every bite, she didn't want to stop eating. It was going to be hard to go back to eating processed foods on Moon Base.

She happily accepted seconds and did her best to keep up with the multiple conversations surrounding her. Toby kept up a running stream of stories of happenings at university and drew Shaine and Morgan into a friendly sports rivalry over the System Soccer League teams. Shaine's father and her brother-in-law talked farming and politics. They occasionally asked Morgan and Shaine their political perspectives as spacers. Jeannette and Leese jumped into whatever conversations seemed to need their two cents and asked Morgan what it was like to live on Moon Base, and if she was enjoying her time on the farm.

It was everything Morgan imagined family dinners should be, and so much more lively and intense than anything she'd known. Growing up, she remembered quiet family dinners when her parents' shiftwork allowed. Later, it had been just her and her dad. Even when she had retreated into sullen teenaged silence, Vinn Rahn insisted they share a meal and somehow manage to touch base.

Jeannette served apple crunch with ice cream after they decimated dinner. Morgan sighed in pleasure, savoring the cold with the hot. The sweet and crunchy flavors and textures made her taste buds do something close to an orgasm. Washed down with fresh-ground coffee, she couldn't imagine anything better.

As the second round of coffee was poured, discussion turned to Toby's latest political cause.

Mike said, "It's pretty far-fetched, if you ask me. There's no good reason to reopen that old nuclear power plant. We don't need it here."

Jeannette agreed. "It's been inactive since before I was born. Seems silly to decide to refit it now."

Toby nodded enthusiastically. "It's all about corporate greed," he said firmly. "That's the only reason they'd try to reopen. It's an environmental danger of the hugest degree! They won't even talk about how they're planning on funding all the upgrades they have to do to get the site back to code."

Morgan asked, "Wasn't nuclear power outlawed on Earth centuries ago?"

Kent Ichiro nodded. "It was. But power plants in operation were allowed to continue. The problem is we've been safe for so long now, people have forgotten the dangers and disasters and the swaths of land left uninhabitable. Or they think that the plants will be safer and more foolproof."

"Exactly!" Toby agreed. "But the technology has hardly changed. There hasn't been any need to upgrade technology that's not in use. There are only three nuclear power plants in the world currently active and supplying power, and those are all in the middle of nowhere."

Shaine shook her head. "Who's pushing this? I can't imagine it's the local population around here."

Mike said, "There are a couple of local council people and a group in the territory senate, but I don't really see what they'd gain. They insist it would help the economy by giving us a new revenue stream, selling the extra power back to the grid, providing about two hundred and fifty permanent jobs, and a lot of construction and ramp-up employment."

"I don't see how they can possibly make it profitable," Kent Ichiro commented. "That reactor has been off-line for almost a hundred years. Seems to me it would be foolish to sink that much money into bringing the plant back to code."

Shaine asked, "If it's not a currently working facility, how can they bring it online anyway?"

"Loophole," Toby said disgustedly. "The original facility still exists, and they say it's still structurally viable, so legally they can still bring it online. The regulations have been quietly relaxed over the years. Backroom corporate politics. Slip an extra line in a bill here or there while nobody is paying any attention. Stupid idiots. Nuclear disasters destroyed three of the largest cities on the planet three hundred years ago, and they want to try it again."

Morgan sighed. "The corporate greed never stops, does it? They just never learn." Shaine raised a brow and Morgan scowled. "And my father is up there with the worst of them."

Kent shook his head. "Tarm Maruchek is nowhere near the worst of the lot."

Toby said, "There's going to be a protest on Saturday, at University Park. It's going to be huge. Everyone is going to be there. You and Morgan should come."

Shaine held up her hands. "I think we'll pass, buddy. We're too old for that kinda stuff."

Toby turned toward Morgan, his youthful face hopeful. "Oh, come on. It's going to be more like a party. They're even going to have a bunch of bands. I know you like music, Morgan. Come and show your support. You don't have to carry a sign or anything. Just be there, okay? It's like a community event, a big picnic."

Morgan glanced at Shaine who shrugged. Toby put on an expectant, hopeful expression, kind of like an excited puppy dog. Morgan sighed. "Aw, heck, Shaine. You wanna go?"

Shaine laughed. "Yeah, we'll go."

CHAPTER SIX

Saturday afternoon Shaine and Morgan strolled across the green expanse of University Park. Shaine pulled a kids' wagon filled with their cooler, a blanket, two beach chairs and a couple of tossing disks—one for her and Morgan, and one for Big George. The excessively furry Newfoundland trundled along with Morgan holding his leash. His tongue lolled and his tail wagged. Shaine thought he seemed very pleased to be out with his people for the day.

Shaine scanned the busy picnic grounds and decided that as protests went, this one was pretty low-key. She saw mostly young families and university students gathered around picnic tables and blankets, playing disk catch and soccer and having lunch. Signs and kiosks were scattered around the park, posting information about the damage that nuclear power plants had caused in the past and the potential dangers of reopening this one. An acoustic band played in the cement amphitheater at the center of the park. Mellow music floated up the low hill.

Morgan and Shaine spread their blanket on the low rise facing the stage, close enough to hear the music but far enough away that they could still chat. Throughout the day there would be people speaking, several bands and a fireworks show in the evening. From their vantage point, Shaine had a good view of all the action, or lack thereof. Old habits lingered, and she needed to have a handle on what was happening around her even if the mild, family-oriented crowd at the protest didn't seem the kind of mob that would be causing any trouble. She wasn't sure that being out in public was wise, since her intention was to keep Morgan in hiding. But with this many people around, it was like hiding in plain sight. They blended into the crowd, just another group of friends hanging out.

Big George flopped down in the grass next to Morgan with a huff and stretched his legs with a low groan. Morgan rubbed his bear-like head. She asked Shaine, "You think Toby and Chelsea will find us?"

"They'll find us." She grinned. "I have the beer."

Morgan laughed. She lounged in one of the low-to-the-ground beach chairs and tilted her face to the sky. Shaine stretched out next to Morgan and tucked her hands behind her head, eyes half-closed.

Morgan said, "I love the way the sun feels. It's amazing."

"I'm glad you like it."

Morgan combed her fingers through Shaine's short hair. "Thank you."

Shaine sighed and smiled. "You're welcome."

Toby and his girlfriend found them about an hour later. Shaine broke out the flying disks and the four of them played disk catch and fetch with George. Whipping the disk side-handed to Toby, she felt about half of her thirty-nine years. Even Morgan seemed to have regressed from the worldly age of twenty-seven to a carefree seventeen. *To hell with being in hiding*, she thought. They both needed this.

She didn't remember the last time she'd played outside and not in a sealed dome. Probably not since she was in Earth Guard, on leave with her buddies or between missions on Earth.

She wanted to run and cheer and shout to the whole universe that it was a perfect day.

She jumped to catch Toby's return throw, turned and fired the disk toward Morgan. It went high. Morgan took a couple running steps and jumped to snag it. George leaped into the air at the same time and bounced soundly into Morgan, capturing the disk in his mouth and taking them both to the ground with a delighted woof.

Morgan laughed as she pushed Big George off her, wiping the slobber from her face while George pranced in circles, barking and growling with the disk in his teeth.

Shaine jogged over. "You okay?"

Morgan grinned. "I'm good." Shaine pulled her easily to her feet.

Not long after, Toby complained piteously of starving to death. Shaine gave him a hard time even though she felt her own stomach rumbling. They broke out the picnic cooler and passed out sandwiches, chips and cookies.

Toby wolfed down half of his first sandwich in two bites while his girlfriend shook her head at him. "Slow down before you choke," she chided.

He shoved another bite into his mouth and protested around it, "Hey, I'm a growing boy."

"Better watch it before you start growing in more than one direction, T."

He flipped Shaine off and grabbed a second sandwich from the container. "I've been playing disks all day. Gotta keep up my energy." He waggled his eyebrows. "Did ya pack any beer in there?" he asked.

"What, you think I'm lame or something? Of course I did. After Mom left," she added with a guilty smirk. "Let's save it for later. Here, have a soda."

Big George bumped Morgan's hand with his nose, getting her attention and turning pleading eyes on her sandwich. He tipped his head hopefully. A long string of drool dripped from the side of his mouth. Morgan ripped a corner off her sandwich and held it out for George. It disappeared in an instant, and she rubbed his head.

Shaine muttered, "Big baby beggar," and gave him a couple chips.

Chelsea said, "You guys are staying for the fireworks, right? Have you ever seen fireworks, Morgan?"

Morgan shook her head. "I'm excited to see them for real."

"You'll love it!"

Toby put in, "My buddy Johan's band is playing right after the fireworks. They're seriously tight, just killin'."

"Is that the recording you sent me a couple weeks ago?" Shaine asked. Toby nodded. Shaine said to Morgan, "It's the prog-slam band I played for you."

Morgan grinned. "Excellent."

The afternoon went quickly. They ate the rest of the picnic lunch and Shaine brought out the beer as night fell and it was time to settle in for the fireworks. Shaine and Morgan got comfortable on their blanket. George curled up in the grass beside them. Toby and Chelsea spread their own blanket just a bit away.

Morgan scrunched up two fleece jackets and made a pillow, which she put under Shaine's head before she stretched out beside her.

"You comfy?" Shaine asked.

Morgan wriggled a little closer. Shaine eased her arm under Morgan's head and helped her settle in. The sky glittered with stars and the moon hadn't yet risen over the trees. Though they were in a crowd, and Toby and Chelsea were only a couple meters away, the darkness made it feel as though she was alone with Morgan. She savored the sensation of Morgan resting against her. She turned her head to kiss Morgan's hair.

Morgan said, "The sky at night is different here. The dark has more colors."

Shaine studied the sky and thought, *Everything has more color with you here*, but it sounded stupid so she bit her tongue and said, "It's a beautiful night."

From the stage, a low rumble of music started up. Shaine recognized the opening notes from an action vid soundtrack. The music crescendoed and the first fireworks arced up and exploded into a shower of white sparkles. Morgan laughed delightedly.

The music changed from orchestral to popular and the fireworks transformed to match it. Shooting stars and expanding globes of color left trails of red, green and gold sparkles across the night. The reports of the explosions echoed over the hill. A few actually vibrated the ground, and Shaine felt the concussions under her back.

She had a momentary flashback to her time in Earth Guard, to a night in the jungle where she lay hidden in thick brush, watching her own handiwork as a terrorist compound blew itself to hell in a blinding flash of light and sound, shaking the ground beneath her.

That was when she noticed some of the pops and bangs she heard didn't match what she saw in the sky. For a second she thought she was still lost in memories. But the screams were wrong. She heard another spate of blasts.

"That's rifle fire," she muttered. Suddenly, blood pumped wildly in her veins. She stood up and she scanned the darkened park.

The fireworks show continued, spewing colorful patterns into the sky.

Morgan got uncertainly to her feet.

"There." Shaine pointed toward small flashes of light at the far edge of the park. She leaned over to Toby and Chelsea and grabbed Toby by the arm. "Call the police. Tell them there's weapons fire at the protest. Tell them to send medical. Now." Turning, she said to Morgan, "Be right back."

Morgan said, "I'm going with."

Shaine opened her mouth to protest, then shrugged and sprinted toward the flashes of light. There wasn't time to argue.

They bolted up the back of the rise, away from the amphitheater. As they cleared the top of the hill onto the expanse of flat picnic grounds in front of the parking area, they had to dodge people scattering in their direction, yelling and frightened, carrying crying children.

The fireworks show continued to build to an ear-shattering finale. The whine of sirens rose in the near distance. Automatic weapons fire cracked and popped along with the wail of screams.

Shaine and Morgan sprinted full-out over the grass. Shaine could see the gunmen at the perimeter of the parking lot, firing into the edge of the crowd. As they approached, Shaine paused behind a tree, crouching and pulling Morgan down beside her. "Multiple shooters," she muttered.

In the haze of smoke and dust, backlit by vehicle headlights, four assailants fired into the park. They didn't advance their position, just kept firing in place. Two dark-colored hover-vans with their side doors open idled behind the gunmen. Shaine could see one driver in each van. She looked at Morgan.

"Stay here."

Morgan opened her mouth to protest. Shaine leaned over and kissed her hard. "Don't move. I'll be right back." She took off in a low run toward the vehicles. Because of the headlights pointed forward, she had the advantage of shadows and darkness and was able to cross the short distance unnoticed.

She reached the first van and wrenched open the driver's door, grabbing him by the front of his shirt and pulling him out. He didn't even have a chance to squeak before her fist connected with his face. She dropped him, unconscious, to the grass.

She took his place behind the wheel, jammed the van into drive and shoved the throttle forward. The first gunman didn't have time to react before he met the van's grille. The second man shouted and started to run, but she hit him too. The third shooter turned toward her.

Bullets shattered the windshield as she dove out the open driver's door, tucking and rolling as she hit the ground. The van careened forward and hit a tree.

Sirens converged around the park.

Shaine felt pain as a distant sensation as she scrambled to her feet. She saw the second van take off, spraying dust behind it. The remaining gunman took off running across the grass toward the crowd. Shaine started after him.

Morgan burst out from behind a tree, cutting across the grass in front of her.

Morgan launched into the man's legs, tackling and clinging to him as he struggled to get free.

Shaine threw herself on the man's back and landed a solid right hook into the side of his face, stunning him.

"Fuck, Shaine, you're bleeding!"

"Windshield." Gritting her teeth, she pulled the guy's belt off and used it to tie his hands behind his back. He started to struggle again and she smacked the back of his head. "Don't move or I'll use real force," she growled.

"Freeze! Halt or we will open fire!" The voice snapped over an exterior speaker from one of the patrol cars.

Shaine straightened slowly, hands open and held out to her sides as the police converged on them en masse. Morgan froze, wide-eyed, her face pale.

Several SWAT team members ran toward them with assault rifles drawn. "On your knees, now! Hands on your heads!"

Shaine and Morgan did as they were told. Four officers moved forward. Two covered Shaine and Morgan with rifles pointed at their heads. The other two men moved in. Shaine clamped down on a cry as one grabbed her arms and pulled them roughly behind her back. Glass shards from the windshield cut through her skin with the movement. Blood dripped down her back under her shirt.

She shot a quick look toward Morgan, feeling absolutely horrible to see the stark fear written on Morgan's pale features as the other officer secured her hands behind her back. Fuck. Now what had she gotten them into? She took a breath, calming herself.

She said quietly, "We are unarmed. My ID is in my back pocket. Ex-EG, making a civilian arrest. Two shooters and one driver down behind us. One shooter and one van got away. She's with me."

The officer dug roughly in her pocket for her wallet, flipping it open to verify her ID while his buddy patted Morgan down. Six other officers held assault rifles pointed at them. Another group checked out the two gunmen Shaine had hit and the gunman who lay groaning beside them.

One of officers holding Shaine asked, "Did you see where they were headed?"

"The van took off out of the parking lot heading north."

Morgan said sharply, "Shaine needs a medic before she bleeds to death."

"Shut up." The man holding her gave her a rough shake.

The officer in charge snapped, "Boroveck, get a medic." He turned to another officer. "Take these two over to the squads. I'm holding them for questioning."

Two officers escorted Shaine and Morgan to where the police air cars were parked. One opened a car door and said to Shaine, "You can sit there if you want."

Shaine leaned against the car with a groan. If she sat, she'd really start feeling the hurt. "I'll just stand quietly," she muttered.

The officer shrugged. "Your choice. Just don't try anything stupid." He and his partner moved a couple steps away from the two women and stood watch over them. His hand rested menacingly close to his firearm.

Morgan turned to her. "Shaine, are you okay?"

Shaine grimaced, but nodded. "Hurts like a bitch, but I'll be fine. The glass is going to need to be picked out."

Morgan muttered, "Then they fucking well better get over here and start picking."

Shaine gave her a wry grin. It warmed her heart when Morgan got her hackles up on her behalf.

Morgan warily eyed the officers watching them. "Are they gonna arrest us for getting involved?" she asked.

Shaine shrugged, winced, and silently cursed the handcuffs. "More likely they just want to know what we saw, what we heard. They're just playing it safe keeping us cuffed."

"I thought they were going to shoot first and ask later. I nearly peed my pants." Morgan shuddered.

Shaine wished she could put her arms around Morgan. "I'm sorry you got involved in this, Morg."

"I'm okay. It's not your fault. I followed you."

Shaine frowned, not convinced. Morgan said, "At least you weren't scared out of your wits."

Shaine choked out a harsh laugh. "Don't believe that for a second. Only idiots aren't scared when a dozen guns are pointed in their face."

"Well, there goes my hero worship."

Shaine snorted.

CHAPTER SEVEN

It was nearly four in the morning when Shaine and Morgan returned to the farm. Shaine was thoroughly exhausted. It had been an endless night. The medics had brought her, under guard and still handcuffed, to a triage tent. The damage wasn't bad. Several shards of glass were removed from her back and shoulder. Three of the larger cuts needed a couple of stitches. The police kept Shaine and Morgan on-site for another four hours, peppering them with questions.

Shaine didn't blame Owens, the officer in charge, for his suspicion and caution. Shaine kept calmly to her story. She felt bad that Morgan was also being questioned, but Morgan seemed to be taking the situation in stride.

Morgan told her that Owens asked if she was "that" Morgan Rahn, Tarm Maruchek's daughter. She confirmed his suspicions and told him that she was trying to stay out of the limelight. He told her she was doing a lousy job of it. All she could do was laugh. He asked Shaine about Morgan as well. Shaine verified Morgan's identity, and he didn't mention it again.

Eventually, Owens released them, requesting that they remain in the area and be available for additional interviews. Shaine gave him the address of the farm and her personal com code.

Shaine pulled the Racer into the wide driveway and immediately noted the extra cars and all the lights on in the house. She and Morgan stumped up the porch stairs and into the kitchen, arms around each others' waists, leaning on each other. Shaine breathed in the wonderful aroma of fresh-brewed coffee.

Muted voices filtered to them from the entertainment room. She and Morgan walked through to find Shaine's parents drinking coffee with her sister and brother-in-law, plus Toby, Chelsea and a woman Shaine assumed was Chelsea's mother. The big vid screen was on, split between two different news feeds. Closed-captions ran along the bottoms of each window.

"Oh, Shaine! Morgan! You're finally home!" Jeannette was on her feet in a second, rushing to greet them.

Shaine grimaced when Jeannette wrapped her into a motherly hug. "Mom, easy, please," she managed, hearing the crack in her voice when her mom squeezed too hard.

Jeannette released her instantly, stepping back. "Oh, my God, what happened to you?"

Everyone surrounded them in a babble of anxious voices and questions. Morgan sagged against the doorframe looking shell-shocked. Shaine managed to sidle over to her and got an arm around her waist again. Morgan leaned against her.

Shaine finally said, "We're fine, really. But we need to sit, okay?"

Leese ordered, "Toby, go get them some coffee and the sandwiches from the fridge."

Shaine smiled thankfully as Jeannette and Kent ushered her and Morgan to the sofa. They gladly settled down with a couple of quilts tucked around them. A few moments later, Toby and Chelsea returned with mugs of coffee and plates full of sandwiches and cookies. Shaine didn't realize how hungry she was until she smelled the food. Morgan sighed as she sipped the hot coffee.

Jeannette hovered around them. Shaine took another bite of her turkey sandwich and spoke around it. "Mom, sit down. You're making me nuts. What have they been saying on the news?"

Kent and Mike filled them in. The media described a mysterious unarmed woman from the crowd who went up against the gunmen to break up the siege. Someone had taken photos of her and Morgan, handcuffed and talking to the police investigators. Shaine was glad they hadn't had to fend off any reporters.

Shaine nodded toward the vid screen. "Have they learned anything yet?"

Her stepfather said, "Four people dead, nine injured. Seems the gunmen were shooting into the ground or the air a lot of the time. Reporters are speculating the intent was to scare people more than kill them."

"I don't know if it was intentional or not, but using conventional weapons instead of using laser rifles helped them blend in with the sound of the fireworks. Have they figured out yet who Morgan is? Or who I am?"

Leese said, "I just heard them identify Morgan. They haven't released your name, but I imagine that's just a matter of time. Enough people around here still remember you."

Shaine sighed. "I should have stayed out of this."

Morgan rubbed Shaine's back. "You saved lives."

"Yeah, well, it's gonna come back and bite our asses. And probably have media here at the farm."

Jeannette said flatly, "They are not going to get any cookies."

Shaine chuckled.

Chelsea sniffled. "I just don't understand why anyone would just start shooting people for no reason." Tears re-formed in her eyes, already red from crying.

Toby wrapped his arms around her. "It was a peaceful protest," he said. "Nobody was hurting anyone, and they just opened fire. It's insane. They killed Benny Hauser's brother Natt! How could they do that? What did it accomplish?"

Shaine studied her nephew. His shoulders slumped and he looked tired and defeated. Both he and Chelsea were pretty sheltered, growing up in the peacefulness of a small town. She'd seen the darker side of humanity. Hell, she'd *been* the darker side of humanity. But these kids—they were innocents. Whether they realized it or not, what they'd experienced tonight had changed them both.

* * *

A couple hours later, Morgan and Shaine finally crawled into bed. The sky showing through the bedroom's dome had begun to lighten toward dawn. Shaine wrapped her arms around Morgan and tucked Morgan's head under her chin. Morgan snuggled in close, one arm thrown across Shaine's stomach. Shaine's back throbbed where she'd been cut, but it helped just to be lying down. The cool sheets felt good against her fevered skin.

Shaine murmured, "Long night, huh?"

"Yeah. This makes it better, though."

Shaine smiled. "Feels good to hold you."

"Mmmm." Morgan kissed the bare skin under her cheek.

They were silent for a long time. Shaine thought Morgan had fallen asleep when Morgan asked, "What are you thinking? I can almost hear the gears grinding up there."

"Thinking about tonight. You and I are going to take some heat for this because I jumped in there."

"Let 'em talk, Shaine. Can't make it any worse than it is."

"I just hope it doesn't make us a target."

"Target?"

"Yeah. For whoever's plans I fucked with tonight."

"Mmmm. That wouldn't be good."

"No."

"I think you worry too much."

Shaine kissed Morgan's head. "Probably."

Morgan nibbled at the base of Shaine's neck. Shaine shivered as Morgan ran a hand up her torso and slid her palm over a hardening nipple. "Worry tomorrow," Morgan whispered.

Shaine groaned and shifted under her, finding Morgan's lips with her own. *Yeah*, she thought, as Morgan stole her breath, *worry tomorrow*.

* * *

The incessant beeping of Shaine's comp pad shattered the morning. Shaine groaned as she snaked a hand out from under the covers to grab the pad on the nightstand. She thumbed the touch-screen, muttering an oath as she recognized the incoming com code. Morgan mumbled and ducked her head below the covers.

Shaine accepted the call and grunted into the mic. "Yeah?" She double-checked to make sure the video send was off. Rogan didn't need any thrills.

The security chief's less than happy tone boomed through the small speaker, "You know, Wendt, you're not making things any simpler by playing the hero."

Shaine sighed. According to the chron on the nightstand, they'd only been asleep for four hours. It was too fucking early to be having this conversation. She said flatly, "I wasn't going to sit back and watch people die."

"No. You wouldn't, would you?"

Shaine felt Morgan snicker under the covers. She yawned and asked, "Who's behind the shootings?" She assumed that he already had his people looking into things, probably had Kyle Ellerand hacking into the local police database. Since she and Morgan had been involved, Rogan was probably all over it, at least to the extent that it might affect them.

Rogan said, "I don't know who's behind it and it's not my problem so I really don't care. My problem is that you were supposed to keep Morgan out of the spotlight, and it would appear the spotlight found her again."

Morgan popped her head out from under the quilt and said, "If you think I was going to sit back and hide when Shaine might have needed backup, you're dumber than I thought."

"You realize your father is having a fit about this? How are we supposed to insulate you if you refuse to stay hidden?"

Morgan yawned and curled up again.

Rogan continued, "Should I assume this is the end of the situation?"

Shaine said, "I don't know that you should assume anything at this point."

"Don't get involved in this, Wendt. It's nothing to do with us."

"I don't plan on getting involved," she said evenly.

"Stay out of it."

"Yeah, yeah. You worry too much, Rogan."

"You give me reason to," he snapped, and ended the call.

Shaine looked up at raindrops splattering against the glass panels, blurring the view of a gray, overcast sky. Rogan wasn't going to look into the situation. He didn't care. Bastard. She cared. And this wasn't over. Not just yet.

But it was still too fucking early for this. She returned the comp pad to the nightstand and squirmed down under the covers, wrapping herself around Morgan's warmth with a sigh. She kissed Morgan's dark head. She didn't know if she'd be able to fall back to sleep, but there was no sense in getting up early if it was going to rain.

CHAPTER EIGHT

Morgan could only describe the day as gray. Gloomy clouds hung low in the sky. The pouring rain washed out the scenery past the barns. She sat on the porch swing and watched the rain. It pattered steadily on the roof, falling in heavy sheets off the porch eaves and collecting in muddy puddles in the driveway. The air felt damp and clammy.

Morgan cuddled into an oversized sweatshirt she'd found in Shaine's closet. She tucked her feet beneath her, pulling the jacket down over her legs and huddling under the soft fleece.

The rain fascinated her. The dampness made her shiver. Moon Base was so dry. Water was carefully rationed. The small park at the center of Moon Base had grass specially developed to require very little moisture. All the plants were drought-resistant. Shower facilities were sonic and used very limited amounts of water.

To see so much water falling from the sky amazed her and she couldn't stop watching it. So many things that Shaine and her family took for granted, she considered wondrous. It made her feel as though she'd lived her life in a sterile cage. She'd seen all these things in vids—rain and hot sunshine and horses and puddles and mud. But the experience was so much more than she'd imagined. When it shone, the sun warmed her through to her bones. Animals snorted and barked and were warm and furry and so much bigger than she'd thought they'd be. Hoss the horse had stiff, coarse fur that lay flat against his muscular body. George's fur was soft and thick and wild and fluffy and he shed constantly. The animals all had their own odor. The dirt was warm where the sun baked it and cool when she dug down. The air was always moving, even when there was no wind, and there were so many different smells.

She was accustomed to the scrubbed, flat taste of Moon Base air and the scent of too many people too close. Body odor and perfume and sweat mingled with the processed restaurant food aromas of many different ethnicities and the sharp tang of grease and oil and machinery. Some days the air-scrubbers worked more efficiently than others.

On Earth the air was endless. And there wasn't a dome over her head. She'd look up, half expecting to see the sky through weathered glassteel. Having experienced Earth, she knew it would be stifling to go back to Moon Base. But she missed her dad and her friends, especially Charri.

She powered up the comp pad she'd brought out on the porch and connected to the net. Almost immediately, Charri's avatar popped up on her screen. The pink and magenta jungle cat with violet eyes growled at her and Morgan grinned. Glancing at the time, she did the math and figured it was close to twenty-two-hundred hours on Moon Base. Charri would be getting ready to work third shift. She initiated her own avatar, a silvery green dragon, and greeted Charri in text mode.

Morgan: Hey, Char!

Charri: Morg!! Miss you!

Morgan: Miss u 2! How are things going up there?

Charri: Same old. Work. Sleep. Work some more. Quiet without u here. Ben's band is playing this weekend at Club Tranquility.

Morgan: Wish I was there. Hug Ben for me?

Charri: I will. How are you? How is Shaine's family? How is the farm?

Morgan: I'm good. The family is really nice. I rode a horse!

Charri: That is so excellent! You and Shaine getting along okay?

Morgan: We're good. Real good.

Charri: When r u coming home?

Morgan: No idea. We haven't talked about it. Waiting to see what happens.

Charri: I really miss ya.

Morgan: Miss u 2. Feels like I've been gone forever. Have you seen my dad?

Charri: I haven't seen him, no. You haven't missed anything here, that's for sure.

Morgan: I need to call him. I feel bad leaving him up there.

Charri: Your dad is okay. He wants you to be happy. He's got lots of friends. You know he keeps busy. He'll be fine.

Morgan: I still worry.

Charri: I can stop by tomorrow and see him, let you know how he is.

Morgan: Thanks.

Charri: I gotta go. Time to head to work. Talk later?

Morgan: I'll be around.

Charri's avatar blinked out of existence. Morgan sighed and closed down her own avatar. There wasn't anyone else she wanted to talk to, though see could see that a few of her other friends were online.

In the last month, she'd been away from her dad and her friends more than she'd been in her whole life. She wasn't homesick, exactly, but she felt guilty leaving her dad. She hadn't lived with him in over ten years, but she still saw him at least a couple times a week. It'd just been the two of them since she was twelve years old, when her mom died.

She felt responsible for him, as though she should be around in case he needed her. She felt guilty and selfish that she was running away from the reporters stalking her on Moon Base and that she was enjoying her time with Shaine. She set the comp pad down beside her and stared out toward the fields, wondering how long the rain would last. And how long she and Shaine would be gone from home.

* * *

Shaine relaxed into the gentle massage Morgan gave her neck. Morgan leaned over her shoulder, peering at the computer terminal on the desk in Shaine's room. Shaine smiled at the feel of Morgan's warm breath in her ear.

"Finding anything interesting?" Morgan asked.

Shaine wondered how such an innocent question could sound so sexy. Morgan's strong fingers worked the muscles at the base of her neck and shoulders. Shaine almost purred. After a few moments, Morgan prompted, "Well?"

Shaine blinked. "Oh." She grinned. "Not really. Just background history."

Morgan kept up her shoulder massage and kissed the top of Shaine's head. "You'll come up with something," she said.

Shaine sighed. "I hope so."

Morgan kissed her cheek. "I'm gonna see if Charri's on the net," she said, and moved back to her spot on the bed, curled up in a blanket with her comp pad. Shaine smiled and turned back to the terminal.

The rain had continued into the afternoon. Shaine decided it was a good time to start researching the nuclear power plant and the company that was trying to put it back into production. What she'd found so far about Global Geo Systems wasn't earth-shattering, or anything she didn't already know.

Most interesting was that Mann-Maru had acquired GGS nearly twenty years ago, though GGS operated as an independent subsidiary. It struck her as odd because Mann-Maru was one of the few companies that had sided with the environmental groups lobbying vocally against GGS bringing old nuclear plants back online.

GGS insisted that it was their right to remain commercially viable and that Mann-Maru and others were just trying to keep the underdogs down to maintain a monopoly, despite the fact that Mann-Maru didn't own or run any nuclear or other power facilities. GGS insisted that in communities struggling for jobs, the power plants would be welcomed.

Shaine didn't think her hometown of Pleasant Valley was a struggling community. The majority of farmers, including her parents, generated their own solar and wind power and were mostly self-sufficient. Even in town, most houses and buildings had solar units supplying power to the grid.

Shaine wondered why Mann-Maru didn't just cut GGS lose. Why keep a subsidiary that was acting against Mann-Maru's interests? Maybe, instead of researching backdoor methods of shutting the power plant down, she should just go to Tarm Maruchek and ask him to get involved. He certainly had the power to do so.

In the meanwhile, though, it made sense to dig up what she could and turn it over to Mann-Maru's best intelligence analyst. Kyle Ellerand excelled at uncovering information. If a loophole existed that they could use to keep the plant shut down, Kyle could find it.

Looking up from her pad, Morgan asked, "Hey, Shaine, is this power plant thing for sure?"

Shaine shrugged. "The process has been started. The sale of the land to GGS is legal. But the request for an operation license is still in deliberation. The land has to be rezoned. Right now it's considered a protected site, so the plant can't be put into active use until that's changed."

Morgan cocked her head. "So, even if GGS owns the land and the buildings, their hands are tied until everything else is done."

"Right."

"Where are you going with this, Shaine?"

Shaine ran her fingers through her short hair and turned in her chair to face Morgan. "Not sure. I just know I want it shut down for good."

Morgan set her pad aside and considered her seriously. "Is there anything we can actually do?"

Shaine frowned. What did she really want to accomplish, and was it even feasible? She'd been away from Pleasant Valley a long time, but she felt the need to do something to keep her hometown safe. Her family was here. She couldn't walk away without at least trying to help. She said, "There has to be a way to keep the plant permanently shut down. Some buried clause or law or statute that would mean they couldn't bring the plant back online."

Morgan said, "You'd think the locals would have found something if it's out there. From what Toby and Chelsea said, they've been working this issue for quite a while."

Shaine shrugged. "Depends on where they're looking and who's doing the searches."

Morgan scratched her cheek. "You could always ask Kyle to take a look for you," she suggested, "because I know that's what you're thinking."

Shaine laughed. Morgan sure had her number. "Damn, I love you."

Morgan grinned back. "Feeling's mutual."

"Good." Shaine picked up her comp pad and tapped in Kyle Ellerand's personal calling code.

After a few seconds the screen cleared and the mousy intel genius grinned back at her. "Hey, Wendt, anyone ever tell ya playin' hero is no way to keep a low profile?"

"Nice to talk to you too, Kyle."

Ellerand laughed. "Rogan's stomping around here having conip-fits. I've been spending all my time trying to cover your sorry ass so the press doesn't find out more than your usual cover story with Mann-Maru. Of course, if you keep playing commando, nobody is going to believe you were a low-level security administrator for ten years. If I were you, I'd lie low. Unfortunately, they've pegged Morgan, so she's not in hiding anymore."

Shaine sighed. "Sorry."

"No worries," he conceded. "I'll do what I can."

"Fuck."

"About sums it up. So, what's going on?"

Shaine asked, "Have any time to do some recreational research?"

"For you, luv, I'd move mountains," he responded graciously.

"Yeah, yeah. Suck up. There's an old nuclear power plant here that GGS bought and wants to refurbish and put into operation. Anyone with a brain knows it's a disaster waiting to happen. Unfortunately, some yahoos on the territory council seem to be determined to push this through. I'm looking for a loophole that gives the people a way to shut it down permanently. It's probably buried under a few tons of bureaucratic muck and I thought you might be able to dig it out."

He grinned. "Ah, my specialty, cutting through red tape. Yeah. I can do that."

"I'll send over a data packet with some background."

"Okay." He leaned back in his chair. "Seriously, though, how are you guys weathering the storm?"

Shaine grinned. "We're doing fine, and my mother loves Morgan. It's been good, up until I was stupid."

"Just keep your head down for a bit and it'll settle. I'll call ya when I have something useful."

"Thanks, Kyle. We appreciate it."

He grinned. "Don't thank me yet. Talk at ya later." He signed off.

Morgan made a face. "I didn't figure we'd caused that much of an issue, being seen."

Shaine scowled. "If I'd have thought about it, I'd have thought better of it."

Morgan chuckled. "Naw, you'd have done it anyway," she said.

"I'll be right back."

Shaine left Morgan in the bedroom talking to Charri on the net and trotted down the stairs to the den. She closed the door behind her and took out her comp pad, holding it and thinking for a moment before she chose the com code for Tarm Maruchek's direct line. She wasn't sure if going to him directly was a good idea, but she did know that she wanted to do it out of Morgan's earshot. She didn't know what, if anything, would come of the conversation, and she didn't want Morgan to see Maruchek in a bad light if the response was negative. Morgan had enough to deal with just knowing the man was her father.

Setting her shoulders, she tapped the com code.

After a few seconds, Tarm Maruchek's face came up on the screen. "Shaine."

She nodded. "Mr. Maruchek."

He frowned at her and she studied his face. There was so little of Morgan in Tarm Maruchek's angular, strong-jawed countenance. Morgan had her birth mother's delicate features and wide gray eyes rather than Tarm's deep-set piercing blue. Tarm asked, "Is something wrong?"

"No. We're fine. I have something I want to talk to you about."

"If you're going to apologize for getting in the middle of a shoot-out, it's a bit late for that."

Shaine wasn't sure if he was being sarcastic or genuinely angry. "I won't apologize for trying to save people. But I will say that I didn't mean for Morgan to be in the middle of it."

Maruchek nodded slowly, his expression stern. "She does have a mind of her own, very much like her mother."

Shaine said nothing. She'd never known Arella Maruchek.

"What can I do for you, Shaine?"

"I'm sure you're aware of the situation here with GGS."

"Yes, I am."

"They're a subsidiary of Mann-Maru, is that correct?"

Maruchek nodded.

Shaine ran her tongue over her lips. "I'll be blunt. I don't want this power plant in my hometown. You have the power to shut the whole thing down. You can lean on GGS, either politically or otherwise, to put a stop to this. I know you're not in favor of GGS opening these nuclear plants. Do the right thing and shut them down."

Maruchek frowned. "It is not that simple, Shaine."

"Isn't it? Sell them off, cut them loose. Put political pressure on them. There must be something you can do to kill this initiative."

"GGS is an independently run subsidiary. We have a controlling interest in their shares, and I have people on their board of directors, but it is not a policy of Mann-Maru to have direct control of our subsidiaries. It would be a breach of the subsidiary contract."

"So cut them loose. I've never asked anything of you in all the years that I've worked for you. I'm asking you this."

Maruchek studied her face. "I will give it some thought. But I will make no promises."

Shaine nodded. "Thank you."

He cocked his head, a small smile turning up his lips. "You're going to look for a way to shut this down whether I get involved or not, aren't you?" he asked.

"It's a possibility."

He nodded. "All I can say is that if anything comes back to Mann-Maru, you're on your own, Shaine. We won't bail you out."

"Understood."

"Keep my daughter out of trouble."

"I'll try."

He nodded and closed the connection.

Shaine frowned at the comp pad and wondered if she'd accomplished anything with that conversation. She very much doubted that Maruchek would intervene to stop GGS. On the other hand, she found it interesting that he didn't seem to intend to stop her from looking into the situation.

With any luck at all, Kyle Ellerand would find something they could use to keep the power plant closed. If not, she wasn't sure what she could do.

* * *

After dinner, Morgan followed Shaine, Kent and Jeannette into the entertainment room to have coffee. Morgan settled on the sofa. Shaine turned on the vid screen and sat beside her. The local evening news focused, as expected, on the shootings at the protest. The death toll had risen to five people—four adults and one child killed.

The faces of the four captured men came on screen. The first gunman was dead, killed when Shaine ran him down with the van. The other two were injured and recovering. The van driver had only minor injuries. The second van driver, who'd escaped with the fourth gunman, was arrested earlier in the day when the others gave up his name.

According to the police liaison, all the men told the same story. The fourth gunman, who remained at large, had arranged the attack and paid them. None of them knew his name. He'd worn a mask the entire time, so they had no facial description. The captured men appeared to have no personal agendas other than to make a fast cash profit. They'd each been paid a half-million credits. The lead gunman instructed them to shoot toward the crowd, but to aim into the ground or into the air. "Scare the hell out of them, but you don't have to kill anyone unless you want to," was the quote they relayed to authorities. All but one of the victims were killed by ricocheting bullets or shrapnel.

Shaine's expression was grim as the news anchor moved on to the next story. She said, "The guy who got away is someone else's errand boy. Considering the amount of money those idiots were paid, it stinks of corporate scare tactics."

Morgan studied Shaine's cold expression. Knowing Shaine's history with Mann-Maru Corporate Security, she figured if Shaine suspected a company's involvement, she probably wasn't far off. She'd long ago learned to believe the worst about corporate tactics. The larger the firm, the more they seemed to be laws unto themselves. It was the one thing that made her uneasy about her birth father. She knew Tarm Maruchek had more power and money than most. She wanted to believe that he used his influence more for good than for his own purposes, but she simply didn't know.

Jeannette asked, "Regardless of who's behind it, why shoot innocent people without saying what they want?"

"Fear is a great motivator. Everyone assumes it was against the protesters. Now maybe fewer people will bring up objections to the power plant." Shaine sipped her coffee and added, "In any case, if it's a corporate-backed attack, GGS isn't going to claim it, and it isn't likely it can be traced back to them anyway. If the protests continue or grow into real political opposition, I can guarantee you there's going to be more trouble."

Jeannette's brow furrowed. Kent nodded thoughtfully. "I'm sure the authorities are thinking the same thing," he said.

"I hope so," Shaine muttered.

Morgan asked, "Why haven't they brought in Earth System Investigations?"

"ESI would only get involved if the incident is more global than local," Shaine replied.

Shaine's mom went to the kitchen for more coffee and her father followed. Morgan glanced at Shaine and whispered, "Hear anything from Kyle?"

Shaine shook her head. "Not yet. I'll call him later."

Morgan nodded and settled back to watch the sports scores.

Kent and Jeannette returned with their coffee and settled back into their recliners. Kent asked, "Do you think it's an issue that your name has come out with this, Shaine?"

She shrugged. "I wouldn't expect so. My plan to keep Morgan hidden is trashed, though. As far as me breaking up the shooting spree, a lot of folks around here know I was in special operations, so they wouldn't think much of it. Whoever set the attack up might not be real happy about it, but I don't see them retaliating."

Her mother's eyes widened. "You think you could be in danger?" she asked.

"Nobody's going to come looking for me, Mom. Don't worry about it."

Morgan looked down at her cooling coffee then across the room at the vid screen. *They might not come looking for Shaine, but chances are, we'll end up looking for them. And if they figure out who Shaine is and what she's capable of, they'll definitely see her as a threat.* She said nothing. She didn't want Shaine's parents to worry. She and Shaine could take care of themselves.

* * *

After the local news finished, Shaine and Morgan retreated to Shaine's room for the remainder of the evening. Morgan flopped onto her stomach on the big bed, reaching for her comp pad on the nightstand. "I need to check my mail," she said.

Shaine settled beside her, leaning back against the headboard and retrieving her own comp pad. "You'd better let Charri and your dad know you're okay," she suggested.

Morgan raised a brow. "You're starting to sound like your mother."

Shaine snorted. "Right," she muttered, but as she played her words back in her head, she had to admit it was true. She sighed heavily. "I gotta call Kyle," she said, and tapped in her encryption key to dial through.

Morgan snickered.

Kyle picked up the call just before it would have gone to his message queue. He greeted her with a grin, pushing sandy brown hair out of his eyes. He reminded her of an adolescent who hadn't combed his hair for a week. "Hey, Wendt, how's things?"

Shaine glanced around, assessing. Girlfriend on her right, comfortable bed, skylight. She grinned into the tiny vid camera. "Can't complain much, Ellerand. Got anything for me?"

"Actually, I was just gonna call ya. Only one possibility I've come up with so far. And I'm not sure it's going to be very helpful."

"Just hit me with it."

"I found the original land sale and zoning documents. They're different than the copies available to the public, because the 'gotcha' clause was removed from the copies. If the original structures of the containment facility or the cooling towers are destroyed or damaged badly enough to make them unusable, the land becomes Territory Protectorate land. It can't ever be developed. I'm sure they expected that if the structure was that badly damaged, what was left would be an uninhabitable, radioactive no man's land."

Morgan looked up from her pad and said, "The original structures are still intact, so this doesn't matter."

"Right." Ellerand nodded, his eyes focused meaningfully on Shaine. "Unless something were to happen to the current structure. I found the original blueprints of the site and buildings. Haven't been able to come up with any additions or extensions to the originals, but I'll keep looking. I'm sure they're out there. I'll send it all to you, encrypted."

"Thanks, Kyle."

"No problem."

Shaine logged off the com session and leaned back on the bed, staring at the ceiling. She got Kyle's thinly veiled suggestion and now her brain was racing ahead with possibilities. It wasn't a long leap to make. She couldn't count on Tarm Maruchek to step in. He'd as much as said he wouldn't. That left it up to her.

She thought aloud, "Wonder how much damage we could do if we got in there with some well-placed explosives? I have some favors I could call in."

Morgan set aside her pad and sat up, facing Shaine. "You're serious."

"Yeah, I am. No good is going to come of this if the power plant comes online again. I don't want to see my family doused in lethal radiation, even if it's only a remote possibility. Nobody else is going to do anything about it, so why not take the situation into our own hands?"

"Because it's illegal?"

Shaine shrugged. "Not like I haven't worked on the dark side of the law before," she commented. "Besides, nobody's going to get hurt. The place is empty. All that happens is GGS loses money they can afford to write off."

"Rogan and my father will know it's you."

"What are they going to do about it? Turn me in?"

Morgan scowled. "What if the local authorities figure out it's us?"

"If we do this right, nobody will even know we were there. Special Ops motto: Leave no trace. I've done this before. We'd be in the clear."

Shaine studied Morgan's face, willing her to believe, hoping she wouldn't scare Morgan away. Because now that this was in her head, she knew she'd go through with it, whether Morgan was part of the plan or not.

Morgan said, "You're not very good at staying out of trouble, are you?"

Shaine shrugged, tried for lighthearted. "I was trying. Then I met you."

"Haha."

"Seriously, though, I've been in the thick of it since I was a nineteen-year-old punk in the EG. I went from Special Ops to being in the middle of Mann-Maru's corporate intrigue. I have been a commando, an assassin, the heavy who threatened those who betrayed Mann-Maru. Most of what I've done was either state-condoned or corporate-condoned murder and blackmail. Being a mechanic is the most honest thing I've done in my adult life. Going back to what I know is easy. It scares the piss out of me that it is. But this is still the right thing to do."

Morgan sat silently for what seemed to Shaine like an eternity. When she finally looked up with serious gray eyes, Shaine was relieved to see no judgment or disgust in her gaze. Morgan asked, "What's the plan?"

Shaine smiled in relief at the implied "we." "For now, I want to wait for the blueprints and info from Kyle. Then I can start making some calls."

"You know people who can blow up buildings?" Morgan asked.

Shaine grinned. "I know some demolitions experts from my days in Special Ops." She had a particular old friend in mind, someone she trusted with her life. She just hoped Grey Tannis would be available.

CHAPTER NINE

Morgan propped open the door to the greenhouse and stepped inside, breathing in the thick, moist, mossy aroma. A few ceiling fans turned lazily, barely stirring the humid air. Morgan looked around at the long rows of work counters covered with plants and seedlings, smiling at the richness of it. Jeannette had asked if she and Shaine would water and thin the new seedlings and deadhead the flowers for the weekend market.

Shaine was going to show Morgan what needed to be done, and then she planned to fix the overhead watering system which had developed a leak. If there was time, she would also extend the piping to the new section of the greenhouse. Morgan was more than happy to help out. She enjoyed working with the plants, even if she still occasionally mistook some for weeds.

Morgan walked over to a worktable just to the side of the entrance. Amidst the clutter, she saw a computer terminal with a net connection and a set of tired-looking speakers. Happily, she linked her comp pad into the terminal. A few seconds later her favorite recording of Ben's hard-core slash-metal band blared into the quiet.

She turned as Shaine walked in. "Did you get a hold of your friend?" she asked.

Shaine shook her head. "Left a message. Nice music."

Morgan grinned and said, "The speed and volume will make the plants grow faster."

Shaine laughed. Her head bobbed to the heavy, driving rhythm. They worked through the morning, took a break at lunch and then returned to the greenhouse for the afternoon. They were in the middle of setting up the additional overhead watering lines when the tone of Shaine's comp pad receiving a call sounded just under the blasting of Morgan's slash tunes.

Shaine grinned when she looked at the call. Morgan dialed down the music as Shaine climbed down the ladder and took the call.

"Hey, Grey! Lookin' good, girl."

Morgan felt a little twist of jealousy in the pit of her stomach at the wide grin on Shaine's face. She moved to Shaine's side to hear the exchange better and see the woman on the pad's vid screen.

Grey had strong, aquiline features and silvery white hair styled in a longish crew cut. Her eyes were an odd, piercing gray blue. Her smile was wide and teasing. Morgan wrapped her arm around Shaine's waist. She knew it was childishly possessive and she didn't care.

"Not lookin' so bad yourself, Wendt. What's going on?"

Shaine pulled Morgan close. "You know, the usual. Got a girl, got a gun, got troubles."

Grey raised a blond brow over disbelieving eyes. "You got a *girl*?" she repeated. "Now, that's a switch. Guns and trouble, that's normal. Girl's gotta be nuts to hang with you, ya crazy bitch."

Shaine laughed. "Fuck off, Tannis. You're so insane you scared 'em off just lookin' at 'em."

They both chuckled, and then Grey Tannis narrowed her eyes. "I bet this isn't just a social call, though, is it?"

Shaine sighed. "No. Wish it was, though."

"What can I do for you?"

"I need your expertise, and also to acquire some equipment."
Grey nodded thoughtfully. "When do you plan on implementing?"

"No set deadline, but I'm thinking in the next week or so. Name your price."

The blond woman smiled. "Well, it happens I have some vacation time. Don't worry about money. This is between friends, and I think I still owe you a couple lives. You at the farm?"

"Yeah."

Grey was quiet for a couple seconds, then nodded. "I'll be there the day after tomorrow and we can talk options."

"Thanks, Grey."

"No problem. See you then."

"See ya." Shaine closed the connection, giving Morgan a squeeze. "Well, Morg, we've got the cavalry coming."

"She seems quite capable."

Shaine smirked. "Grey Tannis is hell on wheels. You're gonna love her."

Morgan made a face. "I'm either gonna love her, or I'm gonna beat the crap out of her if she looks at you that way again."

Shaine exploded in laughter and hugged Morgan against her. "Sweetheart, don't you be worrying about Grey and me. Her wife would blow her head off if she stepped out of line."

* * *

That evening, after dinner, Shaine and Morgan volunteered to do kitchen cleanup, then decided to take a walk up to the top of the low hill bordering the west fields to watch the sunset. The evening still held much of the day's heat. Hazy dust motes hung in humid air that smelled of grass and manure. Shaine and Morgan strolled hand in hand along the path leading up the hill.

They topped the rise and walked through the double row of trees that ran along the top, settling down beneath a tough old silver maple. Shaine sat between two huge roots. Morgan rested between her legs, leaning back against her chest. Shaine wrapped her arms around Morgan's middle. She breathed in Morgan's scent and enjoyed the closeness of Morgan's body against her.

The sun hung just above the horizon, a deep red ball of heat against a white-blue sky that shifted into streaks of muted pinks, oranges and yellows. Shaine listened to the distant calls of birds. She could hear the rustle of squirrels chasing through the trees and the buzz of insects. She loved the familiar smell of dust and hay. It brought back memories of simpler times. She missed that simplicity sometimes. She hoped she and Morgan could spend many more evenings like this and wondered if it was even a possibility. She hugged Morgan. "This is nice. Sometimes I think I could settle here again."

Morgan twisted a little to look up at her. "What keeps you from it?"

"A million things. Nothing. Maybe I'm just too restless to stay in one place. Maybe I just haven't been ready to settle down."

"I think it would be hard for you, being here, separating the past from the present. I mean, being around family, and your old room, and all the things that haven't changed. It would be easy to kind of get lost in the past, forget the need to move forward. I think it's a little like going back to Moon Base is going to be for me. I can pretend to live in my past, but I need to move forward and figure out what I want to do."

"When did you become a psychologist?" Shaine teased.

"Must've been all the alcohol and head injuries over the years."

"Mmmm." Shaine kissed Morgan's hair and squeezed her tighter. "You're right, though, you know. It would be hard. The other reason I've never come back is that until now I hadn't found a person I'd want to stay here with."

"Is that a proposition?" Morgan asked.

Shaine felt her face flush, and after a moment she nodded. "Yeah, I think it is."

Morgan said, "As long as it's with you, I'd live anywhere."

Shaine leaned down, her mouth meeting Morgan's with gentleness that quickly intensified. Morgan wriggled around so she was straddling Shaine's lap, her arms around her neck, fingers twisting in her hair, pulling her closer as the kiss deepened.

Passion and heat flared inside Shaine, and she moaned into Morgan's mouth, seeking more. The need for air forced her to break the kiss, leaving them both gasping. Foreheads touching, they grinned at each other. Shaine lifted a hand to Morgan's cheek, a feather-light touch on her soft, pale skin. "One day at a time, right?" she breathed. "We'll figure out what we want. No rush, no pressure. I love you, Morgan."

"I love you too."

Morgan leaned up for another kiss, then settled comfortably in Shaine's embrace. Shaine sighed contentedly, realizing she no longer had any doubt that they belonged together. She could no longer imagine a life without Morgan. She needed her and loved her in a way she'd never needed or loved another.

They cuddled and watched the sun drop steadily below the horizon. A perfect summer evening. Shaine relaxed, watching the sky shift into dusk.

CHAPTER TEN

Shaine had grabbed an air bike and run out to the north field to bring her dad and Mike some parts and tools to fix the cultivator, which had broken down again. When she returned to the house an hour later, Grey Tannis had arrived at the farm. Shaine swung off the bike and hurried across the yard from the maintenance shed.

Grey, Morgan and Jeannette were sitting on the porch. Morgan and Jeannette swung lazily on the swing. Grey perched sideways on the front railing, her back against a thick post, one foot up on the railing with her arm wrapped loosely around her knee, her other long leg swinging free. All three sipped on glasses of iced tea and looked like the weekly coffee klatch.

Shaine chuckled as she strode up. "Hello, all."

Morgan grinned. "Hey, you."

Jeannette asked, "Dad and Mike doing okay?"

"Yeah. It'll be a quick fix." She turned toward her old friend. "Good to see you, Grey."

The blond woman raised her glass in a salute and returned a warm smile. Grey hadn't changed much over the years. She was still a tough chick, tall and lanky with sinewy muscle, her hair cropped short against her head. She was no older than Shaine, but her hair had always been silvery white. Shaine didn't know if it was a natural mutation, or a purposeful genetic manipulation. Grey had a strong-featured, angular face and piercing pale blue eyes. "Back at ya, Wendt. Been a long time. And your mom is still the best."

"I like to think she is. I guess you've met Morgan, too, huh?"

"I have. Don't know what she sees in ya, though." Grey grinned and laughed. "We've been having a wonderful time telling her all kinds of tales that will embarrass the crap out of you for years."

"You're a bitch, Grey. Any more of that iced tea left, Mom?"

"In the cooler, dear."

"I'll be right back." Shaine hurried into the house and returned a couple minutes later with her own glass. She joined Grey on the railing, leaning against the opposing post. The four chatted amiably for a short bit before Jeannette excused herself. "I've got some calls I need to make, so I'm going to leave you girls to yourselves."

After she'd disappeared into the house, Shaine and Morgan exchanged looks. Morgan asked, "You think she suspects something?"

Shaine laughed. "Of course she does. But she won't ask, and I'm not planning on telling."

Grey grinned. "I love your mother."

"Let's go upstairs. I have blueprints I want you to look at."

"Lead on."

* * *

Grey leaned over the power plant blueprints spread across Shaine's bed. The entire site was about two kilometers square. She studied the diagrams, tracing the structures. As she did, she asked, "Are you thinking about leveling all of the individual structures? How much demolition are we talking about?"

"It needs to be enough to make the containment building and the three cooling towers nonviable and unable to be re-used. I'm open to suggestions and recommendations."

Grey whistled lowly through her teeth. "You're sure there's no contamination in the existing buildings? I don't want to walk out of there glowing like a damned lightning rod."

"Based on all the documentation that Kyle's found, and according to local authorities, all the nuclear materials were removed when they shut the plant down. The whole site is clean." She shrugged. "We were in and out of there as kids and we're all fine."

Grey raised a suspicious brow. "I don't suppose you have a Geiger counter on your person?"

From where she sprawled on a pile of pillows on the floor, Morgan said, "My pad will do that."

"Seriously?"

Morgan grinned at Grey. "I'm a ship's exterior maintenance worker. My pad's an old work unit. We always scan for nuclear leaks from the ships' batteries."

"You two are scary," Grey said.

Shaine laughed.

Grey returned to the blueprints. "It's gonna take a lot of power. The walls are damned thick, layered inner and outer. It'd also be good to know exactly what the definition of structurally unsound is. Are you planning on a remote detonation, or timed?"

"Remote. I want to control when it goes off."

"Problem with remote is if we set charges inside, it could be tricky getting a clean signal through. Depends on distance. We can always set up signal substations to relay. Who's going to be setting charges?"

"Me. You, if you're interested. Morgan. One more thing. I want to use civilian grade explosives—too easy to trace military grade back to me."

Grey nodded again, picking up her comp pad and making a bunch of notes. She said, "I'd really like to get in there before I make any plans. I don't like going in blind. It would help to see what the state of the interior is. It's been closed almost a hundred years, right? It would be worth looking for weak points. After that long, there has to be some structural damage, if only from normal weathering."

Shaine said, "It was kind of creepy and crumbly when I was a kid. I was only on the site a few times, and never actually inside any of the main structures. The maintenance buildings that we got into were all gutted and empty. The pro-power people keep saying the basic structures are intact and only need minimal updating and repair."

Grey asked, "Wishful thinking?"

"I don't know. Let's go over there tonight. There isn't much security. They put a couple of rent-a-cops out there when all this started, sitting in an air car at the entrance. There's a chain-link fence with barbed wire around the whole site. Nothing is electrified."

"Okay, we can work with that. Can we go in on foot? Away from the main road?" She traced the outer edge of the blueprint. "This is the main entrance, looks like administrative. Back here there's a service entrance, near all the garages and storage buildings. I'd want to go in at the rear of the site, midway down the fence line."

Shaine reached for a local aerial topo map and set it down over the blueprint. "It's surrounded by open fields, so not much cover, though the grass is probably at least chest-high, and there's a lot of brush and clusters of small trees, so that'll help. If we go after dark, we should be okay. We can take a couple of all-terrain bikes out to here, tuck them back into the trees out of sight, and walk the rest of the way."

Morgan said, "I'm going too."

Shaine grinned at her. "I was planning on it," she said.

"Good."

"I'll tell my mom we're going to town for beer, so we don't have to sneak out."

Morgan frowned a little. "I don't like lying to her."

Shaine shrugged. "So, we'll stop for beer on the way home."

Grey laughed.

* * *

Shaine felt like a teenager proving to her friends she wasn't afraid to go into the haunted house. The power plant site was dark and shadowy. As a kid, they'd dared each other to get into the site and bring back proof, with pictures. It remained a creepy, empty shell of unused buildings and familiar black shadows of the cooling towers against the sky. Until now, it was ancient history. Other than kids being kids, nobody gave it much thought.

Grey had the blueprints folded into her waist-pack. She and Shaine made quick work of the fence, using laser cutters to open a flap big enough to crawl through. They pulled it closed behind them. Shaine led them across what probably had been a personnel parking lot. The ancient tarmac was pocked and shattered. Weeds and grass and small trees grew up through the cracks. After a hundred years, there was very little left of the surface.

The moon rose high and bright, eliminating the need for flashlights as they crossed the open ground. Grey pointed. "Let's take a look at the first cooling tower."

They wound through the brush to the five-story cylindrical structure. Grey studied the outside as they approached it, pulling on night vision goggles.

Morgan asked, "What are you looking for?"

"Deep cracks in the walls or in the foundation. The cracks can make the demo easier by using existing defects. Ideally, we would rappel up and into the inside, see what's there."

Grey rocked back on her heels. "No way we're going to be able to place enough charges to completely bring it down or collapse the structure. Not without industrial demolition machinery."

Shaine asked, "If we rappelled up the side, could we place a whole line of charges? Try to force a major crack in the structure?"

"I can get self-drilling charges. We'd have to set them into existing cracks to do enough damage to destabilize the structures. Surface damage isn't going to shut this down."

They walked further around the cooling tower. Grey said, "Let's check out the containment building. We should be able to get inside. The aerial shots showed an exterior ladder up to a maintenance hatch at the top of the structure."

They jogged across the site, past a single-story administrative building and some mechanical buildings. The containment facility was a dome-topped cement cylinder. At least half of the structure was below ground level.

Shaine glanced over at Morgan, who looked down at her pad. "No abnormal radiation readings," Morgan said.

Shaine nodded. "Good."

As they picked their way down the overgrown tarmac street, Morgan said, "Seems like we'll have an awful lot to do to get all the charges set in a night."

"Might be two nights setting charges," Grey replied. "After I see the containment building, I'll do some figuring before we decide how we're going to handle this. I can also bring Mia back with me, so we have one more body."

"Mia?"

Grey grinned. "My wife. She's a certified demo professional too. We work together."

Five minutes later they reached the ladder scaling the outside of the containment building. The cylinder rose four stories to its dome. The maintenance hatch was about three stories up, where the ladder ended in a square, railed platform.

Shaine watched Morgan gaze uneasily up the ladder. She touched Morgan's shoulder. "You okay?"

"Yeah, sure." Morgan forced a smile.

Grey swung onto the ladder. "I'm going up. You guys coming?"

Shaine turned to Morgan.

Morgan muttered, "It's not like falling in null gravity."

"You don't have to go up," Shaine said quietly.

Morgan took a breath and squared her shoulders. "Like I'm gonna let you have all the fun."

Shaine grinned. "You go next, I'll take the rear."

Grey had already slithered up a dozen rungs. Morgan pulled herself up onto the ladder and started climbing. Shaine waited until Morgan had gone up a few rungs, then followed. She called up softly, "Feels pretty stable. I think we're good. Just watch your step."

Grey's voice floated down. "Little late to think of that, Wendt."

"Just keep climbing, Tannis."

When they reached the halfway point, Grey paused, turning on the ladder to survey the site with the night vision binoculars. "Security is still just sitting at the main gate." Grey shook her head and started climbing again. A few minutes later, she pulled herself up onto the metal grate platform, edging aside for Morgan and giving her a hand up. Shaine climbed up and hugged the outside edge. It was a tight fit.

The maintenance hatch was manually pressure-sealed and secured with a heavy chain and lock. Grey produced a laser cutter from her pack and handed it to Shaine, then shifted so that she hid the light of the cutter from the rent-a-cops.

Shaine made quick work of the chain. Morgan and Grey pulled it free and looped it around the platform railing. Grey repacked the cutter. Shaine studied the wheel that sealed the hatch, glad it was manual rather than powered. Of course, who knew if they could get it to turn. She said, "Grey, grab a piece of the wheel, and let's see if we can crank this thing."

They strained to turn the wheel, muscles flexing. After a moment, Morgan dropped to her knees between them and took hold of a lower spindle, adding her strength to the effort. It finally gave an inch with a horrible screech that cut sharply through the night.

They froze. "Fuck!" Shaine hissed.

Three sets of eyes scanned for movement from the front gate, nearly two kilometers from them. It seemed far away, but the way sound traveled at night, Shaine swore there was no way they wouldn't have heard. "We need to remember mechanical oil next time," she muttered.

Grey said, "Let's just do it quick and get it over with."

Morgan commented, "Heard that one before."

Shaine snorted and Grey muffled a laugh.

They wrenched the wheel, cringing as the metal-on-metal squeal pierced the silence of the night. Finally it released with a hiss of stale, musty air. The three women stilled. Shaine scanned the area near the gate with her night binocs and saw no movement, no lights aimed at them. The security guys didn't get out of their car, and the headlights remained off.

Grey muttered, "Those guys are either deaf, sleeping or jamming on some good tunes."

"Thank god for rent-a-cops," Shaine said. "Let's take a look inside. Morgan, what's your pad reading?"

"All clear. Hint of residuals. You'd have to be in there for weeks on end before it even registered in your body."

The door creaked and the rusting metal snapped as Shaine pulled the hatch open enough for them to squeeze through. Grey settled the night vision goggles over her eyes again and poked her head inside. "Man, it stinks in here. Step down on your way in. There's a railing."

She stepped through the door and onto the walkway. Shaine followed her in, Morgan behind her, pushing the hatch a little further open. Without night vision goggles it was pitch-black past the immediate circle of moonlight.

Grey described what she could see. "The walkway goes all the way around. There's a structure across the center, accessible by the walkway, with a lift. Probably for removing equipment."

Morgan asked, "At some point, wouldn't this have been a completely sealed structure?"

"Probably before they shut it down and pulled all the nuclear materials out," Shaine said. "Can you see down at all?"

"Too dark." Grey started walking around. "I want to see if that center structure is intact."

Morgan chewed her lip. "Seems like we'll need an awful lot of firepower to do any real damage in here."

Grey's footsteps echoed softly in the musty air as she followed the walkway around. Her voice was quiet as it came back to them. "It'll take a good amount of explosives, but placed correctly, we can take advantage of weak points in the structure to do the most amount of damage. As long as we don't need to bring the structures down completely to make them unusable and unstable."

Shaine watched Grey disappear into the blackness, trying to monitor her movement by listening to the shuffling of her boots on the concrete walkway. After a couple minutes, she heard the dull ring of boots on metal grating.

Shaine called quietly, "What are you seeing?"

"Too dark to see much. I'm on the catwalk. There's a pulley system here they must've used to bring equipment up. No cable or anything though. I'd say they had heavy machinery doing all the work. Too dark to see into the hole. Coming back over."

A couple of minutes later, she joined them at the door in the small wedge of light from the open hatch. Shaine asked, "You have what you need?"

"Yes. All we're going to get tonight, in any case."

Shaine glanced at her chron. "Good. Let's get the hell out of here, then."

CHAPTER ELEVEN

Shaine and Morgan saw Grey off early the next morning. She promised to return in two days with all her equipment and her wife. Turning back toward the farm, Shaine gestured toward the near fields. "Let's take a walk."

They crossed the clearing where the cars were parked, walked past the barn and then along the fence circling the nearest cow field. She caught Morgan's hand and twined their fingers together. "You doing okay, Morg?"

"Sure, why?"

Shaine shrugged. "Just checking. Lots going on, you know?"

"Charri sent a note. She said things have settled down a lot at home. They haven't seen any press hanging around work or by my apartment building. Dad says they haven't bothered him, either. Maybe they're finally getting tired of me."

"Hope so. After this is done we can go back, if you want."

Morgan nodded, but said nothing.

Shaine studied her profile. "What are you thinking?"

"Even if we go back, it's going to be different."

"Probably."

"I know it's weird, but I don't know if I'm ready to go back yet."

"We can stay here as long as you want. There's no rush."

"I know."

Shaine stopped, easing Morgan into a tight embrace, nuzzling her hair, trying with everything in her to let Morgan know that she was safe, that she'd do anything to have Morgan be okay. Morgan relaxed into her body, arms tight around Shaine's waist, face buried into Shaine's chest. "I love you, Morgan."

Morgan's grip tightened convulsively. "Thank you," she mumbled. "Thank you. I love you too."

Shaine wasn't sure what the thank yous were about, but she continued to hold her lover tightly, rubbing her back, hoping it would help. She sensed Morgan was struggling to maintain her composure, but wasn't certain why. She supposed it came down to too much change and not enough time to deal with it. Hell, she wasn't sure what they should do, either. She just knew she wanted to be with Morgan. It wasn't even a question. Whatever Morgan decided, she would be at her side.

Shaine still had questions of her own, though. When they returned to Moon Base, would she return to her job as a mechanic? Or was she destined to remain in the thick of intrigue? Maybe she could simply be Morgan's full-time bodyguard. She had a feeling she'd get bored as hell just doing mechanic work day after day. It'd been a good thing at first, a change she needed to stop the escalating ease with which violence came to her. The last couple of assignments from Rogan had shaken her. It was one thing to kill in cold blood as a sharpshooter in the EG, taking orders from the government in the interest of the greater good. It was another to be asked to do the same for corporate profit. She still wondered if Maruchek was aware of all of the things Rogan asked her to do.

If she were sucked back into Rogan's security group, there would be a line drawn that she would not cross. Unless Morgan's safety was involved. Then all bets were off. As they had been when she'd taken out Tyr Charun, the man who'd tried to murder Morgan when he discovered she was Tarm Maruchek's daughter.

She kissed the top of Morgan's head, combing her fingers through the soft black strands. In the end, it was about Morgan. After some time, Morgan finally pulled away, keeping hold of one of Shaine's hands and leaning against her side. "Let's walk, okay?"

Shaine acquiesced and they continued slowly along the narrow foot trail. Morgan slid her arm around Shaine's waist, and Shaine kept an arm around Morgan's shoulders. It made it harder to walk, but they both seemed to need the contact.

They walked in comfortable silence, turning back toward the house when they reached the end of the first section of fencing.

Morgan asked, "Do you really think this plan with Grey is going to work?"

"We'll make it work. Grey is good. So is Mia. I want the whole situation over with and this is the fastest way to finish it."

"Provided we don't get caught."

"We won't get caught." Shaine squeezed Morgan's shoulders. "But if you want to stay back, that's okay, Morg. I don't want to force you into going along."

"No, I'm in. But how can you be so sure?"

"Practically speaking, they have no security. This is a cakewalk compared to some of the stuff Grey and I have done in terms of getting in and out undetected. Then there's the part where it's so ludicrous, nobody is going to even imagine that it'd happen, so they're not looking for it. Right now, they're worrying about the attack on the protest. Somebody blowing the crap out of the power plant isn't even on their radar."

Morgan nodded, accepting the explanations. They came up over the rise closest to the farmhouse. Morgan pointed. "Hey, that's Toby's air bike, isn't it?"

"Yeah, it is. Let's go see what he's up to."

* * *

Toby had come for dinner because Leese was out of town on business. She'd told him and his dad that if they wanted to eat, they may as well eat at the farm. Left to their own devices, the two men would likely starve. Shaine was happy to have her nephew around to harass. Toby gave back as good as he got. He even turned his boisterous teasing onto Morgan.

Shaine, Morgan and Toby set the table and helped bring the food out before taking their seats. Conversation started before eating and continued through the meal. Morgan passed the bowl of mashed potatoes down to Toby. He scooped a sizable pile onto his plate then reached for the gravy boat. "Oh, yeah, I forgot—my friend Billy said that they're planning another protest for the day after tomorrow. A bunch of the council members and some project people from GGS are going to the power plant site. I guess there's going to be press and stuff. They're going into the old administration building."

Jeannette asked, "What are they going to do there?"

Toby shrugged. "The message I got said it was supposed to be some kind of media thing. Like just for promotion or something." He stuffed a forkful of meat and potatoes into his mouth and talked through it. "They want protesters at the front gate to meet the press and the company representatives."

Jeannette scolded, "Toby, your mother didn't raise you with those kinds of manners."

He swallowed and grinned sheepishly. "Sorry, Grandma."

Shaine snickered. Toby glared at her. Shaine said, "Seriously, I hope you aren't planning on being there, Toby."

"Why not? Our whole group is going."

Jeannette raised a brow. "After what happened at the park? I agree with Shaine. You shouldn't be going there."

Toby huffed impatiently. "They're not going to do the same thing twice. Besides, it's not like it's a big deal. This will just be maybe thirty of us with signs in front of the entrance gates in the middle of the day." He looked across the table to his father and grandfather for support. "You agree with me, right?"

Kent Ichiro held up his hands, staying out of it.

Mike frowned. "I'd rather have you stay away from there."

"I'm not a child."

"No, you're not. And the choice, ultimately, is yours. But my advice to you is to stay out of it."

Toby shook his head. "You guys really think they're going to send gunmen in broad daylight? Seriously?"

Shaine said, "Doesn't need to be gunmen."

"You're paranoid, Shaine."

She shrugged. "I'm also older and more experienced than you. Take it however you want."

CHAPTER TWELVE

Jeannette stopped Shaine and Morgan the next morning as they came downstairs on their way out the door to take a walk. "Shaine, honey, I need you to run into town for me," she said.

Shaine stopped. Morgan pulled up beside her, recognizing Shaine's flash of concern. Now that Morgan's cover was blown, they'd discussed not going out in public unless they really needed to. Because of the media's continued interest in Morgan, Shaine felt that there was still a threat.

Morgan pointed out that they hadn't had any reporters at the farm. Shaine was fairly certain it was because Maruchek had put covert security around the farm to keep outsiders out. She hadn't seen anyone, and Rogan hadn't discussed it with her, but she would have put money on it. Probably they had all the incoming com lines bugged. Though she'd called Grey on an encrypted line, it was a Mann-Maru encryption on her com, so they could have listened in easily enough. Especially if it'd been Ellerand doing the spying for them. All the intrigue made Morgan's head swim. Were they ever really alone?

Shaine put a smile on her face. "Sure, Mom. What do you need?"

Jeannette pointed to a small pile of letters and flat packages. "That paperwork for the farm needs to get to the lawyers today. I need to take Grandma Richards to the clinic, so I can't take them over."

"Sure, we can run those into town for you. Over to Justin and Justin, right?"

Jeannette nodded. "Yes. Thank you, Shaine. Grandma just called. Her stomach is acting up again and Grace can't take her." She was already gathering her bag and jacket and heading toward the door. She stopped to give both women a hug and disappeared in a whirlwind of fluttering energy.

Morgan glanced at Shaine. "Change of plans, huh?"

"Yeah. Lemme get my stuff. We'll take the Racer."

Shaine ran up to her room and returned wearing a long-sleeved camouflage shirt that hung untucked over her tank top and cargo shorts. Morgan couldn't help but appreciate the view until Shaine opened the shirt to show a small laser pistol in a snug shoulder holster.

Morgan frowned. Shaine wouldn't wear a gun if there wasn't a real threat. Right? She swallowed, feeling slightly nauseous. "You really think you're going to need that?"

Shaine covered the gun again. "Probably not. But I'd rather have it and not need it."

"It makes me nervous."

Shaine took Morgan's hands in hers. Morgan was always surprised at the warmth of Shaine's skin and the strength behind her gentle grip. "I'll do everything I can to keep both of us safe," Shaine said seriously.

"I know that."

Shaine gave her hands a squeeze.

Morgan concentrated on the feel of Shaine's hands holding hers, on the strength and sureness in her voice. She wanted to trust Shaine. She didn't want to be afraid. And she sure as hell wasn't going to let Shaine go into town without her. She squeezed back. "Okay," she said. "Let's go."

Shaine smiled and slid an arm around Morgan's shoulder. "Sooner we leave, sooner we get back," she said.

Despite her misgivings, Morgan enjoyed the ride. They drove past University Park and into what seemed to Morgan to be a picture-perfect small town. Most of the houses lining the road appeared to have been built decades ago, but seemed neat and tidy.

Shaine pointed as they passed a corner convenience store. "The school I went to is just down that way."

Morgan got a glimpse of a tree-lined lane with houses on either side. They continued down the main street. There were businesses on both sides and a handful of people walked along the street. Cement flowerpots at every corner and in the middle of the blocks overflowed with vibrant yellow and pink flowers. Shaine pulled into an open street space. "The lawyers are just a block down," she said. She grabbed Jeannette's envelopes and got out of the car.

Morgan popped open the passenger door. They had parked outside a candy shop. The smell of chocolate and caramel corn made Morgan's mouth water.

Shaine came around the car and took Morgan's hand. She nodded toward the candy store window. "You wanna stop in on our way back?"

Morgan grinned. "Definitely!"

They made their way quickly to the lawyer's office and delivered the papers then headed back to the candy shop. The bell on the door rang as they walked in. The woman behind the counter smiled. "Welcome to Cathy's Candy," she greeted them.

Morgan grinned. "Thanks." All she could smell was chocolate. The display counters near the checkout had every kind she could imagine. The shelves on the sides had colorful collections of suckers and treats and gifts. Another counter had popcorn, caramel corn and cheese corn.

Morgan peered into one of the chocolate displays. There was a place on Moon Base that had candy, but not a whole store. This was pure sugar heaven. Shaine came to stand beside her. "What'cha gonna get?"

"Not sure. It all looks good."

The woman behind the counter said, "The nut clusters are always a favorite." She paused and stared for a second. "Shaine Wendt?"

Shaine looked up.

The woman smiled widely. "Wow! I haven't seen you in years! Cathy Denner. We graduated together."

Shaine smiled. Morgan noticed that it didn't go to her eyes. "Hello. Good to see you," Shaine said.

Morgan jumped in, intending to take the focus off Shaine. "I think I'd like a half dozen of the dark chocolate nut clusters. Shaine, you want anything?"

"How about a half dozen of the coconut ones?"

Cathy said excitedly, "That was really incredible, what you did, Shaine. You're a real hero!"

Shaine's face flushed and she shrugged uncomfortably. "It wasn't a big thing, really," she said. "But thanks."

Morgan handed the woman her credit chit, and Shaine took the opportunity to drift away to look at other things.

The woman looked from Shaine to Morgan. Morgan could tell she was put off by Shaine stepping away, but she started putting the candy in a package. She focused on Morgan as she finished ringing up the sale. She saw recognition in the woman's dark eyes. Morgan kept her expression neutral as she pocketed her credit chit, inviting no further conversation. Morgan took her candy and she and Shaine quickly exited the store.

Shaine opened Morgan's car door for her, then got in behind the wheel. She started the engine and glanced at Morgan.

"That was awkward," she muttered. "Thanks for jumping in."

Morgan shrugged. "She recognized me too. Did you remember her?"

"I recognized her name. She wasn't anyone I hung out with. I don't think I really knew her."

"You were tense. I've never seen you that way around people."

Shaine frowned. "Yeah. I hate that hero crap. Let's drive a bit. I'll show you around town."

"Okay." Morgan settled into the soft leather of the passenger seat. "I want to see where you used to hang out." She smiled at Shaine. She'd been curious to know what kind of place had created such a complex woman as Shaine Wendt. Certainly, she'd had a good stable home life. But Shaine had never talked much about school or her friends.

As they drove slowly down the main street, Morgan thought it would have been hard for someone with a restless spirit to grow up in such a small town. Granted, it was bigger than the closed environment of either Moon Base or a mining facility in the Asteroid Belt, but it was so quiet. Even Moon Base felt more crowded and bustling than this small town.

Shaine seemed to relax as they drove. She pointed out her favorite restaurants from when she was a teenager, going out with friends on the weekends. They drove by her senior school and a small shopping center that had a busy parking lot and people milling between stores.

Morgan took it all in. It was like places she'd seen in vids, almost unreal to her, and so incredibly different from her own experience. She felt no jealousy or envy—only an odd sense of the surreal that she couldn't quite place.

Shaine said, "There's a place I want to show you." She took a turn that brought them to a park on the edge of the main part of town and pulled into a small, empty parking lot. "Come on."

Shaine popped her door and came around Morgan's side, taking her hand as Morgan stepped out and shut her door. Shaine gestured ahead. "It's a little way in," she said.

Morgan was glad to get out and walk. The park was filled with huge old shade trees—maples and ashes and oaks. As they walked further into the trees, the sunlight shifted into thin beams of dappled brilliance filtering through the leaves, rather like having a loosely thatched roof overhead. The grass underfoot was short and thin. Shaine led Morgan into the small woodland, through a narrow clearing to a cluster of gnarled oak trees.

Morgan studied the trees and thought if she were a kid in books she'd read, they'd be great for climbing.

Shaine said, "This is where we used to come when we cut school."

"You cut school?"

"Didn't everyone?" Shaine grinned at her. "Come on, I'll boost you up."

Morgan looked up a little uneasily. In space, without full gravity, falling wasn't nearly as big an issue.

Shaine pointed. "See the second fork, where there are three branches going out? Climb up to there. I'll give you a boost and I'll be right behind you."

Morgan nodded. Shaine cupped her hands, and Morgan stepped in and took the lift, grabbing a sturdy lower branch and pulling herself up into the tree. The bark was scarred and rough under her fingers. There were plenty of hand- and footholds, and she made her way up to the wide crotch where the gnarled trunk split three ways.

Morgan pulled herself up to stand among the branches, leaning against the thick trunk and hanging onto a couple of small branches to keep her balance. She watched Shaine haul herself onto the lowest limb and clamber quickly the rest of the way. She wondered if her partner was part monkey and grinned at the thought.

Shaine pulled herself up beside her and pointed up. "See that flat branch, just over your head?"

Morgan kept a hold of the trunk and looked up. "Sure."

"That's where we're going. I'll go first and help you up."

Morgan eyed the flat branch. It was quite thick—nearly as thick as the trunk itself—so likely it would support their weight. She glanced toward the ground, which suddenly seemed a long way down.

Shaine leaned in and gave Morgan a gentle kiss. Morgan closed her eyes and felt tingles run down her spine. Shaine whispered against her lips, "I won't let you fall."

Morgan took a breath.

Shaine murmured, "Don't move."

Morgan felt the branch under her feet bounce a bit and opened her eyes to see Shaine reach to a handhold above her head and simply swing herself up to the flat limb above them. She hooked one leg around the limb and settled herself, straddling the limb with her legs wrapped around it. Grinning, she reached a hand down to Morgan.

"Take my hand and I'll pull you up."

Morgan clasped wrists with Shaine, got a solid grip, then grabbed for the branch above her as well.

"Up we go."

Shaine hauled her up. Morgan also pulled with her other hand. In a second, she was seated next to Shaine. She shifted to get more comfortably settled and kept one hand on Shaine's thigh.

"This is what I wanted to show you," Shaine said. "This was our favorite place to hang out." She traced a group of initials carved into the rough trunk at head height.

"*SW, JM, LT.*"

"Me and my two best friends," Shaine explained. "Jill Monson and Laney Thoms. We'd come up here and drink on the weekends, sometimes score some weed."

Morgan twined their fingers together, feeling a closeness, a commonality, though she wondered if Shaine's teenaged idea of drinking and scoring drugs was as wild as hers had been. She said, "We hid out behind the air circulators. There was a break in the fencing and an old maintenance shed they didn't use any more. We sat in there and smoked synth and drank beer, or whatever we could get our hands on."

"Guess we both sowed some wild oats, huh?"

"I was out of control," Morgan admitted. She had three years filled with foggy memories of drunken and drugged up binges. She had no count of the number of times she'd been so fucked up she barely even knew her name. She spent those three years falling into a dark, spiraling, aching sadness that nearly swallowed her whole. She remembered blood dripping slowly from the carefully spaced cuts along the inside of her left arm, hoping that oblivion would make the wrenching ache go away.

"Morgan?"

She shook herself, took a quick breath and blinked away the darkness. "Sorry. Memories."

Shaine squeezed her hand. "You okay?"

"Yeah." Morgan smiled at their hands together. "I am now."

They were silent for a long time and Morgan slid a little closer, leaning lightly against Shaine, feeling the comforting heat of her body.

After a while Shaine said, "Got my first kiss in this tree."

"Who from?"

"Laney. On a dare. We were both drunk. Lucky we didn't fall out of the tree. We ended up dating most of our senior year."

"Was she your first?"

"Yeah."

"Shaine, you're blushing," Morgan teased.

Shaine blushed all the more and Morgan laughed. "So, kiss me and add my initials to the tree," Morgan said.

Shaine chuckled and captured Morgan's mouth, sliding her tongue inside, one hand cupping Morgan's cheek, the other on Morgan's thigh to steady her. Morgan moaned into the kiss, feeling the passion pulse straight to her groin. Her free hand covered Shaine's on her thigh, clinging on as Shaine's mouth moved down her neck, nibbling on her pulse point, sending shivers along her skin.

Shaine slowly eased back, resting her forehead against Morgan's. "Mmmm."

"Yeah."

"Let's not fall out of this tree."

Morgan snickered. "Necking in null grav is much safer."

Shaine grinned. "Hang on, okay?" She released Morgan's leg and fished in the pocket of her cargo shorts, coming up with a small laser cutter and flipping it on. Twisting around, she carved Morgan's initials above her own and added a heart around them. The air smelled of burnt wood. A puff or two of smoke wafted between them. The original carvings had been done with a knife, but Shaine was willing to forgo tradition for execution. After a couple minutes she flicked off the cutter and pocketed it, smiling at the results.

"What do you think?" she asked.

Morgan grinned. "Perfect."

Shaine smiled. "Yes, you are," she agreed. "Come on, let's get down."

Morgan sighed. "S'pose we better."

They clambered down the tree, Shaine going first and helping guide Morgan's feet into the right step holds. They ambled slowly across the park, holding hands.

"Seems like a nice place to grow up," Morgan said.

Shaine shrugged. "It was okay. Kinda slow. I wanted to get out, get away. I felt a little lost here, bored most of the time. The EG was the easiest way out, so that's what I did. Sounded exciting, right? I wanted to do something worthwhile. School wasn't my thing, so I didn't want to go to university."

"I just expected to do what my parents did," Morgan said. "Be a spacer like them. It never really occurred to me to want anything else." Shaine gave her a warm one-armed hug and she leaned into it. "I guess now I have a chance to consider other things."

"If you want to," Shaine said. "You have the means, that's for sure." She kissed Morgan's head. "You need to do what feels right for you. You don't have to decide until you're ready, and you don't have to do anything different at all if you don't want to."

"The hardest part is I don't even know what I'd want to do, or what I'd be any good at."

"The right thing will fall your way," Shaine said. "Not like there's a time limit or anything."

Morgan shrugged. "True. I guess I don't need to worry about it right now."

"Nope."

They strolled through the trees, taking a roundabout path back out of the park to where they'd left the car.

Morgan sighed. "You know, it's going to be hard to go back to Moon Base after all this. I never realized how lifeless it is there. I never knew what I was missing."

"We could move back here," Shaine offered.

Morgan shrugged. "I'm not sure I want that. Not sure what I want, really. I never realized that there was anything so wonderful as all this. You can watch all the vids you want, but until you experience it, it's just not real."

"Guess I never thought about that before," Shaine admitted.

Morgan grinned. "Well, no matter what we decide to do, this has been great, staying here with you."

"I've liked it too."

Morgan swung their arms. "We better get back to the farm, huh?"

"Yeah. Come on, I'll show ya the back roads home."

CHAPTER THIRTEEN

Shaine wasn't surprised that Toby and Chelsea decided to go to the protest with their friends. She figured they would succumb to the lure of being part of a civil protest, so she knew it was her job to do what she could to keep them safe. It was also an excuse to check out the power plant site in the daylight since Grey and Mia would be returning later that afternoon.

The morning had dawned bright and sunny, promising midday heat. Shaine and Morgan woke reasonably early, had breakfast and showered. Shaine finished dressing and stood in front of the mirror on the back of her bedroom door, running a comb through her short red hair.

Morgan sat on the edge of the bed, pulling on a pair of socks. "You think it'd be easier if we just went with them to the protest?" she asked.

"It might be easier, but it would mean outing ourselves again, and I'd just as soon avoid notice. Better for both of us to keep a low profile. Besides, if anything goes down, I don't want to be in the middle of a bunch of civilians. I want to be on the outside where we might be able to do some good."

"I get that."

Shaine grinned, feeling the beginnings of low-key mission adrenaline.

"What do you expect to happen?"

"Not sure, really. Since it's daylight, my guess is that if there is an attack, it would be from a safe distance, or they'd have to scream in, do something and get out before they could be stopped. Thing is, though, there'll be council and GGS people there, so it can't be indiscriminate. Maybe a sniper, maybe someone planted in their midst or someone in a vehicle that can make a quick getaway. There's only the one road to the front gate, so their options are limited. Most likely nothing will happen." She flopped down on the bed, leaning on the pillows propped against the headboard. "I figure, we creep in, stay low in the grass, put up a telescope camera that feeds to the pads. I'm going to bring a sniper rifle and a compact long-range automatic."

Morgan frowned. "What about local police? Or territory authorities? Won't they be doing the same thing?"

Shaine shrugged. "I don't know. I'm not sure how serious they're taking all this. I imagine there will be a fairly heavy police presence. I was going to give Kyle a call before we leave, see if he's heard anything."

Shaine glanced at the chron on her nightstand, then patted the bed beside her. "Come and sit with me."

Morgan crawled over the bed, settling beside her. Shaine shifted to straddle Morgan's legs, putting one hand to either side of her head on the headboard. She dropped a playful kiss on Morgan's mouth, and Morgan wrapped her arms around Shaine's neck, parting Shaine's lips with her tongue and turning playful into passionate. Shaine sighed into the kiss.

Morgan pulled Shaine's body down over her own, capturing her mouth hungrily. Shaine returned the kiss, reveling in the taste of Morgan's mouth and the slick feel of their tongues dueling. Blood pounded through her veins and pulsed between her legs. Good thing they weren't in a hurry to get anywhere.

* * *

They took two all-terrain air bikes from the machine shed and followed ground-level back roads to the fields surrounding the power plant. The roads quickly deteriorated into narrow overgrown tracks. Kids on dirt bikes or all-terrain vehicles were probably the only people coming out here.

They tucked the bikes into a stand of tall grass, covering them with brush, and hiked toward the spot where Shaine thought they'd have the best chance of seeing what was going on.

For once, Shaine was glad of the old combat fatigues she'd left in her closet at home. She had enough for her and, with some rolling of sleeves and pant legs, for Morgan, too. Dressed in camouflage head to toe, including hats, they crossed the fields relatively hidden from plain sight. The fields that Shaine remembered being just open grassy areas had grown up into the beginnings of forestland. Thick copses of brush and clusters of young maples, poplars and quick-growing ash scattered throughout the fields. They didn't provide any real cover, but it did break up the landscape.

Shaine led the way to a slight rise about two hundred meters from the nuclear plant's front gates. They bedded down in the tall grass, creating a small blind. Shaine set up the tiny three-sixty degree vid camera at the top of a finger-thin telescoping stake. The video feed played back to both Morgan's comp pad and her own. She removed her high-powered laser sniper rifle from its case, snapped on the scope and slapped in a power cartridge. She checked the safety and set it between them.

She broke out her compact laser machine gun. Probably serious overkill, but it was identical to her old workhorse from Earth Guard. Not long after she'd been discharged from service, she'd gotten the gun through a friend of a friend who knew a dealer. After all those years in the military, there was no way she was going into civilian life unarmed. She shook her head. Damn, she'd been paranoid back then. Smiling, she checked the power pack and the safety and set the machine gun beside her as well.

Her comp pad lay on the ground at her knees. Shaine glanced down at the video feed. The protesters were starting to gather in front of the still-locked gates, circling with their signs. Some carried plain paperboard signs, others had high-tech holo signs that flashed with multiple messages and images. There was a single police hover-van immediately to the right of the gates. The two officers remained in the vehicle.

Morgan scanned the sky. Even standing, she was short enough to remain hidden behind the tall grass. After a while she sat down with her pad, taking remote control of the camera and setting it to do a three-sixty degree scan.

Shaine watched Morgan, her face serious as she watched the images on the pad in her lap. It felt incredibly natural to have Morgan at her side. She realized in that moment she completely trusted Morgan to have her back. When she worked for Mann-Maru she'd preferred to work alone. As a commando, she'd always been part of a team. Morgan felt like a partner. She didn't have the training, but she had good instincts.

"There's another van coming in," Morgan murmured, stopping the camera and zooming it in. Shaine glanced at her pad to see Toby and Chelsea climbing out of an air van with several others who appeared to be about their same age.

"Leave the camera there, and I'll take it, if you can watch the sky?"

Morgan nodded. She put her pad in her pocket, scooping up a pair of binoculars as she stood, turning a slow three-sixty.

"Helijet, Shaine, way out. Three o'clock."

Shaine focused the camera on the black spot and zoomed it in. "Police," she said. "Glad they're going to be in the air."

Morgan nodded and continued her scanning without comment.

Shaine said, "Here comes another van." She watched a second vehicle float up the road and stop at the entry to the drive. Another group of seven protesters piled out with signs and exuberant energy for the cause.

"There's another helijet, too. About seven o'clock. Not sure if it's incoming."

Shaine shifted the camera. The police HJ was still to their right and looked to be just hovering and watching. The second helijet was off in the distance and didn't appear to be coming any closer. Shaine zeroed in on it and decided it looked like a local farmer's crop duster. She frowned. "Keep an eye on that second one, make sure it stays out there."

"Sure."

Three local media vans floated up the road. They pulled in and started setting up cameras pointed toward the gates. Two police squad cars arrived shortly after. Four officers got out, watchful but not getting involved with either the press or the protesters. The protesters marched in a long narrow oval in front of the gates.

Shaine focused the camera on the road leading to the power plant's entrance. A group of dark vehicles came over the rise from town, headed in their direction, creating a growing puff of dust against the bright blue sky. She glanced at her chron. Thirteen forty-five hours. Right on time. It had to be the GGS people and the city officials.

Well, that should liven things up, she thought.

She grabbed her binoculars and followed Morgan's line of sight. The two HJs hadn't moved from their general area or distance. Also encouraging. Hopefully she and Morgan were just out here on a lark.

The four city vehicles hovered into the driveway, whipping up the dusty ground. The protesters increased the volume of their chanting and held their signs higher. Shaine could hear the fervent tones of their mantra. Media cameras and reporters shifted closer to cover the action, and the police moved in.

The city vehicles disgorged their passengers—four men and a woman in expensive-looking business suits, four city officials, and two maintenance engineers wearing yellow jumpsuits.

The protesters shouted, "Don't risk our future! Keep the doors shut!"

The city officials strode toward the gate. A group of protesters, including Toby and Chelsea, broke off and rushed to link arms and sit in front of the gates. As the GGS group approached the gates, heated words were exchanged with the marching protesters. One of the GGS people gestured to the police.

The police didn't rush to their aid, but did start to talk to the group blocking the gate. Shaine watched as two of the officers started pulling the protesters away from the gates, handcuffing them and dragging them by the armpits toward the big police hover-van. The protesters didn't fight the removal, but didn't help, either.

Shaine observed until they took her nephew and his girlfriend away, then shifted her focus. One of the city people undid the cable and locks holding the gates shut. The two engineers pushed the heavy, barred gates into openings in the gate walls. The protesters yelled louder but didn't interfere as the GGS group followed the engineers and city officials through the open gate and down the overgrown path toward the administration building some fifty meters further in.

Four officers took up positions at the gate. The police van drove off with the arrested protesters a few minutes later.

Morgan said, "Toby's going to be in a crapload of trouble when he has to make that phone call home."

Shaine snickered. "Yup."

Morgan grimaced. "My dad kicked my ass the first time it happened to me."

"Didn't seem to have helped much, huh?" Shaine teased.

"Smart-ass."

"Yup."

Morgan chuckled, then sobered. "What are they gonna do in there, anyway? Nothing's online. There isn't even any power."

Shaine scanned the fields around them. "I think it's a political move. Just a show of intentions, make it seem like things are heating up."

They watched silently for a while.

Morgan said, "I think that other HJ is coming closer."

"Hmmmmm. Think you're right." Shaine tracked the flyer. It seemed to be slowly easing closer as it ran what appeared to be crop dusting patterns, as though it were a new pilot practicing. She turned back to the power plant, but there was no change there. She glanced at her chron. They'd only been inside for about ten minutes. She figured they'd kill at least an hour wandering around in the facility, though she had no idea what they could be looking at.

The place was empty. Any working tech had been gutted decades ago. There was no power. Probably just rats and cockroaches. She remembered from her youth that the outbuildings they'd gotten into were empty, gutted shells.

She settled in to wait. At least Toby and Chelsea were out of the trouble zone, even if there was going to be hell to pay for getting arrested. The movement around the media vans had quieted as everyone waited for the people to come out of the admin building. There were no additional vehicles around, and Shaine didn't see anyone in the area that looked out of place. She was a bit surprised that they hadn't taken any press into the buildings with them, then decided they probably didn't want to publicize the fact that the place was trashed.

"Shaine," Morgan said quietly.

Shaine turned to face the fields to the east. Sure enough, the smaller HJ had changed its patterns and was heading toward the power plant. Shaine hefted the compact machine gun and flicked off the safety. Focused on the HJ, she sighted it through the scope. "Where's the police HJ?"

Morgan scanned behind them. "Still back there. Hasn't come in yet."

"Let me know what they're doing." Shaine remained focused on the incoming HJ.

A few seconds later, Morgan reported, "Police HJ incoming, seven o'clock."

The smaller HJ put on a burst of speed toward the gates. Staying high in the air, it did a flyby, raining laser fire across the driveway in front of the gate. The HJ was too high to do a lot of damage, but the effect was phenomenal. Protesters and media people scattered in an eruption of screams and chaos.

Shaine sighted through the scope as the fast-moving helijet flew over the gates, firing steadily. The police HJ came in from the rear of the site.

Morgan squeaked, "Fuck!" and pulled Shaine to the ground as a mini-missile from the police jet whistled over their heads. A second missile hit the smaller HJ and it veered away, spewing smoke from its tail. Shaine looked up after a few beats. The police helijet was following the intruder. She glanced over toward the power plant gates. There were police yelling orders, trying to assess the damage. Shaine looked at Morgan. "You okay?"

"I'm good. You?"

"Let's get the hell out of here."

"Lead the way, baby, I'm right behind you."

They grabbed their gear and packed it quickly into Shaine's equipment bag. Crouching low and staying under cover as much as they could, they ran through the fields. She hoped everyone would be too preoccupied to notice her and Morgan running through the field.

* * *

Shaine and Morgan raced the air bikes toward the farmhouse and pulled into the driveway. Shaine made a point of slewing sideways as she braked, showering Morgan with a wash of dust and gravel. Morgan came to a more sedate stop and flipped Shaine off with a gloved hand as she slung her leg over the bike and climbed off.

Shaine laughed, sliding off her own vehicle. She pulled off her gloves and helmet, running her fingers back through her hair. She nodded toward a nondescript air car parked nearer to the house. "Think Grey's here," she commented.

Morgan nodded and removed her own gloves and helmet. "On the back porch with your mom."

"And she brought Mia." Shaine grinned and waved a hand in greeting to Grey, her wife Mia and Jeannette. She unhooked her equipment bag from the back of her bike and shouldered it, and she and Morgan crossed the driveway toward the house.

Grey Tannis sprawled on the porch swing, all long legs and muscle, her silvery hair shining in the sunlight. She wore cargo pants and a tank top, her lightweight work boots propped up on the porch railing. The woman beside her was petite but muscular, of partly Asian descent, with shoulder-length light brown hair pulled into a tail. She leaned comfortably against her counterpart.

"Hey, all," Shaine greeted them.

Grey raised a half-full glass of iced tea. "Afternoon."

Jeannette gave Shaine and Morgan a once-over from her perch on the edge of a high-backed rocker. "How did it go?" she asked.

Shaine made a so-so motion, waggling her hand. "You have the news on?" she asked.

Jeannette shook her head. "Should we?"

Morgan and Shaine both nodded. Shaine said, "Probably."

Jeannette frowned at them and stood up. "Let's go in then, and see what's on the news." She led the way through the back door.

Grey raised a pale brow. "Always exciting around you, isn't it, Wendt?"

Shaine shrugged and smiled at Grey's companion. "Mia, it's good to see you again."

Mia Tannis smiled, almond-shaped dark eyes lighting. "You too, Shaine." She gave Shaine a hug then stepped back.

Shaine said, "This is my partner, Morgan Rahn. Morgan, this is Grey's wife Mia. We go way back, so just ignore the fact that they think I'm an idiot."

Morgan grinned, taking Mia's proffered hand in a firm grip. "Hey."

Shaine gestured toward the door. "Let's go see what they're saying about the latest protest fiasco," she suggested.

What the reporters were saying wasn't as important as the footage they were showing as the four women joined Jeannette in the kitchen. They watched a clear shot of the protesters, including Toby and Chelsea, being dragged away from the gate in handcuffs.

Jeannette turned an accusing glare on her daughter. "Arrested? Shaine, you were supposed to keep them out of trouble!"

Shaine sighed. "We were hiding in the field a ways away, keeping an eye on things. There wasn't anything we could do to prevent that. Besides, Toby's just gonna call it a feather in his liberal hat."

Jeannette glowered at her. "Leese is going to have a fit."

"And Toby and Chelsea are going to have learned a lesson. Besides, at least it got them out of there before the shooting started."

"WHAT?"

Grey and Mia also looked at Shaine, who pointed at the small vid screen suspended from the bottom of the kitchen cupboard. "I think that's what's on now."

Jeannette turned up the volume as a shaking video showed a helijet swooping down over the driveway. Laser fire strafed across the crumbling tarmac, throwing up clots of dirt and gravel. The announcer's voice said, "Fortunately there were only minor injuries sustained in the chaos. The helijet was shot down by the police and crashed in a field about a kilometer away. Investigators are currently on the scene, trying to determine who was behind this new attack."

Jeannette turned away from the screen and sat down heavily on a stool at the breakfast bar, shaking her head. "This is all just a bit much," she said quietly.

Morgan laid a hand on her shoulder and simply nodded.

Mia said, "At least none of the protesters were badly hurt."

Grey looked at Shaine. "Can you back that vid up? I want to see it again."

Shaine nodded and grabbed the remote off the counter, rewinding the vid. When she got to where the helijet came into view, Grey said, "Stop there. Run it slow."

Shaine did so, and they studied the unfolding images. Shaine observed, "The line of fire is at least four meters out in front of the people by the gates."

Grey nodded. "They weren't planning on killing anyone."

"First protest was like that, too. Limited casualties when it could easily have been a bloodbath."

Morgan asked, "Why even bother?"

Shaine shrugged. "No idea." *And, honestly, I don't give a crap, as long as it all stops after we blow the damned place up.*

Jeannette stood. "I'd better head over to Leese's to keep her from killing her son."

Shaine said, "If she needs help with cash for bail, tell her to call me."

Jeannette nodded shortly. "You girls have a good afternoon," she said, and strode quickly from the room.

The four women looked at each other. Shaine sighed heavily. "Well. Guess we have some planning to do, huh?"

CHAPTER FOURTEEN

Morgan crouched in the brush outside the fence at the back of the former nuclear site. They had returned to where they'd already made a cut in the fence. The darkness was nearly complete. Heavy clouds blocked out the moon and stars. In the dimness, Morgan could barely make out the features of the women beside her. All of them were dressed in black and wore black face paint.

Grey looked at each member of the group as she spoke. "Last-minute questions?" she asked.

Shaine shook her head, shifting her heavy pack more evenly on her shoulders. "We're good."

Grey nodded. "Okay. You have the blueprints on your pads. Use the micro GPS to put the charges where they're indicated, and how we showed you. If you run into anything, we have the radios."

Shaine agreed. "Back here in three hours. Stay cool, stay low, and we have this covered."

Grey held the fence open where it was cut. Shaine and Morgan scooted through first, followed by Mia, and finally

Grey. They picked their way across the broken, overgrown tarmac at a fast jog. The lack of moonlight increased the density of the shadows. A steady breeze blew warm, damp air from the south. The high grass and spindly trees swayed and rustled around them.

They split up when they reached the first of the three cooling towers. Shaine and Morgan hung back while Grey and Mia continued toward the containment facility. Morgan followed Shaine as they circled around the thirty-story cement tower. Shaine crouched and slid the backpack off, pulling it around in front of her. Morgan knelt beside her and opened her own pack. She removed a winch-and-cable pistol and released the grapnel's claw.

Morgan wore a full climbing rig, black cargo pants with plenty of pockets and a tool pouch around her waist. Shaine passed her a set of explosives, which she pocketed.

"You know what to do, right?"

Morgan nodded. "Sure. No issues." Her comp pad contained a 3D rendering of the tower with all the explosives placements marked. The micro GPS built into the blueprint display would tell her when she reached each point. It was relatively foolproof. The self-mounting explosives would bore into the surface. All she had to do was place and activate them.

Shaine grinned at her. "Good."

Morgan passed Shaine the winch gun, and the taller woman backed away from the tower and aimed for the top of the tower structure. The grapnel-ended line shot upward into the night. They heard the muffled crump of the claws digging into the surface, lodging solidly into the cement. Shaine pulled on the thin line, checking to make sure it was secure. She returned to Morgan's side, handing her the gun, setting the line lock.

"Remember, this button to reel up, this one down."

Morgan nodded and clipped the butt of the pistol to the front of her climbing rig. She was the smaller and lighter of the two, so she took the option to do the rappelling while Shaine covered her. Truthfully, she was much happier to be doing something, rather than being the lookout, and she'd told Shaine the same.

"Okay, here I go." She tapped on the miniature comp pad attached to her forearm to bring it to life, then closed her hands around the winch controls. A touch of her finger and the winch gun started reeling her slowly upward. When her feet left the ground she shifted, leaning back into the climbing rig the way Shaine and Grey had taught her, walking the wall with her feet, letting the winch do the work.

The cement smelled damp and musty. The surface was rough and weather-worn and felt almost sandy under her boots. She climbed slowly through the gloom. Above her, she could see the deep crack in the tower's outer shell. Her feet slipped a couple times as she climbed. Each time, her heart skittered, fear pulsing through her until she realized the cord would hold her, even when she ended up face-first against the cement.

She let the winch pull her until the comp pad beeped quietly. She stopped the winch, settling her stance as solidly as she could, and wrangled the first of the charges out of her pocket. She took a quick look at the wrist comp to double-check the placement and grabbed at the edge of the crack, pulling herself over a half-meter. She tapped the winch's up button for just a second, until she could get a foothold inside the meter-deep crack. She lodged the explosive into the back of the crack and tapped the raised button. The device bored into the surface with a slight vibration. When it stopped, she set the arming mechanism. It blinked red three times before going out.

One down. Four to go. She placed the rest of the charges at the intervals that Grey requested, and let the winch reel her back down to the ground. She lost her footing a couple times on the way down and was relieved to have solid ground beneath her feet as she released her climbing rig from the link on the winch gun. She twisted the barrel and pulled the trigger, releasing the grapnel at the top. She gave the line a solid jerk to pull it down.

The rubber-coated prongs hit the ground a few meters away with a heavy thunk. Morgan made quick work of reeling the line back in.

Shaine led the way toward the next cooling tower. This one would require both of them to go up. They crossed the grounds, careful to stay low and moving quickly between the clumps of high brush and small trees. Shaine kept an eye toward the main gate. Morgan looked that way a few times as well, but she'd seen no movement or lights in that direction. She was glad that the gate was more than a kilometer away from them. She hoped what little noise they made would be lost in the steady breeze that hissed across the site.

They reached the next tower and moved around to the side facing away from the main gate. Grey wanted the charges on the inside of this tower. A satellite photo had shown a significant crack in the inner wall. Shaine and Morgan would both climb up. Morgan would again place the charges while Shaine kept watch.

Shaine set both grapnels and they ascended side by side. When they reached the top, Shaine pulled herself onto the two-meter-wide rim before helping Morgan up. Morgan hooked a leg over the rim and shimmied onto it. She stayed on her belly and peered into the black gloom on the inside. She couldn't see down more than a few meters. Shaine pulled out her night-vision binoculars and scanned the area.

"Security is still sitting in their car," she reported. "I don't see Grey and Mia. They must be inside the containment facility." She returned the binocs to her side pants pocket. "You ready?" she asked.

Morgan nodded. "Sure." The blackness inside the tower made her a little uneasy, but she shook it off. It was a little late to be afraid of the dark. She trusted the comp pad to tell her when to stop. She would also have to get past a heavy grate bisecting the tower about a quarter of the way down. She rechecked the clip holding the winch gun to her harness and wriggled to the inside edge of the wall.

Shaine said, "Let me double-check the grapnel." She crawled to where Morgan's grapnel lodged into the cement, giving it a good tug. It held solid. "You should be okay."

Morgan scowled at her. "Gee, thanks," she muttered.

Shaine patted her leg. "You'll be fine. Turn on your headlamp once you're below the rim."

Morgan took a deep breath and checked the winch gun, letting out a short bit of line. She dropped her legs over the inside of the rim and hung for a couple seconds with her feet dangling and her torso still on top. Finally, she slid over the edge, hanging onto the top until the line was taut. She gave Shaine a grin. "Wish me luck."

"Be careful," Shaine said softly.

"I will." One hand on the winch gun, the other gripping the line, she got her feet against the wall and started slowly descending. When she was a couple of meters below the top, she flipped on her headlamp. She blinked in the light, but was glad to be able to see the surface under her feet.

The crack started about ten meters below the rim. It quickly opened into a meter-wide break that reached more than a meter into the surface. According to Grey's aerial photos, it extended at least halfway down the tower. The cement around the edges was crumbly and rough. Morgan felt it scraping the palms of her gloved hands and it made her boots slip when it crumbled under her weight.

Her comp pad GPS beeped softly when she'd descended about twenty meters.

Morgan stopped and retrieved an explosive from her pouch, reaching into the crack to secure and arm it. She placed two more charges before her feet hit the metal grating stretching across the tower. Morgan stopped the winch and looked around.

Shaine's voice was a whisper in the transceiver in her ear. "You reached the grating, what are you seeing?"

Morgan gave herself a little slack on the line and turned, balancing on the metal rungs, placing her boots carefully. The grating was made of steel wire perhaps six centimeters in diameter, woven into half-meter squares. The rusted metal seemed solid except for where it intersected the crack. Morgan could feel the give as she bounced a little bit where the cement had broken away from the rungs. She panned her light around and spoke softly.

"The grating is intact here, and too small for me to get through with the pack on. I'll have to cut a piece free. There's a big fan below this." She could see the shadowy outline of a monster-sized fan blade and shivered to think about what she'd have been up against if the damned thing was actually running. She'd be mincemeat if she fell into that. Ugh.

"Okay. Still all quiet up here."

"Good. Gonna cut through now."

Morgan decided to take out a piece of the grate closest to the wall. She crouched and dug in her tool pouch for the laser cutter. She'd wielded one hundreds of times at work, so it wasn't a stretch to do so now. She made the first cut, then hung onto the wire crosspiece as she made the second cut, not wanting the metal to go crashing and banging all the way to the bottom. She shoved the heavy piece of wire into her belt and replaced the cutter. "Heading down now."

"Roger that."

Morgan sat on the edge of the grating, resettled her harness, checked the clips, then dropped down through the hole she'd created. The winch reeled her past the rusting fan blade. She studied the broken cement as she walked down it. Spiders skittered out of the headlamp's light. Webs glittered inside the crack.

When her pad beeped again she jammed a charge into the crevice and armed it. One to go. She dropped down another ten meters to set the last charge then reversed the winch and let it haul her back up.

She slowed as she approached the fan and the grating, careful as she passed the sharp blade. She wriggled back through the grate, feeling the rough wire catch at her clothing.

Shaine's voice rumbled quietly in her ear. "Make sure to turn off your headlamp and stay low when you get to the top. I'm seeing some movement by the guards' car. Not sure what's going on."

"Okay."

Shaine was lying flat on the surface when Morgan hauled herself to the rim. Shaine whispered, "Another car pulled up."

Morgan pulled herself onto the rim. Shaine had her night vision binocs focused on the gate. Morgan squinted through the darkness. A second set of headlights faced the gate. Shaine murmured, "Three guys standing out there, just talking. I alerted Grey."

"Think they can see us from there?"

Shaine shrugged. "If they were using night vision binocs they might. They're not even looking this way. Let's wait a bit before we go down."

Morgan nodded. Shaine kept the binoculars focused on the security guards. Morgan didn't bother to use her own, just silently scanned the darkness. She could smell dampness in the air. The light breeze brought the musty scent of old cement and dust from inside the huge tower. Morgan felt as though she were at the top of an ancient watchtower, keeping guard in a desolate, silent realm. The three towers and the containment facility were enormous. The security cars seemed like miniscule threats to the huge presence and bulk of the buildings.

Shaine said, "They're leaving."

Morgan saw the second rent-a-cop air car reverse and drive away. The headlights flicked off on the parked car. Shaine watched a while longer before pocketing her binocs. "Let's go."

They rappelled back down, released the claws and reeled them back in, then headed for the final cooling tower. They needed to set a line of charges inside and outside of the third tower to try to create a break in the structure because there were no faults apparent. As they jogged through the brush and grass, Morgan asked, "How are we doing on time?"

Shaine glanced at her chron. "We're okay. No need to rush."

Morgan nodded. "Good. I don't like to hurry when I work."

Shaine grinned. "Damn, I like your style."

Morgan swatted her backside playfully. "So, do you want me to take this one alone, or are you coming up too?"

"Let's both go. I'll set the outer charges, you set the inner ones. Don't wait for me when you get to the top, just head down and set yours. I'll wait for you on top, and we'll go back down together."

"Works for me." Morgan smiled. "We make a good team."

"Yeah, we do."

They made fairly quick work of setting the charges on the third tower. In no time they were back on the ground. Morgan said, "I still have five charges left. Should we just set them all down here at the base, below the others? Seems a waste not to use them up."

Shaine laughed. "You're getting way too into this demolition stuff. Let's do it. I've got a couple too."

They attached all the remaining charges in a cluster a couple meters from the ground and set them. Shaine had no idea if it would do any real structural damage, but it would definitely make a big bang.

When they finished, Shaine checked in with Grey.

"We're done here and on our way out. Meet you at the fence."

"Roger that. We're out in about ten minutes."

Morgan and Shaine hurried across the overgrown property. They reached the cut in the fence and crouched in the darkness behind the brush and weeds. Grey and Mia jogged up about fifteen minutes later.

Grey said, "We're set. Let's blow this joint."

They ducked through the opening and Shaine made quick work of resoldering the chain links. Grey took a small control unit from her pouch and held it up. "You guys ready?"

Shaine nodded. "Do it, Master Destructor."

Grey flashed her a grinning salute. "Yes, sir, Captain Commando." She pressed her thumb on the print-reader and the unit came alive. "Three, two, one." She keyed the firing button. For about three seconds they held their breath.

The explosions started as a low thundering of muffled whuffs and quickly expanded into a deafening roar of destruction. Debris flew. Clouds of white cement dust mushroomed up and out. Shards of building rubble started showering down on them.

Morgan choked, "Holy fuck!"

Shaine grabbed her arm. "Go, go, go!"

Grey muttered, "Maybe I should have moved us out farther, huh?"

"Where's the fun in that?"

"Ow! Fuck, cover your head!"

They raced away from the site while debris and dust rained down. Shaine shouted to Grey, "Overestimate a little?"

The tall blond woman just laughed. "Naw, sounds worse than it is—dry cement makes a damned mess!"

The high grass whipped at their faces as they ran. Morgan stayed a step behind Shaine. She couldn't decide if she felt like they'd just cut loose with the world's greatest prank, or if she felt like a criminal running from the law. If they got caught, they were screwed. On the other hand, they had done this for a good cause. Besides, Morgan thought, blowing stuff up was fun. She stifled a crazy urge to laugh gleefully.

"There's the bikes!"

They had two air bikes and doubled up on them, moving out of the area as fast as they dared. It was still fully dark and Shaine had disconnected the automatic headlights on the bikes. The riding was treacherous. Morgan gritted her teeth and held on as Shaine led the way through fields and back trails to the farm and straight into the equipment barn.

"Holy shit," Morgan muttered as they dismounted. Her legs were shaking and she leaned against the wall. Shaine came up beside her and wrapped an arm around her shoulders.

"You okay?"

"Yeah. Adrenaline crash."

Grey said, "Good job, you guys. That was flawless."

Mia gave her a raised brow. "Honey, you don't even know what happened after we left."

Grey shrugged. "It sounded right," she said.

Shaine passed out wipes so that they could clean the black camouflage makeup off their faces. The wind from their ride had blown off the worst of the debris dust. Morgan looked around at the group. They all needed baths.

Shaine said, "Let's go inside and see if there's anything on the news yet."

Morgan slid her arm around Shaine's waist as they headed toward the house. Knowing what they'd just done, she felt like a guilty adolescent. Her hope that nobody would be home was dashed as they strode into the kitchen. Jeannette Ichiro stood at the counter, pouring herself a cup of coffee. She gave them a raised brow stare as they trooped into the house.

Shaine smiled innocently. "Hi, Mom. What's up?"

"As if you need to ask me," Jeannette said.

Grey, Mia and Morgan all put on their best "who me?" looks, and Shaine smirked. "Is it on the news?" she asked.

Her mother sighed. "I felt the explosions all the way over here, Shaine."

"Heh."

"They just broke into regular programming with the news alert that terrorists had attacked the nuclear reactor site."

The women exchanged glances.

"Terrorists?" Morgan repeated.

Grey scratched her head. "Little paranoid, huh?"

Jeannette frowned at her. "We don't often have buildings blowing up around here," she said dryly.

Shaine looked at Grey and Mia. "Hope nobody noticed you guys showing up in town."

Mia smiled. "We are practically invisible," she said. "Nobody knew where we were going, and we didn't stop anywhere on our way. Besides, who would think to worry about the comings and goings of the owners of a legitimate construction demolition company?"

Jeannette sighed again. "Would anyone care for some coffee?"

"All around, Mom."

Morgan said, "I'll help."

Jeannette shooed them out of the room. "I've got it. You girls get comfortable and see what havoc you've created." She shook her head at her daughter. "You're lucky your father's not home."

Shaine grinned. She dropped into the oversized recliner in the entertainment room and pulled Morgan down on her lap. Grey and Mia settled on the sofa, not quite as close, but comfortable nonetheless.

"Oooh, we done good, ladies," Grey said, studying the video on the screen. It was a panoramic view of the damage from a media helijet. The site was still thick with dust in the air, illuminated by the helijet's floodlights. A gray blanket of snow covered the whole site and extended into the fields beyond. Fire suppression vehicles and law enforcement cars lined the road into the reactor site. A handful of police and firefighters scouted around inside the gate. Most of the fire troops loitered near their vehicles. With no electric and no power there was no fire at the site.

The camera panned across the cooling towers. One had partially collapsed on one side, a whole span of the curved wall reduced to rubble. The second had a very visible open crack from top to nearly bottom. The third had a very large hole in the side at the base, and the wall above that was rent with a deep crack and fissures.

The top of the reactor building had been blown from the inside out, leaving concentric piles of cement around the building. The dome was mostly gone. The worst of the debris field was mostly contained within the site grounds. Shaine nodded at that, satisfied. The intent hadn't been to do damage to the surrounding area, and in that, Grey had done well. They had done plenty of damage to the site itself. Shaine hoped it was enough to scuttle the plan to restart the reactor plant.

The comp pad in her pocket vibrated. She pulled it out and frowned. Shaine sighed and mouthed to Morgan, "Rogan." She then held up the pad and said, "Got a call I need to take."

Morgan slid off her lap and Shaine pushed off the chair, taking the pad up the back stairs to her bedroom and closing the door before she answered it. Rogan's dark visage glared at her from the small screen.

Without preamble, he demanded, "What the fuck are you doing up there?"

Shaine looked blankly at him. "I was sitting with my girlfriend until you interrupted. What are you doing?"

He actually growled at her. "Do not fuck with me, Wendt."

"Wouldn't dream of it, Rogan."

The door opened behind her and Morgan poked her head into the room.

Rogan said, "If ANY of this comes back to you or Morgan, you are a dead woman walking. I will have you drawn and quartered and blown into minuscule bits!"

Morgan's eyes widened.

Shaine managed to look bored. "You worry too much, Rogan. Bad for your heart."

He glared. "I am not joking," he snapped, and the connection cut off.

Shaine dropped the pad back into the pocket of her cargo pants. "Well, that was fun," she said dryly.

Morgan frowned. "How much trouble are we in?" she asked.

Shaine shrugged. "None, technically."

"What if they figure out who did it?"

"They won't."

"How can you be so sure?"

"Nobody knows Grey and Mia are here. There is no reason for anyone to look at us for something like blowing up buildings. We're just visiting my family. The explosives are all civilian-grade self-destruct and leave no evidence behind."

"But they know who you are, Shaine. It's not that hard to find out what people do, that you have a background in Special Ops and security."

Shaine shook her head slowly. "Actually, they don't know much at all about me. Because there isn't anything about me out there. They can find my service record, but most of it is classified. Because we were Special Ops, our identities were wiped, all records of us cleared or rewritten. My time at Mann-Maru will show me working as a midlevel security manager at corporate before I became a mechanic. There's no record of my real function." She shrugged. "Essentially, I'm off the grid."

Morgan considered this for a few moments. "You're accustomed to working outside the system, aren't you? Outside the rules. You just do what you want and assume that the law can't get to you."

Shaine licked her lips. "I've been doing this for most of my adult life, Morg. It's second nature."

"It should scare the piss out of me, Shaine, but, honestly, it doesn't."

"Thank you."

"Sometimes I think it bothers you, though."

Shaine sighed. "Sometimes it does. A lot of why I was trying to get out of it." She took Morgan's hand and pulled her to sit beside her on the bed. "Seems like old habits die hard, huh?"

Morgan reached up, tracing the taut line of Shaine's jaw. "It isn't necessarily a bad thing, hon. I mean, it's all for a good reason." Shaine made no comment, sitting quiet and still. Morgan cocked her head. "What are you thinking?"

"Everything. Nothing. You're honestly okay with this? With me?"

Morgan gently turned Shaine's face toward her, cupping her cheek with one hand. "Shaine, I love you. Whether you're under the radar or not. I love that you're brave enough to do what's right, like what we did tonight. I love that you care. I love that you love me and trust me enough to include me in your plans."

Shaine turned her head, kissing Morgan's palm, and then pulled her into a tight hug. "God, I love you."

Morgan leaned up and captured Shaine's lips in a kiss that quickly turned passionate. She reveled in the taste and feel of Shaine's tongue twisting against her own. The pulse of desire radiated down to her groin. She moaned against Shaine's mouth and pulled her closer. Shaine's hands slid under Morgan's T-shirt and chills ran up and down Morgan's spine.

"I want you so much," Shaine breathed.

Morgan pushed Shaine back on the bed and crawled on top of her, sucking hard on the pulse-point at her neck. Suddenly desperate with need, she pulled at Shaine's clothes, wanting them off, now.

Shaine arched against her, hands at Morgan's waist, fumbling at the buttons on her pants, pushing them impatiently down and out of the way. Morgan wriggled to get free, doing the same for Shaine, finally giving up and just sliding her hand into Shaine's pants, between hot skin and the soft, dampened fabric of her silk boxers. She sighed as her fingers slid into warm, slick folds.

Shaine choked on a cry as Morgan entered her, her hips jerking up for more contact. Morgan was more than happy to oblige. Shaine's fingers found Morgan's center in turn and she gasped. Panting, they fell into a rhythm, straining against each other, trading open-mouthed kisses, climbing frantically toward climax until they came together, collapsing against each other, gasping for air.

Morgan dropped her head onto Shaine's chest, feeling Shaine's long arms wrap around her tightly. "Damn," she whispered.

Shaine kissed her hair. "Yeah."

They lay like that for a few minutes, until Morgan sighed. "They're probably wondering what happened to us."

Shaine chuckled lowly. "Yeah, probably not, Morg. Probably not."

Morgan shook her head with a groan and rolled off Shaine, sitting up on the bed. Shaine got her own self up. They got themselves sorted and respectable. Morgan caught sight of them in the mirror on the back of the door. Both their faces remained flushed with exertion. *Yeah*, she thought. *They won't have to guess too hard to figure out what we were doing.*

* * *

Grey and Mia slipped out of town early the next morning after grabbing a couple hours of sleep in the guest bedroom and a quick breakfast courtesy of Jeannette. Shaine and Morgan headed back upstairs after they left, wanting to nap a while longer before facing the day. They'd all been up watching the news until nearly dawn.

Morgan woke some hours later, content and comfortable, wrapped in Shaine's arms. It was a wonderful feeling, waking with Shaine curled around her. When she slept alone, she wrapped herself in her quilt like a mummy, curled on her side. When she'd been with her ex-girlfriend, Gina, her sleeping habits had been a serious point of contention between them. Gina hated Morgan's tendency to steal all the covers, wrapping herself in blankets instead of wrapping herself up in her companion. Gina resented the separation. Morgan tried, but couldn't change, and always woke up having cloaked herself in isolation.

Sleeping with Shaine, she never woke wrapped alone in the quilts. For better or worse, Shaine had become her security blanket. She felt protected, but not smothered. Safe.

She wriggled a little closer into Shaine's warmth. Shaine's arm tightened around her waist and Morgan felt a sigh of warm breath on the back of her neck. The skin-on-skin contact made her feel so wonderfully content, on the edge of arousal, as though they shared one skin. She wished she could remain right where she was, not caring to move, for the rest of her days. She smiled to herself, closed her fingers over Shaine's and closed her eyes again.

CHAPTER FIFTEEN

The next evening Shaine got a call on her comp pad after dinner. Morgan was sprawled on the sofa in the entertainment room while Shaine stretched out on the floor with a pillow. She leaned over to look at Shaine's pad to see who'd called.

Shaine frowned at the com code and shrugged. Morgan watched, wondering who it might be.

They were both surprised when the screen cleared to show Morgan's older brother, Garren Maruchek, smiling at them from behind a desk. He leaned back in what looked like a very comfortable conform chair. He was a tall man, built like his father. His long black hair was pulled into a neat ponytail at the nape of his neck. He had his father's piercing blue eyes and strong, aquiline features. His deep voice came clearly over the pad's speaker. "Hey, how are you two doing?"

Morgan grinned from her position leaning over Shaine. "Hey, Garren, what's going on?"

Garren shrugged. "Just working. I've been putting together the details of Father's latest big project. We've gotten the go-ahead to start mining on Mars. Earth Assembly decided Mann-

Maru was the lesser evil fighting for mining rights, so I'm working to get the project off the ground."

"Sounds pretty intense," Morgan commented.

Shaine said, "Actually, Rogan mentioned it too. I wondered when they'd finally give into Maruchek on that."

"I stay out of the politics," Garren admitted. "That's not my forte. I'm an organizer, not a lobbyist. Father is much better suited to that role." He grimaced. "Actually, the organizing is kind of the reason I'm calling."

Morgan frowned, suddenly suspicious. "What do you mean?"

"Actually, I'm hoping that the two of you might help me."

"I'm not sure we want to know what you're about to ask," Shaine commented dryly.

Garren managed an embarrassed smile. "Well, I'm only calling you before Rogan does. He'll ask the same thing, I'm hoping you might actually listen to me."

Morgan frowned. "Hell, Garr. Better you than Rogan any day. But what in the universe can we do for you?"

He smiled. "You can drag Shaine's ass to Mars with you. I need a head of security on the project and I want to bring in my own people and have them report to me directly rather than deal with Rogan as a middleman, second-guessing me all the way."

Shaine cleared her throat. "Very direct of you, Garren. But I'm not in the security business anymore."

He raised a brow. Morgan thought he looked just like their father. He said, "Could have fooled me. Nice demolition project, by the way."

Shaine snorted. "Been talking to Kyle lately?"

Garren grinned at her. "Actually, he and I have had a couple of very enlightening conversations."

Morgan's hackles went up. "I don't appreciate you spying on either me or Shaine, and if that's what you're about, this conversation is over."

"No, wait, Morgan, I wasn't spying!" He pushed anxiously to his feet in front of the screen. "That came out wrong. Please, hear me out."

Morgan glared angrily at him. "Say your piece, but it better be good."

Garren nodded. "I knew that Kyle was an ally of Shaine's. I went to him in the hope that he might be able to suggest someone who would be best suited to run security on the Mars project. We got to talking and he said that I should talk to you and Morgan. He said that you'd probably want to stay out of the limelight and this would be a great way to do it."

Shaine sighed.

Morgan asked, "What did he tell you about what's going on here?"

Garren held up his hands. "Nothing, really. I had a couple of 'bots out keeping me apprised of news of both of you. So I heard about Shaine stopping the shootings in her hometown. Then, yesterday I got a blurb in my inbox about someone blowing up an empty nuclear power plant near Shaine's home. I put two and two together." He grinned. "Did I get four? Or have I miscalculated?"

Shaine chuckled. "You got four. You were never stupid, Garren."

"So, would you consider it?" he asked. "I really would love to have you guys on board here. I think you've got the brains and the experience for the job, Shaine, and I would truly rather not have to deal with Rogan on a regular basis."

Shaine looked to Morgan questioningly. Morgan shrugged. "If you want to go, I'm there with you," she said.

Shaine turned a serious expression on Garren. "If I accepted, would I have complete control over the security department?"

"Absolutely."

"Give us a day to talk about it," Shaine said.

Garren nodded. "You know where to find me."

Morgan said, "We'll call tomorrow."

"Thanks."

Garren signed off. Morgan and Shaine turned to each other and said at the same time, "What do you think?" They broke into giggles.

"Well?" Shaine asked.

Morgan cocked her head thoughtfully. "We did talk about needing to get out of here. I suppose Mars is as good a place as any to hide out. But, really, the question goes to you. Do you want to be Garren's head of security?"

Shaine frowned. "Honestly, I don't know." She ran a hand through her hair. "On the upside, it wouldn't be undercover work. I'd be as much an administrator as anything. I'm not big on administration, but I could keep my force small and be more hands on."

"You're good at this, Shaine, and you know it. You're better at security than you are a mechanic." She grinned.

Shaine stuck her tongue out. "Yeah. I know. But what about you? I don't want to drag you halfway around the solar system if it isn't what you want."

Morgan wrapped her arms around Shaine's shoulders. "I don't know what I want at this point. I know I can't go back to my old life, but I don't know what the possibilities are. I'm sure I can find something to do while we're there. As long as we're together, it'll work out."

"You're sure?"

"I'm sure."

Shaine smiled. "We'll talk to Garren tomorrow, then."

CHAPTER SIXTEEN

Morgan was sad to leave the farm. She'd started to think of it as home. She liked working in the garden and the greenhouse, and treasured the walks she took with Shaine. It had been so wonderful to have so much time just for themselves.

Shaine's family made her feel so comfortable. Jeannette was almost like having her own mom back again. When she'd slipped and called her "Mom," Jeannette had smiled brilliantly and told her to keep calling her that. "You're family here, Morgan," she'd said. They had a final meal with Leese, her husband and Toby.

Morgan tried hard not to cry as they were getting in the air car, but ended up swiping away tears anyway. Jeannette hugged her hard and kissed her cheek and told her she was always welcome, and she was very glad that Shaine had found such a wonderful partner. Morgan sniffled until the farm had long disappeared from the rearview vid screen, and Shaine had shifted into the upper sky lanes.

So much had happened while they'd been at the farm—a lifetime of experiences and excitement in a couple short weeks.

She wanted to return to find out what winter was like and to see Toby graduate from the university. Shaine promised they'd return when they could, maybe for Winter Solstice the following year.

In the end, the furor around the nuclear plant ended reasonably favorably. The destruction at the plant site remained under investigation. Local authorities had no suspects and no traceable evidence. Because of the damage, GGS had to forfeit the option to reopen the plant. Toby was ecstatic. Shaine and Morgan didn't tell him about their involvement. He, like the media, speculated that GGS had decided it wasn't worth their while to go through with the deal and sabotaged it themselves to save face.

Shaine and Morgan's plan was to leave the air car at the Mann-Maru space terminal in New York City and catch a shuttle back to Moon Base. Both women had loose ends to tie up there and plans to make before they headed to Mars. Morgan wanted to spend a bit of quiet time with her dad and see Charri. Even though they'd talked via their net avatars or emailed nearly every day, it wasn't the same as being with her best friend in person.

Fifteen hours later Morgan and Shaine reached Moon Base and disembarked from the Mann-Maru shuttle. Morgan trudged down the short ramp with her duffel bag on her shoulder. Shaine carried an oversized backpack and had arranged for the equipment bag with her guns to be delivered to her apartment by a courier from Mann-Maru Security.

A black-uniformed Mann-Maru Security guard met them at the bottom of the shuttle's ramp and escorted them to the landing bay airlock, which he opened with a key-code. Once Shaine and Morgan were inside, he nodded to them and sealed the small compartment. A couple minutes later, the door at the back of the airlock opened to the inner part of the private corporate terminal.

The Mann-Maru terminal was virtually empty. A couple of employees staffed the main desk, but the seating area and the coffee station were empty of travelers. Both employees nodded politely to Shaine and Morgan as they walked through.

The smoky glass door to the main spaceport slid open as they approached. Shaine and Morgan stepped into the bustling dome of the Moon Base spaceport. Travelers moved between the many terminals attached all the way around the dome. Announcements boomed over loudspeakers, accenting the general hubbub of noise and voices. Music and enticing aromas drifted from the various bars and restaurants. Everywhere she looked, Morgan saw small air carts darting about between pedestrians, moving luggage or carrying people to and from the different terminals and seating areas scattered through the spaceport.

Shaine said, "Let's head to the tram." She slid an arm around Morgan's waist, and they ambled toward the tram station across the dome. The trams ran every twenty minutes or so between the spaceport and the Moon Base dome almost forty kilometers away.

The two women hadn't gone more than ten meters from the Mann-Maru terminal when a group of about twelve reporters rushed them, shoving recording devices in their faces and yelling out questions.

"Come on, Ms. Rahn, just a simple statement! Will you be working for Mann-Maru? What does Tarm Maruchek think of having found his daughter? Do you speak with him often? How does your adopted family feel about your birth father?

"Ms. Wendt, that was a courageous thing you did in your hometown! What possessed you to get involved against gunmen? Is it true you were in Special Operations in the EG?"

Shaine glowered at the reporters, caught Morgan by the arm and shouldered roughly through the small group. Morgan ducked her head and followed Shaine's lead. The reporters followed them through the terminal to the tram station.

When they reached the ticketing kiosk, Shaine slid her credit chit through the reader, requested two rides, then jammed her laser cutter through the chit reader. She and Morgan rushed through the turnstile and jumped on the tram a half-second before the door slammed shut, leaving behind frustrated, shouting reporters. Morgan sighed and leaned against her partner. "You are the best," she murmured.

Shaine hugged her one-armed while she hung on to the overhead bar with her other hand. "Only for you, love."

"So, my place first, or yours?"

Shaine shrugged. "Mine first? I can grab some clothes. We can stay at your place and you can call your dad. Hell, tell him to come over. We'll order out dinner."

Morgan grinned. "Sounds like a good plan to me."

* * *

Vinn Rahn, Morgan and Shaine sat around the small table in Morgan's apartment, sharing the noodle and meat stew they'd had delivered. Morgan was glad her dad agreed to join them.

His careworn face held a content smile. Vinn Rahn wasn't much older than Tarm Maruchek, but life had been much harder on his aging body. He was paying for all the years he worked in null or near-null gravity in the Asteroid Belt mines, without the time, energy or facilities to do workouts in full gravity to keep his muscles and bone structure built up. Morgan hated to see him more hunched over every year. His hazel eyes had faded and arthritis gnarled his fingers. He used a cane now, and she worried about him getting around.

Vinn pointed a fork at his daughter. "So you're leaving again, then?"

Morgan said, "In a few days, yeah. Shaine needs to organize her security team before we can go, and I want to tie up some loose ends too. There isn't a transport going out until next week anyway."

Vinn frowned as he stabbed at a piece of vegetable. "I had hoped you'd stay around a while. I've missed you. How long will you be gone?"

Shaine answered, "It's hard to say. Initially, I'd guess we'll be on Mars for a few months, though I'm sure we can get back for visits from time to time."

"It won't be forever, Dad."

He put on a brave smile. "I know it won't," he said. "I've been spoiled, having you around as long as I have. Most parents aren't that lucky."

Morgan felt her heart breaking, tightening uncomfortably in her chest, and looked down at her dinner, no longer hungry. She blinked back hot tears and fought to get control of her emotions.

Vinn said, "I'm sorry, Morgan. I don't mean to make you feel bad." He patted her arm. "I want you to live your life and be happy. You're happy with Shaine. I'm not so old I can't see that." He smiled. "You girls go to Mars and have an adventure. And you, Shaine Wendt. You keep my daughter out of trouble, okay?"

Shaine flushed and grinned. "I'll do my best," she said.

Morgan muttered, "I'm not the troublemaker in this relationship."

Vinn laughed. "Then you'll have to fill me in on the trouble you make," he decided, and scooped up a forkful of noodles. "This is very tasty."

Morgan managed a weak smile. Her dad was trying to tell her he'd be all right. She wanted to believe that, though the guilt remained. Until now, she'd never been away from him for more than a few days at a time. She had never traveled, other than the occasional jaunt to the Luna City dome with her friends.

Shaine squeezed her leg under the table and Morgan took a deep breath, finding strength in Shaine's touch. It would be all right. She would keep in touch with her dad, and it would be fine. Vinn had a lot of friends here, and he kept busy. He didn't need a babysitter. She would miss him, and he would miss her. Change was tough.

CHAPTER SEVENTEEN

"It's been a long time, Captain Wendt," the man on the screen said with a smile.

Shaine grinned at her former Earth Guard sergeant. He'd aged some over the years, his brown hair speckled with gray. A few more lines traced his face, but his eyes still had the same piercing glint, and his well-muscled frame remained strong. "Too long, Sarge. How've you been?"

"Eh, can't complain, you know? The civvy thing has gone pretty well for me. But I bet this isn't a social call, is it?"

She shrugged, a bit chagrined. "Unfortunately, no. I need to put together a core security team I can trust. I hoped you'd be able to help me."

"I think we can work something out."

"Thanks, Jens. I'm looking for a group of six to start with. We'll be setting up security at the Mann-Maru mining site on Mars."

He nodded thoughtfully. "So, people with spacer background. What kind of trouble are you expecting?"

Shaine laughed. "Expecting? The usual, I suppose. Trouble among the workers, possibly outside threats, though being on Mars should minimize that issue."

"Will you need pilots? Fighter support?"

"Eventually, but not right away. We don't have any fighter ships yet, just ground transport and the supply shuttles in and out."

He glanced down and tapped a couple notes into a pad. "I have a couple people in mind already," he said.

Shaine smiled. "Excellent. I need to do interviews and have the core group set five days from now. Is that possible?"

"Absolutely. Can I use this com code for them to contact you?"

"Yeah, this'll do." She tapped a couple of commands into her pad. "I just sent you an info packet with the job recs. If you need anything else, let me know."

"Sounds good. I'll be in touch."

"Thanks, Sarge."

"No problem, Captain."

* * *

Shaine had her core security staff hired within three days. On the fourth day, the new team gathered at her apartment. Shaine stood in the kitchen going over her notes and observed the group as they chatted amongst themselves in her sitting room. Two were ex-Earth Guard. One was a former police officer. The others had trained with private security organizations. All were martial artists, sharpshooters and had spent time in space.

She was glad she'd gone through Sarge's security staffing agency. Garren asked why she didn't just pull people from Rogan's Security Department. But she wanted her own people, loyal to her, and not with Rogan's biases built in. She didn't want Mann-Maru corporate involved any more than they needed to be. She wanted corporate to write the paychecks and handle the human resources. The rules of security operation would be hers and hers alone.

She planned to make Josef Waylin her second in command. He was the most experienced in the group, and she'd worked with him in Earth Guard Special Ops. Serious, intelligent, loyal and reliable, Josef was broad-shouldered, had no neck and hair still cut into a regulation flattop. She trusted him. She trusted his judgment. He'd been a good friend and a damned good soldier.

Seated on the couch next to Josef was a whip-thin young man with bright blue eyes and an intense gaze. His short golden hair crowned his head in wild disarray. His name was Thomas Reede, but Sarge referred to him as Whippet.

Ben Wycheski, Allim Haahn and Lukas Fells sat on the kitchen chairs she'd moved into the living room. All three men were straightforward security specialists. Nothing standout about them, though they were all very competent and motivated. Shaine considered them interchangeable. Each had solid skills and experience and would fit in anywhere she needed him.

Del Marin, the final member of the team, sat on the floor opposite the couch. She had honey-brown skin, black eyes and dreadlocks tied loosely at the nape of her neck. Del wasn't tall, but under the form-fitting T-shirt she wore, Shaine could see the hard definition of muscle in her arms and upper body. Shaine noted the alert tension in the way Marin held herself and how she took in every detail of the room as she talked to Josef. Marin was only two years out of Earth Guard and had been in Special Ops as well.

When everyone was settled, Shaine walked over to join them. "Welcome," she said. They nodded in response. She sat down next to Josef on the sofa. "I'll assume you all know the purpose of this assignment and that you've all read the packets you were sent. I wanted to get us all together before we leave so that we can get to know each other a little bit and understand the chain of command. Everyone answers to me. Josef is my second on this team. If I'm unavailable, he will provide direction. Del is third in the command chain, and will act as my second if Josef is unavailable." She looked around the group for confirmation, then turned and gestured to Morgan, who was sitting at the desk at the back of the room, working on her pad. Morgan stood and joined Shaine.

"This is my partner, Morgan Rahn. If I am unavailable, and she says that she speaks for me, her word is as good as mine. She'll be my right hand outside the security chain of command."

Again, she looked around the group, waiting for confirmations. She grinned. "Good. We're going to have plenty of time to put things into place. We'll be staying in the temporary dome while the primary facility is being completed. There is a group of geologists on-site doing core drilling and mapping. Sys ops is in charge of facilities and construction. We'll be working with them to make sure the security systems are put into place as the new facilities are brought online. There is a skeleton maintenance crew on-site as well."

Josef asked, "I assume that external site monitoring will be remote?"

"Initially, yes. No sense in being outside if we don't need to be."

Allim Haahn asked, "How long until they actually bring the mine online?"

Shaine shrugged. "There isn't a set date. It'll be at least a year or more. At this point, they're still defining the breadth of the ore deposits, so there's a lot of work to be done first."

Whippet asked, "What's on the immediate agenda?"

"Sys ops has started work on an emergency radiation shelter and the permanent living dome. So construction is first in terms of bringing more people up to the site."

Whippet nodded. "Will we be vetting the incoming workers or is Mann-Maru corporate handling that?"

Shaine smiled. She liked the way this kid thought. She said, "We'll have complete control over vetting security personnel. For site employees and construction personnel, Mann-Maru will do the usual background verification, but I want to take a look at everyone. We need to know who's on-site." Shaine narrowed her eyes at Whippet. "You have a hacking background. You want to take point on checking people out?"

He nodded. "Sure."

Del Marin cocked her head. "What about Garren Maruchek? Does he have a clue, or are we babysitting him, too?"

Shaine felt Morgan stiffen beside her. "Garren's good at what he does. He's good at administration, at making the whole project work. He doesn't need babysitting. He won't have any direct control over security, but I'll work with him and keep him in the loop. He's coordinating construction plans and administrative functions. We won't be at cross purposes. He can be trusted to have our best interests in mind."

Del nodded, satisfied. Shaine knew Del had been in a situation where upper management had sabotaged security, and her caution was warranted. Being as far out as Mars, if the shit hit the fan, they needed management to be behind security, not getting in the way of keeping people safe.

Shaine was aware of each of the new security team giving Morgan the once-over, obviously trying to decide what her place was in the scheme of things, other than simply Shaine's partner. Shaine had anticipated this, and told Morgan to expect it.

They took a break from the discussion and Morgan volunteered to fetch drinks for everyone. Whippet offered to help, and Shaine watched him follow Morgan to the small kitchen. She listened in on their interaction and watched out of the corner of her eye while the others talked quietly.

"Your ability to keep the press out of your face is amazing," he commented.

Morgan looked at him, her expression blank. She said, "I have nothing to say to them."

"You're a security risk," he countered.

"No more than Garren or Shaine. I'm neither helpless nor stupid."

He cocked his head. "If you're Wendt's partner, I'd say you're probably worth more than your shipping weight. From what Josef said, she wouldn't waste her time with useless baggage."

Morgan lifted her chin, met his gaze without flinching. "I'm going to assume that's a compliment, because if it isn't I'm going to kick your little blond ass."

Laughing, he grinned and held his hands up in surrender. "And I don't doubt for a second that you could. Seriously, those other guys, they don't keep up with pop culture too much. I'm not sure if they've caught on to who you are. Del's gonna be annoyed. The guys won't care."

"Why should she be annoyed?"

"She doesn't like dealing with celebrities."

Morgan laughed. "I'm no celebrity. I'm a mechanic with dubious parentage."

"Yeah, well, your dubious parentage makes you untrust-worthy in her eyes."

Morgan shook her head. "Whatever." They returned to the group with a bucket of iced bottles of beer, which Morgan set on the coffee table in the center of the sitting area. Grabbing a beer for herself, she retreated to Shaine's desk with her pad.

Shaine continued to lead the discussion of the situation at the Martian mining site. Morgan listened while she surfed the net and wrote in her journal. She and Shaine had talked about what her role would be when they got to Mars. Technically, there was a lot she could do to be useful. She could help monitor the security cameras and communications. With her mechanic's training, there would be work she could do in systems operations or maintenance. If any ships needed emergency servicing, she could help there too. Whatever happened, she wouldn't be tagging along for the ride. She'd find something to do.

She knew it wasn't likely she could simply go back to life the way it had been before Tarm Maruchek came into it. As much as she didn't want to admit it, her status in life had changed. She'd gone from being just an average, ordinary systems mechanic to being the long-lost daughter of one of the wealthiest, most powerful men in the world. The press called it a "Cinderella Story" though they still insisted on trying to dig up dirt about her life.

She had to disconnect her personal com code to keep reporters from calling her. People she didn't know wanted to know who she was, what she was like, what she did and how she felt about being Maruchek's lost daughter. Even her friends got calls about her.

She knew that Tarm's people—like Kyle Ellerand and others in security—worked hard to keep her off-limits from the press. At this very moment, there were probably Mann-Maru security operatives skulking about the apartment building, monitoring her whereabouts and keeping unwanted reporters from knocking on the door. For that she was thankful.

Going to Mars with Shaine helped everyone. It got her out of the spotlight. And maybe it would give her a new niche in life to call her own, because right now, she felt at loose ends.

Since she graduated from trade school, she'd been paying her own way, taking care of herself and working. Even when she still lived with her father, she worked and helped with expenses as much as he let her. Staying at the farm had been like being on vacation.

Morgan knew a permanent vacation wasn't going to work for her. She couldn't hide out for the rest of her life. Her father's people didn't want her working on the docks. They still worried about the threat of random terrorism against Mann-Maru, like the sabotaged space suit that had killed her best friend. She still shivered to think that she was the one who should have died. And she knew her father worried that more of his enemies would try to murder her the way Tyr Charun had.

Perhaps in a couple of years, when the novelty of her sudden celebrity had worn off, she could go back to her old job. For now, that wasn't going to happen. And she wasn't content to just sit back and wait it out.

Going to Mars was going to be a good thing, especially since she'd be there with Shaine.

CHAPTER EIGHTEEN

Wearing a brand-new custom-fitted mechanic's vac suit, Morgan stepped off the ramp of the supply shuttle and onto the rocky Martian surface. The sun glared dully and she blinked until her faceplate tinted to shade her eyes. The landscape was stark and barren. The sky was a pale blue instead of black, and the ground a rusty brown-red instead of gray. At least they'd have a true day/night cycle here, though, and gravity was a little closer to Earth-normal.

Morgan shuffled forward to stand beside Shaine. The rest of the security team disembarked behind them. Even if she was fully outfitted in a vac suit, she was glad to be out of the supply ship. The trip from Moon Base to Mars took a full three and a half days, with nothing to do but drink coffee, sleep or read. There was no net connection in transit and very little in the way of creature comforts since they were on a supply ship. They'd been restricted to a small barracks room separate from the ship's crew and a tiny lounge with a processed food and beverage dispenser and a single vid screen, but only room for three to sit at a time.

Morgan looked curiously around the new construction.

A few hundred meters in front of her and to the right, the bare bones of a new living dome was framed in steel and concrete. Four stories high and about the size of a large city block, it would house and provide for several hundred people. To the right of the new dome was the foundation of a structure that would eventually be part of the ore processing facility. Beyond that, Morgan could see posts and flags stretching out toward the horizon and marking the mining site itself.

To the left, about fifty meters away, was the temporary working dome where they would be staying. It was prefab. Its curved walls were solid steel rather than transparent glassteel like the Moon Base dome. It was only a third the size of the new dome, but big enough to house nearly two hundred people. Facing them was an airlock entrance with a manual umbilical tunnel folded against it. When they were ready to unload supplies from the shuttle, the tunnel would be attached to the shuttle's cargo bay hatch so that supplies could be unloaded directly into the dome without the need for vacuum suits.

Morgan felt the slight pressure of Shaine's gloved hand on her shoulder. Her partner's voice came across clearly in her helmet speakers.

"Home sweet home, huh?"

"I wouldn't go that far."

Shaine laughed.

Morgan smiled. She was with Shaine, she was out of reach of the media and she was reasonably happy. If they were here on Mars, well, whatever. The living situation would be similar enough to Moon Base, even if space and creature comforts were more limited.

Besides, her brother Garren was on-site, and she was looking forward to seeing him. She enjoyed his dry, sarcastic sense of humor. He didn't talk down to her and never treated her as being less worthy than him. They had a common interest in sports. Garren had played some grav ball in school. They both liked music, and, oddly enough, both liked similar slam-thrash bands.

"Come on, let's get inside."

Shaine led the small group across the gravel-strewn surface to the temporary dome. She keyed the controls for the outer airlock and they moved quickly into the tight space. The hatch slid shut and sealed behind them. Morgan automatically focused on the red light in the ceiling. After a minute or two, the light shifted to orange, then yellow and finally green. The inner door slid open.

Morgan stepped into a warehouse space lined with all manner of supplies and building materials. The back of the warehouse contained shelves of tools and three work bays. The entire storage area was well lit and tidy. She glanced down at the atmosphere readout on her wrist, then reached up and popped the seal on her helmet and lifted it off. She held her helmet at her side as she took a better look around. Shaine and the others did the same.

A man strode toward them from across the warehouse. He was a large fellow with a beefy build. Strong arms and big hands extruded from his cut-off work shirt. Morgan thought he looked perhaps a little younger than her dad. He was dark-skinned, his black hair peppered with gray.

"Hello," he called, his face breaking into a wide, white smile as he spotted Shaine. "Captain Wendt! Welcome!"

Shaine stepped toward him and clasped his outstretched hand in her still-gloved one. "Hey, Joe. Been a while. You're looking good, old man."

"And you're still a smart-ass, Captain. Good to see you." He stepped back. "Welcome, all of you. Glad to have a few more hands here. I'm Joe Hailey, Head of Maintenance. This is the maintenance bay and the supply warehouse, so if you're looking for supplies or need things fixed, this is the first stop." He pointed to a small area of lockers and shelves off to one side. "You can stow your suits over there. Just grab an empty locker."

"Thanks." Shaine nodded toward her team and they obediently headed over toward the lockers. Shaine hung back a moment and Morgan remained at her side. Shaine regarded Joe Hailey with a broad smile. "Joe, this is my partner, Morgan Rahn.

She'll be joining us as a jack-of-all-trades. She's a mechanic, so she can probably help you out down here if you need an extra hand. Morgan, this is Joe Hailey. Joe was my first drill sergeant. One of the guys who kicked my ass all over basic training and then again when I was rehabbing before they decommissioned me." She grinned at him. "Stubborn bastard."

He grinned back, skin creasing around his eyes and mouth. "Takes one to know one, Wendt," he returned easily. Hailey smiled at Morgan and she shook his hand. He said, "Stop down here any time, Morgan, and we can chat. I've got stories you're gonna love to hear."

Shaine shook her head and Morgan chuckled, thinking it was going to be fun to get some stories about her lover. Morgan was certain whatever she heard from Joe Hailey would be damned interesting.

Hailey said to Shaine, "Grapevine said you'd gotten out of the security game. I was surprised to see your name come up in the memo here."

Shaine shrugged as they walked toward the lockers. "I got out. Rogan sucked me back in." They reached a long bench where the rest of the group was getting unsuited. Shaine set down her helmet and she and Morgan started stripping out of their vac suits.

As Shaine sat down to unseal her boots, she glanced up at her old friend. "So, what's the scoop around here, Joe? Things going okay?"

"As can be expected. Had a couple bad sandstorms blow up over the past couple of weeks. Locked things down here, but no damage other than a lot of cleanup."

"Got any troublemakers on board?"

Hailey scratched his head thoughtfully. "Not so far. Some tension between the science geeks and the core drillers, but nothing to worry about. We've only got about fifty people on-site. Maruchek's been here quite a bit. He's here now, probably in the control center."

Morgan asked, "Garren?"

Joe nodded. "Garren Maruchek, yeah."

Shaine said, "We'll check in with him before we do a walk-through of the site. We've got building supplies on the transport. Do you have anyone for that, or do you need me to send a couple of my guys back to help out?"

"I've got crew here to unload, so don't worry about that."

"Excellent. Thanks, Joe."

He nodded and sent Morgan a grin. "See you around later, hey?"

"Absolutely."

* * *

Later that day, Shaine, Morgan, Josef Waylin, Garren and Amaar Ahmed, the primary System Operations and Site Engineer, sat around a table in a cramped conference room. Plas-sheets of data covered the dark, faux-wood surface along with architectural and engineering designs. To the side of the table, a touch screen easel had a handwritten list of the meeting notes and a column of action items scrawled along one side.

Amaar tapped on his pad and the image on the easel changed to a basic diagram of the mining site.

He used a laser pointer to indicate the area he was interested in. "You are thinking that here, here and here, we'd have external security cameras, yes?"

Shaine nodded. "For now, that will be enough. They're out of the way of the construction crews, but we'd still get visual of the whole area."

"Sounds good," Garren agreed. "First priority, though, we need that underground shelter finished."

Amaar confirmed, "We should have it done within the next week. The dig is programmed into the rock borer and it's in process." He glanced at his pad. "There haven't been any issues so far." He flipped to another blueprint and highlighted a part of it. "We're creating a living area, an emergency medical unit, a secondary control center and a docking and maintenance space that should allow room for two regular transport shuttles and a workspace. The shelter will be linked to both the temporary living dome and then to the permanent dome after it's been sealed. There will also be an underground connection to the processing plant when that's ready."

"Good," Garren said, leaning back in his chair. "I think that about covers what we need to discuss for now. Anyone need anything else?" He got back negative indications and smiled. "Excellent. We're on schedule, so that's a good thing." He looked at Shaine and Morgan. "Are you staying here for the duration, or headed back to Moon Base?"

Shaine said, "We'll stay here. I've got new hire résumés coming to me to start filling out the security team. I won't bring people out right away. There's no rush yet."

Garren frowned. "Is Rogan going to be involved?"

Shaine shook her head. "Peripherally. He'll need to know what's happening at a high level, but I'm doing the hiring. He won't have any say on a day-to-day basis."

The dark-haired man smiled. "Thanks, Shaine. Nothing against Rogan, of course."

Morgan choked on a dry laugh. Garren frowned at her and she shook her head. "Later," she muttered.

Shaine looked between the two, searching for similarities between siblings. Garren resembled his father in the broadness of his stature and his chiseled features, where Morgan had the almost elfin look of her mother—wiry and fine-boned. Her pale complexion was a result of growing up in space rather than on Earth. The only thing they had in common physically was their black hair. But where Morgan's was fine and straight, Garren's was thick and wavy. It was also much longer and tied with a metal clip at the nape of his neck. The ponytail hung halfway down his back.

They didn't look alike, but they both did that little head-cocking thing when they were amused or teasing. They both tended to fidget if they had to wait for anything. Morgan played with her adopted mother's wedding ring and Garren twirled his stylus through his long fingers.

Garren shuffled his plas-sheets into a folder and grabbed his pad. "I need to make a few calls before it gets too late."

Morgan said, "Say hi to our father if you talk to him."

Garren grinned. "I will. Hey, maybe later, you guys want to play some pool in the game room and have a beer?"

Morgan glanced at Shaine, who shrugged amiably. "Yeah, that'd be okay," she agreed. "We'll see you later."

Garren nodded and headed to the tiny space across the hall he called an office. Morgan thought it wasn't much bigger than a broom closet. Shaine turned to her. "How about we finish getting our stuff put away and relax a while before we find something to eat?"

"Sure. I'm wasted. Wonder if there's anything in the mess hall other than military surplus meals?"

"What, you don't like eating tasteless cardboard? You'da starved in the EG."

Morgan backhanded Shaine in the stomach. "Some of us like food that tastes like food," she teased.

Shaine laughed and dropped an arm over Morgan's shoulder as they sauntered down the hallway toward their living quarters. They shared a single room toward the end of the hallway. Shaine used the palm-reader to unlock the door. It slid open with a catch and an ear-popping squeal.

Morgan made a face. "Guess I won't be sneaking in and out without you knowing, huh?"

"Gotta love temporary housing," Shaine muttered.

Morgan walked in and shut the door behind them, making a mental note to see if Joe Hailey had any spray lubricant down in the warehouse.

Their very spartan quarters had a double bed and a single dresser against one wall, and two chairs with a square end table between them on the opposite wall. Morgan walked to the back of the room. A sliding door revealed a bathroom complete with a sink, a vacuum toilet and a sonic shower. She sighed. Damn, she was going to miss the long, hot showers at Shaine's family home.

When they'd arrived, they'd left their bags unpacked on the bed. Now they made quick work of putting away their clothes and toiletries. Morgan laid the quilt she brought across the bottom of the bed. She sighed as she straightened.

Shaine leaned against the frame of the bathroom door, rubbing her hands over her face. She pushed off and strode the two paces to the bed, holding a hand out to Morgan. "Let's lie down for a while."

Morgan didn't need any encouragement. Shaine stretched out on the bed and scooted toward the wall, making room. Morgan sat down beside her then reached to the foot of the bed and pulled the quilt over them as she settled back. She squirmed to get comfortable on the mattress. It wasn't as form-fitting as she would have liked. She wriggled until she was curled around Shaine. Using Shaine's shoulder for a pillow, she draped one arm loosely around Shaine's middle. Shaine wrapped Morgan in her arms, giving her a squeeze.

"This is nice," Morgan murmured, eyes already closed.

Shaine rubbed her back and kissed her head. "It is." She leaned back, said a little louder, "Lights, off."

Morgan felt Shaine's body relax as the room darkened and heard her sigh. Smiling contentedly, Morgan dozed off.

CHAPTER NINETEEN

The next morning found Morgan and Shaine in the main operations control room. The primary communication and ops console was a half-circle workspace that took up most of the center of the room. Systems monitors for the facility's power, life-support, electrical, water and heat covered the wall to the right of the ops desk. Operations staff in blue work suits manned the row of control stations facing the monitors.

Amaar had set aside space for Shaine's group in the back left corner of the control room where a couple maintenance guys were putting together another half-circle counter. Shaine claimed the small office built out behind the counter.

Morgan loitered against the wall by Shaine's office, purposely staying off to the side and observing.

Josef and Del stood with Shaine at the main ops desk. The three talked with Amaar as they looked over the work list for the day. Amaar had just posted the core drilling schedule to the main vid screen.

Shaine asked, "Do the scientists go out with the drilling teams?"

Amaar nodded. "Most of the time, yes. They confirm the core placements against the site surveys."

"And get in our way."

They all turned to face the woman who strode into the room. She was stocky, with dirty blond hair and blue eyes. The newcomer held out a hand. "Anya Bjork," she introduced herself.

Shaine shook her hand. "Shaine Wendt, Head of Security. My second, Josef Waylin, Specialist Del Marin." She gestured toward Morgan, who raised a hand in greeting. "Morgan Rahn."

Anya nodded a greeting, and glanced at the work board. "I'm on the first drill shift," she said. "Just need to log in." She glanced around. "I take it the noble and all-knowing Dr. Ulm hasn't checked in yet?"

Amaar shook his head. "I haven't seen him this morning."

Anya logged into one of the terminals facing outward, then held her comp pad against a data port for a couple of seconds to download the information she needed. Turning from the terminal, she said, "Tell the good doctor I'll be getting suited up and checking our gear. Nice meeting all of you." She strode out the door.

Del raised a brow. "Trouble among the natives?" she queried.

Amaar shrugged. "Never been in a place where the scientists didn't piss off the workers," he observed. "It's nothing to worry about."

Del frowned.

Shaine said, "First thing I want to do is get all our personal coms synced and start installing the cameras." She looked to Amaar. "Do you have anyone who can set up monitors and systems here while we get hardware in place on-site?"

"Sure, I'll get Ruddy down here. He's good."

Morgan walked over and asked Shaine, "You mind if I go down to maintenance? Maybe I'll go with Anya to the drill site."

Shaine nodded. "Yeah, sure."

Morgan gave Shaine's arm a pat. "I'll probably be more useful there," she commented.

Shaine smiled. "Don't cause any trouble," she murmured.

Morgan grinned and left the room. She headed down the circular outer hallway toward the maintenance space and palmed the hatch into the warehouse. It beeped and the door slid open. She strode through, shivering with the sudden change in temperature. She could see her breath in the air and pulled down the sleeves of her heavy tunic to cover her hands.

She looked around. The part of the warehouse she was in seemed to be primarily storage. Sheets of building materials for interior walls, stacks of piping and raw cable spools were piled neatly. Crates were stacked in low rows, each marked with an inventory sheet.

Morgan walked further into the warehouse, impressed by its organization. Along the outside wall, several shop tables were set up in separate work bays. Tools lined the walls above the counters. Joe Hailey stood in one of the bays, wielding a fuser and wearing a pair of goggles as he leaned over the innards of a ground skimmer.

On the other side of the warehouse, Anya Bjork was setting out her vac suit.

Morgan stopped a few feet from Joe Hailey's work bay, not wanting to interrupt. After a few moments, he looked up and smiled. "Hey, Morgan, what can I do for ya?"

"Nothing. Just saying hello. I was going to see if I could go out to the site with Anya. Maybe I'd be able to lend a hand."

"Sure. But if she doesn't want you to go along, I can always use another hand down here."

"Thanks, Joe." She shoved her hands into her pockets. "What's with the heat in here? I'm gonna freeze my fingers off."

"I already called sys ops twice. I'm sure the heat exchangar is acting up. If they don't do anything about it in the next hour or so, I'm gonna start doing it on my own."

"Well, hell, if Anya doesn't want company, I'll help you out."

Hailey grinned and Morgan gave him a wave as she crossed over to where Anya Bjork worked on her vac suit.

"Hey."

The blond head came up. "What do you want?" The question sounded sharp and annoyed.

Morgan held up her hands in a peace gesture. "Chill, man. I was just wondering if you would mind some company on the site today. I need to get a feel for things, and thought it'd be interesting to see the coring process."

Bjork stared at her, looked her up and down, then shrugged. "Whatever. Just stay out of the way."

Morgan grinned. "No worries. On Moon Base I'm a dockworker, external ship systems maintenance."

Bjork's expression was unimpressed, bordering on hostile. "If you're a dockworker, then what the hell are you doing out here? Tagging on your girlfriend? Oh, wait a minute, you don't have to tag on anyone. You've got more money than you know what to do with, don't you, Morgan Rahn? Or are you going by Maruchek these days?"

Morgan's smile slid away, her hands clenching into fists. "I go by Rahn. It's my name." She turned and walked back toward Joe Hailey, hoping he was as decent as he seemed.

The big man looked up as she strode over. "Problem?"

Morgan scowled. "Fucking bitch," she muttered. She looked at him, accusation in her eyes. "If you have an issue with the fact that Tarm Maruchek is my father, tell me now."

He studied her, assessing. "Don't see that it makes a whole hell of a lot of difference to me who your daddy is," he drawled. "Shaine holds you in high esteem and that says a lot. She's good people. I trust that woman with my life." He squinted at her. "Any friend of Shaine's is a friend of mine."

Morgan sucked in a long breath, taking a couple seconds to push down her anger. "Thanks, Joe. So, what can I do here?"

He smiled. "How are ya with a fuser, kid?"

"Passable," she returned with a smile of her own.

"Good, 'cause I'm gonna start using a damned sledgehammer on this piece of crap in about five minutes. Why don't you have a go at it? Damned sand everywhere and it's got the whole drive mechanism hanked up."

Morgan took the fuser from him and leaned over the skimmer's engine. It'd been a while since she worked on small engines, but what she'd learned early on came back quickly. She considered what Joe had done so far and then went to the workbench against the wall for a few more tools.

An hour and a half later, the skimmer engine hummed to life. She could still hear some grating as it shifted gears, but that kind of wear and tear wasn't something she could fix. Eventually the transmission components would need to be replaced. She didn't usually see this kind of problem on Moon Base. With no atmosphere, there was no wind, so the gray rock dust wasn't as invasive as the wind-blasted sand here.

Joe returned to where Morgan was working when he heard the engine crank up. He cocked an ear and nodded, impressed. "Nice work, kid. You're now my go-to skimmer mechanic."

Morgan grinned. "Thanks." She brought her hands up and blew on her fingers, trying to warm them up before she shoved her hands into her pockets, stifling a shiver. "Damn, it's cold in here."

He nodded. "That it is. What do you say we go grab some lunch and then head up to the operations center and see if anyone is doing anything about it. If they're not, we can get our hands in there and see if we can figure out what's going on."

"Works for me."

* * *

When Morgan and Joe arrived at the mess hall, the lunch rush had already begun. Several site workers had gathered to eat, grouped around the bench tables, mostly segregated by occupation. Morgan recognized Anya Bjork sitting with three other men dressed in standard gray work overalls. Another table held a couple of women in lab coats. Amaar Ahmed, Whippet and Del Marin sat together at the last table.

Whippet lifted a hand in greeting, which Morgan returned with a smile. She and Joe went to the serving counter, which consisted of a prepared-meal and beverage dispenser, some condiments and eating utensils. There were facilities for a real kitchen, but it was closed. Morgan supposed they hadn't hired cooks yet.

Frowning, she punched in a food request. The dispenser dropped out a hot sealed container with her cheeseburger, a bag of chips and a juice bottle. Morgan put everything on a tray, grabbed sauce for her chips and a napkin. She squeezed in at the table with the security team. Joe followed behind her. Morgan sighed as she swallowed her first bite. She hadn't realized how hungry she was until she inhaled the slightly greasy smell— even if it was just a prepackaged sandwich with unidentified processed protein.

Whippet teased, "Geeze, Morgan, you'd think you actually enjoy eating this crap."

She balled up her napkin and threw it at him. "I'm starving. Raw protein flakes would be good at this point."

He laughed and threw it back. "You've been in space too long, you nutcase. You probably like military MREs too."

She pointedly took a big bite of her sandwich and replied as she chewed, "If you'd eat once in a while you wouldn't look like a damned bag of bones, Whip."

Del laughed.

Joe Hailey shook his head and muttered, "Children."

They all concentrated on eating. After a while, Morgan asked, "Is Shaine still out placing cameras?"

"Yeah, she's with Josef and Allim. They took a skimmer over to where they've been drilling the latest batch of cores. I think they were setting up some trip-beacons at the site perimeter." Del took a sip of her coffee. "Not sure why they'd bother. Only things out there are wind and sand."

Morgan shrugged. "Better safe than sorry, I guess. I think Garren is concerned about sabotage."

Joe Hailey said, "There's that religious colony, hunkered under the ridge about four hours west of us. They were pretty angry about us being here. I suppose they could come down and cause trouble."

Del snorted dismissively. "I think we could handle them." Then she shrugged. "Ah, well. Not in my job description to question why. Just to do what needs doing."

"There's an enthusiastic employee," Whippet commented, adding a grin to lessen the sting.

Morgan laughed. She liked Whippet. He reminded her of an older and more experienced Toby.

Hailey said to Amaar, "So, what's the story with the heat exchanger? You got anyone looking at why I'm freezin' my butt off the last two days?"

"Leo was going to get to it later today. You want to have a go at it sooner, feel free."

Joe nodded. "Me and Morgan will take it on, then."

Shaine and Josef strode into the cafeteria. They chose their food and joined the others. Shaine cupped her hands around her coffee mug and shivered. "Damn, it's cold in here. Cold everywhere."

Morgan frowned. "Your vac suit heater not working right?" she asked.

Shaine shook her head. "Naw. Suit's okay. Just cold in here. What's up with the heat?"

Amaar sighed. "The heat exchangar isn't working at full capacity for some reason. Joe and Morgan have volunteered to take a look at it after lunch."

Shaine nodded. "Thanks."

"Sure. What's on your agenda this afternoon?"

"Need to go back out to the site to finish up what we were doing." She glanced around the room, then said quietly, for their table only, "Got an interesting earful while we were out this morning."

Del raised a dark brow. "Do tell."

Shaine shook her head. "Not here. In any case, it's just pissing and moaning." She caught Morgan's eye, and Morgan knew she'd been listening to Anya Bjork. Morgan shrugged and finished off her bottle of juice. Fuck Anya Bjork and her attitude problem.

Joe Hailey stood up, stretching his back. "Well, Morgan, guess we oughta get at it. Talk to you all later." He moved away, pausing to empty his tray into the recycler.

Morgan pushed to her feet. "Later, kids," she offered with a smile. She let one hand brush Shaine's shoulder as she passed. Shaine smiled up at her.

CHAPTER TWENTY

Morgan and Shaine fell into an easy routine over the next few days. Morgan divided her time between assisting Joe Hailey and helping monitor the security cameras for Shaine's group. She preferred working with Joe since it was hands-on instead of watching live video feeds that showed nothing other than people working or sand blowing.

A week into their stay, Morgan found herself in ops covering the security desk. Three ops personnel staffed the facility monitors. Ahmed's second in command, Gohste Rocke, was at the main ops console at the center of the room. Morgan listened in while he helped one of the field techs control the rock borer carving out the underground emergency shelter.

Morgan liked working with Gohste. They had a lot in common, and his sense of humor made her laugh. She hated to admit it, but she was also fascinated by his looks—it wasn't every day she met an albino. Gohste's pink eyes and the complete pallor of his skin took some getting used to. She tried hard not to stare.

Gohste leaned over the terminal he monitored, his fingers flicking over the keyboard and the touch screen in rapid succession. He frowned at the monitor and tapped some more before speaking into his mic. "I see it, Ket. Back the drill off."

Ket's voice responded over the overhead speakers. "Roger that. Pulling back. I'm going to have to switch drill bits. This one is toast."

"Go ahead and do that. You're hitting solid bedrock there." He fiddled with the touch screen. "Think it's just the one spot. I'm sending you the scanner feed so you can see it, too. The rest should be a lot softer."

"I'm shutting down to switch out the bits. Back on in a few."

"Roger that, Ket. Standing by." Gohste leaned back in his chair and stretched long arms over his head.

From the security station slightly behind and to his left, Morgan heard his back pop and crack and she cringed. "You oughta see a chiropractor about that," she commented wryly.

The albino laughed. "Yeah. Should probably do a lot of things." Cocking his head left and right, he popped his neck then rubbed his face as he yawned. Running his fingers back through short white hair, he sighed. "On the upside, once Ket gets through this one tough spot, we should have the underground space cleared out in another day and they can start putting in the interior infrastructure. It'll be good to have a real radiation bunker set up."

"What's the timeline once it's bored out?"

He shrugged. "On paper, a couple of weeks if they work three shifts a day. Real life, we'll see."

She blanked one of the monitors and pulled up the Space Administration Weather site. She poked around until she found the weather for Mars and the Asteroid Belt, then marked the site for future reference. A quick look at the forecast data told her that there weren't any imminent sunspot storms.

The main ops door hissed open. A tall woman with dark hair strode in, looking ready to bang heads. Her lab jacket swished behind her as she stopped in front of Gohste. "What in the hell are you doing out there?" she demanded. "You're upsetting important experiments in the lab! I can't get reliable readings when the seismometers are bouncing off the scale!"

Gohste stretched out in his chair and regarded her with a bored expression. "Good evening, Dr. Hurtz," he offered with a smile.

She glared. "Don't fuck with me, Rocke. Just stop the disturbances."

Morgan turned in her chair to watch, not bothering to hide her interest.

Gohste shrugged. "No can do. We're digging out the underground shelter, and that's a safety priority. We should be finished with the main shelter tomorrow. Unless you like radiation poisoning?"

"That is NOT satisfactory! Where is Ahmed?"

Morgan piped up, "I saw him earlier with Joe in the warehouse."

The scientist sneered at Morgan, then turned and stalked out of the room.

Morgan smirked. "Bitch," she muttered.

Gohste laughed. "You got that right. Maybe I'll tell Ket to use a really dull drill."

* * *

Morgan was still staffing the security desk later that night when her partner strode into ops. Shaine's brows rose as she saw Morgan.

"Babe, what are you still doing down here?"

Morgan had her feet up on the desk, her personal comp pad in her lap, while she flipped through the security cameras with one hand. She smiled. "Hey, hon. I told Del I'd sit in for her tonight. She's got the crud that's going around. She looked like shit and could barely talk."

Shaine sighed. "All the medical miracles we've come up with and we're still fighting the common cold and flu."

"I was gonna com ya, but I figured you were still on rounds. I'm on until oh-four-hundred, then Lukas will be in the rest of the shift."

"Thanks, Morg." She sighed dramatically. "It's gonna be cold tonight, sleeping all by myself."

Morgan leered at her. "Oh, I'll warm ya up just fine when I get home."

Shaine laughed. "Good."

Morgan flicked through the screens again and frowned. "Hey, site camera three is down," she said. She tapped a couple controls and ran a diagnostic. "I can't connect to it at all. Maybe the power pack drained. Should I send someone out there?"

Shaine shook her head. "Add it to the priority task list for tomorrow. I don't want to send anyone out in the dark. Camera two should be able to pick up at least part of that area."

Morgan nodded. "Will do."

"Anything else going on?"

"Nothing. Nobody's even down in the rec room. A couple folks in and out of the mess hall, but that's about it. Pretty much everyone's hunkered down for the night. Hurtz and Ulm are down in the lab, as usual."

"Okay. Well, if you need anything, just com me."

"I'll wake you up every hour with stupid questions," Morgan teased.

Shaine grinned and started toward the door.

"Hey!"

Shaine spun around.

Morgan cocked her head and opened her arms. "What, no kiss good night?"

Shaine considered for a moment then sashayed across the floor. Very deliberately, she leaned over Morgan's chair. Morgan looked up to see pure lust darkening Shaine's green eyes. As Shaine slowly lowered her mouth, she tangled her fingers in Morgan's short black hair. She teased with the tip of her tongue until Morgan felt a growl at the back of her throat. Her body heated up as she opened to Shaine's advance, demanding a passionate response, returning Shaine's kiss. Minutes passed before they separated, breathing each other's air.

Shaine cupped Morgan's cheek with one hand. "God, I love you," she murmured against Morgan's lips.

"Love you too."

Shaine grinned and backed slowly and reluctantly away. With a wink and a wave, she slipped out of the ops, leaving Morgan sprawled in her chair with her eyes closed, blood pulsing in her groin, and four hours before she could do anything about it.

CHAPTER TWENTY-ONE

Morgan pulled on a warm undershirt and grabbed a heavy long-sleeved tunic before sitting down on the bed to pull on an extra pair of socks.

Shaine paused in the bathroom door. "Planning on being in the warehouse today?" she asked.

Morgan shook her head. "Actually, I'm going to suit up and shadow Piper and Wrenn on the site. They're going to start sealing up the new dome today. Piper said he could use an extra hand since the shuttle with the extra construction guys got held up. I figured I may as well be useful."

"Love, you're always useful."

Morgan shrugged. "You know what I mean."

Shaine smiled and sat down next to her, giving Morgan a hug and a kiss on the temple. "I know what you mean."

"What's on your agenda?"

"The shuttle from Moon Base should be here in a couple of hours, so Josef and I will be processing the security newbies."

"I'll see you at supper then?"

"Yes."

"Good."

* * *

Morgan suited up with the rest of the crew and joined them on the skimmer that took them to the construction-site. They hadn't worked in three days because of a sandstorm that had blown through. Yesterday they'd had to do cleanup and sand removal. She'd be working again with Alec, Piper and Wrenn, who'd taken her on as an impromptu apprentice. She enjoyed the work, and since Joe didn't have things for her to do every day, she was glad to be able to lend an extra hand.

The crew jumped off the skimmer and started toward their respective jobs on the site. Alec headed to the construction crane. Morgan followed Piper and Wrenn toward the empty frame of the new dome.

Sixteen curved girders rose from the foundation like curved steel bones, meeting at a sixteen-sided steel plate at the top. Laid out around the empty frame, the glassteel dome sections rested on the gravel like gigantic clear slices of an orange peel.

Piper and Wrenn started to secure the hydraulic clamp at the end of the crane cable to the top of a glassteel slice. There were rivet holes in the girders and matching holes in the glassteel. The bottom of the glassteel slice had a lip the width of the foundation and holes matching the rivets poking up from the foundation. It would be Morgan's job to fuse the rivets once the slice was in place on the girders. Alec mounted the side ladder to the crane's open control cockpit. He called over his helmet's open com channel, "Let me know when you're ready, Piper."

Piper lifted a hand in response. "Yeah, be a couple minutes."

Morgan joined Piper and Wrenn. "Just tell me what you want me to do."

"You and Wrenn are going to guide the glassteel from the bottom. I'll be at the top of the dome and will lock it into place there."

"Sure."

Piper double-checked the clamp's lock on the glassteel. "Alec, it's connected. I'm going up top."

"Got it. Waiting on you, then."

Wrenn helped Piper get into a climbing harness. Piper connected to a winch line connected to the platform at the top of the dome. He used a remote on his wrist to start the winch and rose slowly to the top where he climbed up and connected his safety line. "Okay, I'm ready. Let's do this."

Alec's rough voice crackled over their headsets. "Righto, gents. Wrenn, Morgan, you ready?"

"We're set," Wrenn replied.

"Starting up, real easy."

Alec brought tension to the cable and eased the glassteel upright. "Coming forward now," he warned them.

Wrenn said, "Roger that. We're clear."

Morgan took another step away from the four-story piece of clear metal as it rose off the ground. She looked up past the glassteel into the hazy orange-hued sky. Thin, fast-moving clouds hissed overhead. She decided the landscape had a certain beauty. It felt warmer than the blackness of the moonscape. But it wasn't Earth. She smiled, glad she'd experienced all three places, then shook herself into the present. She was working and she needed to stay alert.

The four-story piece of curved glassteel swung very slowly toward the dome's base, barely a dozen centimeters above the ground. Wrenn and Morgan walked along a few feet from its side, watching closely.

Wrenn warned, "Slow it down, Alec. You've got about three meters to the base."

"Roger that. Slowing."

"Two meters," Wrenn counted. "Bring it up twenty centimeters to clear the base."

The movement of the piece slowed to a stop. It rose a little more, swinging slightly. Suddenly Piper shouted, "Cable!"

In an instant, the crane cable shredded and snapped. The top half whipped back toward the crane and the lower half snapped against the glassteel, cracking the clear metal as it dropped onto its edge.

Morgan dove away from the glassteel. Something heavy slammed the back of her helmet and shoulders. Her nose slammed against the faceplate in an explosion of light and pain before everything went dark.

CHAPTER TWENTY-TWO

"Morgan! Morgan!"

Voices penetrated her consciousness. She was aware, first, of the pounding in her head and her nose, then of the cold, then of the metallic taste of blood. She groaned.

"Morgan, talk to me!"

She managed a pained grunt, blinking her eyes into focus and seeing red gravel under her faceplate. "Uh. Damn." Thinking hard, she started making a checklist. She was breathing. She had air. Cold. Suit heater damaged? Not good. She tried to move her arms to get to the diagnostic readout on her wrist, but her arm was trapped under her. She could move her legs but she seemed to be pinned in place.

"Morgan! Talk to me!"

Morgan blinked again, shivered, and took a breath. She could hear the panic in Shaine's voice. Shaine? "Here," she croaked.

"Thank God! Morgan, hang in there—just a little longer. We need to use a lifter to get that piece of glassteel off you. You have air?"

"Yeah, I have air." Morgan could see blood splattered on the inside of the faceplate. Her nose didn't hurt enough to be broken, at least. "Think my suit heater is damaged." She shivered again. "I'm losing heat fast." She felt strangely calm.

"Just hang in there, love."

Shaine's voice was a warm blanket over her soul. She closed her eyes against the pounding in her skull. *Concussion*, she thought. *I must've really hit my head on the helmet when I went down. Lucky the faceplate didn't break.*

She thought she could hear the grinding of machinery. Maybe it was just vibrations on the ground. Voices buzzed in her helmet speakers—Shaine's voice, muffled, barking orders, other voices, an urgency in the tones that she couldn't feel herself.

She lay there, staring at the ground, watching the blood drip from her nose onto her faceplate, knowing she could die lying here. She could freeze to death before they could get the metal off her and get her to safety. She supposed she was lucky it hadn't crushed her or cut through her air lines. Perhaps the concave of the glassteel was her savior. She wasn't ready to die. She didn't want to leave Shaine. Not so soon. They'd only just got started. She thought she should be panicking. Instead, she simply waited. And shivered. Her hands and feet were starting to feel numb. She listened to the voices buzzing in her helmet. She could hear their panic.

Seconds passed. Perhaps minutes. She wasn't certain. She felt the shift of the weight pinning her down.

"Morgan, stay still." Shaine's voice, firm but comforting. "We're going to lift the glassteel up, then pull you free."

"Okay," Morgan mumbled. Her lips felt stiff and frozen. She was shivering constantly now. Her breath fogged the faceplate. She couldn't see the sand anymore. Tiny crystals of ice formed on the glass and in the blood splattered on it. Pretty.

Morgan felt the weight lifted from her back. Sand grated under her faceplate as she was dragged backward. The world shifted and she was on her back. She almost threw up from the motion. Sunlight glared on the ice covering her faceplate. She closed her eyes. It hurt. Shaine's voice echoed vaguely in her ears. "Morgan, talk to me, can you hear me?"

Morgan tried to nod, but didn't have the energy. She tried to say something, but managed only a weak grunt. She wasn't cold anymore.

"Hang in there. Three more minutes."

Morgan felt them lift her onto the back of a skimmer. Dizziness washed over her. She wished she could hold Shaine's hand. The world slid from gray to black.

* * *

Shaine snapped out orders as she rode toward the temporary dome. Sitting beside Morgan's prone, suited form on the flatbed, she took in the information fed to her, automatically assessing and delegating. "Get the area locked down and guards on it."

Josef's voice responded in her helmet speakers, gruff and brusque. "Doing that now."

"Shaine, the cable's been cut!" Whippet reported.

"What?"

"We just pulled the crane cable down. The break is too clean for it to be anything else. There's a cut about three quarters through. The other strands are stretched and twisted apart."

Shaine took a deep breath and let it out slowly. "Lock down the whole site. Now. Everyone in quarters. I want to know who was out on the site and when. I need to know who had access to that crane. Del and Whippet, go through background checks again for everyone on-site."

"We're on it."

"I'll be with Morgan. Josef, you're on point."

"Roger that, Shaine."

Shaine rested a gloved hand on Morgan's arm. Morgan's faceplate was frosted over and it scared the hell out of her. Shaine demanded, "Can't this damned thing go any faster?"

"Doing the best I can, ma'am," the driver replied, but she felt a slight increase in their speed. The skimmer kicked up a little extra red dust as they sped toward the temporary dome.

* * *

Cold. Why am I so damned cold? Morgan blinked gritty eyes open to a dimly lit room. Her head pounded. Cautiously, she tried to move her body. She could move her fingers. She could wiggle her toes. She felt the softness of blankets tucked up to her chin.

She remembered the instant when she saw the cable snap, diving to the ground and waking up facedown in the red gravel. She trembled, partly out of delayed shock and relief that she was alive, and partly because she was freezing. The shivering made her whole body feel tense and achy. She wondered just how close she'd come to dying. She tried to look around without moving her throbbing head. She heard and sensed movement beside her.

Shaine said, "Morgan, you're awake."

"Uh."

Morgan realized she was in the infirmary. Shaine tapped a com unit on the wall at the head of the bed and said quietly, "Lei, she's awake." Then she turned concerned eyes on Morgan. "How do you feel?" She caressed Morgan's face with a feather-light touch. "You scared the shit out of me, babe."

"Cold," Morgan whispered.

Shaine nodded. "I'll get more blankets."

Morgan shook her head just a tiny bit. "Just climb in," she whispered. "Body heat is good."

Shaine grinned. "Okay. In just a minute. I want the doc to check on you first, okay? You want some water?"

"Yeah."

Shaine got a cup with a straw from the bedside tray. Morgan managed a couple sips of the warm water before turning away. "Alec and the guys okay?" she asked.

Shaine's expression darkened and she took a long breath. Morgan felt her stomach churn. Shaine said, "Wrenn and Piper are okay. Alec—um—the crane cable broke through the windshield and sliced through his suit. We couldn't get him back inside fast enough. I'm sorry, Morgan."

Morgan swallowed and a tight wave of pain contracted around her heart. *Fuck. Alec, man, you didn't deserve that. Fuck. Fuck. Fuck.* She didn't bother to try to stop the tears that spilled down her cheeks. *And here I am, again, surviving. I don't know why I deserve it.*

Shaine gently wiped Morgan's tears away. "I'm so sorry."

The door to the room opened, and Dr. Nguyen strode in, pausing as she studied the scene before her. "Is everything all right?" she asked quietly.

Shaine looked up. "I told her about Alec," she said.

Lei frowned. "Ah. Sometimes I hate this job," she muttered.

Shaine said, "There was nothing you could have done, Lei. He was gone before we got him to you. The suit was compromised. He was frozen before we even got him out of the crane cockpit."

Lei sighed, then visibly shook it off as she turned to Morgan, running a body scanner over her. "How do you feel, Morgan?"

"Cold. My head hurts."

Lei nodded, reading the scanner. "Your body temp is still down a little, but the concussion seems stable." She shined a light into Morgan's eyes, and nodded. "Your pupils are starting to respond to light," she noted briskly. "You need to rest and stay warm." She looked at Shaine. "You're going to stay with her? I want you to wake her up every hour or so, make sure that she doesn't fall unconscious again."

Shaine nodded. "I'll set my chron."

Lei nodded. "I'll leave you to it then. I'll be in my office. Call if you need anything."

"Thanks, Lei."

The small doctor nodded and slipped from the room. Shaine looked down at Morgan. "Want more water?"

"Please."

Shaine gave her another drink from the straw, and Morgan smiled tiredly. Shaine set the cup aside. She stripped down to her boxers and a tank, folding her clothes into a neat pile on the floor. She peeled back the thick pile of blankets tucked around Morgan's body and slipped under them, wrapping herself around Morgan and the blankets back around both of them.

Morgan relaxed into Shaine's warmth, breathing her in, feeling better just from the contact, feeling her body slowly stop shivering. She wrapped her arms around Shaine and slid her hands under the tank to feel Shaine's warm skin. Settling her head on Shaine's chest, she could hear the strong beating of her partner's heart and let it lull her. Closing her eyes, she drifted to sleep.

* * *

Shaine dutifully woke Morgan every hour, just long enough to get her to say something coherent before she let her partner slide back into sleep. She lay awake most of the time, overly warm under the piled blankets but dealing with it because she knew it was for Morgan's benefit, and Morgan hadn't complained of being too warm.

Her brain was on overload. When she let herself think about how close she'd come to losing Morgan, it sent shudders of dread through her heart. Another five minutes, maybe ten, and Morgan would have frozen to death. Just the thought of not having Morgan in her life made her almost physically ill. Holding Morgan in her arms felt so right and so comfortable and so complete. When the call went out about the accident, fear had nearly sapped her ability to think. It had taken all her military training to function and take control.

Morgan mumbled in her sleep, shifting and wrapping herself tighter around Shaine's middle. Shaine kissed the top of her dark head. "I love you, Morgan Rahn," she whispered. "I want to spend the rest of my life with you."

She hadn't expected those words to come out. It was something of a revelation—certain and final. With sudden, crystalline clarity, she knew what she wanted and needed. To be with Morgan. To be married to her. Forever. She wondered if Morgan felt the same way. She knew Morgan loved her. But they'd never talked about marriage.

She caressed the soft skin under her fingers. *Would you spend your life with me?*

She didn't know if they were ready, yet, for that. Maybe it was too soon. There'd been so much change, so much upset in their short time together. They were still learning each other. Even so, Shaine knew in her heart she'd never felt so certain of anything in her life.

* * *

The next time Shaine woke, Morgan was lying awake beside her, a sleepy smile on her face as she regarded Shaine. Shaine smiled back, relieved to see a sparkle back in Morgan's wide gray eyes. "Hey, love," she said softly, reaching up to brush a few strands of dark hair from Morgan's face.

"Hey." Morgan's voice was rough with sleep.

"How are you feeling? Warm enough?"

"Yeah. But thirsty."

Shaine pushed up on her elbow to reach the bedside tray table and the cup of water on it. She got the cup for Morgan and put the straw within reach of her lips.

Morgan took a few sips. "Thank you."

Shaine returned the cup, then settled on her back, pulling Morgan down on top of her. Morgan sighed and rested her head on Shaine's chest. "Mmmm. That's nice." Morgan snuggled in. "You warmed me all up."

"Glad I could be of service," Shaine teased lightly.

Morgan gave her stomach a tickle. "I'm hungry, too. Any food over there?"

"Sadly, no. But I can get us some."

"Eh. Stay here a while. Then maybe I'll get up too. I feel okay."

Shaine said, "We'll check with the doc first."

Morgan sighed. "So, what happened? How in the hell did the cable snap?"

Shaine frowned. "The crane cable was cut three-quarters of the way through."

Morgan stiffened and pulled back so she could look Shaine in the eye. "Seriously?"

Shaine nodded.

"What the hell, Shaine."

"Yeah. Well, the gang is on it, and I trust Josef to do what needs to be done. We're on full lockdown."

Morgan studied Shaine's expression for a few seconds, then sighed and lay back against her chest. "You stayed here with me," she said.

"I did." Shaine kissed Morgan's hair. "You're more important than any of this other crap."

Morgan felt tightness in her throat and tears burned her eyes. "I love you," she whispered thickly, hugging Shaine tightly.

Shaine returned the hug. "I love you too, babe."

They stayed like that for some time before Morgan shifted. "I hate to say this, but I really have to pee," she muttered.

Shaine chuckled. "Let me get Lei. She'll want to check you out before you get up."

Shaine managed to untangle herself from Morgan and the blankets and slid out of bed. She quickly pulled on her pants and tunic and went in search of Dr. Nguyen. She found her in the office inside the infirmary.

Lei looked up when Shaine knocked and walked through the open door. "How is Morgan doing?"

"Pretty good I think. She needs to go to the bathroom, but I told her you needed to check her out before she got up."

Lei stood. "Good. Let's do that."

They returned to the infirmary where Morgan was the only patient in the room of four beds. She was sitting up with the blankets still wrapped around her.

Lei ran her diagnostic scanner up and down Morgan's body. Morgan asked, "Will I live?"

Dr. Nguyen's serious demeanor didn't shift. "Yes, you will live. Your head looks good. The concussion was minor. Your body temp is back to normal."

"Can I leave then? I'm starving."

The petite doctor nodded, pocketing her scanner. "You may leave. Don't do anything strenuous. You should rest. If your head hurts, take a couple painkillers. If you start having blurred vision or dizziness come back and see me."

Morgan nodded. She knew the drill. She'd had enough concussions to know what to do.

Morgan pushed the blankets off and shivered in the cool air. Shaine handed her a tunic, which she pulled on gratefully. Shaine hovered over her when she stood, a little shaky, and walked her to the small restroom. She took a couple minutes to splash warm water on her face and dry off with one of the towels on the narrow counter. She felt much better just doing that and moving around. Food, she thought, and then a nap. She'd be good as new.

CHAPTER TWENTY-THREE

Shaine's gaze took in her core security group, gathered around the conference table. "What do we have?" she asked.

Del said, "So far, nothing popping up on the deep background checks."

Josef handed across a folder of plas-sheets. "These are the crane maintenance records, which included cable replacement. That was five days ago."

Shaine asked, "The replacement cable was certified?"

"And the packaging was sealed," Josef said. "They used the crane the day after they did maintenance, when they were placing the primary girders and when they unloaded the glassteel plates from the supply shuttle and brought them to the construction-site. The cable would have given out on them when they were doing that if it had been cut at that point. Piper said this is the first time they've used the crane since then because of the sandstorm."

Whippet added, "Someone went out and came back in when that number three camera was down two nights ago. Nobody should have been out after dark."

Shaine said, "I hope I'm stating the obvious when I say we need to know who went out."

Josef nodded. "We've started interviewing people, seeing who was doing what at that time, who might have been missing."

"Who's doing the interviews?"

"Del and me."

Shaine nodded. "I want in on those. Somebody saw something."

Del nodded. "The natives are getting restless being in lockdown," she noted. "So we'd better find something before they start beating the crap out of each other."

"What about com logs? Anything interesting incoming or outgoing?"

"Ben and Allim have been sifting through those. Nothing so far. We put 'bots on the net links, and they're monitoring those."

"No way to identify who was in and out when that camera was down?"

Josef shook his head. "The airlock should have been logging suit IDs going in and out, but the software isn't there. I don't know if it was purposely removed or if it was missing to begin with, but nothing has been logged since day one. There's no surveillance camera in the airlock. The outgoing and incoming codes recorded on the lock's keypad are just general use codes that everyone has access to. So all we really have is time and date."

Shaine scowled. "Okay, well, let's just stay on it. And get some fucking security on the airlocks. I don't care if it's two guys standing there twenty-four hours a day with a fucking clipboard logging people in and out. What else?"

"Garren is talking with Maruchek and Rogan right now," Del said.

Shaine rubbed her forehead, a headache coming on. "I'm glad I'm not on that call," she muttered. "Maruchek's gonna be pissed and Rogan's going to blame it all on me."

Josef said, "You've been running this by the book. No blame. Whatever we missed, Rogan would have missed too."

"Maybe yes, maybe no. Still on my head." Shaine pushed to her feet. "Okay, let's get a few more interviews done."

* * *

Morgan walked slowly down quiet hallways. With the whole place in lockdown, all nonessential personnel were restricted to quarters. It felt a little creepy. Shaine hadn't answered her com call, so she assumed she was in the middle of something. After she'd been released from the infirmary, she and Shaine grabbed a bite to eat, and then she had napped for a couple of hours. Now she was bored.

Bundled in an insulated jacket because she was still chilled, she made her way toward the operations center to see what was going on, hoping there was something she could do to help. She figured she could at least take over monitoring coms and video so the others could do more important work.

The door hissed shut behind her. Amaar was at the main communications console. Over at the security console, Ben was watching vid feeds and monitoring net traffic. Del and Lukas had their heads together on the other side of the console, several windows open on their monitors. Del had a stylus in one hand, making notes on a virtual white board behind them.

Morgan stepped into the security area. "Hey, Ben, what's up?"

The security specialist smiled. "Hey, Morgan. How are you doing?"

"I'm good, thanks. Anything I can help with?"

"I've got this. Things are pretty quiet with everyone in quarters. Del and Lukas might need another set of eyes."

Morgan nodded. Lukas was a good guy. However, Del wasn't one of her greatest fans. Del decided early on that Morgan was just there to accompany Shaine, with no value of her own. It annoyed the hell out of Morgan, but it did seem that over the last couple of weeks Del's attitude toward her had improved.

She reminded herself that she wasn't out to impress Del Marin. Fuck that. Even so, she wanted to prove to Del and everyone else that she was more than just Shaine's girlfriend. It helped her cause that she was working with Joe Hailey, doing construction and monitoring the security cameras.

She walked up to Del and Lukas and waited for a break in their conversation.

After a few moments, Del looked up. "Something we can do for you?" she asked.

Morgan met her slightly challenging gaze and shook her head. "Actually, I wondered if there was anything I could help with."

Lukas shot her a grin before he ducked his head to type another query into the console.

Del cocked her head. "Depends on what you can do."

Morgan said, "Well, dancing is out of the question."

Lukas snorted and Del shot him a dark look.

Morgan sighed. "Look, I'm not sure what you're doing, but I've got a brain, so maybe there's something I can help with."

Del shrugged. "Okay. Lukas, send a few of those background checks to that terminal." She pointed to the one on Lukas's other side. "We're going through background checks again, to see if we missed anything. Read through it. If anything seems odd, flag it. Run some net searches, see if anything comes back. The standard search queries are in a dropdown in the query app. You can modify them if you want."

Morgan nodded. "Okay." She moved past Del to the seat next to Lukas and settled in front of the monitor. With a quick swipe of her finger on the screen, she enlarged the first of the background reports and settled in to read.

After a silent half hour, Lukas said, "Hey, I might have something here."

Del looked over from her screen.

He said, "This guy, Mathew McKillan. He's part of that last group that came up. This is his first out system construction job as a full guild member. He finished training on one of the mining sites before he applied to this posting."

"Nothing odd about that," Del commented, "other than the fact I'm surprised they brought in a newbie for this kind of project."

"That's what I thought. So I went out to the net and ran some queries on his name, checking the social sites, the kind of stuff that wouldn't come up in a job quals lookup. And this comes up." He tapped at his screen, and sent the information to their screens as well. "The guy has ties to the Unified Martian Temple of God."

Del said, "I'm sure a lot of people do. They're not exactly a small organization."

"Yeah, but his brother is one of their Elders—living here in the Temple's biodome. I ran a search on our com logs, to see if he was talking to anyone. Nothing comes up with his ID, and that just seems odd. Almost everyone here has at least one or two calls in and out to somebody."

"You're not impressing me here, Lukas."

"I just have a feeling. Let's flag this guy."

Del shrugged. "Consider him flagged." She grabbed the stylus and added the name to their running list.

CHAPTER TWENTY-FOUR

The aging construction worker leaned back in his chair and watched Shaine and Josef. His eyes had deep crinkles around them. His skin had a ruddy, lined texture, as though he'd spent time outdoors rather than doing construction in a vac suit in space. Perhaps, earlier in his life, he'd worked on Earth. Shaine got the sense that Mischan Dorovitch had been around a long time, seen of lot of life, and was smart enough to learn from what he'd experienced.

Josef said, "I'm gonna be up front with you. The crane's winch cable was sawed three-quarters of the way through. That's why it snapped. You're not a suspect, Mischan. But we want to know where you were and who you were with Thursday night, around twenty-three fifty hours."

Mischan nodded thoughtfully. "Well, guess I'm surprised it took this long," he drawled. "Knew this was going to be an interesting ride. Lots of people don't want Mann-Maru getting another stronghold on the market." He shrugged. "Figured something was going to go down at some point."

Shaine leaned back. Mischan was the kind of guy you didn't push. He'd tell what he knew, but he wasn't going to be hurried. He understood the politics and he understood his place in the scheme of things.

He said, "I was down in the mess hall, grabbing a sandwich. I just got off shift. I was working on wiring the underground shelter. Zulu and Piper were in the mess hall too, havin' coffee or something. From there, I went back to the barracks and got ready for sleepin'."

Shaine asked, "Do you remember who was in the barracks at the time?"

Mischan pondered that, then slowly rattled off a list of names. It seemed to Shaine he was thinking his way around the room, picturing it in his head and naming the people he saw. When he finished, he paused for a moment, then added, "I fell asleep pretty soon after that, so if there were people coming and going, I wasn't paying them any attention. Got up my usual time. Didn't notice anyone missing who I would have expected to see."

"Okay. Thanks, Mischan. If you think of anything else, let either me or Shaine know, okay?"

"Sure."

Shaine said, "Thanks for your time."

Mischan nodded, pushed to his feet, and ducked out the door. Josef cast a glance at Shaine, who was stretching her back and reaching her arms over her head with a heavy sigh. She asked, "How many more?"

"About a dozen."

"Let's see if we can get through them all tonight. I have a feeling we're going to see something once we start analyzing the information."

He nodded. "Me too." He tapped on the screen of his comp pad, looked at the list and then tapped the com. "Hey, Jordan, bring Nels Wilson up here."

"Got it, boss."

* * *

Morgan walked back to their quarters, more exhausted than she expected to be after a few hours of poring through data. But at least she wasn't cold anymore. She palmed the lock and the door squeaked open. A wave of disappointment washed over her as she entered the darkened room. Shaine wasn't home yet. "Lights," she said into the quiet. "Dim."

She wondered how the interviews were going, and hoped they were learning more than she and Lukas and Del had. There were no smoking guns in the background checks or in anything else they managed to dig up. Del was frustrated as hell and ready to start banging heads indiscriminately. Lukas didn't show it as much. Morgan thought that she should have felt more frustrated with not finding out who had killed Alec, but she just didn't seem to be able to drag up the emotion or the energy.

Tired, she thought. *I'm just tired. I should have crashed a long time ago.* The slight concussion and the cold were taking their toll. She sat down on the bed and pulled off her boots, undressed and used the bathroom. She found a warm pajama top, pulled up the extra quilt and snuggled under the covers. As the blankets warmed to her body, she felt the tension relax out of her muscles.

She yawned and closed her eyes but her brain refused to settle. Sadness and anger pulled at her heart over Alec's death. He was a great guy. What was it about good people dying before their time? Just another reminder of how transient and unfair life could be. She wondered how many more friends and loved ones she would lose to violent death.

Old, familiar questions plagued her brain. Why was her life spared when Alec's was not? Part of her was glad to be alive. Another part of her was glad Alec wasn't a close friend like Digger had been, and then she felt bad about that, too.

She felt guilty that she'd scared the crap out of Shaine, but was also incredibly thankful that she had Shaine in her life to love her and take care of her. She could hardly fathom being alone. It had only been a few months that they'd known each other, and yet it seemed so much longer. She missed Shaine even now, though it seemed silly. But she wanted Shaine with her, wanted to feel Shaine's warmth against her skin and the strength of Shaine's arms wrapped around her.

She snuggled further into the blankets and imagined Shaine was holding her. She smiled at the imagined warmth and let out a long sigh as she closed her eyes.

CHAPTER TWENTY-FIVE

Shaine didn't bother with pleasantries as she strode into the conference room the next morning. Her security team was assembled around the table. "Okay, talk to me, people."

Josef rubbed a big, meaty hand over the reddish-brown stubble of his crew cut. "We think we have him." He tossed Shaine a small data chip, which she caught and popped into her comp pad.

"Thanks. What've you got?"

Josef gestured to Del, who picked up the narrative. "We went through the interviews and mapped out where everyone was and when, and who was potentially unaccounted for when that camera was down. Only two people haven't been placed. One of those is Joe Hailey, and I think we can pretty safely eliminate him as a suspect. He's got his own quarters and he said he was sleeping at that time. He has no motive and no criminal background. The other is Mathew McKillan. His background check is on that data chip. He's got family ties to the Unified Martian Temple of God. His brother, Isaiah Abraham, is the spiritual Elder of the group. It's basically Abraham's church. That in itself doesn't mean McKillan's the saboteur, but it is a possible motive. The Temple folks do not want us here, and they've been pretty vocal about it."

Shaine nodded, picturing the guy in her head. She remembered him being quiet and unassuming—the kind of guy that didn't get noticed in a crowd. "The interview with him is on the chip?"

Del nodded. "It is. We watched it again. He's good, I'll tell you that. I don't think I would have suspected him in a million years based on the interview."

Whippet added, "You don't suspect him until you really look at the bio-scans I was taking. Then you can see the inconsistencies. He was working hard to keep his cool."

"Let's bring him in again," Shaine said. "Up the ante a little bit, see if we can get him to break."

* * *

He didn't break. He seemed completely amazed that they thought he was capable of something so awful. He was just a working guy, he minded his own business. He had no reason to do something like that.

Shaine drilled him about his brother, the Elder in the Unified Martian Church. Mathew repeatedly insisted he wasn't close to his brother, who was fifteen years older. He said he didn't know much about the Temple, nor did he particularly care. He didn't believe in God, and he didn't follow any organized religion.

Shaine thought he was too cool about it, but they had no choice but to let him go, at least until they could analyze the bio-scans that Whippet was taking as they talked. But even if there were suspicious changes, bio-scan evidence wasn't enough to hold him or charge him. Shaine assigned Ben and Allim to keep an eye on McKillan. They tracked him via remote security cameras and watched the net and the com logs for any messages he might have coming or going.

Shaine lifted the lockdown order and crews were allowed on the construction-site to work again. Morgan took her turn at the security console, scrolling through the internal and external camera feeds. She was flipping through cameras in the living quarters when she saw Mathew McKillan looking generally pissed off as he entered the barracks.

She reached over to grab her pad and punched in a preset calling code. "Hey, Ben."

"What'cha got, Morgan?"

"Just saw McKillan go into barracks. He looked pretty pissed."

"We've got him on the private feed. Thanks, Morgan."

"No problem." She signed off and set the pad aside. Living and personal quarters were monitored, but on a closed, private system that only the primary security team could access. She continued watching the screens as they switched randomly through the cameras.

She could hear Amaar's deep tones as he spoke on the com to somebody, but other than that, the ops center was quiet. Morgan didn't mind it, but she would much rather be in the warehouse with Joe or on the construction-site doing something physical.

Shaine and Josef strode into ops. Morgan could feel Shaine's frustration as soon as she walked in. She was practically bristling with it. Shaine dropped gracelessly into the chair beside Morgan. Josef leaned on the edge of the desk, arms crossed over his chest.

Morgan raised a questioning brow. "I take it the interview didn't go the way you wanted it to?"

Josef said, "Not exactly."

"There has to be a way to get him to crack," Shaine muttered. "Maybe we're going about this the wrong way." She reached for a keyboard and logged into the system. "What about this guy's brother? What do we know about him? McKillan says they aren't close. There's got to be something on the net that we can find on the brother's side to prove whether he's lying to us."

Morgan watched as Shaine started a couple of 'bots to query the net on Isaiah Abraham. Morgan and Lukas hadn't found much personal data on McKillan when they'd done a similar search. McKillan didn't even have a registered avatar. Of course, it didn't mean that he didn't have one under a different name. They'd searched through Abraham's information too, looking for any references to McKillan, but other than a couple general references to family, they hadn't found anything there, either.

"Do you think the Temple people know he's here?" Morgan asked.

Josef shrugged. "Does it make a difference?"

Shaine cocked her head. "What are you thinking?" she asked.

"I'm not sure. Just wondering if that was something you could use as a game piece. If they know he's here, maybe it's because they planted him here. What if we contacted the colony and asked them about him?"

Shaine cocked her head. "It depends on if he's closer to his brother and the Temple than he's leading us to believe."

Josef muttered, "I feel like we're missing something. Are we jumping to conclusions?"

Shaine shrugged. "The others are still digging. Let's see if these 'bots come up with anything. In the meantime, I think I have an idea."

CHAPTER TWENTY-SIX

"Get dressed. You're going for a little ride."

Shaine tossed a pair of work pants and a shirt on top of Mathew McKillan's sleeping form. He blinked. For an instant she thought she saw a hint of something other than sleepy curiosity in his eyes.

"I don't understand," he murmured, sitting up. He looked around the barracks room. All but two or three of the beds were empty. Of those who remained, two were sound asleep and snoring. From across the room, Mischan Dorovitch looked on silently for a few moments before he rolled over and closed his eyes again.

Shaine said shortly, "Get dressed. I'll be waiting in the hallway." She stalked from the room and joined Del and Josef in the corridor. "Well, this will be interesting," she said.

Del smiled dangerously. "I want to see the little shit squirm."

A couple minutes later, McKillan stepped into the hallway, still disheveled from sleep and surprised to see the security team waiting for him. Shaine gestured for him to start down the corridor. He frowned. "What's going on?" he asked.

"I told you. We're going for a ride."

McKillan stopped, dark eyes flashing at Shaine. "Is this is some kind of a threat?" he demanded.

Shaine's smile was predatory. "Threat? No. Just a little visit to see your family. No threat."

He stiffened. "I don't understand," he said.

Del smirked. "Sure you do, Matty. You're not that stupid. We thought we'd zip out to visit your big brother, Isaiah, see how he's doing. Thought that might be nice, like old home week, you know?"

"I have nothing to say to my brother," he said shortly. He turned away, as though to head back to the barracks room. Shaine caught him by the arm, her grip like iron, stopping him midmotion.

"Let's go." She pushed him in front of her and he didn't fight it, but the glare he gave her was just shy of murderous.

Del grinned at Shaine. Josef's lips tightened into a line. The three of them escorted McKillan to the warehouse and across to the hangar connected at the far side. They stepped into the airlock and Del sealed it behind them. It only took a minute for the opposite door into the hangar to release since the hangar was at full atmosphere. They guided McKillan toward a small surface transport. Josef keyed the ramp down and strode aboard. Shaine gestured McKillan to follow, and she and Del jogged up behind him.

The ramp led into a small seating area in the center of the transport. There were four padded bench seats facing forward. Each bench had four headrests and four sets of four-point restraints. A row of wall lockers lined the back of the compartment. The cockpit could be sealed off, but stood open for the moment.

Shaine and Del ducked into the cockpit. Josef remained in the seating area with McKillan. He smiled at the younger man. "Take a seat," he instructed tersely, and leaned against the fuselage beside the cockpit hatch with his arms folded across his oversized chest.

McKillan sat stiffly on the front bench in the seat farthest from Josef.

"Better strap in, McKillan. It's gonna be a rough ride."

Dark eyes flashed his way. "What about you?"

Josef's grin was taunting. "If you strap in, I don't have to worry about a rough ride," he said. "You need any help with that?"

"No."

McKillan grabbed the restraints and clipped them around his body. The engines revved and settled into a vibrating hum. Shaine's clipped tones echoed against the metal hull. "Runner One to ops. Gohste, open the exterior hangar bay door."

Even through the thick hull, they could hear the warning claxons sounding in the hanger. The lights beyond the cockpit window shifted to red. The warning gave anyone in the hangar three minutes to vacate before the main doors opened to the thin Martian atmosphere.

"Ops to Runner One. Interior bay hatch is now sealed and locked. Opening main hangar door."

"Thanks. We'll check in to let you know what's going on."

"Ops standing by. Good luck."

Shaine signed off the com. "Let's get this show on the road." She took the throttles and eased the surface transport from the hanger. Once out and away from the construction-site, she kicked in the turbos and sent them shooting across the sand basin to the west.

Josef poked his head into the cockpit. "All good here," he said in an undertone. "Our boy is not happy."

Del looked over her shoulder and shot Josef a grin. "Good."

Shaine nodded, her attention on the landscape as she shot across the rocky sand. She hoped they were doing the right thing, bringing McKillan to the Temple's colony dome.

At this point they didn't have anything on the guy other than circumstantial evidence that suggested he wasn't where he should have been. Whippet tracked down a number of messages and blogs from Isaiah Abraham. Again, there were only a handful of references to Mathew McKillan, and most in passing, listing family members.

Abraham authored several vitriolic rants against the development of mining in their pristine Martian utopia and against Mann-Maru for being the implementer of that development. His tirades railed against corporate culture generally, the immorality of corporate political power and the sin of wanting money and power more than the love of God.

Shaine wasn't sure what they would accomplish by bringing McKillan to the colony. She hoped it might shock him into admitting to the sabotage of the crane cable. A good man was dead. If she could prove McKillan was the culprit, she could prosecute and at least feel like justice had been done.

If he wouldn't talk, she was tempted to just leave the guy with his relatives at the Temple colony and call it done. That felt like punishment enough; stuck in a "utopian society'" without access to the outside world.

They hadn't announced their pending arrival to the Temple colony, so that in itself could prove interesting. Josef said he'd do the talking, that it would be better than Shaine potentially antagonizing them. One of the Temple precepts was that women were for making babies and being wives, and the men ran the show. They would respond more readily to Josef being the leader. Shaine agreed although it grated on her sensibilities.

It was a four-hour trip to the Unified Martian Temple of God dome, roughly six hundred and fifty kilometers from the mining site. Time dragged. Shaine concluded that the Martian landscape wasn't any more interesting than the lunar one. It just had different colored rocks and sky. Del and Josef switched between acting as copilot and keeping an eye on their reluctant and silent passenger. McKillan seemed to get more uncomfortable as they got closer to the colony dome.

Shaine wasn't convinced that his discomfort was significant. Four hours was a long time to sit on a hard bench seat, especially with either a big, muscular guy standing over you, or a really hot, tough chick glaring at you like you were a speck of dirt on her shoes.

Shaine glanced at the GPS map. They were about twenty kilometers out from the colony dome. She eased the skimmer between a couple of rocky sand dunes and onto a flat plain. The sun was a dim orange-yellow ball in the hazy bluish sky, painting the landscape with vague light and shadows. In the distance, she could see the Temple dome rising up from the horizon.

Del said, "I'll get Josef up here to contact them," and pushed herself up from the copilot's seat. She ducked out of the cockpit and Shaine could hear her as she tapped Josef on the shoulder. "Your turn, man. We're coming up on the colony."

Josef dropped heavily into the seat beside Shaine. He grabbed a headset and pulled it on with one hand. He flipped on the com and scanned through the channels.

"Incoming land transport to Unified Martian Temple of God colony. Do you read? Over."

Incoming transport, we do not want visitors. Please leave the area."

"Unified Martian Temple, we have a passenger whom we believe you'd be interested in. The passenger is requesting asylum at the colony."

Shaine glanced at Josef. They hadn't talked a lot about the approach they were going to take.

"We don't want indigents. Go away."

Josef smiled. "Tell your Elder, Isaiah Abraham, that his brother Mathew is here to see him."

Silence for several seconds, then another voice came on the line, deeper and more commanding. "Mathew?"

Shaine heard shuffling behind her in the cabin and a thump that sounded like Del shoving McKillan back into his seat.

Josef keyed the com. "If you want to talk to him, you'll either have to come out to us, or let us in to you."

"If you've done anything to him, you will pay for it," came the growling reply. "When you arrive, we will open the hangar bay door. You may bring your transport in."

"Roger that." Josef killed the com.

Shaine said, "You and I go in with McKillan. Del stays and keeps the shuttle on hot standby."

A couple minutes later Shaine eased the ground transport up to the colony dome, hovering in front of the hangar bay door. The dome's outer shell was scratched and dusty from the blowing sand, the glassteel cloudy and reddish. The hangar door opened slowly, jerking its way up. Shaine imagined she could hear it creaking and squealing as it rolled upward and she wondered what kind of maintenance they were doing.

When the door was fully open, she eased the transport into the hanger. The center of the hangar was open and she spun the small ship around so they were facing the door before she set down. Along the sides of the hanger, she noted various small skimmers but no spacecraft, and she thought it odd that they would have no way out if anything were to happen to the dome. At the mining site, they had a couple of emergency shuttles.

As she idled the main engines, the hangar door clanged shut. The red emergency lights continued on, but started flashing blue as the atmosphere in the hangar was restored. Shaine glanced at the exterior scanners, watching the temperature and oxygen levels slowly come up to Earth-normal. She had no intention of cracking the hatch on the transport until she saw people in the hangar to greet them.

Del reported, "Exterior life support reading normal."

Shaine nodded. "We'll sit tight until they show up to greet us." She watched the wide-angle rear camera view, currently showing the airlock hatch in the back of the hanger. They waited nearly ten minutes before the hatch opened. Five men created a half circle behind a tall, dark-haired man in a long black tunic and loose black pants. He was clean-shaven and had dark, deep-set eyes. Shaine recognized Elder Brother Isaiah Abraham from the photos they'd seen. She smiled to herself. At least they were going straight to the top of the food chain, and not dealing with underlings.

She stood up and dropped a hand on Del's shoulder. "Keep an eye on things."

Del nodded. "Not a problem. I've got the guns warmed up, just in case."

Shaine grinned. It was good to have people who thought the way she did. The ground transport had hidden guns in the upper rear of the ship as well as on either side and to the front. They were well-armed, whether it appeared that way or not.

Shaine stepped from the cockpit. Josef waited by the hatch with McKillan, one hand wrapped around the young man's bicep. McKillan faced the door.

Shaine couldn't see McKillan's face, but she read tension in the tight set of his shoulders and neck. Good. She nodded to Josef. "Let's go."

Josef palmed the exit controls, extending the short ramp as the hatch unsealed with a hiss and slid open. He pulled McKillan along beside him as he strode down the ramp. Shaine stayed a step behind on McKillan's other side. For a left cross-draw, she had a sidearm in a waistband holster only slightly hidden under her jacket.

They stopped at the bottom of the ramp.

The Temple group came to a halt about three meters from them. The men around Abraham stood silent, arms crossed over thick chests, standing at parade rest, watching their visitors closely. Abraham took a step forward. His eyes were on the young man between Shaine and Josef.

"Mathew, are you well?"

McKillan nodded but said nothing.

He addressed Josef. "Why do you bring my brother to me?"

Josef said, "We suspect your brother has killed a man on our construction-site."

Abraham lifted a brow. "Indeed? Has Mathew admitted to this accusation?"

McKillan hissed, "Of course not!"

Shaine grabbed McKillan's other arm and snapped, "Shut up."

Josef said, "We thought perhaps you would take him in since he is family. We have no use for troublemakers."

Abraham seemed to consider this, dark eyes piercing as he studied his younger brother. McKillan seemed to shrink under the glare, dropping his gaze and hanging his head. "If we were to take my brother in, there would need to be a trial, of course. We do not abide murderers here."

Shaine raised a brow. "Even to save their souls?" she asked.

Abraham frowned. "Do not mock me, woman."

Shaine shrugged.

"When would you have this trial?" Josef asked.

McKillan said, "I didn't do anything, Brother. I should go back with them."

Abraham glared at McKillan and the young man fell silent, his eyes returning to the floor. Abraham said to Josef, "We can have the trial here and now. We have witnesses." He gestured to the men around him. "As the Vessel of God, I am judge and jury in this colony."

Shaine had to work hard not to laugh. *What an arrogant, power-hungry bastard.*

She heard McKillan swallow audibly, though he never lifted his eyes from the ground. *Yes*, she thought, *this might just shake the truth loose.*

Josef nodded, accepting Abraham's statement. "All right. We accuse Mathew McKillan of cutting into the crane cable on the construction-site, causing it to snap and killing one man. We know someone was outside while the camera surveying the area around the crane was out of order. By interviewing all of our people, we have placed all but two men for the time that the crime would have taken place. The other has an alibi. Which leaves Mathew McKillan as the only man unaccounted for during that time. He has a motive—his ties to your organization, which is very much against our presence on this planet. He has the skills to have both disabled the camera and to have cut the crane cable. He doesn't have an alibi, other than that he was sleeping, and we have witnesses to say that he was not in the barracks at that time. During his interview, bio-scans indicated agitation and fear when questioned about his whereabouts and his ties to your organization."

Abraham said, "Your evidence is quite circumstantial."

"It's only a matter of time before we find definitive evidence," Josef said. "Meanwhile, we'd have to keep him in lockup at the construction-site."

Abraham nodded slowly. Dark eyes assessed his brother like a hawk eyeing its prey. Shaine tried to read his expression, but all she could sense was a coldness that made her glad she wasn't the focus of his attention.

"Look at me, Mathew," Abraham ordered.

McKillan raised his head hesitantly. Shaine could almost smell the fear coming off him in waves.

"Tell me."

McKillan remained silent.

"Tell me!"

"I failed, Brother!" McKillan's head dropped. "Forgive me, please!"

Abraham walked forward and grabbed McKillan by the chin, forcing the younger man to meet his forbidding dark gaze. "Are you guilty?" he demanded.

Tears leaked at the corners of McKillan's eyes.

Abraham shook him. "Tell me!"

"Yes! Yes! I am guilty! I have failed!" McKillan sagged between Josef and Shaine, and they were forced to hold him up to keep him on his feet.

Abraham gestured to his officers. "Take him. He will be punished by our laws." Two men stepped forward.

Josef held up a hand to stop them and turned to McKillan. "You say you failed. What does that mean?"

McKillan's voice broke. "I did not complete my mission for God," he whispered.

"What was your mission?" Josef asked.

"To stop you all. To make you leave this Holy place. Mars is for the righteous, not for immoral corporate sinners. But I did not succeed." He hung his head.

Shaine looked from McKillan to Abraham, but her gaze lingered on the elder. "I hope to hell you didn't have anything to do with this mission."

Abraham glowered at her. "Watch your mouth, woman."

Shaine shook her head. "Whatever."

Josef looked seriously at Abraham. "Did you send Mathew on a mission to sabotage us?"

"I did not set him on this course. God did," he said. "You should not be on this world, but I would not resort to murder to remove you."

Josef nodded. "Thank you."

Abraham glanced at the two men who'd stepped forward, and they took McKillan by his arms. "Come, sinner, to your punishment," one of them intoned. As they pulled him away, McKillan broke down sobbing.

Abraham said to Josef. "Thank you for bringing my brother to me. He must be punished for his failures and be brought back to redemption."

Josef nodded and turned, striding back up the ramp. Shaine gave Abraham a final warning glare and followed Josef into the shuttle, sealing the hatch behind her. As the hatch closed she called, "Del, fire this puppy up as soon as they're clear. I want out of this place."

"Roger that, boss. These people are fucking creepy."

Josef said, "You record that whole thing?"

"Absolutely."

Shaine dropped into the pilot's seat. Josef braced himself behind them. "Fucking cultists," she muttered. "Be interesting to know what McKillan's punishment will be. He was practically wetting his pants."

Del's hands darted over her controls, starting to bring the primary systems back up to full power. "They can kill him as far as I'm concerned. That would pay for Alec's death."

"Gotta love frontier justice," Josef commented. "Very efficient."

Shaine glanced at the vid monitor. "The interior hatch is sealed."

They waited impatiently for the hangar door to open. After a couple of minutes, it started to jerk upward. Del engaged the engines. Shaine was relieved they weren't going to have to shoot their way out.

As soon as the hangar door cleared, Shaine gunned the throttles, hurtling out of the hangar and over the sand.

Josef asked, "You think that was just a show for our benefit? Or are they actually going to punish him?"

Shaine considered. She would have liked a real, legal confession out of McKillan, but she supposed this was as close as they could get. "You saw Abraham's eyes. He was cold. And there's no way McKillan was faking that kind of fear."

Del added, "These guys are into hard-core corporal punishment. I read a couple accounts of whippings and even eye for an eye kind of stuff. Out here, who's going to stop them, right?"

Josef nodded.

Shaine frowned as she guided the transport away from the Temple dome. She didn't condone their kind of justice. She didn't agree with the way they lived their lives. Of course, they didn't agree with the way she lived hers, either. She shook her head. Had they done the right thing, leaving McKillan at the colony? Was she any better than Abraham and his goons? She and Josef decided to log this officially as McKillan returning to his family. There would be no accusations of wrongdoing. They had nothing other than circumstantial evidence, and his confession in front of Abraham wouldn't stand up in court. It would be considered coercion.

Del smacked Shaine's arm. "Your girlfriend had the right idea. Smart one, bringing him here."

Shaine managed a weak smile and continued guiding the ship toward home. And Morgan.

CHAPTER TWENTY-SEVEN

Shaine worked dutifully at the desk in her tiny office. The month following Alec's death had gone quickly and smoothly. The new living dome was sealed and life support brought online. It wasn't fully commissioned yet, but at least they didn't need to wear full vac suits to work inside. The emergency radiation shelter was ready and available if needed.

The days had become frighteningly routine. Shaine was happy that she and Morgan had at least a little time just to themselves. They'd settled into a very comfortable existence, though both of them seemed to be working a lot of extra hours lately.

Tonight Shaine flipped through paperwork from the group of twenty workers who'd come in today. They were taking on more personnel as construction ramped up inside the primary dome. Everyone was cheering the fact that they'd finally brought in real kitchen staff and had started to serve fresh "home cooked" food as well as the preprocessed packaged meals from the dispensers. She'd hired additional security personnel to balance out the numbers. Five had come up today with a supply ship. Ten more would be along on the next supply run, but it was still a relatively small security team.

Someone rapped on the doorframe.

Shaine looked up. "Come in."

The door slid open and Morgan walked in, dropping heavily into the chair in front of the desk. "Hey."

Shaine smiled. "Hey, yourself. What's up?"

"Nothing. I wanted to see how you were doing. And let you know there was still food in the cafeteria, if you wanted to eat."

"Ah. Food. Guess I forgot about dinner. Did you eat?"

"Naw. I was waiting for you."

Shaine grinned. "You are way too sweet, hon."

"Yeah, well don't tell anyone, right?"

"My lips are sealed." Shaine grinned. "Unless of course, I'm using them on you," she added.

Morgan flushed and let her head fall back. "Oh, baby," she intoned.

Shaine chuckled and got to her feet as she logged out of her terminal. "Let's go find some grub. I've had enough for one day."

Morgan sighed dramatically. "Work, work, work. You're turning into a regular corporate administrator," she teased.

"Watch it, Rahn."

"Watching." Morgan waited until Shaine preceded her out the door. "Nice ass, Wendt."

Shaine laughed as she strolled into ops. Gohste was at the com desk, feet up on the console and a pad in his lap. He lifted it up. "There's a new weather bulletin coming in from the System Space Administration."

"That's never a good thing. What's going on?"

"Solar flares. Big ones. They're predicting we're going to catch it full on."

Shaine walked over to his monitors and put the alert up on the main wall screen. She skimmed the reports from the SSA Observatory on the moon. Based on their path around the sun, the full force of the flares' energy was going to smack right into them.

Shaine said, "Put an alert out. We need to start battening down after this shift and move everyone into the underground shelter before this hits us."

Gohste said, "According to the SSA, we have seventeen hours and fifteen minutes to get to shelter. I'll check in with Ahmed and let him know what's going on."

Shaine nodded. "Sounds good. Thanks, Ghoste."

* * *

Morgan sat behind the security monitors, flipping through the interior cameras. She was filling in while the rest of the security team monitored the final move of personnel to the underground shelter. The solar storm was ratcheting up. They'd lost all com and net feeds from Moon Base and Earth.

She glanced up at the red countdown clock displayed on the main ops screen. Three hours, forty-six minutes. Not a lot of time, but they were nearly done transferring all their personnel into the underground shelter. She wasn't worried about the process. She was more concerned about dealing with the boredom of being stuck underground for a few days.

Shaine had been flitting back and forth between the security station and talking with Gohste, Ahmed and Garren, who were at the main ops console, coordinating the move and monitoring systems between the temporary dome and the shelter.

Gohste's voice carried over the general hubbub, and Morgan looked his way.

"This is the Mann-Maru Mining Facility, yes." His fingers flickered over his communications console. He put a hand to his earpiece. "Please repeat. Your signal is breaking up." He listened again, frowning. "Unified Martian Temple, come in! Do you read? Can you hear me?" With a frustrated curse, he said, "I lost the call. Shaine, I patched the recording through to your station. The Temple colony reported that one of their kids ran off with a personal ground skimmer, maybe an hour ago, maybe two. They think the kid may be headed toward us."

Shaine looked up from her terminal with an incredulous expression. "Do they know we've got a major solar storm less than four hours out?"

Gohste shrugged.

Garren said, "Try to send them a weather update, Gohste. Then they can't say we didn't."

"Even if it isn't our problem if they're that stupid," Morgan muttered. She brought up the views from the outermost cameras and set them panning the area. "I'll see if anyone's within camera range."

Shaine ran a hand through her hair. "No way they'd have gotten this far in a couple of hours," she said. "Not on a skimmer."

Morgan said, "We could take a rescue vehicle out and see if we can find them."

Del looked up from the security boards. "Great idea, but we don't have anyone free."

"I could go out," Morgan said.

Shaine's eyebrows rose toward her hairline. "I don't think so."

Morgan ignored her and said to Gohste, "Who's the pilot on call?"

He tapped a screen. "Mojo's on."

"Tell him to meet me down in the hanger," she said, pushing to her feet.

Shaine said, "Morgan, we need to lock down the shelter in three hours. The radiation levels are starting to rise faster. I'll give you half an hour out and half an hour back. That's it."

Morgan nodded. "One hour," she acknowledged. "Thanks, Shaine."

Shaine pursed her lips, her expression grim, and Morgan knew she wasn't happy about the excursion. She also knew it was probably the only chance the kid had of staying alive. She headed toward the door.

"Morg?"

Morgan stopped and turned back.

"Be careful, okay?"

Morgan smiled. "I will. Love you too."

* * *

The rescue transport had room for the pilot and copilot up front. Morgan took the copilot's seat though she wasn't able to fly. She could handle the coms and the scanners. She and Mojo wore vac suits on the off chance that they would actually find the missing kid. For the ride out, though, they'd left their helmets and gloves secured in the midship lockers.

Morgan was glad Mojo was the pilot on call. The tall man was one of the most laid-back guys she knew. His strong, flat-planed face suggested his descent from the South American continent. He wore his black hair pulled into a braid that hung almost to his waist.

Mojo revved up the engines and Morgan flipped on the com. "Flyer One to base, over."

"Go ahead, Flyer One."

Morgan recognized Gohste's voice. She said, "Just letting you know we're heading out."

"Roger that. Good hunting."

Shaine broke in, "Watch your time, Morgan."

"Got it. Flyer One out." Morgan tapped off the com.

Mojo eased the compact rescue transport out of the hangar and opened up the throttle as they passed through the construction-site. He picked up enough altitude for a decent view while staying low enough to see a small personal skimmer. He said, "If the kid's already been out a couple hours, he can't have more than three hours of air left if he's in a standard suit."

"Yeah. Not good. I've got thermal scanners up, as long range as I can get them."

"I've got a grid plotted." He put a flight pattern up on the cockpit HUD.

"I'm scanning the com channels, too. Hopefully we'll pick something up."

* * *

Shaine's voice crackled over the increasingly static-filled com. "Morgan, you need to turn back."

Morgan could hear the agitation in Shaine's voice, but they'd finally got a hint of their runaway, and she wasn't ready to give up yet. She frowned as she tried to focus the thermal scanners in on the heat indication she'd just picked up. "Just a few more minutes. We've got a signal on the thermal scan, a couple minutes from us."

"Damn it, the radiation readings are climbing."

"Just a few more minutes."

Mojo pointed with one hand, the other still on the control stick. "I think I see something. About two o'clock."

"Shaine, I think we got the kid! Back in two and two."

Mojo swung the transport directly at the target and swore as the skimmer came into view. Riderless, it lay on its side in the sand. "Do you see the kid?" He hovered, slowly pivoting the ship as they visually scanned the area, looking for a suited body.

"There!" Morgan saw the dull glint of sunlight off a faceplate near a pile of rocks a couple meters from the crashed skimmer. "Put down. I'll go out." She sealed the cockpit hatch behind her as she went through to the cabin.

She pulled on her helmet and gloves, sealed up her suit and checked the suit's diagnostics a final time before she opened the airlock. Not waiting for the short boarding ramp to finish extending, she jumped down onto the hard-packed sand. She jogged toward the rock near the crashed skimmer. When she caught sight of the suit leg extending past the rocks, she slowed and hoped like hell the kid wasn't splattered. She stepped around the rock. The vacuum suit was intact, with no frost on the mirrored faceplate. She took in a breath. The suit was probably functioning.

Morgan knelt by the helmet, frustrated that she couldn't see the face through the mirroring. She picked up the kid's arm, looking at the small diagnostic computer on the suit's wrist. All the basic functions were running in the yellow. She frowned and switched to a more detailed graph mode. *Fuck*. The suit was nearly out of air and power.

She got behind the kid and picked him up under the arms. "Mojo, I'm coming in! Kid's alive, but his suit is gonna crash and burn in about three minutes."

"Hurry up, then. Shaine's bitchin' at me to get us back."

"Got it." Morgan chastised herself for not thinking to bring a gurney or something with her as she dragged the runaway to the ship. She pulled the body up the short ramp and laid him on the floor, then reached back to shut the hatch. As the airlock sealed, she yelled, "We're in! Go!"

The life support system started cycling in the cabin, pumping heat and air into the midsection of the ship. She knew it would only take a couple minutes, but the wait seemed interminable. As she dropped to her knees beside the kid, she felt the transport lift off, rocking as Mojo hit the throttle and picked up altitude.

She grabbed the kid's wrist, splitting her attention between the suit diagnostics and the indicators above the hatch, waiting anxiously to pop the suit's helmet and get the kid some decent air. The suit's life-support was running in the red now. Clean air was depleted and the unit was recycling what was left in the suit itself. It would be toxic in three minutes.

The compartment indicators finally flashed green. Morgan ripped off her own gloves and made quick work of popping the seals on the kid's helmet, pulling it off to reveal a teenaged girl with wildly curly blond hair.

The girl's head lolled back. Morgan slapped her pale cheeks. "Come on, wake up!"

She could feel the girl's breath, shallow and weak, against the back of her hand. She laid her back down and started unsealing the girl's suit, talking to her the whole time and wishing she was a medic instead of a mechanic.

Mojo's voice came over the compartment speakers, "How's she doing?"

"Still out. Trying to get her unsuited so I can see what's going on. Make sure to pull into the barn, hey?"

"Roger that. We're about twenty minutes out. Shaine's having a fit."

"She'll get over it. Just get us back there."

Morgan got the girl's suit open, pulling back the front panels without actually taking it off her. The suit was basic and didn't have any biofeedback diagnostics. At least the girl was breathing. She had a solid pulse and some color coming back to her face. Morgan didn't see any blood or obvious trauma, so she could only assume that she either smacked her head on the inside of the helmet when she went down, or she was out because of the low oxygen content. Maybe both.

She brushed the girl's hair out of her eyes. The girl groaned and blue eyes blinked open to look around in bleary panic. Morgan said, as reassuringly as she could, "Hey, you're okay. It's okay. We're headed to the mining site. My name is Morgan."

The kid stared at her, and Morgan realized she still had her own helmet on. Shaking her head, she undid the seal and pulled it off, setting it on the floor next to her. "Sorry."

Blue eyes studied her face intently. "Please don't take me back to the colony," she pleaded.

"Not if you don't want to go."

The girl nodded.

"Are you okay? What happened?"

The girl frowned. "The skimmer hit a big rut in the sand and I caught a cross gust at the same time. I tried to recover, but it dumped. I think I smacked my head." She lifted her arm, realizing she was still mostly suited. "How did you find me?"

"We got a call from the colony saying someone ran off. We were searching with a thermal scanner. With the sunspot radiation about to hit us, we figured we should find you before you got your brains fried."

The kid looked sufficiently spooked. "Oh."

"So, what's your name?"

"Um. Friday. It's Friday."

Morgan blinked. "Interesting name," she commented.

Friday made a face. "I think it's stupid. My parents said it's some kind of ancient literary reference."

"Are your parents at the colony?"

"My parents are dead. My sister dragged me out here. And I'm not going back."

Morgan nodded, accepting the hard determination in Friday's expression.

The ship lurched, shifting hard to port and up before it settled again. Morgan grabbed at the loose helmet beside her as it slid away. They could hear Mojo's fluent curses as he wrestled the ship back under control.

"Morgan, get our visitor strapped in. It's getting a little dicey with these winds, and I could use an extra set of hands."

"Be there in a sec, Mo." Morgan looked at Friday. "Can you get up, so we can strap ya in?"

Friday nodded. "Yeah."

Morgan got to her feet and reached down to give Friday a hand up. The ship continued to shift under them, but Morgan managed to keep her balance and got Friday settled on one of the trauma beds built into the wall. She secured the girl with four-point restraints and patted her on the shoulder. "Just hang on, okay?"

Friday nodded. "Thanks."

Morgan gave her a grin and turned away to unseal the cockpit hatch and join Mojo.

Shaine sent them directly into the underground docking bay. Radiation levels had increased frighteningly quickly while they'd been gone. Ops had shifted control to the underground ops center, and all staff were checked into their shelter quarters. Rather than waiting for the docking bay to pressurize and heat up, the maintenance crew hooked up an umbilical to get Morgan, Mojo and Friday into the sealed underground shelter.

Mojo ducked out of the umbilical first, still suited except for helmet and gloves. Shaine greeted him with a slap on the shoulder. "Good job, Mojo."

He grinned at her. "Take it easy on your girlfriend, hey?"

Morgan and Friday stumbled out of the umbilical just a step behind Mojo. Morgan supported her counterpart, who was taller than she was, with an arm around her waist. Both were free of helmets and gloves. Morgan's focus was on the girl, who looked around with wide eyes. Morgan said, "It's okay, you're safe here. It's an underground bunker."

"And you won't send me back?"

"No, I told you that. It'll be okay."

Shaine stepped in front of them. "Jesus Christ, Morgan, if you cut things that close again, I'll kill you myself."

Morgan grinned and pulled Shaine into an awkward hug, kissing her cheek. "I love you too, Shaine."

Shaine managed another frown before shaking her head with a sigh and turning her attention to the young woman at Morgan's side. Morgan patted the girl's shoulder. "This is Friday. Friday, this is our Head of Security, Shaine Wendt."

Shaine looked Friday up and down. "Hello, Friday. Welcome. Are you all right? Do you need to see a medic?"

Friday shook her head. "I'm okay, as long as you don't send me back to that hellhole."

Shaine glanced at Morgan. "No chance of that while we're in the middle of a solar radiation storm," she returned evenly.

Friday's sharp blue eyes flashed up. "What about after the storm?" she asked.

Morgan said, "We won't force you to do anything you don't want to."

Shaine cautioned, "We'll cross that bridge when we get to it."

Morgan said to Friday, "Let's get out of this gear and get some food. Then we can talk, okay?"

They crossed over to the lockers on the far wall. Shaine helped Friday out of her vac suit while Morgan shed hers and ran her diagnostics before stowing it in her locker. Shaine waved a maintenance tech over. "I need you to check Friday's suit, Mitch. Make sure it's functioning properly and file the report to my pad."

"Yes, ma'am."

Shaine shook her head at the ma'am, then shooed Morgan and Friday ahead of her toward the cafeteria. They passed a number of personnel milling about the narrow hallways as they headed further into the shelter's interior.

Morgan asked, "Any updates at all as to how long this storm is going to last?"

"The last report from the SSA said it would last at least four days. The scientists are thinking it'll be closer to a week. In any case, radiation is breaking up all our com streams, so we're on our own until it passes."

"Well," Morgan observed, "at least we won't have corporate breathing down our throats for a few days."

"Or any news from the outside."

Friday looked from one to the other. "Are you both in charge here?" she asked.

Morgan shook her head. "I'm sure as hell not," she said. "I'm just a working grunt."

Shaine laughed. "I'm Head of Security, so reasonably high on the in-charge list."

They strode through a set of auto-opening double doors into the cafeteria. There were several rows of solid plastic picnic tables. The serving counter spanned the back of the room, providing fresh food from the kitchen as well as a bank of automated food and beverage dispensers. A board with the day's menu written out hung on the wall.

Morgan grinned. "Looks like burgers and fries if you want live food."

The expression on Friday's face was near to swooning. "Please? All we get are vegetables and processed proteins at the colony."

"Burgers it is, then," Shaine agreed. They got their food and drinks and Shaine guided them to a quiet corner where they could talk without interruption. She had already noticed how Friday watched Morgan for cues and how the girl's intense, blue eyes scanned the room warily, taking in every detail.

Morgan dug into her food and Friday followed her lead. Shaine picked up a fry and chewed it thoughtfully. After a few seconds, she asked, "So, what brings you to us, Friday? What made you leave the colony? Were you intending to reach us here? Or had you not thought that far ahead?"

Friday set her burger down, her expression serious. "Of course I intended to get here," she said. "I am not stupid."

Shaine shrugged, "Just asking."

Morgan gave Shaine a curious frown, but said nothing. Shaine sent Morgan an almost imperceptible head shake.

Friday said, "I had a chance to get out, so I took it. I knew I was taking a chance because of the storm, but I worked out my route and I knew I could make it in time. Even if I didn't make it, I would rather die than slowly lose my mind in that asylum."

Shaine studied her. "That's a pretty strong statement."

Friday's expression darkened and she pushed her food away. She glared at Shaine and snapped, "If I wanted an interrogation, I could go back to the colony."

Shaine held up her hands. "Sorry. Relax, okay. Look, I just want to understand what's going on. And, honestly, I'd like to know what I'm going to be dealing with when we have communications back and the colony decides to ask about you."

Friday scowled. "They're freaks, okay? I don't belong there. I don't believe in their bizarre religious shit, and I never will. They think I'm dangerous because I think for myself and I want to learn and I'm not afraid to say it. Every drawing I've done, they've destroyed. They say art is heresy. At least, my art is. I tried to get into an apprentice program for mechanics or computer diagnostics. They won't let me because girls aren't supposed to do that. They don't want people with brains, especially women. They want zombies they can control who will believe all their crap."

Morgan asked quietly, "What do they do about people they can't control?"

Friday's intensity went inward for a moment and she swallowed. "They have a lot of ways to try to make you toe the line," she said flatly, and, after a beat added almost inaudibly, "Sometimes you just let them think they've won."

Shaine frowned, but said nothing.

Morgan laid a hand on Friday's arm. "We won't send you back there," she said firmly. She flashed a glance up at Shaine, who nodded. Morgan smiled at her. Shaine returned the smile, but wasn't certain they could keep the girl with them legally. If the kid was a minor the decision could be taken out of their hands. She changed the subject.

"Okay, next thing," Shaine said. "We need to find quarters for our new friend here. I'm not sure what the status on free space is, so let me find out what's available." She pushed up from the table. "You two finish up here. Morgan, will you run Friday by the infirmary, just to make sure she's okay after that crash?"

"I'm fine! I don't need—"

"Humor me, okay? It'll make me feel better to know for sure that you're not injured. The doc should probably check your radiation levels, anyway."

Friday narrowed her eyes at Shaine, who simply smiled and strode away. As she walked, she overheard their next exchange and chuckled to herself.

"Your girlfriend can be a bitch," Friday observed.

"She just takes charge. Don't worry about it."

Friday snorted. "You're whipped."

"Finish your dinner and we can go meet the doc."

CHAPTER TWENTY-EIGHT

Shaine strode down the corridor from the cafeteria toward the small underground ops center. She keyed her com as she walked. "Garren?"

"Ayah. What's up?"

"Are you in the control room?"

"I am."

"Good. I'm on my way. We need to talk."

"I'll be here."

Shaine pulled up a chair in front of the desk in Garren's tiny office and straddled it, leaning her arms on the back. "I think we need to anticipate some trouble with the Temple over our young runaway."

Garren leaned back in his chair and frowned. "Do tell."

"I just have a bad feeling. She absolutely does not want to go back there. I think there's more going on than just a kid who's not happy. I'm having Morgan take her to see the doc. I told

Friday I wanted to make sure her radiation levels were okay, but Lei will do a full scan. I want to know everything I can."

"Do you think they're going to come after her?"

"I'm not sure. I think they're more likely to try to create a big stink out of it, make it all public. I don't think they want her back, but I think they'll use her to cause trouble for us."

Garren ran a hand through his long black hair. "As soon as we get coms back, I'll let legal know what might be coming our way."

"Good. I just don't want to get caught unawares. Morgan isn't going to let anyone mess with this kid. I don't think I've ever seen her in protective mode before. It's kinda cute."

Garren chuckled. "Messing with Morgan is not on my to-do list."

Shaine sighed and stood. "I'd better go find them. We need to figure out where Friday's going to stay."

"Good luck with that."

"Thanks, Garren. You're all heart."

Shaine found Morgan pacing in the corridor outside the temporary infirmary. "How's it going?"

Morgan shrugged. "Okay I guess. She's been in with Lei for about fifteen minutes. You figured out where Friday's gonna stay?"

Shaine made a face. "Space is pretty tight. No singles, and I don't want her in with everyone else. I can put her in with Del, but not sure I feel comfortable with that."

Morgan said, "No telling what Del might teach her. Probably end up drunk and learning how to throw a dagger. She could probably bunk in with us, though, couldn't she? We can grab an extra cot. It'd be crowded, but—"

Shaine sighed. She knew it was the obvious answer, but it sure as hell wasn't her first choice. "Crowded?" she repeated. A glance told her they were alone in the hallway and she stepped in front of Morgan, easily picking her up and trapping her against the wall. Morgan grinned, wrapping her legs around

Shaine's waist, her arms around her neck. Shaine leaned into her, playfully nibbling at Morgan's neck. "You realize there's not going to be any of this with a roommate, hmmmm?"

Morgan groaned softly, twisting her fingers in Shaine's hair, pulling Shaine's mouth to her own. Lips parted, Shaine explored Morgan's mouth, kissing her deeply. Shaine felt the heat pooling between her legs. Morgan ground against her. A flood of need shut down everything but the taste of Morgan's mouth and the heat of Morgan's center against her abdomen.

A throat cleared, rather sharply. "Are you two about done?"

Shaine groaned, sighing as she rested her forehead against Morgan's. "Damn."

Morgan unhooked her legs from Shaine's waist and found her footing. "Shit."

Dr. Nguyen raised a thin brow. "You could at least find a room," she commented, only barely managing to hide her grin.

Shaine felt her face flush. "Actually, that's kinda what started it," she muttered.

Morgan snickered. "So, what's the word, Lei? Is Friday okay?"

Lei waggled her hand. "Yes and no. I'm glad you're both here."

Morgan frowned. Shaine wasn't sure she wanted to hear the rest.

"I wish we had a more private place to talk, but there isn't consulting space down here. I ran a full diagnostic scan. Her radiation levels are fine. She didn't get any exposure." She pushed her hands into her pockets and frowned. "Let's be clear. Friday has not admitted to, confirmed or denied what I'm going to say. I can only attest to what I see. I can suggest what the causes might be, but I am only speculating. Are we clear with that?" Lei looked seriously at both women, who nodded. Morgan's expression darkened and she leaned against the wall, staying close to Shaine.

Lei said, "She's got bruises and welts up and down her back, some new, some older. The scan showed three cracked ribs. They're healed now, but she was probably injured within the last year or so. From a forensics point of view, the welts were likely from a cane or even a whip. She's also been concussed at least twice. Now, the hard part." She paused, taking a breath. "I think she's been raped. There's suspicious bruising and some internal scarring. Friday denied it when I asked if she was injured or attacked either at the colony or previous to being there. But I wanted you to know what I found."

Shaine blew out a long breath.

Morgan paled and swallowed, crossing her arms over her stomach. "Those fucking sons of bitches," she whispered. Her expression was stricken. "Shaine, we have to help her."

"We will."

Morgan put a hand on Shaine's arm. Shaine could feel Morgan's hand shaking even through the fabric of her tunic. Morgan pleaded, "You can't send her back there. Promise me, Shaine."

Shaine looked at her partner. "Take a deep breath, babe. She's not going anywhere. But we're going to need to know where we stand legally on this."

Anger flashed across Morgan's face. "Fuck that. When did you get all politically correct?"

Shaine shook her head ruefully. "When I decided to take on this position." She took Morgan's hands and held them. "Just trust me on this."

Morgan swallowed. "And you need to trust me." She pushed up the left sleeve of her shirt, turning the bared inside of her arm toward Shaine. "Have you ever wondered why this happened?"

Shaine nodded slowly, tracing with one finger the line of tiny, raised vertical scars that tracked from the inside of Morgan's wrist halfway up her forearm. Perfectly spaced lines about two centimeters long, probably a hundred of them, which stopped just before the artery at her wrist.

Morgan said quietly, "I was in a really fucked-up relationship. I was seventeen. She was teaching me to fight so I could compete in the freestyle competition, but everything got out of hand. She said she wanted to toughen me up, and she'd follow the beatings with all this doting attention, and I wanted so badly to be the fighter she wanted me to be. I thought I loved her and I thought I needed her. I thought I deserved the beatings because I wasn't good enough. And it just escalated. I was taking painkillers like crazy, so I could function. I lost more than a year, all hopped up on painkillers, chasing them with hard liquor and swimming into a spiral of blackness. The night I did this, I'd promised Charri I'd go home, but I didn't. I went back to Christie's. When I got there, she was with another woman. I was furious. She challenged me to fight for her. She beat the crap out of me, raped me until I bled, then laughed at me while I laid there, barely conscious, and she fucked her girlfriend in front of me before they both walked out. I don't remember how I got home. I was lucky because I passed out from the drugs and alcohol before I could finish what I started. Another five or ten minutes, and I'd have bled out. As it was, Charri and my dad found me facedown at my kitchen table in a pool of blood."

"Damn, Morgan."

She shrugged. "It was a long time ago. But at least I have an idea what Friday might be going through, if what Lei suspects is true. We need to help her, Shaine. What she needs right now are friends and people she can trust. She needs to feel safe."

Dr. Nguyen nodded. "I'm sorry for what happened to you, Morgan. But you're right. You, more than any of us, are most likely to be able to help Friday."

Morgan nodded.

Shaine put an arm around Morgan's narrow shoulders. She was so out of her depth here. Physical pain and loss, those were things she knew. Friends dying in the line of duty she understood. For a moment it hurt that she hadn't known this huge piece of Morgan's past. Why hadn't Morgan told her? Maybe because it still hurt, she thought. She hoped they might have time to talk about it later. For now, though, they needed to deal with the situation at hand.

She asked, "What do we do? We don't want to tell her what we've talked about here, do we?"

Morgan shook her head. "No. She'd see it as betrayal. She needs friends and protectors right now, and that's what we'll be."

* * *

Shaine watched Morgan and Friday. After only a day, the two were acting like siblings and Morgan had taken on the role of the protective older sister. They had retreated to a corner of the ops center, sitting side by side at an empty work table, heads bent over a comp pad on the table between them. Friday was showing something to Morgan. Shaine assumed that it had something to do with the 3D art and virtual game worlds Friday created. The lanky blond teen spoke animatedly and Morgan nodded, interested and attentive, occasionally asking questions.

Shaine worried about their options for keeping Friday safe. The girl hadn't mentioned her treatment at the colony, other than that they wouldn't let her think for herself or learn anything useful. Friday said she was tired of everyone around her telling her she was wrong or evil or doomed to hell. She had no friends, trusted nobody and had run away out of pure and simple desperation.

Shaine had no intention of returning Friday to the colony, though she wasn't sure how she was going to pull that off. On the upside, Friday was seventeen years old, eighteen in a few months when the issue would be moot. Unfortunately, the radiation storm wasn't going to last that long, so she'd have to figure something else out.

With communications down because of the solar storm, she wasn't able to get word to the colony that Friday had been found. Nor could she contact Earth or Moon Base for any weather updates. She didn't like being so cut off.

She scanned the security monitors. The hardwired outside cameras showed steady, if somewhat static-laden signals, though there wasn't much to see through the fury of the sandstorm that had been blowing for a day. The scientists had set up radiation monitors as well. The external radiation was off the charts. The internal monitors in the above-ground bio-dome showed some uptick in radiation, but nothing damaging or worrisome. The radiation levels underground remained normal.

It was maddening not knowing how long the storm would last. All they could do was monitor the radiation and weather and wait it out. She wished she were better at being patient.

CHAPTER TWENTY-NINE

It took another five days before Ahmed, Shaine and Garren decided, after lengthy discussion with their scientists, that it was safe to release everyone from the underground radiation shelter. By that time, tensions were running high. They'd broken up a dozen fights between bored personnel and the holding cells were full. Everyone had cabin fever and even though they were only moving back to the small temporary dome, there was at least room to breathe. Construction and maintenance work resumed. Everyone had something to do. They had communications and net connections again so there was news from Earth and Moon Base.

Shaine's first task was to contact the Unified Martian Temple of God colony to let them know that Friday was safe at the mining site. She was surprised nobody from the colony had called to check on her. She wondered if their communications were still down. She shook her head and queried for the correct com code to the Unified Martian Temple of God colony.

Morgan walked up behind her. "Hey, Shaine. You going to call the colony?"

"Yeah. Was just about to."

"Fri's freaking out, worried about having to go back."

Shaine sighed. "I'm not sending her back. I told her that. I take it she doesn't want to talk to anyone there?"

Morgan jammed her hands into her pockets and leaned against the edge of the counter beside Shaine's monitor. "She says they can all go straight to hell."

"I think they're already there."

Morgan grinned. "You mind if I listen in?"

"No, I was hoping you would." Glancing at the number on her pad, Shaine punched the calling code into her com board. It took a couple of tries to get the call through, and when it did, the image on the screen was static-filled and scratchy. Shaine squinted at the fuzzy image of a thin-faced woman wearing a dark scarf over her hair. "Good morning. I'm Shaine Wendt, Head of Security at the Mann-Maru construction-site. I wanted to let you know that we rescued your runaway before the storm. Friday is here, and is safe and well."

The woman on screen gaped at her. "You! My God, she's with YOU?"

Shaine blinked and did a double take with her mouth half open.

Morgan looked from one to the other, seeing recognition in both sets of eyes, though with very different reactions.

Shaine shook off her surprise. A cold, businesslike mask fell over her sharp features. "Hello, Flower."

"I want to talk to Friday," the woman demanded.

Shaine considered for several seconds before replying, "Friday's not with me right now. She didn't want to speak to anyone at the colony. In fact, she didn't even want me to let anyone there know she was alive." She fixed an icy gaze on the other woman. "Why would she feel that way?" she asked.

"I don't know. I want to see my sister. She needs some sense talked into her. When will you be returning her?"

Sister? What the fuck? Shaine sensed Morgan stiffen and glanced her way with a tiny shake of her head. She said to Flower, "It may be a while. The radiation is still too high to travel safely." That was a boldfaced lie, but she didn't care.

Flower looked frustrated, then angry. "I'll be in touch," she said and killed the connection.

Shaine sat shaking her head at the blanked screen. "Damn."

Morgan frowned. "Who the fuck was that?"

Shaine rubbed her hands over her face. "My past, haunting me. An ex, actually, who fucked me up for a long time."

Morgan cocked her head. "Didn't look much like your type," she commented dryly. "I mean, Flower? Jesus. Who'd name their kid Flower?"

"Apparently the same people who'd name their other kid Friday." Shaine let her head fall back against the headrest. "Aw, hell, Morg. This is gonna get ugly."

Morgan shrugged. "Might. So, tell me how you knew this person?"

"Ummm, first, can we go and talk to Garren? I want legal in on this mess sooner than later."

Morgan gave her a raised brow. "That bad, huh?"

Shaine grinned and patted her on the butt. "Nope, not that bad, really. I just wanna make sure that I have my ducks in a row before the shit starts hitting the fan."

"Whatever the fuck that means," Morgan muttered.

Shaine laughed and grabbed Morgan's hand, pulling her along toward Garren's office.

Garren looked up from what he was reading when they walked into the tiny space. He smiled. "To what do I owe this visit?" he asked.

Shaine smiled. "Just wanting to brighten your day with my presence," she said. "Have you gotten a message through to legal?"

"I did. Jahn said I'd hear back in a day or two."

"We may need to hear back sooner than that."

Garren raised a brow, and Shaine thought how much it reminded her of his father. "Well, it's like this," she said, and continued to fill him in on the conversation she'd just had with Flower.

* * *

Morgan staffed the security desk with Lukas. She watched the monitors and the com board while Lukas sat at one of the computer stations running background checks on a group of construction workers Garren's people were considering hiring. Gohste was at ops. Shaine was out on the construction-site, doing rounds with Garren and Allim, assessing damage from the storm. Morgan had dropped Friday off in the workshop with Mojo and Joe Hailey, tinkering with a skimmer. Friday loved learning and getting her hands on anything that needed fixing, and the guys had taken to her like a little sister.

Morgan's pad buzzed at her, a message from Shaine with a download included. *Hey Morg. Can u take a look at the attchd file? Thx. Ly S.*

Morgan typed back an acknowledgment and opened the file. It was from Shaine's friend, Kyle Ellerand. Morgan skimmed the document. It contained a brief bio/background on Flower MacKiern. Flower was a former journalist and had worked for UniNet Media as an entertainment reporter. She had walked away from that successful career a little more than three years previously when she married a young man named Alfred MacKiern and joined the Unified Martian Temple of God.

Prior to that, Flower had been awarded custody and guardianship of her younger sister, Friday Whiteson, when their parents were killed in an air car accident on Earth. At the time, Friday had been twelve years old. Friday was seventeen now.

Morgan sat back and considered the information. Being a former journalist, Flower could be in a position to disseminate misinformation if she still had contacts in the industry. She could cause a lot of trouble for all of them.

Morgan was torn about how she felt about this former relationship of Shaine's. Her initial reaction had been jealousy and anger when Shaine had told the story of her disastrous relationship with Flower. The jealously quickly dissipated, but it still pissed her off that Flower had been so cold. She didn't understand how, when dating an ex-EG commando, the woman would be so offended by a little violence—in her defense, no less. Shaine never lifted a finger against Flower. So what if she'd beaten the crap out of a jerk who was harassing Flower in a bar—hell, any decent person would have done the same to defend the honor of her girl. It just seemed extreme to her that Flower could turn on Shaine because of it. Shaine wasn't a monster, or a vicious, dangerous person. Flower, on the other hand, was a freak.

Morgan shook her head. The past was the past. She pushed the thoughts away. What counted now was that they were able to protect Friday from any more violence and give her a chance at making her life what she wanted it to be.

Morgan had seen the effects of violence, long before she'd experienced it herself. Her friend Jaimie had been beaten unconscious by her father. The shock of seeing her lying in that infirmary bed, her face black and blue and bandaged, ribs and arm broken—Morgan shuddered at the memory. She'd been thirteen. It wasn't the first time Jaimie had been beaten by her father. It wouldn't be the last. Morgan had been furious.

She remembered going off half-cocked at Jaimie's father when he came into the hospital room. She'd screamed at him, hauled off and started pounding on him. Josef Leighman was a very large man and simply held her at arm's length once he got hold of her, and called for security.

That had been her first incarceration. Fortunately, no charges were filed. It wouldn't be her last run-in with the authorities, but her self-destructive anger had started about then. With a sigh, Morgan shook off the memories and tried to concentrate on the security screens she was supposed to be monitoring.

When a com call came into the security station, Morgan frowned at the ID, trying to decide if she should take the call from the colony or if she should let it slide through to the main ops console. Finally, she took the call. "Mann-Maru Security."

She recognized the woman on the screen as Flower, and she didn't look particularly happy, nor particularly well-rested. Her blond hair wisped haphazardly out from under her black headscarf. Her face was haggard and she had dark circles under her eyes.

"I want to speak with Friday," she said.

Morgan felt her anger rising. "Friday doesn't want to speak with you," she said. All she could see were the bruises and scars on the girl's back. She wanted to jump through the screen and beat the crap out of this woman who allowed it to happen.

"Who are you to say that? Where is my sister? I demand to talk to her!"

"I'm Friday's friend. She's here. She's safe. And she has nothing to say to you."

"How dare you!"

"I don't 'dare' anything. I'm just telling you what Fri told me. If you want to talk to Shaine, she'll be back in a couple of hours."

Flower glared. "I don't want to talk to Shaine. I want to talk to my sister. What's your name?"

"Morgan. Morgan Rahn. R-A-H-N."

"You'll hear back from me, Ms. Rahn."

"Fine. I'll let Shaine know you called." She cut off the connection, knowing she hadn't handled that well, and not giving a shit, either. No way those people were going to get Friday back. No fucking way.

* * *

Morgan was happy that Shaine joined her and Friday in the cafeteria for dinner that night. She studied Shaine as she set down her tray and eased her long frame onto the bench. She looked tired. Her shoulders slumped a little. Morgan asked, "Long day?"

Shaine nodded and shoveled a forkful of vegetables into her mouth. She chewed and swallowed, then said, "I've forgotten what it's like to spend that many damned hours in a vacuum suit. It weighs on you. I have the headache from hell."

Morgan nodded. "Yeah. Vac suits, even in partial gravity, suck. Those helmets are a bitch. I noticed it right away when I was out on the site." She dipped a chunk of bread into her stew. "I'll give you a shoulder rub when we get back to the room."

Shaine smiled. "Thanks."

Friday said, "My sister called here today."

Shaine's smile faded.

Morgan frowned at Friday. She had planned to tell Shaine, but was going to wait until later. She said, "I took the call. She wanted to talk to Fri. I told her that Fri didn't want to talk to her. I asked if she wanted to talk to you, and she said no."

Shaine sighed. She lifted her container of juice and said, "Maybe I should've had beer."

Morgan grinned. "Actually, if you sweet-talk me, I have some in our room."

Friday's eyes brightened. Morgan gave her a look. "Not for you, kiddo."

The blue eyes narrowed, "Like you were such an angel at my age," she muttered.

Morgan smiled serenely. "I learned from my mistakes so you don't have to. Besides, there isn't enough for three."

Shaine snickered and continued eating.

CHAPTER THIRTY

Tarm Maruchek was pissed. Morgan could tell by the set of his shoulders, the flat line of his mouth and the intensity of his gaze as he faced them over the vid com. "Have either of you seen today's news?" he asked sharply. His question was aimed at Shaine and Garren, but Morgan felt the bite of it as well.

Shaine sat up in the chair beside Garren's. She looked as though she'd just woken up, which she had, and was nursing a double-caff. Morgan knew she too looked like she'd barely had time to throw on yesterday's clothes. Shaine said, "I haven't had a chance to check the vid feeds yet. We were up most of the night dealing with a power generator issue."

Maruchek didn't appear mollified. He said sharply, "The Unified Martian Temple of God is accusing you of kidnapping one of their members. A juvenile." He glared daggers at them. "I assume you can explain this situation?"

Garren leaned forward against his desk and said, "She ran away from the colony just before the radiation storm. Morgan and Mojo rescued her and she's staying here until it's safe to return her."

"Why do I believe there is more to the story than that?"
Shaine rubbed her temples. "Because there is."

"Care to enlighten me?"

Shaine managed a twisted smile. "Not really."

Maruchek didn't look amused. He simply waited.

Morgan stepped in front of the camera. She said angrily, "They were beating her. They probably raped her, too, but she won't say. Friday's got bruises all across her back and sides. No way she's going back to those bastards."

"That's quite a charge, Morgan."

"It's the truth."

Shaine said quietly, "Friday ran from them. She hijacked a personal skimmer and dismantled their regular transports so that they couldn't follow her. They called us to see if we could find her before the storm broke, which we did, but barely. Doc Lei took a look at her to make sure she was okay. The injuries Friday has are more consistent with beatings over time than any damage from the skimmer crash. She's even had her ribs broken. We have it all documented. Garren put in a call to legal to see what our options were, and we were keeping her here until we heard back."

"And now our hand is being forced. If they were hurting her, why would they put themselves out there like this?"

Shaine sipped slowly at her coffee. "Who reported the kidnapping?" she asked. "Did they give a name?"

Maruchek glanced down at his desktop. "Flower MacKiern, the sister of the kidnapped girl. She was also a reporter with UniNet Media."

Shaine sighed. "Yeah. Great. In this case, I think the accusations are probably aimed at me personally."

Maruchek gave her an impatient glare. "And why would you think that, Ms. Wendt?"

Shaine ran her hands through her hair. It didn't help to make it less messy, nor did it hide the flush on her face. "Because I dated her, a long time ago, and it ended rather badly."

Maruchek shook his head and muttered a string of oaths under his breath.

Morgan protested, "It's not Shaine's fault. We're trying to do the right thing for Friday. If Flower's being a bitch, it's because she's afraid someone will find out they're a bunch of cold-hearted cultists."

"You put the company into a difficult position."

Garren said evenly, "Legally, they can't fault us on this, Father. Friday's injuries were well documented when she came to us. Up until yesterday, it wasn't safe to go out of the radiation shelter, so we can't be blamed for holding her unduly. We've kept her safe. She'd have died out on the surface if we hadn't found her."

"That may be true, and certainly we will get our legal people on this issue. In the meanwhile I need the facts so we can put them out there appropriately. I don't like it when my own publicity people come to me with these kinds of issues. A heads-up would have been a good thing. You, of all people, should have known that, Garren."

Shaine said, "By the time Garren knew about the situation, our coms were jammed by the sun storm. We got a call in to legal as soon as we had a signal, so it's not as if we weren't dealing with the situation."

Maruchek said, "I want a complete report, with all the sordid details."

Shaine and Garren nodded. Shaine said, "It'll be in your hands in an hour."

"Good." Maruchek cut the com link.

Garren rolled his head, popping the vertebrae in his neck. "Well, that wasn't as bad as I thought it would be," he commented.

Shaine scowled. "I'm gonna go and get that report written."

"I'll get you some more coffee," Morgan offered.

Shaine leaned down and kissed her. "You are the best," she said, and, patting Morgan's butt, she slipped out the door.

Morgan flushed and Garren laughed. "You guys are sad," he accused lightly.

"Asshole. You just wish you had such a good-looking girlfriend. I'll drop a coffee off for you too." Morgan grinned and swept out of his small office.

* * *

Morgan joined Shaine in her office the following morning. She leaned against the doorframe, arms crossed over her chest. Shaine leaned back in the desk chair. Morgan could clearly see the vid screen on the desk. Tarm Maruchek frowned slightly as he regarded them from behind his own desk.

The previous day had been a long one. The overindustrious media had run away with the story of Friday being "kidnapped" and held at the Mann-Maru construction-site. They learned that Morgan was on-site, and she was with the Head of Security. Someone made the connection between Shaine and the photos of her and Morgan in the zero-G cube, and then to Shaine having "stopped" the gunmen on Earth. They referred to her as a "security cowboy." The rumors and innuendos ran rampant, fueled by "sources" from the colony describing how "confused and lost" their young Friday was, and how she would be "ruined" by the barbaric infidels at the construction-site. All those rough construction workers, men and women alike—what would they do to poor, innocent Friday? And what was Mann-Maru going to do about it?

The last straw for Morgan was the message she'd received from her best friend Charri, asking what was really going on. At least Charri didn't accuse them of kidnapping. But for Charri to ask, the media had to be absolutely rabid.

Morgan had seen some of the coverage. She and Shaine had walked through the rec room to grab an entertainment pad for Friday and she'd barely restrained herself from putting her fist through the screen in reaction to an "Entertainment Universe" story. Her fury felt like a wild thing inside her, wanting to lash out.

Meanwhile, the Mann-Maru legal and PR departments were busy trying to refute the allegations without making specific claims that Friday was being ill-treated by the colony.

Now Tarm Maruchek faced them, serious and concerned. He wanted Morgan and Shaine to talk to Friday and get her to either admit or deny that she was being abused at the colony. Without a statement from Friday, if she didn't press charges, they had no case and she would have to return to the colony because she was still underage.

Maruchek wanted Friday to press charges against her rapists and torturers. His people would do their best to keep it all under the radar if it were to go to trial. He was convinced if they could bring a legitimate case against the colony, Abraham and his Temple would back down and do everything they could to keep it out of the courts and downplay it in the press. Morgan could see the logic in that, though she hated to put Friday through the trauma.

Shaine said, "We'll talk to Friday tonight."

Morgan added, "If she wants to talk. I don't want to push her."

Maruchek frowned but nodded. "Do what you can." He glanced down at his desk. "I have another meeting. Let me know what happens."

Shaine said, "I'll call."

"Thank you. We'll talk later. Morgan, Shaine." He cut off the connection.

Shaine ran her long fingers through her hair with a sigh, turning in her chair to face Morgan. "As much as you'd rather not, we're probably going to have to be pretty blunt with her about this."

"Yeah. I don't like it, but I think you're right." She straightened and glanced at her wrist chron. "I'd better get going. Joe needed me to help in the equipment warehouse today. Lots of repairs after the storm."

"I've got meetings with Garren and Ahmed most of the morning. Things are ramping up, so we've got a lot of preparation to do. The scientists turned in their final maps of the iron veins, so we're ready to start final plans for the strip mining process. It's going to get really crowded around here before they get the workers' quarters finished in the new dome."

Morgan smiled. "Glad I'm not the one coordinating all that." She dropped a quick kiss on Shaine's cheek and slipped out the door.

Shaine smiled. It was good to have Morgan on-site with her. She felt so much more settled having her around. She loved the connection between them. Some days, though, she worried that she was more focused on her work than Morgan. Not that Morgan seemed to be bothered by it. Besides, Morgan was nearly as busy as she was.

What about the future, though? What would she and Morgan do after this gig? Return to Moon Base? Go back to Earth? She had all but proposed to Morgan back at the farm, and Morgan had accepted. But they hadn't made it official. And they hadn't talked about it since. Is that still what Morgan wanted? To be married to her?

It still didn't answer the question of where they would end up. What did Morgan want? Morgan had skills she could use anywhere. She was a good all-around mechanic. She learned fast. They needed to talk about the future, but they'd been too caught up in the present.

Shaking away the thoughts, Shaine opened the task list on her computer. There were a handful of reports from her security team she needed to read through and sign off on. They were a good group, doing a good job.

Since the incident with the crane and Alec's death, everyone had been on much higher alert. Following the protocols they'd started in the radiation shelter, they continued with frequent, random patrols of the entire complex. She'd instituted site patrols on foot and on personal skimmers during the day. She'd also set a strict guard on the entrance to the warehouse and the external airlocks. The guards were responsible for logging all incoming and outgoing personnel.

She opened the first of the reports and settled in.

The com beeped, a single beep for an internal call. Absently, and without looking up from her work, she opened the connection. "Wendt."

"Got a vid call for you on the main switchboard. From the colony. You want to take it?"

"Yeah, send it through. Thanks, Rita."

The vid screen on her desk flickered to life with the serious faces of Flower and Elder Brother Abraham. Shaine decided to play it pleasant and nonconfrontational, despite the obvious hostility on Flower's face. "Good morning. What can I do for you?"

Abraham said, "The situation with Friday has gone on long enough, Ms. Wendt. She must be returned home. If you cannot bring her to us, we will come to retrieve her."

Shaine nodded thoughtfully and slowly took a sip of her coffee. "I didn't know you had transport there. I didn't see it in the docking bay."

"Just because you didn't see it doesn't mean that we don't have it, Ms. Wendt," Abraham replied. "When do you plan on bringing Friday back to us?"

"Frankly, I will only return her when, and if, I am convinced it is a safe place for her to be. That has not yet happened."

Flower glared. "I demand you return Friday to us! She belongs here!"

Abraham leaned forward and said more evenly, "You have no right to keep the girl. She is a minor and belongs with her family. It is not your choice to make."

Shaine managed to keep her face blank despite her boiling rage. "Unfortunately, Friday has refused to return to your colony. She doesn't want to be there."

There was a knock on Shaine's door. It slid open, and Friday poked her head in. "Shaine, have you seen Morgan? I thought she was—" She stopped short with a gasp as she recognized the faces on the screen.

"Friday! My God, are you all right?" Flower exclaimed.

The tall girl stepped guardedly into the room, folding her arms over her chest. She licked her lips and her blue eyes hardened with dislike and disgust. "Of course I'm all right," she said. "Better than I've been in a long time."

Shaine watched Friday with concern. The girl's focus was solely on the screen.

Flower said, "You must come back to us, sister."

Abraham added, "Yes. Your family is here, young Friday. You belong with your family."

Friday choked on a laugh. "You are not my family. Family doesn't beat and rape their children. I'll die before I go back to that hellhole."

Shaine stifled her reaction to Friday's very flat statement.

"You lie!" Abraham hissed.

"Fuck you, Brother Abraham. I don't lie. I've got the scars to prove it."

"Shameful, ungrateful heretic! I am sure you got the scars from them!"

Shaine stood, leaning into the camera, and said firmly, "Friday will stay with us. This discussion is over." She killed the connection with a vicious stab at the console and turned toward the young woman in the doorway.

Friday shuddered, practically falling into Shaine's tight embrace, all her bravado dissolving into gasping sobs. Shaine held her and stroked her hair, and whispered into her ear. "It's gonna be okay, Fri. We're your family, if you want us. Me and Morgan." She knew as she said the words that she meant it more than she'd ever meant anything in her life.

Shaine took Friday back to their quarters. After their stay in the radiation shelter, Friday had moved in with Shaine and Morgan in their regular quarters. Shaine considered Friday too vulnerable to be on her own, and since she was now her and Morgan's responsibility, Shaine wanted the teen where she could keep an eye on her. Not because she was afraid Friday would do anything wrong, but because she was afraid someone else would make Friday a victim. Shaine wondered if she were becoming her mother.

She got Friday settled with the entertainment pad.

"If you need anything, call me, okay? Or call Del. She's in ops all day. Morgan is in the warehouse, so as long as she's not out in a vac suit, you can call her too. Are you sure you'll be okay?"

"Yeah. I'm okay. Thanks, Shaine. I just need some time to chill."

"All right. I'll come get you for dinner later, then."

Friday managed a weak grin. "I'll be here."

* * *

After dinner, Morgan put on water for tea and went down to the cafeteria to get cookies. Everything was better when it involved cookies and tea. And she wanted Friday to feel comfortable and loved and cared for. They all settled on Shaine and Morgan's bed. Friday sat cross-legged at the foot with a blanket pulled around her shoulders. Shaine stretched out, propped on a pile of pillows. Morgan sat beside her, leaning against the headboard, a quilt pulled up over her lap. They all held their tea in spill-proof mugs and the cookies were on a plate in the middle of the bed.

Slowly, Friday told them about her parents' death in an air-car accident. As her only remaining family, Flower became her guardian. It had been okay for a while, until Flower married and joined the Unified Martian Temple of God with her husband. Flower quit her job and they moved into a small commune in Phoenix run by the Temple. Her peacenik sister changed from being "normal" to spouting all the narrow, strict dogma that her husband believed.

Flower tried to get Friday to believe it too. Friday fought back, but what could a fourteen-year-old kid do? She just quietly played along and secretly clung to her personal beliefs, her books, her drawing and her computers. But even that fell apart when Flower and her husband moved them to the colony on Mars two years ago. Because the commune had been small and in the city, she'd at least had some freedom and she was still enrolled in public school. At the colony, education was replaced with religious dogma. Her computer and books were taken away.

Friday had been on a fast track in computer science and engineering, creating virtual holo-worlds for gaming and media production. At the colony, she was not allowed to pursue what was seen as "unsuitable" work. She tried to work secretly on a computer that she put together with scavenged and stolen parts, but when that was discovered she was severely beaten and punished.

After that, she stole a comp pad from a distracted maintenance worker and started working with that. When her sister's husband found the pad hidden in her room, she was beaten again, this time so severely she ended up in the infirmary. When her drawings were discovered, her sister was outraged at the subject matter. A great deal of it was fantastical, with dragons and fairies, and erotic depictions of women with women. This time, rather than beatings, the punishment was rape, to teach her the correct role of a woman in a relationship.

Morgan was sickened and angry. Sometime during the telling, Friday crawled up between Morgan and Shaine, and they held her tightly while she told her story. Morgan struggled not to transfer her fury to Friday by verbally lashing out at the Temple Elders or her sister. This was Friday's time to be angry or sad or hateful or shamed. She and Shaine repeatedly assured Friday that no matter what happened she would always have a place with them

"You guys are the best, really." Friday hugged them both as tears slid down her cheeks. "You don't know how much this means, having you."

Morgan smiled. "We're just glad to be here for you."

After a few more sniffles, Friday wiped her eyes with the back of her hand and got up off the bed. She went to the small trunk at the end of her cot and opened it. When she returned to take her place again between Morgan and Shaine, she had two things in her hands. One was an older model comp pad. The other was a data chip. She handed the data chip to Shaine.

Shaine looked at her questioningly.

Friday licked her lips. "There's a couple other reasons they might want me back there," she said. "Some of it's on that chip."

"What's on here?" Shaine asked.

Friday frowned. "I got really angry after the rape," she said. "I figured, with all that was going on, there had to be something they were hiding. So I went fishing. I ran some 'bots and hacked into their systems. They're really clueless about security. Abraham has been siphoning off funds for years, mostly to support all his wives and children. There's also record of all the payoffs to authority justices to look the other way anytime anything was reported. And records of the punishments dealt out. A lot of women have been raped and beaten. And minors, too. Like me. Not just girls. There've been boys too. It's all on there. If you want to remote connect to their systems, I have that set up too. I tried it last night, and the connection is still available."

Shaine leaned her head back against the pillows, considering.

Morgan asked, "Do they know you have this information?"

Friday shrugged. "They probably suspect. I'm pretty sure they were afraid I could hack their systems. I think that's the real reason they didn't want me to have access to a computer. They didn't trust me."

Shaine gestured to the comp pad. "And that?"

Friday handed it over. "It's Abraham's top man's personal comp pad. Brother Daniel John. He kept a journal. I'm in it. He included descriptions of all the women and girls he's raped. The beatings he's given. It's pretty sick. He gets off on it. He left it unattended on a park bench. It went missing."

Morgan whistled.

Shaine sighed. "You do realize that stealing is illegal? And because the diary is stolen, it can't be admissible in court?"

Friday nodded. "I know. But if the information could be leaked to the press, unofficially…" She shrugged. "Maybe it would get them off my back, or start a real criminal investigation."

Shaine rubbed her face with her hands.

Morgan tried very hard not to laugh. It wasn't funny, but, honestly, the kid was just too much. With Shaine's contacts—with Kyle Ellerand—it would be so easy to do just what Friday suggested.

Shaine sighed. "Okay. I need to talk to Maruchek about this stuff. I don't think we can do anything with it from a legal standpoint."

Friday muttered, "Maybe it'll accidentally go missing from here, too."

"Maybe Kyle would have some ideas," Morgan added quietly to Shaine.

Shaine gave her a glare, then said to Friday, "The first thing you need to do is disconnect that remote access."

"Why?"

"Because it's suspicious, it looks bad for you, and it's probably illegal. I'd like to get through this without going to jail."

Friday scowled. "I'll do it tonight."

"Thank you."

Morgan added, "I'll stand over her shoulder and make sure she does it."

Friday glared at her, and Morgan grinned. "Hey, I was your age once," she said. "I know all the tricks."

* * *

Shaine called Maruchek the next morning, not really looking forward to the conversation. Maruchek answered the vid-call from his own desk.

"Good morning, Shaine."

"And good evening to you," she replied.

"Should I assume you were able to talk to Friday?" he asked.

Shaine stopped smiling. "We did, yes."

"Why do I get the feeling I don't want to hear any of this?"

"Because you probably don't." Shaine sighed. "The short version first, then we can talk details and what you want to do about it. Friday told us about the rapes and beatings. I think she'll agree to give a statement to the authorities. Second, she came into possession of a comp pad belonging to one of Abraham's right-hand boys, as well as a data chip full of hacked data that she intended to use against Abraham. She said there's a lot of damning evidence in it. I haven't looked at it yet."

Maruchek pinched the bridge of his nose with a heavy sigh. "Okay. I'll contact my lawyers when we get off this call. Make sure that Friday is okay to give a statement and answer questions about what happened. They will want names and dates if she can give them. The interview will be with the system authorities, our lawyers and Friday. Either you and/or Morgan are also allowed since she's a minor. Friday can press charges if we feel we have enough information, and that should squash this whole thing."

Shaine nodded. "I'm sure she'll be okay with that. I get the feeling she wants to deal with this instead of ignoring it. She's a tough kid."

"A lot like you and Morgan," he commented with a smile. "Now, the comp pad. That's not permissible evidence. But you know that."

Shaine nodded. "I know that. Friday does too, but seems to think that it can be 'leaked' to the media, to fuel the fire against Abraham and his people."

Maruchek blew out another heavy sigh and leaned back in his chair. Shaine thought he was getting tired of dealing with high maintenance women. Not that Morgan was high maintenance—she just brought a whole new serving of issues to his already full plate. And now they'd brought Friday into their collective lives. Shaine didn't figure Maruchek was ready to have a seventeen-year-old added to his list of responsibilities. He had the same look her stepfather used to have when she was Friday's age and had just gotten on his last nerve.

Shaine said, "I was going to talk to Kyle Ellerand."

Maruchek actually closed his eyes and rubbed his forehead for a moment before nodding slowly. "Whatever you talk about, I don't want to know," he said flatly.

"I'll talk to Friday again about making a formal statement to the authorities. Let me know when you have a meeting time set up."

"I will. Thank you, Shaine."

"Sure. Have a good evening, Mr. Maruchek."

He shook his head and smiled at her. "I think you can probably just call me Tarm," he offered. "After all these years, and now that you and Morgan are together."

Shaine felt her face flush, but she nodded. "Tarm, then."

"Good night, Shaine." He logged off, still smiling.

Shaine blew out a breath. She double-checked her encrypted line and speed-dialed Kyle Ellerand's com code.

CHAPTER THIRTY-ONE

While Friday was showering, Morgan took the time to spend a few minutes with her journal. She jotted a date on her pad with her favorite lime-green stylus. She thought about the past couple of days, which had been busy. After cloning its internal data cache, Shaine sent the stolen comp pad in a sealed package to Kyle Ellerand via supply shuttle. Friday met in a vid conference with Maruchek's lawyers and the system authorities to press charges against Elder Brother Isaiah Abraham and Brother Daniel John.

About the time the media got wind of the charges against Abraham and John, they also received copies of a diary that made Abraham and his people look very bad, and underlined the charges Friday filed against them. The names of the other victims were removed from the accounts, but it was clear who the perpetrators were alleged to be.

Abraham insisted the diary was a fake, and described Friday as a delusional teenager, angry with her elders and egged on by Mann-Maru employees at the mining site where she was being held. They focused on Morgan and Shaine as dangerous influences on the girl, citing Morgan's penchant for fighting in grav ball games, the inappropriate violence Shaine learned in the EG and their "unnatural" relationship. Snippets of Abraham's impassioned speeches played in regular rotation in the entertainment gossip media.

Morgan was glad that, so far, neither she, Friday nor Shaine had been harassed by the workers on-site. Of course, many of them knew the story of how Mojo and Morgan had rescued Friday from the radiation storm. Enough of them had worked with Morgan and Friday to know the accusations didn't ring true. Friday seemed happy and relaxed with both Shaine and Morgan, and was settling in well at the base. Morgan and Shaine were valued and trusted members of the staff. Shaine had a reputation for being fair and even-handed, Morgan for being an easy-going and hard-working crew member. Morgan hoped attitudes wouldn't change.

Friday finally emerged from the sonic shower. Morgan finished her journal entry and shut down her pad as Friday dressed, then they headed to breakfast.

The cafeteria was busier than usual. Morgan left their jackets at one of the bench tables to save them a couple seats while they went to the dispensers to get their breakfast. Morgan watched people come and go as they ate. She noticed a lot of new faces—mostly men, but also a few women. There always seemed to be more men out system. On Moon Base, it was fairly even between the sexes. Guys just seemed to be more comfortable with the temporary nature of out system construction work.

Friday asked, "We gonna finish up those two skimmers today?"

Morgan nodded. "Yeah. We'll start there, then we'll see what else Joe has for us. Shaine said Garren started running a midnight shift in the new dome for building construction, so we may end up over there if they need extra hands or gofers."

"I haven't been in there, so that'd be cool."

"I was, day before yesterday, but they were having issues with the life support system, so everyone was in suits, just in case."

Friday said, "I got that game code to run last night."

"Yeah? How late were you hiding under your blankets doing that?"

Friday grinned. "I don't know. I didn't check the chron. You guys were out cold though."

"Well, if you're falling asleep on me later, I'm sending you back to quarters, right? I can't have you out of it if we go outside. That's rules."

"I know. I'm good. I'm not an old lady like you."

"Smart-ass kid." Morgan pointed a fork at her younger charge. "You better mind your manners."

Friday made a face and giggled. Morgan gave her a mock angry glare and they both laughed.

Morgan swallowed the last of her pancakes and licked her lips. Suddenly, Friday set her fork down very carefully, her eyes focused across the room. Her smile was gone and her brow furrowed.

"What's up?" Morgan asked quietly.

"That guy over there looks really familiar."

"Which one?" There had to have been twenty guys in the general direction Friday was looking.

"Next table, facing us, third guy in, shoveling food into his mouth."

Morgan tried to look surreptitiously. He was an average guy with dark hair cut short and neat, clean shaven, nothing stand-out about him. Morgan asked, "Familiar from where?"

Friday hesitated. "From the colony, I think. I'm not sure what his name was. They kind of all looked and acted alike. I think he did maintenance in the colony dome."

"You're sure?"

"I think so, yeah."

Morgan took a good look at him. She'd tell Shaine about him if they ran into her at lunch, or if she got a chance to com her. Later on, they could show Friday photos of the new personnel who'd come in during the last couple weeks and Friday could point him out. If he was really from the colony, they needed to take a closer look at how in the hell he got hired in the first place.

* * *

Shaine had breakfast with Morgan and Friday the next morning. She perused her work mail via her comp pad as she sipped her coffee and finished her toast.

Morgan asked, "Anything on the guy Friday recognized?"

"Just reading the report now." Shaine scanned through the rest of the document and finally shook her head. "Nothing. Everything about him checks out. Hired from Earth. He's an electrician. We brought him on for work in the new dome. His name is Andy Lenz. Fingerprints and palm-scan all checked out. He has a verified transcript from one of the North Am trade schools. Last job was on Moon Base, doing electrical systems upgrades at the spaceport. Lukas ran standard backgrounds, which come up clean. No criminal record. Lukas did some deep searches and digging around and got nothing."

Morgan asked, "What about Ellerand?"

"I sent him the pic and what I had to see if he could come up with anything else. I haven't heard back yet. I'll check in with him when I get to my office."

"I'm sure it was him, Shaine," Friday said. Her expression was serious and earnest. She set her fork down.

Shaine sighed. "I believe, you, Fri, I really do, but unless I can actually prove that he isn't who he claims to be, there's nothing I can do but have my people keep an eye on him."

Friday nodded but didn't look convinced.

"We'll keep our eyes open, too," Morgan said, touching Friday's arm. "Come on, we need to get down to the warehouse."

Shaine said, "If there's anything on this guy, we'll find it."

Morgan smiled. "I know. See you later, Shaine."

* * *

Morgan and Friday caught a closed skimmer ride into the new dome's docking bay along with Joe Hailey and three others.

They were partially suited, carrying their gloves and helmets. Some sections of the new dome were still having intermittent issues with life support as new sections came online, and there were occasional power outages for system updates. Morgan was only slightly annoyed with the need for suits. She took the vagaries of maintenance work in stride, but she could see Friday was struggling with the weight of her suit and the restriction of movement. As they trudged out of the docking bay, helmets in hand, Morgan said, "Depending on what's going on in our work area, we may be able to take the suits off."

Friday muttered, "I sure hope so."

Joe Hailey laughed and said, "The maintenance bay is sealed and powered separately, so we can take the suits off."

"What are we working on today, Joe?" Friday asked.

"We got all the rest of the bunks and self-standing closet units for the barracks. You guys are helping my crew put them together."

Friday's disappointment was palpable. "Grunt work," she groaned.

Morgan gently swatted her arm. "Get over it, kid. Life is full of grunt work."

When they got to the maintenance bay, there were already three others working on unboxing all the parts. Morgan grinned, recognizing Nate, Lauren and Annie. She and Friday unsuited and pitched in. Morgan was happy to be busy. She took charge of Friday, giving instruction and direction when needed and trying her best not to hover. For the most part, Friday did well.

As they finished building the bunk frames, they lined them up near the bay door. Other crews came to pick them up and transport them on indoor skimmers to the barracks building. Morgan wasn't paying a lot of attention to who was coming and going, but at one point, Friday stopped working.

Frozen in place, still holding a power screwdriver, Friday stared wide-eyed toward the door. Morgan followed her gaze. The man Friday had pointed out, Andy Lenz, stood with one hand on a bunk. He was staring back at Friday, and for an instant,

Morgan would have sworn she saw something—some not quite definable emotion—flit across his face before he turned quickly away, pushing a hand-skimmer out of the maintenance bay.

Friday's face was pale, her eyes wide. "We need to leave now," she said.

Morgan stepped over to stand beside her. "He's gone now, Fri. And you're here with us. Let's just keep focused on what we're doing okay?" *Oh, that's lame,* she thought.

Friday said, "He recognized me, Morgan."

"It's possible. Let's talk to Shaine again after shift."

"I'm serious. I have a really bad feeling about him."

Morgan could feel the panic, hear it in Friday's voice. How could she defuse this and reassure Friday, without making her think she didn't believe her? She touched Friday's arm. "I know you're serious, and I know you're freaked out. But we can't do anything about it right now. We need to talk to Shaine and figure out what's going on, okay? For right now, you're safe, and we're with friends."

Friday relaxed slowly. After a few moments, she nodded. "Okay." She lifted the screwdriver. "Guess we should get back to it, then."

Morgan grinned. "Let's do that."

When they'd done about half of the bunks, Morgan glanced at her wrist chron. Almost done with their shift. Joe Hailey came back toward them. "Hey, Morgan, can you and Friday deliver a skimmer back to the temporary warehouse? You can call it a day, then."

Morgan shrugged. "Sure, we can do that. Hey, Fri, let's suit up. Where's the skimmer, Joe?"

"Over in the hangar bay."

Morgan sighed. Well, that'd be a bit of a walk. The hangar bay was on the other side of the dome from where they were. No wonder she and Friday were volunteered. "Thanks, Joe," she muttered.

He grinned. "I owe ya a beer," he said, and headed back to the maintenance office.

Morgan and Friday trudged across the open grounds of the dome. There were no paved streets yet, the ground just plain Martian gravel, but several buildings had been finished, including the maintenance bay, the flight hanger, and the workers' apartments and communal barracks. Several other buildings were in process, but it was difficult to determine what they were. To Morgan, it felt like a miniature Moon Base. There wouldn't be room for a park or much open space, but at least they could see the sky and the landscape beyond the dome's clear glassteel panels.

They got to the hangar bay attached to the outer wall of the dome. The control room at the rear of the hangar was empty. Once the site was up and running, there would be at least a couple operators monitoring and handling the opening and closing of the bay doors and life support. Morgan glanced around and shrugged. She walked to the row of glassteel windows overlooking the outer bay. One skimmer rested near the personal vehicle exit.

"Guess that's the one we're delivering," she said. "Let's get this done and get some dinner." She helped Friday seal her helmet and gloves and watched as she ran through her diagnostic checks, then got suited up herself. She checked her own diagnostics, making sure all her life support was running correctly, then motioned toward the airlock into the outer bay. She keyed on her com. "Can you hear me?"

"Yeah, I hear ya."

Morgan cleared her throat.

Friday sighed audibly. "Roger that," she amended.

Morgan grinned and started toward the airlock. She could see Friday's suited form just to her left and a step behind her. She keyed the airlock entrance, punching in her personal ID to log her exit. She waited until Friday preceded her into the small airlock and sealed the hatch. The door locked behind them and the inner door released almost immediately. The outer bay was still pressurized since the bay doors were shut. As she led the way toward the skimmer, Morgan said, "We'll make sure the skimmer runs before we pop the outer door. No sense in venting the area if it doesn't."

Friday giggled, "Roger that."

"Smart-ass."

They reached the open bed skimmer. Morgan gestured. "Go ahead and crank it up, Fri."

"Cool."

Friday pulled herself up into the driver's seat. Morgan smiled as she watched Friday's gloved hands touch the different controls and finally press the ignition. She was proud that Friday went through the order she'd taught her, turning on the electrics, checking the power feed, making sure she was in neutral and then finally hitting the ignition. It wasn't a big deal, really, but it made her feel good that Friday cared enough to listen and follow directions.

"Good job, Fri. Leave it running and I'll open the small bay door."

Friday asked, "Can I drive?"

"Sure. Why don't you pull up to the door?"

She watched as Friday eased the skimmer to idle in front of the door. Morgan walked over to the controls at the side of the garage-sized door and punched in her ID again. Only certain people had authorization to open the outer doors, primarily shift leads and security or ops personnel. Morgan was glad she was among them. As she was about to hit the open button, the lights flickered. Morgan turned.

A figure in a standard-issue vac suit stood in the hangar bay, the airlock door still open behind him. The suit's faceplate was clear and Morgan recognized Andy Lenz immediately because he turned to face her.

Morgan punched the button to open the small bay door. It rolled up, venting the atmosphere in the hanger. As Morgan climbed into the passenger seat, she said, "Pull out and stop so I can close the bay door."

Friday eased the skimmer through the door and parked just beyond it. Morgan swung down to the sand and walked back to the doorframe. She keyed outer control panel.

As the door began to shut, she looked to the back of the bay. Andy Lenz still stood at the airlock, watching. Morgan felt a chill run through her. Frowning, she pulled herself back up onto the skimmer, standing just behind Friday's shoulder. "Let's go, Fri."

CHAPTER THIRTY-TWO

Morgan leaned against the bathroom door as Shaine brushed her teeth. Their quarters were quiet and dark. Friday was half-asleep in her cot, blankets pulled up to her chin. Morgan could hear the music blaring in the teen's ear pods. It made her smile to herself, thinking about how many times her dad had told her she was going to go deaf with that "damned crap you call music" blaring in her ears.

In this case, it was good to know that Friday wasn't listening to their conversation. Morgan said quietly, "I don't know, Shaine. It was really creepy. He was just standing there, watching us. There's something going on with that guy."

Shaine spit out toothpaste. "I'll talk to Kyle again. But the guy checks out." She rinsed out her mouth, frowning. "I don't like it, either. I don't like that the data is so damned clean. No dirt, no nothing. He hardly has a presence on the net at all. No avatar, no social sites, couldn't even find a mail account for him. Unfortunately, you can't prosecute someone for being a hermit. Hell, I don't even have a reason to pull him in for questioning."

Morgan nodded. "I know. I just want to make sure that someone's watching this guy."

Shaine smiled as she turned out the bathroom light. Morgan led the way toward their bed. "I've already got him listed as a close watch. I'll keep our people on him."

Morgan slid beneath the covers.

Shaine crawled in and stretched out on her back and Morgan curled up against her. "No more business, okay?" Shaine murmured.

"No more business." Morgan leaned up for a kiss. "Love you, Shaine."

"Love you, Morgan."

* * *

Morgan left the maintenance bay and hurried down to ops and Shaine's office. She wasn't upset at the sudden call down to security, but she had to wonder what was so important that Tarm Maruchek wanted to talk to both of them. She figured it had to be something to do with Friday.

She gave Gohste a wave as she strode into ops and along the wall to Shaine's office. She knocked on the door, then palmed the opener on the frame and entered the room.

Shaine turned from her desk. The monitor was on, and Tarm was already on the line. "Hey, Morg," Shaine greeted.

Morgan smiled. "Hi, Shaine. Hello, Dad. What's going on?" She pulled over a chair and sat down next to Shaine.

Tarm said, "We were discussing public relations."

"Public relations?" Morgan frowned.

"All of the blowback from this situation with Friday has put you back in the limelight, Morgan," Tarm said. "Everyone is asking questions, and aside from 'no comment,' we aren't giving them the answers they want."

Morgan folded her arms over her chest, not liking the direction the conversation was headed. "I have nothing to say to the press," she said flatly.

Maruchek continued, "We've got the media on our side with the investigations and the leaks that have come out regarding the behavior of the Temple Elders. But we need to put a face on what's happening."

"What do you mean, 'put a face on it?'" Morgan asked warily.

"If the public is going to get behind a cause and support it, it makes it easier if there is a face they can associate with that cause, and a real person behind it. In this case, that person is you, Morgan."

Morgan's eyes formed slits and she shook her head. "Uh, no. I don't think so."

Maruchek said, "I know you're not comfortable with this, but it's important. I set up an interview with Kathryn Leer. You need to do this, Morgan. It will let people see you for who you are. They'll see that you're not the bad guy, that you're just an everyday person. You're not a kidnapper, or someone who's playing up to me just for the money. In the long run, this will keep the press off your back far more effectively than you avoiding the whole situation."

"Meanwhile, I'm plastered on the vid screen, and everyone is staring at me and making up what they want to believe anyway. No way. Let them think what they want. The people who know me know the truth."

"Which is precisely the point," Maruchek countered. "The public wants to know you, Morgan. They've heard rumor and innuendo and false accusations. Let them hear your side of it and see you as you are and not as they imagine you to be."

Morgan scowled. She looked to Shaine. "How about some help here?"

Shaine managed an apologetic shrug. "I think he's right, Morg."

"It's just one interview," Maruchek said. "I know Kathryn Leer well. She won't back you into any corners or ask trick questions. You can vet all the questions ahead of time."

Morgan sighed heavily and slouched in the chair. She felt like a whiny kid, but couldn't shake the reaction. "I don't want to be a celebrity. I don't want everyone knowing all my business. It's my life, damn it."

"And right now everyone is poking into your life, trying to figure out who you are. They want to know you. In my experience, I've found that giving the public something, even a single interview, will take the pressure off and they'll leave you alone. They'll have their answers."

"You're sure?"

"I've been doing this for decades, Morgan."

"And Kathryn Leer is coming to us? To Mars?"

"Yes. She could do it via a vid-link, but we agreed it would be better to do the interview in person."

"Okay. But just this once."

Maruchek smiled. "I will arrange things, and let you know when to expect Kathryn. She'll probably have a small crew with her."

Shaine nodded. "We'll be ready."

Morgan just frowned.

* * *

Five days later, Morgan reached across the security communications board and pinged Shaine's rom. Shaine acknowledged her page. Morgan said, "Hey. The shuttle's on its way down. I'm going to let Garren know and see if Fri wants to go down and meet Kathryn Leer. Are you meeting us?"

"I'll meet you there, yeah. I'm at the labs. Make sure the docking crew puts an umbilical out to the supply ship, okay?"

"Roger that. See you down there." Morgan made a quick call to Garren and another to Friday, who was in the middle of something on her computer, and opted out of the meet and greet. Despite her discontent with the interview situation, she realized she was looking forward to actually meeting the famous Kathryn Leer. The Universal News Syndicate reporter had risen up the ranks from a local anchorperson to handling in-depth investigative reporting and later, interviews of high-ranking political figures and celebrities. She was known for her sharp wit and pointed questions, as well as her ability to tell incredibly haunting stories about ordinary people doing extraordinary things.

By the time Morgan got to the warehouse, the supply shuttle had landed. Joe Hailey's docking crew was finishing connecting the umbilical between the ship and the airlock. Garren came in just after Morgan arrived. Shaine jogged up to join them a couple minutes later.

Kathryn Leer led the group emerging from the airlock and into the warehouse. She stopped and looked around with interest, smiling widely when she saw Morgan, Shaine and Garren. She walked quickly toward them and they met her halfway.

Garren stepped forward, holding out a hand in greeting. "Welcome to Mars, Ms. Leer."

"Thank you. I'm pleased to be here." Kathryn gripped his hand firmly.

"I'm Garren Maruchek, the site administrator. This is Shaine Wendt, our head of security. And this is Morgan Rahn."

Morgan was surprised that the famous interviewer was barely taller than herself. And yet Leer seemed large than life, despite being rumpled from the three-day flight from Earth. She wore her sandy brown hair in a short, sophisticated style, a bit tousled, but attractive. She had gentle blue eyes and a genuine smile. She wore a casual shipboard jumpsuit, in tones of blue, and low boots.

Leer turned her attention to Morgan. "Ms. Rahn, I'm glad to meet you. Your father speaks very highly of you."

Morgan felt her face flush. "Um, good to meet you too," she responded. She wasn't sure what else to say.

"I hope you and I will have a chance to sit and chat a bit before we do the interview. Then you'll have a chance to ask any questions and get a little more comfortable."

"Sure, we can do that."

Garren asked, "Where do you want to set up for the interview?"

One of the crew behind Kathryn spoke up, "Would it be all right to take a look around to find a good spot for filming? I want to get a feel for this place."

Garren nodded. "Absolutely."

Shaine said, "I can assign someone to show you around the public spaces. We set up a secure area here in the maintenance bay where you can store your gear."

The man nodded and held out a hand. "Rog Metlend, head videographer."

Shaine grasped it.

Garren said, "We have guest quarters set aside for you, if you'd like me to show you where they are?"

Kathryn Leer nodded. "That would be wonderful, thank you. I think we could all use some time to freshen up before we get started."

"We also have dinner set for six p.m. in the cafeteria, if that's all right?"

Kathryn Leer answered for her group. "That would be lovely."

Garren smiled. "Excellent. I'll show you where you're staying and where the cafeteria is as well."

He offered an arm, which Leer took with a smile, and led them off down the hall.

Morgan and Shaine exchanged glances. "Well," Shaine said, "he's quite charming when he wants to be, isn't he?"

Morgan grinned. "He's a guy, Shaine. And she's a lovely woman and a celebrity. Of course he's going to be all gallant and charming."

"Come on, let's get some coffee before I have to go back to meetings."

"And before I bring Friday to work on a couple flatbed skimmers."

Shaine made a chivalrous gesture of offering Morgan her arm, which Morgan took with a flourish, and they followed the entourage down the hallway.

* * *

In the warehouse workshop, Morgan held a diagnostic comp pad over a skimmer with its engine cover off. Friday stood beside her. Morgan grabbed a couple tools from the workbench behind her, then leaned over the engine, tracing a hairline fracture in the housing.

"See that? The housing is cracked." She glanced at Friday, who nodded. "Gonna be full of sand and dust. That's why it's not firing. The contacts are either dirty or, depending on how long this has been cracked, they're scratched beyond redemption."

Friday cocked her head. "How do you get the housing off? Do you have to remove the whole thing?"

"We have to take the whole module out. We'll have to replace the module housing, or at the very least, seal that crack. To clean the circuit board, we have to pull it out of the module. And hope we can get the housing open without having to use a laser cutter on it. Some of the older ones are built sealed, so there's no other way to get them open."

Friday grinned. "When in doubt, use brute force?"

"Sometimes it saves time," Morgan admitted. She leaned in to loosen a couple of the bolts holding the starter module down, then straightened. "Gotta get the other two from underneath," she explained. She folded herself onto the floor and shimmied on her back under the skimmer.

Friday watched from above as Morgan twisted her hand into the engine to reach the first of the bolts, using a small ratchet to loosen it. Friday said, "Guess it helps to have small hands, huh?"

Morgan swore as the nut popped off and skittered away across the floor. "Small hands help. And bendable tools." She got the other bolt without losing the nut. "Okay, pull the module straight up and out."

"Sure."

Friday got her hands around the starter module and pulled gently, but it didn't move.

"Rock it just a little as you pull, and don't worry about breaking anything."

"Oh!" The part came off in to Friday's hands.

Morgan caught the two bolts that fell loose and shimmied back out from under the skimmer. As she sat up on the floor, she saw Friday freeze in mid-movement. Morgan followed her gaze and saw Rog Metlend near the doorway with a camera focused on her and Friday. She pushed herself to her feet and faced him.

"What're you doing?" she asked. She tried to sound friendly, but the wariness in her voice was more than obvious.

He dropped the camera off his shoulder and smiled. "Just getting some casual film—everyday work stuff, you know? Is that okay?"

Morgan frowned. "I guess it's okay with me. But you'd have to ask Friday if she wants to be on film."

Friday frowned. "Everyone might see me?" she asked.

He shrugged. "If we use the footage, anyone who watched the program would," he said.

"So, if you film me and I'm fine, and I'm happy, they'd see that, right?"

"Sure."

Friday glanced at Morgan. "If everyone sees that I'm okay, then whatever my sister says, they'll know it's all lies."

Morgan thought about that. "It's possible." She looked to the cameraman. "Are we going to be able to see exactly what goes out in the final version? To okay it or not?"

He nodded. "That's my understanding. You'd need to ask Ms. Leer, though."

Friday said, "I don't mind if you film me, then."

Morgan cautioned, "You're sure?"

"Yes. I'm sure."

The man walked over to join them. "So, what are you working on?" he asked.

Morgan said, "Skimmer wouldn't start. We have a lot of issues here with sand getting into things. I was showing Fri how to get the starter module out, and I'll show her how to clean it and test it. Basic mechanics. She's good at it, picks stuff up fast."

"So, you're a mechanic?"

"I am. Schooled for it. I was doing ship systems outer maintenance at the Moon Base docks before we came here. Now I'm kind of a jack-of-all-trades."

He looked at Friday. "You're that kid they're saying is being held against her will, right?"

She straightened her shoulders. "I'm not a kid. And I'm not being held against my will. I will never go back to that place. I like it here, and I like the people here. They let me learn here— like what Morgan's doing now. And I can do my artwork."

He nodded again. "Well, just do your thing. I'm going to be around, okay? If you see me filming something you don't want, tell me, and I'll trash it."

"Fair enough," Morgan agreed, then added, to Friday, "Come on, this thing isn't going to fix itself."

Metlend backed out of their space, wandering around the workshop a bit, shooting snippets of film. Morgan was aware of his presence in her peripheral vision, but as she started showing Friday how to clean the starter and the engine's circuit board, she forgot about Metlend. When she looked for him a while later, he'd disappeared.

It made her think of Andy Lenz, standing in the hangar bay a few days ago, and she frowned, wondering again what he'd been doing there. Friday asked a question, and she put on her game face, pushing the musings away.

* * *

Morgan leaned back a little from the table, feeling comfortably full. The cooks had put together a special meal in honor of their celebrity guests, so everyone had real meat and gravy over mashed potatoes, with cranberry sauce and vegetables. They even had apple pie. It wasn't Jeannette's pie, but Morgan was in heaven just the same, and she couldn't help laughing at Friday who was all but swooning over hers.

All in all, dinner with Kathryn and her crew went very smoothly. Everyone seemed to enjoy themselves. Kathryn was gracious when any of the workers wandered over to say hello and ask for an autograph. Sitting across from her, Morgan was able to observe without being rude, and was impressed by Kathryn's ability to deal so easily with her admirers. Rog Metlend sat beside Kathryn, but spent most of his time talking to Garren, who sat beside him. Shaine sat on Kathryn's other side.

Morgan could see the tension in Shaine's shoulders. Her eyes didn't stop moving the whole time they ate, watching the people around them, assessing, guarding. Morgan decided to grab some leftovers for Shaine to eat later, since she'd hardly touched her dinner. After dessert, Kathryn asked Morgan if she had time to sit down and chat.

Since the cafeteria was still busy, Morgan suggested that they use the quarters she shared with Shaine and Friday. It was crowded, but at least it was quiet.

Morgan led Kathryn down the halls. The reporter was dressed in comfortable but smart-looking black slacks and a turquoise silk tunic with a black leather jacket and low black boots. She walked with her hands in her jacket pockets, and Morgan noticed that she seemed to observe everything. Her eyes never stilled and her expression was interested and curious.

Morgan palmed the lock and the door slid open. Morgan gestured for Kathryn to precede her. "It isn't much," she said, "but it's home." She crossed the room to pull out the chair at the built-in desk. "You can sit here. I'll just pull up a spot on the bed."

Kathryn smiled her thanks and sat down as she looked around. "Will the permanent dome have larger quarters?" she asked.

Morgan nodded. "I'm sure it will. Temporary workers will still stay in the communal barracks. Singles will have at least a small kitchen area, and for families there'll be one or two bedrooms. It's still cramped, but it's better than this."

"A minimalist existence, then?"

Morgan shrugged. "I guess. It's all I've ever known. You value your friends and family more than any stuff you might collect. Even on Moon Base it's like that. There just isn't room for a lot of extras."

"Do you live with Shaine on Moon Base, too? How long have the two of you been a couple?"

Morgan felt her face flush. "Actually, we've only been together a little while, just a few months, really. We both have our own apartments on Moon Base, but we'll consolidate when we go back. There just wasn't time before we ended up here."

Kathryn nodded thoughtfully. She gestured to the small cot against the far wall. "You have an extra bed?" she asked curiously.

Morgan grinned and said, "That's where Friday's crashing. We didn't want her in the barracks with everyone else or all alone, either. She's our responsibility, so it seemed right to just keep her with us."

"Friday is okay with that?"

Morgan sensed a certain amount of disbelief, as though Kathryn was looking for dirt and conflict. She felt her hackles go up and frowned. "We talked with her about it. She was pretty traumatized by what was going on in her life. She didn't want to be alone, either. She needs to feel safe and to have people around her who care and who will protect her. Right now, that's me and Shaine."

Kathryn smiled. "A lot of people wouldn't go so far out of their way to help a stranger."

Morgan shrugged. "Friday's a good kid. She's family now."

"How does Tarm Maruchek feel about the situation?"

"I'm sure he would prefer not to have the extra excitement." Morgan chuckled. "But I think he's glad to be able to help Friday out since she landed in our laps."

Kathryn smiled. "Off the record, how do you feel about your birth father? I don't mean to be forward, but if I know where you stand, I can work around that in the interview. Nothing we say in this room goes beyond this room."

Morgan met Kathryn's deep blue gaze for a few moments. Kathryn's expression was comfortable and open. Morgan sensed sincerity and honesty and wondered if it was real, or just a façade. Her gut told her Kathryn was on the level. Finally, she said, "Maruchek seems to be a decent man. He's been up front and fair with me. I think he's gone out of his way to be very frank with me. He hasn't pushed about anything. He's my father, but he'll never be my dad. I have a dad, Vinn Rahn. I've lived with him all my life, and I love him with all my heart."

Kathryn said, "This must be difficult for you."

Morgan shrugged. For the most part, she realized, she'd come to terms with it. "Sometimes it can be. I was happy the way my life was. But I don't think I can go back to that same life again, and that's hard. What pisses me off is everyone being so interested in my business and judging me when they don't even know me. I don't want fame and fortune. I just want to go to work and have my friends and play some grav-ball and have my life, you know? Still, the thing that's been wonderful about this is that it brought Shaine into my life."

Kathryn smiled. "The two of you seem to be handling things well together."

"So far, yeah. I don't think I could have done this without her."

"You and your brother seem to get on well from what I saw at dinner tonight."

Morgan grinned. "Garren's a good guy. Sometimes I think he's a little naive about the ugly realities of life. He hasn't had to live them. I mean, there's some pretty harsh stuff going on out there. I've seen it firsthand, and I don't think Garren has. But he's not one of those arrogant rich boy types. We have fun. I never had a brother or sister, so it's great to have someone to tease."

"What about the money, Morgan? Will you be inheriting a great deal?"

Morgan frowned. "I don't want the money. I don't need it. I work for a living. And, honestly, we haven't talked about it. Tarm's tried, but I don't want to get into it. He said there's a trust fund for me. I don't even know what's in it."

"Aren't you even curious?"

"I lived my life taking care of myself. Working for a living. Like my dad and mom did. I live in a studio apartment on Moon Base. Money is just trouble. It makes you a target. I don't want that. I don't want to have to wonder if everyone I meet wants something from me."

Kathryn Leer raised a skeptical blond brow. "Don't you expect that to be the case, with or without the money?"

"Maybe. Probably."

Kathryn said, "I will do all I can to keep your privacy yours, Morgan. We don't have to talk about anything you'd rather not share." She smiled. "I have to say, it's a pleasure to interview someone I respect and find to be an honest, decent person. You are one of the few."

Morgan returned the smile. "Thank you."

"One final question, and this one is a more difficult one."

Morgan frowned, but nodded. "Okay."

"There are a lot of rumors and accusations going around about how Friday got to be here, and why she's not gone back to the Unified Martian Temple of God colony. The people from the colony are accusing you of keeping her against her will and turning her against her church. Meanwhile, Mann-Maru is providing legal support for Friday, and she has pressed charges against Abraham and two other Elders, accusing them of child abuse and molestation. Can you talk about what's really happening?"

Morgan ran a hand through her hair. Maruchek had cautioned them about what they said since there was a legal case pending, but at the same time, she knew Friday was anxious to have her side of the story told. Morgan chose her words carefully. "Friday's here because she ran away. She wanted the freedom to live her life, and they weren't allowing it. We're not holding her here. She refuses to return to the colony. We won't make her do something she feels so strongly about, especially if it potentially puts her in danger."

Kathryn nodded. "Are you comfortable talking about this?"

"I know that Maruchek and his lawyers would probably prefer me not to."

"And Friday?"

"What I was going to suggest was that I go and find Friday and we talk to her. She may want to make a statement, or join the interview."

"And your father would be okay with this?"

"That I don't know."

Kathryn laughed. "I like you, Morgan Rahn. Let's find Friday and talk to her."

CHAPTER THIRTY-THREE

Kathryn and Rog Metlend decided to film the interview in the main cafeteria. They liked the normalcy of people wandering in and out, showing the day-to-day workings of the site. Morgan wasn't sure she liked the idea of an audience, but she didn't have any say in the matter. Shaine insisted on a heavy security presence. Since it wasn't a live taping, any belligerent audience members could be removed.

They set up a stage area around one of the bench tables on the side of the room. Someone pulled in a more comfortable chair for Kathryn. The video techs set up lights and microphones around the stage area. There were two stationary cameras and one handheld.

Metlend marked the floor to indicate where personnel should NOT be. Shaine decided not to put up a physical barrier. She had enough security in place that they wouldn't need to worry about anyone crossing the line.

Off to the left side of the stage, Kathryn's hair and makeup artist had his station set up. On another table there was a video monitor for each camera and a soundboard for monitoring and tweaking the input from the microphones.

Morgan stood out of the way, sipping a cup of coffee and watching the tech crew setting up. Friday leaned against the wall at her side, munching on a bag of baked vegetable chips from the dispenser. Morgan thought it was an awful lot of bother for one little interview. But at the same time she was fascinated by all the details.

Friday said through a mouthful of chips, "You nervous?"

Morgan shrugged. "Not so much about the interview. More about what it will bring about. Maruchek said that this will keep the media off my back in the long run, but I don't know if I believe that."

Friday chewed thoughtfully. "I can kinda see his point. You'd be kind of answering their curiosity. Once you do that, they'll know what they want to know and might leave you alone."

"Now you sound like Shaine," Morgan commented.

"I'll take that as a compliment."

"It's annoying, Fri."

"Aw, you love me and you know it." Friday laughed and shoved another chip in her mouth, crunching loudly. She hip-checked Morgan and Morgan hip-checked her back.

Kathryn Leer strode into the cafeteria, pausing at the entrance to scan the room. Seeing the two women, she joined them with a smile. "Hello, ladies."

Friday smiled. Morgan said, "Hi, Kathryn."

"Looks like the crew has things well in hand," she commented. She leaned against the wall beside them and crossed her arms over her chest. Morgan thought she was the epitome of a woman very comfortable in her body and her place in the world. A couple months ago, Morgan could have said the same about herself. She felt like was finally returning to that equilibrium and accepting all the changes in her life, but she still hadn't quite gotten a handle on where exactly she was going.

"Guess I didn't realize how much goes into an interview on the back end," Morgan commented.

Kathryn chuckled. "I've been around it so long, I don't think about it too much. I got a chance earlier to walk around with Del." She shook her head. "I think it would be very difficult to be trapped inside all the time. Even when you go outside, you're trapped in a vacuum suit. Del got me all suited up, and we walked over to the construction-site. I have to say, it was exciting and awing to be out on the planet's surface, seeing the sun from here, and the barren beauty of the landscape. But it was also a little scary and claustrophobic. I've been in a vac suit before, but I don't find it comfortable."

Morgan said, "The colors are interesting here. It's different than on the Moon. Brighter. More dynamic."

Kathryn turned her gaze on Friday. "How do you feel about living out here, Friday?"

The teen shoved her hands into her pockets. "It's okay. I miss Earth, though. Too many rules here. Too trapped in."

"You still annoyed with me for yesterday?" Morgan asked.

Friday scowled. "Yeah, I am still annoyed with you from yesterday. I would have been fine out there, you know."

Kathryn raised a questioning brow. Morgan grinned. "Fri's pissed 'cause I wouldn't let her suit up with me when I went out to the construction-site. She'd been up half the night working on her pad, and was yawning and tired and not concentrating. Rule is, if you're not at a hundred percent, you don't suit up. Period."

Friday said, "There is no such rule."

"I said that was the rule, so that's the rule," Morgan said flatly. "You don't screw around with your safety or the safety of your crewmates."

Friday swallowed and looked away. Morgan took a breath and let go of the surge of anger flowing through her. She was aware of Kathryn watching the exchange. Morgan said quietly, "Careless mistakes kill people. I've seen it. I would rather not see it again, and I would rather not see you go through it, Fri."

Friday simply nodded, staring at her feet.

Kathryn commented, "We tend to forget that the work you do is dangerous."

"Most of the time it's not so bad. But it's easy to get careless. That's when the stupid stuff happens. On Moon Base we have a lot of safety regs and a two-strike safety policy. First time you screw up, you get a warning. Second time you screw up the same thing, you're fired on the spot."

"Harsh," Kathryn commented.

Morgan shook her head. "Necessary." She lifted a hand to point to Kathryn's assistant, who was fussing over the hair and makeup station. "That makeup stuff, is that just for you, or do we all have to do it?" she asked.

Kathryn grinned. "We'll all do a little. It'll keep you from having shiny faces in the lights, or from being so washed out you look sickly. I promise not to let Howard overdo it, okay?"

Morgan laughed and flushed. "Okay."

* * *

Shaine observed the room from the side of the stage area. She was out of the way of the stagehands, but able to see the whole room. She was also close enough that she felt she could be a bodyguard for the women onstage.

By the time Metlend decided they were ready to start taping, the cafeteria had filled with personnel. Most were just there to watch. A few were grabbing a meal or snacks. Shaine scanned the room. Everyone appeared interested and calm. She didn't notice anybody loud or overzealous.

She shifted her focus to Morgan, who sat stiffly in Howard's makeup chair. Morgan looked very typically Morgan—no glitz, nothing different from her usual style. She wore gray cargo pants, her favorite work boots and a faded forest-green tunic with a zippered, high-collared neck, which she left open. Howard fussed with Morgan's short dark hair, much to her chagrin. Shaine could hear Howard grumbling that he could make her look like a princess if she'd just let him. Morgan smiled sweetly and offered to rearrange his face if he tried, while Friday stood near the chair giggling.

Shaine shook her head, glad as hell she wasn't going to be in front of the cameras, and a little guilty that she found Morgan's discomfort amusing.

She scanned the room again, noting her people within the crowd and around the edges. Three sat in the front row. She still didn't approve of the decision for an open taping. But Rog Metlend wanted a realistic setting and to include the workers. He called it artistic license. He wanted to be able to show personnel doing what they did, eating, hanging out, demonstrating to the outside world what it was like to work on Mars. He insisted that it would make Morgan more accessible to the masses, knowing she was living in the same conditions that they did.

Shaine had to admit that other than being paranoid, she didn't have a solid reason to close the taping. After all, Morgan and Friday were with these folks on a daily basis. Kathryn and her crew had been wandering around the halls for the past day without any problems. There would have been ample opportunity for anyone who wanted to cause trouble to have done so already. Garren thought it would be great for morale if the staff got to see Kathryn Leer doing an interview, especially since the camera crew had been wandering around getting random film of the workers.

But she was still spooked by the thought of McKillan sabotaging the crane. And Friday continued to insist that Andy Lenz was from the colony. She had people watching him round the clock, but he hadn't done anything untoward. She told security at the door that she didn't want him at the taping, and that if he showed up, they needed to have someone with him at arm's length every second.

It drove her crazy that even Kyle hadn't found any more than what she and her people had found. She'd been sorely tempted to have Friday reconnect the remote connection into the colony network. But that was a lesson she didn't want Friday to learn—that it was okay to ignore the law just because they wanted to. It was bad enough they'd let her get away with stealing the comp pad. Probably worse that Friday knew they had underhanded ways of getting information through her friend Kyle.

A few years ago, she wouldn't have thought twice about playing fast and loose with the law. Now she felt like she needed to be a good role model. She felt the need to follow the law instead of avoiding it. Well, most of the time, anyway.

Metlend and Kathryn stopped to talk to Morgan and Friday. Metlend pointed to the side of the stage near where Shaine stood then went to talk to one of the camera operators. Morgan slipped out of Howard's chair.

Morgan shot Shaine a nervous grin as she and Friday approached. Shaine smiled back. "How are you doing?" she asked.

Friday said, "Morgan's nervous."

Morgan scowled at her. "I'm not nervous," she returned flatly. "Rog says we're going to get started in a few minutes."

Shaine wrapped her arm around Morgan's shoulders. "Seems like they have everything in hand."

Metlend walked to the front of the crowd, motioning for quiet. "Okay. Can I have your attention, people? We're ready to get started. Everyone see the green light there?" He pointed to a green light on a pole off to the far left. "If the green light is on, you're free to talk. When the light turns red," he paused, and the light turned to red, "that means we're rolling, and we need you to be quiet. You can move around quietly, but please, no talking, and no loud noises."

He waited until there were nods and general sounds of agreement, then smiled. "Great. Thanks, everyone." He turned and went to stand behind the woman who was controlling the camera feeds on the small monitors.

The three camera operators positioned themselves.

Metlend said, "Okay, let's do the intro segment. Kathryn, I need a casual walk onto the set. Do the intro standing."

One of the assistants with a clip pad took her place at the center of the set. "Red set, please." The light turned red and the audience hushed. She held up a digital board with several numbers on it. "Take one. Roll." She strode quickly off the stage.

Shaine could still hear the light clinking of silverware on dishes, the rustle of clothing and the benches squeaking as people shifted. She watched Kathryn take a deep breath, put on her game face and walk confidently onto the set, beginning her opening monologue as she did so.

Shaine divided her attention between the stage and the audience. Kathryn stopped and started the monologue a handful of times before Metlend called it a take. The green light came back on, and the audience breathed and clapped a little bit. Kathryn smiled at them and walked over to the left side of the stage to talk to Metlend.

After a few moments, he said, "Let's do the initial introduction and bring Morgan on." He looked to Morgan. "You ready?"

Shaine grinned encouragingly at her. Morgan returned a rather tight smile before she nodded at Metlend. "Sure."

"Kathryn will introduce you, then you'll walk onto the stage, greet her, and you'll both sit down. Remember, this is casual, so be yourself. It's not live, so there are do-overs, okay?"

Morgan nodded. "Okay."

The assistant with the clipboard took Morgan by the elbow and positioned her just to the edge of the camera's view. "Wait here until Kathryn invites you over."

Morgan nodded again. Kathryn gave her a warm smile. "You'll do just fine, Morgan," she said.

The assistant called for the red light, announced the take number, and they were rolling.

After the introduction they moved into the interview itself. Filming continued to go smoothly. The audience continued to behave. Shaine forced herself to watch the room rather than focusing only on Morgan. At one point, filming had to stop because both Kathryn and Morgan broke into hysterical giggles over a phrase that Kathryn butchered into being incredibly crude. The whole audience laughed with them.

Eventually, Kathryn introduced Friday and she joined the interview. Shaine couldn't help but smile at Friday's youthful enthusiasm. Friday seemed to enjoy her moment in the sun. The tall blond teenager grinned at Kathryn as they talked, then would become serious while making a point. She was animated, but not in an obnoxious way.

Sitting on the other side of Friday, Morgan leaned back with her elbows on the table, hands hanging loose. Morgan's expression was one of amused affection toward Friday most of the time, though Shaine noticed the anger simmering behind Morgan's eyes when Friday talked about her treatment at the colony. Morgan didn't cover her emotions well, and in this case it was probably a good thing.

Metlend called a couple of breaks for everyone to stretch and relax between groups of questions so that he and his techs could review the footage.

Shaine rocked back on her heels. It was becoming a long day. Her people still seemed alert, watching the crowd. The faces in the audience had changed as workers came and left, though the majority stayed for the duration, enjoying a novelty in a place that had a great deal of sameness.

Shaine returned her focus to the interview. Kathryn addressed a question to both Morgan and Friday, eliciting an excited grin and animated talk from Friday and more complacent input from Morgan as she described teaching Friday about being a mechanic and some of the things they did during the day.

While Morgan was talking, Shaine saw a movement at the entrance. She looked across the room to see Andy Lenz storm into the cafeteria. As he cleared the doorway he screamed, "Kill the heretics!" and fired toward the stage.

Morgan grabbed Friday and rolled them both off the bench and onto the floor.

A stream of laser beams seared the air where the women had been a split second ago. Shaine dove past Morgan and Friday and tackled Kathryn to the floor. Stage lighting exploded, showering them all with glass shards.

The room erupted into chaos.

Someone shouted, "Clear! All clear! We got him!"

Shaine rolled off Kathryn with an apologetic grimace. "You okay?" she asked.

Kathryn nodded, wide-eyed. "I think so, yes."

"Morgan!" Friday shouted.

Shaine spun around on her knees, crawling to Morgan's side, ignoring the glass on the floor. "Oh, God, Morgan." Fear made her chest hurt. She snapped at the security guard that rushed toward them, "Get a medic in here, now!" She touched Morgan's cheek. "Baby, talk to me," she whispered.

Morgan swallowed and blinked. "Hurts," she rasped. Her shirt was charred where a hole was burnt through her upper bicep. Shaine could see the reddened, blistered and blackened wound through the hole in the fabric.

"I swear, I'll kill him myself," Shaine muttered.

Morgan managed a watery smile. "My hero."

Shaine leaned down and kissed her forehead.

Another surge of movement and noise came from the entrance. Shaine looked over her shoulder to see three of her people drag the handcuffed gunman to his feet and lead him, stumbling, toward the door. A splash of blood ran down his back from his upper right shoulder where his shirt was ripped. Shaine looked away and brushed a light kiss on Morgan's lips. "Relax. Medical is on the way, okay?"

Morgan nodded.

Shaine turned to Friday. "Are you okay, Fri?"

Friday nodded, wide-eyed. "Scared shitless but fine."

"Stay with Morgan, okay?"

"Sure."

Shaine pushed to her feet.

"Move people! Excitement is over!" Josef and two other men started to break up the crowd and move them out of the cafeteria.

"Josef!" He paused as Shaine caught up to them. "What the fuck, man? How'd he get past our people? And who took him down?"

Josef frowned. "They stopped him at the door and told him he needed to wait to go in because they were filming. Lee said he complied, and was turning away, like he was going to leave or wait off to the side. Lee looked back to the room, and next thing he knew, Lenz was firing. Laney Chrisse was leaning against the back wall. She threw a knife into his back when he ran in and started shooting." He tried hard not to grin. "A steak knife. She was waiting for a break to get rid of her food tray."

"Jesus Christ," Shaine muttered.

"Is Morgan okay?"

"She will be." She glanced over to where Friday sat on the floor with Morgan. "I'll meet you down in security."

"Right." He started to join the other two security officers moving people toward the doors.

Shaine caught his arm and added, "And tell Lee he's officially fired." Shaine returned to the stage area.

Kathryn's crew crowded around her, all talking at once.

Shaine strode up to Metlend. "I think we're done here for the day," she said.

He ran his hands through his hair. "Uh, yeah. Jesus. Maybe we can pick up tomorrow. There isn't much left to do. We've got to clean up those lights and everything anyway. Holy hell."

Kathryn stepped toward Shaine, looking a bit shaky. "Does this happen often?" she asked uneasily.

"No. It doesn't. Are you sure you're okay, Kathryn?"

"Yes, I'm fine. Just a bit shaken up. For all the interviews and reporting I've done, I've never been shot at."

Shaine said quietly, "I don't think you were the target."

Friday looked stricken. "He was one of Abraham's wasn't he?" she asked.

Shaine frowned. "I don't know."

The medics entered the cafeteria at a run with a hover-gurney floating between them and Lei Nguyen in the lead. They stopped at Morgan's side and started taking her vitals and examining the burns on her arm. Dr. Lei shook her head. "You cause me too much work, Morgan Rahn," she said, then to her assistants, "lift her onto the gurney."

Morgan winced as they lifted her. Shaine stepped to the gurney. "I'll be there as soon as I can," she said. She kissed Morgan's forehead again. "Love you," she whispered.

Morgan managed a smile. "Love you too."

The medics started pushing the gurney toward the door, with Friday a step behind them. Shaine put a hand on Friday's arm, stopping her for a moment. "You were right, Fri. I'm sorry."

Friday swallowed. "Just nail the bastard."

"We will."

Friday hurried after Morgan and the medics.

Shaine watched them leave. She turned again to Kathryn. "You're sure you're okay?"

The woman nodded and managed a wan smile. "I'm fine, thank you. Though I think I'd like to go back to my quarters and decompress a bit."

Shaine lifted a hand toward one of the security guards directing people from the cafeteria. "Ben! Come and escort Ms. Leer to her quarters."

He hurried over. "Yes, ma'am." He offered a gallant arm to Kathryn, which she took with a grateful smile. He led her away.

Shaine looked around the room, making sure that things were in hand. Lukas and Whippet rushed in and she motioned to them. "Keep an eye on things here. If anyone needs anything, send others to take care of it. Josef will probably send Keegan down to document and photograph the crime scene. The whole thing should be on video anyway, between the cameras we have in here and what they shot onstage."

"Will do."

"I'm going to ops. If it's an emergency, com me. Otherwise, don't."

"Yes, ma'am."

Shaine left the room, jogging down the halls to ops. When she strode through the doors, Josef and two others had Andy Lenz sitting in a chair in front of one of the jail cells. His shirt was off and his hands were cuffed to the arms of the chair. He leaned forward as a medic attended to the cut on his back. Two armed guards stood at either side of him, guns ready. Josef stood in front of him.

Josef frowned grimly at Shaine as she strode up to him.

The medic straightened. "Six stitches. It's cleaned and bandaged. I'll stop by in the morning to take another look at it and change the dressing."

Josef nodded. "Thanks, Steve."

The medic nodded and packed up his gear.

Shaine said, "Josef, let's talk." She lifted her chin toward her office, and he followed her inside. She leaned against the front of her desk. "What's the story?" she asked.

He scowled. "No story. He won't say a word. On the other hand, I think we know why we can't track this guy."

Shaine raised an eyebrow.

"When we go back in there, take a look at his hands—his palms and fingertips. All completely acid burnt. No prints. He's been wearing synth-skin over the burns. Expensive and practically invisible synth-skin gloves, with someone else's finger and palm prints. Steve cut the gloves off and I bagged them. They're locked in the evidence closet."

Shaine closed her eyes and pinched the bridge of her nose, feeling a headache coming on. "Great. Make sure the doc gets them so she can get a DNA swab. Let's see if we can get anything out of him. Otherwise, we'll throw him in the brig and send him back to the Out System Authority substation on Moon Base and they can figure out what to do with him. My biggest concern is that he isn't alone here."

Josef said, "Right. And if he won't talk now, maybe after sitting in a cell for a day or so, he'll talk later."

Shaine nodded and they left her office. The mystery man Andy Lenz appeared not to have moved a muscle. Shaine said, "Take off the cuffs. I want to see his hands."

Josef gave the two guards a glance, and they brought their weapons up while he uncuffed the detainee. He ordered, "Put your hands in front of you."

Lenz did so without comment. The blank expression on his face didn't change, and he didn't look at either Shaine or Josef.

Shaine took one of his hands in hers, turning it palm up. The skin was smooth and unlined. There were creases where his joints flexed, but even those looked odd. Along the line where the burnt skin and his true skin connected was a ragged, raised scar line, standing out pink against the paleness of the rest of his hands. She noticed he was missing fingernails on at least three fingers.

She asked, "How did this happen?"

He didn't even blink in response.

She tried another tack. "Who were you shooting at? Who was your target?"

Again, she got no response. She nodded to the guards. "Put him in cell one. Let him sit. The authorities can deal with him."

The two men each grabbed an arm and put Lenz in the cell. Shaine turned to Josef. "Did he have anything on him?"

"Yeah. I locked it in the evidence closet with the gun and the gloves. Just a wrist chron, a wallet with his ID and a few credit chits. I sent Ben and Del to go through his belongings in the barracks and his work locker, see if there's anything there."

"Okay. Good. Let me know if they come up with anything. Have Lukas or Whippet do another data search if they come up with any names or anything. Keep Lenz on twenty-four-hour surveillance. I'm going to check on Morgan."

Josef nodded. "Will do."

Shaine strode out of ops.

CHAPTER THIRTY-FOUR

Shaine jogged down the hall toward the infirmary. She could feel the anxiety sitting high in her chest, making her feel slightly nauseous. And angry. Dammit, she was tired of Morgan being shot at. Even if Friday was the target, Morgan was the one who was hurt. Would this bullshit never end? When were they going to be able to find a safe place to stop running?

She reached the infirmary and stopped at the door, taking a few deep breaths to calm herself down. She didn't need to make Morgan crazy too. And she figured Friday was already freaking out. She shook off her anger and frustration and palmed open the door.

The main room, where there were four beds, was empty. Shaine strode through to the trauma bay. Dr. Nguyen leaned over the raised table where Morgan lay. One of her assistants passed her supplies and instruments. Friday stood to the side, watching closely and looking pale.

Shaine asked, "How is Morgan doing?"

From the operating table, Morgan replied weakly, "She's going to live."

Shaine grinned. She rested a hand on Friday's shoulder. "You doing okay, kid?"

Friday nodded. "Yeah. This sucks, Shaine."

"I couldn't agree with you more," Shaine muttered. She moved to the side of the bed. Morgan smiled up at her and met her gaze for a couple of seconds before her eyes fluttered shut.

Lei said, "I've numbed her shoulder and given her a bit of a sedative while I clean and remove the burned skin. When the numbing wears off, she's going to be hurting. I'll send you back to quarters with painkillers. I don't think she needs to stay here. She'll be more comfortable with you. But I will need to check on the wounds tomorrow."

Shaine peered at what Lei was doing. The damaged skin ranged from the outside of Morgan's right bicep all the way up to her shoulder. There were two reddened gouges and one very deep hole where the laser shot had burned further into Morgan's shoulder. Several lines of blackened and charred skin ran along the outside of her bicep. Shaine could also see lightly blistered lines among the more serious burns.

Shaine scowled. She should have been able to stop the attack. Should have seen it coming, predicted it. She shouldn't have allowed the live audience. What the fuck had she been thinking? No matter how much Leer's people had protested, no matter that Garren thought it would be great for the on-site morale, she should have put her foot down.

But she hadn't. Damn it. Her fault. In the end, it had to be her responsibility. She hadn't stopped Lenz. Even worse, she hadn't kept Morgan safe. It crossed her mind to send Morgan back to Moon Base, or to Earth. But there was no way she was letting Morgan out of her sight. It may seem safer at a glance to have Morgan somewhere else, but Shaine didn't think she could handle not having Morgan close.

"Shaine."

She blinked out of her thoughts at the sound of Morgan's voice. "Hey, sweetie," she said, and gently brushed her fingers along Morgan's cheek.

Morgan turned her head and kissed Shaine's fingers. "I know that scowl," she whispered. "It's not your fault. Don't blame yourself."

Shaine sighed. She appreciated the sentiment but she didn't believe it for a minute. She was head of security. Of course the responsibility fell on her.

Friday asked, "What are you gonna do with that guy?"

Shaine thought about it for a few seconds. "Most likely, we'll send him and all the evidence back to the Out System Authorities on Moon Base. There should be enough to convict, between the weapon and the video and eyewitness accounts."

"Did he confess?"

"Not unless he's done so since I left. I doubt he will. We'll file charges and leave it up to the OSA."

Friday sighed heavily and shook her head. "Pretty anticlimactic, isn't it?"

"We're not judge and jury here, Fri, much as we might want it to be that way."

Friday frowned at her. "What about what you did with that McKillan guy? Just bringing him over to the colony? That wasn't exactly what the law would have done."

Shaine sighed. "No, it wasn't. On the other hand, we didn't have enough evidence for charges or a conviction, so it seemed like the next best thing to do. In any case, he couldn't stay here."

"So you follow the rules when it suits you," Friday returned.

Shaine took a deep breath, closing her eyes in frustration. She remembered why teenagers drove her nuts. "Look. When you're my age, and in charge of a security detail, you can make the decisions. Right now, I don't want to hear anymore about it, okay?"

She heard Morgan and Lei chuckle. She sent them both dirty looks.

Friday sulked against the wall. "Whatever," she muttered.

Lei stepped back from the operating table. "I think we've got you all fixed up," she said. "I want you to stay here and relax a little bit, okay?" Morgan nodded and closed her eyes again.

Shaine gently brushed her fingers through the hair on Morgan's forehead, leaned down and kissed her lightly.

Lei turned to her two orderlies. "Please transfer Morgan to a front bed. She'll be more comfortable there."

Lei gestured for Shaine to follow her. Friday remained leaning against the wall.

In the outer room, Lei crossed to the med station and unlocked a cabinet, removing a small container of pills.

"She can have one every four hours. No more than that."

Shaine nodded. "Right." She turned to watch the two orderlies wheel the trauma bed into the room and gently transfer Morgan to one of the beds.

"I want her to rest here for at least a couple hours. If she feels up to it after that, she can go back with you."

"That's fine." Shaine crossed the med bay and sat down on the edge of Morgan's bed. "Hey, Morg," she said softly, taking Morgan's hand in hers.

Morgan smiled tiredly at her. "Hey."

"Doc says you need to get a little sleep before I can take you back to quarters."

Morgan's eyes fluttered. She was having trouble keeping them open. "Okay," she mumbled.

"I'm gonna go and make a few calls back to Earth. You okay if I take off for a bit? Then I'll come back and get you."

Morgan nodded. "Yeah, that's okay." Her eyes shut for a few seconds. "Tired," she breathed.

Shaine kissed her forehead. "You sleep. I'll be back shortly. Love you, Morg."

"Love you too," came the sleepy reply as Morgan's eyes shut again. Moments later, her breathing evened out. Shaine held her hand for a couple minutes more before she stood up. Friday sat down on the bed next to Morgan's.

The teenager gave Shaine a slightly wary look. "I'll stay with Morgan," she said.

Shaine nodded. "Thank you, Friday."

The girl shrugged. "Actually, I can use a nap," she admitted.

"I'll be back in a little while. Com me if you need anything."

"Sure," Friday said, and stretched herself out on the bed.

Shaine hesitated a moment, then smiled encouragingly at the teenager. "It'll all work out, Fri."

"I know. Thanks, Shaine."

Shaine nodded and left the infirmary. As the door shut behind her, she pulled out her com and tapped in Garren's com code. "Garren?"

"Hey, Shaine. I just talked with Josef."

"We need to talk to Rogan and your father," she said.

"Meet me in my office. I'll get them on the line."

"On my way." She tapped the com off and pocketed it.

When she palmed open the door to Garren's office, Tarm Maruchek and Duncan Rogan were already on Garren's vid screen. Josef was on the screen as well, in a second window. She joined Garren, standing slightly behind him at his desk.

Rogan said, "Josef sent an initial report, which we've read."

Tarm looked at Shaine. "Is Morgan all right?" he asked.

Shaine nodded. "She'll be fine. A few bad laser burns, but Dr. Nguyen took care of it. She's sleeping in the infirmary now, and I'll bring her back to quarters in a couple of hours or so."

Tarm's tight-lipped nod told her that he wasn't happy.

Shaine addressed her question to Josef. "When I left Security, Lenz wasn't talking. Any changes?"

"No. He's sitting in his cell, very quiet."

Rogan asked, "Have you interrogated him at all?"

Josef said, "By the books, Mr. Rogan. We read him his rights. We asked him questions. He refused to say anything. It's all in the report and the recordings."

Rogan lifted a dark brow. "You could have been a bit more forceful."

Josef frowned. "We did what we could. Our legal option is to turn over Lenz and all the evidence to the Out System Authorities."

Rogan muttered, "Send him to me and I'll get some answers out of him."

Maruchek turned a dark glare on him. "Enough."

Shaine asked, "Josef, have our people found anything yet? Was there anything in Lenz's belongings? Anything we can try to track?"

"Very little. He had a personal comp pad, but other than standard applications, not much on it. He didn't even have a mail program running. Dr. Nguyen got a DNA sample, which will probably tell us more about who he really is than anything else we have."

Maruchek said, "At the very least, he can be charged with the attempted murder of Friday and Morgan."

Shaine said, "Kathryn Leer was in the line of fire as well. We don't actually know who he was shooting at. He gave no names."

Maruchek frowned, his expression grim. Rogan glared. Josef said, "That about sums it up."

Rogan snapped, "How in the hell did you let this happen, Wendt?"

"He passed all our background checks. The guy's record is clean. Ellerand couldn't even find anything on him. He had faked finger and palm prints. You tell me how the fuck we'd have caught the synth-skin gloves without a full diagnostic medical check when he came aboard? All his records matched. Nothing set off any alerts."

Tarm cut them off with a slice of his hand. "Enough arguing. When will you be sending Lenz and the data back to Moon Base?"

Josef said, "There's a shuttle coming in late tomorrow to pick up Ms. Leer and her people. We can send Lenz back on that shuttle with a couple men to keep an eye on him and the evidence."

Shaine said, "The alternative would be to send our emergency shuttle back sooner. But I don't think that's necessary."

Maruchek said, "Send him on the shuttle with Kathryn and her people. Make sure the OSA knows he's on his way."

Shaine nodded. "Done."

Rogan said, "Find out what his ties are to Abraham's people."

"We'll continue to investigate, but with no further leads, I don't know how much we'll come up with. As Andy Lenz he has no ties to the colony. If his DNA can identify him, maybe there will be a link, but until we get that back, we don't know."

The call ended shortly after that. Shaine headed back to the infirmary, her mind moving faster than her feet. It drove her crazy to know she probably had a way to find out more about Andy Lenz. Friday knew the way into the colony's computer network. Unfortunately, she didn't want Friday going back into that system. First of all, it was illegal. Second, she didn't want Friday taking the chance of getting caught. Third, she knew she was a fucking hypocrite for wanting to use an illegal back door to find out who the hell Andy Lenz was.

Friday was positive she'd seen him at the colony. Shaine had believed her from the start, but without any proof, her hands had been tied. She should have just brought him in. She strode past the hallway to the infirmary and jogged down to ops. She gave the on-duty security members a quick wave and locked herself into her office.

Sitting down at her desk, she opened an encrypted com channel. The vid screen cleared and Shaine grinned at a disheveled-looking Kyle Ellerand. His hair was going in a hundred directions and he was rubbing sleep out of his eyes. He glared at her.

"This better be good, Wendt," he muttered.

She smiled. "How would you feel about doing some hacking for me?"

His mood shifted instantly and he grinned. "I think I would feel very good about it," he replied.

"Okay, this is the deal."

CHAPTER THIRTY-FIVE

Morgan woke late in the morning, slowly swimming up to consciousness. The first thing she noticed was that the painkillers had worn off, because the burns on her upper arm and shoulder were throbbing in time with her pulse. The second thing she noticed was that she was alone in bed. She frowned. She remembered Shaine waking her earlier to give her another round of painkillers.

Friday's cot was empty, the blanket thrown haphazardly up over the pillows. Morgan hoped Friday was following orders and had someone from security with her wherever she'd gone.

She stretched tentatively and untwisted from the quilt she'd wrapped around herself. Overall, she didn't feel too bad. Favoring her right side, she pushed herself to a sitting position and swung her legs over the side of the bed with a groan. She reached up to push her bangs out of her eyes and couldn't stifle the squeak that passed her lips when she lifted her right arm.

Time to find the sling Lei had given her so she wouldn't try using her damned arm again. She glanced at the chron on the wall. They were supposed to be doing the final part of the interview today. Shaine made the executive decision that the final section of the interview would be done on a closed set in the warehouse. Metlend wasn't happy about it from an artistic point of view, but apparently he was spooked enough from the previous day's incident that he didn't put up much of a fight. Morgan thought Metlend could have fought all he wanted, but he wasn't going to budge Shaine from her decision.

Morgan was relieved not to have an audience. Her nerves felt raw and prickly. Being shot at was unnerving, even if the intended target may have been Friday and not her.

It made her worry about the future. Was her life with Shaine going to be a series of dangerous situations? Was her newly discovered birth family going to make her a target for the rest of her life? How in the hell could she live her life constantly looking over her shoulder? Even so, it was better to be always running with Shaine than without her. She couldn't even fathom life without her.

She shook off the thoughts and decided to take a shower. Dr. Nguyen said she'd sealed the burns from water, so showering was okay.

As she started to struggle out of the button up pajama top, the door to their quarters slid open and Shaine walked in holding two thermos mugs and carrying a small grocery sack.

"Honey, wait, let me help you."

Morgan sighed, relieved to see her partner. She'd been about to get seriously frustrated with being one-handed and not very flexible. "Thanks." She sniffed the air.

Shaine smiled and kissed her as she started undoing the buttons on the pajamas. "I ran out for coffee and doughnuts," she said. "I didn't figure you'd be up before I got back."

Morgan nodded and let Shaine gently remove her shirt, wincing as she lifted her arm a little bit.

"Sorry," Shaine murmured. "I'll get the painkillers, okay? Is it pretty bad?"

"It burns and throbs, but I'll live," Morgan said. "Food and coffee should help a lot. I was going to shower, then go see Doc Nguyen."

Shaine asked, "Shower first or food first?"

"Shower, I think, since I'm already half-naked." Morgan grinned and leered at Shaine. "Maybe you can help, hmmm? I seem to be having issues undressing."

Shaine grinned. "Oh, I think I can manage that," she chuckled. She traced gentle fingers lightly over the clear nu-skin dressing covering the burns on Morgan's right shoulder.

Morgan shivered at the touch and felt a flush of warmth flow to her center. Her shoulder ached but her nipples were hard and ached in a different way.

Shaine trailed her fingers down to Morgan's breasts. Morgan sucked in air as Shaine's hands drifted down her sides. Shaine dropped to her knees as she hooked her fingers in the waistband of Morgan's boxers and pulled them down. Morgan felt the goose pimples follow the paths of Shaine's warm hands down her legs.

Shaine looked up at her, green eyes darkened with desire. "You are so beautiful, Morg," she murmured.

Morgan swallowed, used her good hand to grab a fistful of Shaine's shirt and pull her back to her feet. Shaine rose gracefully. Morgan yanked on the shirt. "Off," she said. "Now."

Shaine mock saluted. "Yes, ma'am," she whispered, and pulled her tunic over her head, leaving her upper body bare. Morgan never tired of the view. Small firm breasts, solid muscular abs, strong shoulders and arms.

Shaine kicked off her boots, pants, boxers and socks, then folded Morgan into her arms.

Morgan sighed, melting into the skin-on-skin contact, the heat of Shaine's body, the strength and hardness of muscle and the softness of her skin. She leaned up for a kiss, and Shaine teased her lips with her tongue.

Morgan pulled Shaine's head down with her good arm, deepening the kiss. Desire washed through her. She slid her tongue against Shaine's, wanting more. Needing more.

Shaine's large hands cupped her ass, pulling her close, holding her up as Morgan wrapped her legs around Shaine's waist. She could feel the wet heat as she pressed her center against Shaine's abdomen.

Shaine didn't break the kiss as she carried Morgan into the tiny bathroom. Still holding Morgan against her, she reached into the sonic shower and turned it on, turning up the heat setting on the lamp and the steamer.

Morgan pressed harder into Shaine. Her sore arm was trapped safely between them, her other arm wrapped around Shaine's neck.

Shaine stepped into the shower and the warm steam hissed around them, enhanced by the heat lamp above. Shaine moved her lips down Morgan's neck, her hands kneading Morgan's ass. Morgan moaned. Shaine pressed Morgan's back against the shower wall, and Morgan let one leg down, finding her footing, but keeping her other leg wrapped around, giving Shaine access. Any pain she felt disappeared as Shaine slid inside her, filling her.

Morgan gasped and thrust against Shaine's hand. "More," she breathed.

Shaine captured her lips again and increased the force and speed of her plunging fingers. Morgan felt the wave building and pushed hard against Shaine. Shaine's thumb slid against her clit and Morgan cried out against Shaine's mouth as she came, clinging to Shaine as her body shuddered with pleasure. Her knees went rubbery, and Shaine held her up, kissing her face, holding her close until the spasms stopped.

The hot spray blew lightly against them.

Shaine whispered into Morgan's ear, "I love you so much."

Morgan felt tears joining the dampness on her face. "I love you too." She felt as though her heart might explode with love. She buried her face against Shaine's shoulder.

Shaine supported her with one arm and rubbed her back with her other hand, murmuring quiet assurances against her damp hair.

Morgan wasn't sure how long they stood that way. Eventually they finished showering. Shaine helped Morgan dress, and they lingered over coffee and pastries before Shaine walked Morgan to the infirmary. As they approached the med center, Shaine said, "I really need to go down and check on the prisoner. Will you be okay on your own? I'll meet you down in the warehouse for the filming."

Morgan smiled. "I'm good."

Shaine hugged her carefully, and Morgan returned a slightly more forceful one-armed hug and leaned her head against Shaine's chest. "Thank you for earlier," she said softly.

Shaine gave her a quick kiss. "Thank *you*," she said, and slipped away down the hall.

Morgan watched her for a few moments before turning to palm the door.

* * *

After her stop at the infirmary, Morgan walked slowly to the warehouse, thinking she should have grabbed an indoor skimmer. Her shoulder throbbed and pinched under her clothes, probably because of Dr. Nguyen's ministrations. The energy she'd had in the shower with Shaine was long gone. Maybe it was the painkillers wiping her out. Maybe it was because it just hurt that damned bad, and her body needed sleep to heal.

As the door opened, Morgan trudged inside the warehouse and looked around. The stage had been set up just to the left of the entrance. All the lights and cameras were set up around a couch and a chair. The vid monitors and soundboard were set up on a worktable, and Metlend and a couple of the techs crowded around the controls. Kathryn Leer sat in Howard's makeup chair, but they were just talking and drinking coffee and it appeared her makeup had already been done.

Morgan crossed the floor to where Friday stood off to the side with Del and Joe Hailey.

Del looked her up and down as she approached. "You look like shit, Rahn."

"Thanks. I feel like shit, so it's appropriate."

Friday gave her a hug. Morgan returned it as best she could, not even minding that it hurt like a bitch when Friday hugged too hard. "I gotta sit down, you guys."

Joe grabbed a stackable chair from behind one of the worktables. "Sit, kid."

"Thanks." She sank onto the chair with a sigh of relief and leaned back, closing her eyes for a few seconds. She really wasn't feeling like being interviewed, even if it was only a short segment.

Metlend and Kathryn walked over to join them. Kathryn gave Morgan a concerned once-over. "How are you doing?" she asked. "Are you up for this?"

Morgan nodded. "Sore and tired, but I'm okay to finish the interview." She managed a brave smile. "Are you guys all doing okay?"

Kathryn grinned. "We're all fine. Of course, we weren't shot." She turned her smile on Friday. "What about you, Friday? How are you feeling today?"

Friday's smile was somewhat less excited than it had been the previous day but there was a hard determination in her blue eyes. "I'm not that easily scared off," she said. "I've come this far, and I'm not going to stop now."

Morgan grinned proudly at her. Del slapped the teen's shoulder. "You said it kid. Never show 'em they won. You are one tough cookie."

Friday flushed and her smile intensified.

Kathryn said, "You're both brave, and I'm glad we're going to finish the interview. I want to be able to show the world that you're both really special, strong women."

Morgan said quietly, "I'm not special. Friday's the special one. She's a super-smart, talented person, and given the chance she's going to go far."

Kathryn clapped her hands together. "Let's get going then," she said decisively. "Rog, get everyone on set and ready to go."

* * *

Later that evening, Morgan stood with Shaine and Josef at a small portal in the warehouse, watching the chartered supply shuttle fire up its turbo engines and surge down the short runway outside the temporary dome. It lumbered for a couple seconds before it lifted off the ground and rumbled into the sky, taking with it yet another episode of their lives.

Morgan felt an odd sense of finality and relief knowing that Andy Lenz was on that ship under the watchful guard of Del, Lukas and two others. They also had the sealed evidence case. One more threat eliminated. She wondered when there would be another, but didn't have the energy to pursue the thought. It would happen, or it wouldn't.

Kathryn Leer and her crew had left on the shuttle as well. Morgan was glad to have had a chance to say goodbye to her, and to thank her again for making the interview so painless. Friday sent along her thanks, but didn't want to be in the vicinity when security brought Andy Lenz down to the shuttle. Morgan understood. She'd kept her distance when they'd escorted him to the airlock, purposely staying out of his direct line of sight.

Shaine's com buzzed as they watched the shuttle lights disappear into the stars. Morgan raised a brow at Shaine in a silent question. Shaine mouthed, "Kyle Ellerand," as she tapped the com and engaged her earbud rather than the speaker. She greeted him, adding, "Let me get to my office and I'll call you back."

She listened to the reply and nodded. "Okay. Give me about half an hour." She closed the connection and said, "Let's get Friday. Kyle might have something on Lenz. Josef, you too. Meet us in my office."

* * *

Shaine had her monitor split, with Ellerand in one window and the document that he'd sent in the other. Morgan, Friday and Josef crowded around her desk.

Friday knelt in front, leaning toward the monitor as she studied the second window, slowly scrolling through a series of stills taken by a surveillance camera in the colony. "That's him. I'm sure of it," she said. She sent a suspicious glance at Kyle Ellerand. "Where'd you get these?"

He smiled. "For me to know and you not to, kid," he replied easily.

She stuck her tongue out at him.

He continued, "Obviously, this isn't going to be allowable in court, since I've got no warrants, but someone could follow up on it and go through legal means to get the information."

Shaine nodded in agreement.

Ellerand continued, "Nice thing about shoddy network security is that you can do a lot of random digging around in people's stuff. The name Lenz used at the colony is Bart Michaels. Not sure if that's another alias. I found the most info about him in communications between Abraham and Daniel John. The transcripts are with the data I sent.

"Michaels touted himself as a private undercover investigator. His thing was blending in and not being noticed. Having no prints made him that much more untraceable."

Friday asked, "How'd he lose his fingerprints?"

"He got caught in a chemical spill that killed at least thirty others. He got chemical burns all over his hands. Apparently he nearly died from inhaling the fumes. He got religion when he was recovering and ended up joining the Unified Martian Temple. He was a member of the church for quite a while before Abraham discovered him and hired him to investigate a couple of people he wanted to bring into the fold."

Shaine said, "Okay, that all makes sense. But it doesn't get us any closer to hanging him. Other than the fact that we have him on tape shooting at Morgan and Friday."

Kyle grinned and held up his hands. "I know. It gets more interesting. Abraham was pissed as hell about the mining facility being built so close to his colony. He wanted Mars, or at least that piece of it, for himself. There are documents and communications that suggest he wanted to spread the colony out so that Mann-Maru would have to buy land from him. There are records of him inquiring about buying more land for expansion. The problem is, the planet is in trust of the Out System Government, so there isn't commercial land available unless the OSG grants the land. OSG wasn't interested in dealing with Abraham and shot him down outright.

"So Abraham sent Michaels back to Moon Base to get on one of the work crews going to the new site. Michaels was supposed to wait for Abraham to tell him what to do. I don't know what Abraham actually had planned. Daniel John talked vaguely about wiping out the whole mining site."

Morgan said, "I thought Lenz had no outside contact while he was here."

"He didn't. He was supposed to just wait for orders. By the time he arrived at the mining site, Friday was already there. It's not clear, but I'd guess he decided to take the matter into his own hands."

"Maybe he realized Friday recognized him and he panicked," Shaine suggested.

Ellerand shrugged. "I sent all the documents to you. The important parts are bookmarked, so they're easy to find. One thing's for sure, these guys are not smart. I don't know why they insist on keeping written journals and traceable records. Idiots. Maybe they thought being on Mars would insulate them. They had everything encrypted, but it only took me about three minutes to crack it." He shook his head. "Man, a child could've done it."

Friday muttered, "No kidding."

Ellerand laughed. "I gotta go. I'm already late for a meeting with Barill about something or other."

"Thanks, Kyle."

He shrugged. "No problem. Later, ladies, Josef."

He killed the connection, and his window went blank.

Shaine and Morgan exchanged glances. Josef scratched his head. Shaine said, "Another nail in Abraham's coffin."

Josef shrugged. "Possible. It's all disallowed evidence."

Friday muttered, "As long as he goes to jail, I'm happy. Fucking bastard."

Shaine raised at brow at the language, and Friday scowled. "Just speaking the truth."

Morgan asked, "What are you going to do with the data he sent? You can't really send it to the authorities."

"I'll send it to Maruchek's lawyers. They can get someone to start a legitimate investigation. If they do it right, they can tie this guy to Abraham."

Friday asked, "Do you suppose they're going to want me to testify in person at some point?"

Shaine shrugged. "If there's a trial, it's a good possibility," she admitted. "But we'd be there with you. We'd never let you go by yourself, Fri. I'm guessing it's more likely to be settled out of court. For Michaels, it could go either way. Depends on how he pleads. If he pleads guilty, they won't bother with a full court trial."

"You guys really promise to be there?"

Morgan hugged her hard with her good arm. "We'll be there. Promise."

Friday grinned. "You guys are the best."

CHAPTER THIRTY-SIX

Morgan used the remote to turn on the vid screen. Friday had moved the end table from the other side of the room and put the vid screen on top of it. Shaine and Morgan settled on the bed, leaning against the wall with their legs stretched out. Friday was on the floor in front of the bed, wrapped in a blanket and holding a bowl of chips.

The rec center down the hall was packed with just about everyone who wasn't on shift, but Morgan, Shaine and Friday decided to watch Kathryn Leer's interview on the small vid screen in their quarters.

Morgan shifted to get comfortable. Even after a week, she was still using the sling to keep her arm immobile. She made sure Shaine was on her good side so she could lean in and cuddle. She pulled the quilt up over their legs and twined her fingers with Shaine's. She wanted—needed—the contact. She didn't admit to being nervous about watching the interview, but Shaine seemed to know anyway, and squeezed her hand.

The show opened with eye-catching footage filmed from the shuttle's cockpit as they flew over the construction-site and swooped down to the red gravel for a landing. Kathryn's smooth contralto introduced the show and described the setting. They showed a group of construction workers outside on the site grounds, the geologists in the lab, people lounging around the rec room and eating in the cafeteria. Morgan thought they did a good job of making the place seem relatively hospitable. After the intro and a commercial break, Kathryn introduced Morgan.

Morgan frowned. It was bizarre seeing herself. She wondered what people would think. Shaine patted her hand. Morgan leaned into Shaine's side and rested her head on her shoulder. Shaine slid an arm around her, pulling her close.

Shaine said quietly, "You look good, baby."

"I look like I'm going to throw up."

"No you don't."

Morgan sighed.

Shaine whispered, "I love you."

Morgan cuddled closer, watching herself talk to Kathryn Leer, answering questions about her life, her family and the sudden discovery of her true birthright. They discussed how she didn't want to change or become someone she wasn't because of the sudden fortune and fame. It seemed a familiar theme lately, as did her plea for the media to leave her alone to live her life.

God, I sound like a damned whiny baby, she thought. At least the plea was an honest one.

When Kathryn introduced Friday, the feel of the interview changed. Morgan was surprised by the interaction between herself and Friday. She hadn't realized how protective she was of the younger woman. Or how the two of them interacted the way she'd imagined sisters would act.

Friday came across as comfortable, confident and happy. She talked excitedly about her intention to make something of her life and pursue her interests in 3D graphic arts and mechanics. Her young face lit up with the possibilities. The obvious admiration and fondness she felt toward Morgan and Shaine was evident any time she mentioned them.

The interview progressed to the point where Bart Michaels, a.k.a. Andy Lenz, started shooting at the stage.

Even though she knew it was coming, Morgan jerked as the laser blasts flew. She held her breath as she watched herself push Friday down and winced as the lasers hit her exposed shoulder. Had she not reacted, Lenz would have fried holes in Friday's head.

Shaine's form blurred across the screen, tackling a wide-eyed Kathryn Leer. There was panicked shouting and the popping explosions of the lights behind them before the screen faded to black for the next commercial break.

Morgan found herself shaking uncontrollably. It had been much closer than she'd thought. *Bloody freaking hell.*

Friday turned and crawled onto the bed, her face pale with shock and fear. Morgan pulled Friday between her and Shaine, hugging her close. Friday sobbed. Shaine wrapped both of them in her long arms, murmuring, "It'll be okay, Fri. It'll all work out, and we're here for you."

Morgan fumbled with the remote and turned off the vid screen. They'd seen enough.

They lay cuddled together for a long time before Friday finally shifted away.

Morgan asked, "You okay?"

Friday sniffled. "Yeah. Just shocking to actually see it." She frowned and played with the quilt. "It's weird, because at the time, I don't remember being scared. Now, all of a sudden, it's like, that guy was really trying to kill me." She shuddered.

Morgan patted her arm. "It's an unnerving feeling, I know."

"All because I can tell the world what assholes Abraham and his buddies are."

Shaine said quietly, "Knowledge is power. If you have it, you can use it as collateral, or use it against someone. Abraham knows that. That's why he's afraid of you. Because he can't control you."

"I don't want to run from him for the rest of my life."

"You won't have to," Shaine said. "One way or another, he'll leave you alone."

Morgan shot Shaine a look. The last time Shaine said that, she killed the man threatening Morgan's life. It reassured her that Shaine would be willing to do the same to protect Friday, though she had to admit it was a little frightening to know Shaine was capable of so much violence.

Shaine met Morgan's quick glance and smiled gently. "The law will put both Michaels and Abraham away for a long time. We've got a good case against both of them. If Maruchek's lawyers and investigators follow up on Michaels' involvement with Abraham, that's just more years that he'll be put away."

Friday wasn't convinced. "What if Abraham doesn't go to jail, though? What if he manages to buy his way out or something?"

Shaine's expression darkened. "He won't."

Friday frowned, then finally nodded, though she didn't look entirely appeased.

Morgan decided it was time for a change of subject and suggested that they find a grav-ball game on one of the sports streams. Everyone agreed and they watched for a while before Friday decided to turn in for the night. Ten minutes later, Friday curled up in her own bed with her comp pad, and was asleep shortly after that.

* * *

Late into the night, Shaine lay in bed with Morgan curled against her. Morgan's head rested on her chest, her good arm draped over Shaine's stomach while the other was nestled comfortably between them. Shaine sighed, completely content. She could hear Friday snoring softly in her cot against the far wall. She tightened her hold on Morgan, who sighed against her skin. Shaine kissed the top of Morgan's head.

"Mmmmm, what's that for?" Morgan murmured.

Shaine smiled into the darkness. "I love you."

"Love you too."

"I've been thinking. When we're done here, and after all the court stuff with Friday is over, let's build us a place near my folks' farm. Settle down there, where it's quiet. We can work the farm, I can maybe do some security work. You can maybe do some mechanic work. We can just chill, you know? Would you like that?"

Morgan shifted so they lay facing each other. Shaine could see Morgan's sleepy smile in the green glow of the night-light near the bathroom door. Morgan said softly, "Yeah, I'd like that. Can we have a couple extra rooms? For Friday if she stays with us, and maybe my dad, if he comes to visit?"

"Definitely."

Morgan grinned and leaned in for a long, leisurely kiss.

Shaine lifted Morgan onto her chest, holding her close. Damn, it felt good, even if Morgan's sling dug into her side. She knew it might be a while before they'd finally be able to settle down and have some time to themselves, but at least she knew they both wanted that. She closed her eyes with a sigh.

Morgan asked, "You okay?"

"It scared the hell out of me to see that shooting again. I don't know what I'd do if I lost you."

Morgan wriggled closer, nuzzling her skin. "I'm not going anywhere."

Shaine let go of Morgan for a moment and reached up to remove one of the two chains she wore around her neck. She slid it over Morgan's head.

Morgan squinted through the gloom at the titanium dog tag hanging from the silver rope chain. She traced the deep engraving of Shaine's name and service number and touched her lips to the skin-warmed tag.

"Marry me, Morgan. Be with me forever."

Morgan met her gaze, gray eyes wide. "Forever. Yes."

Shaine captured her lips in a hard, passionate kiss before pulling regretfully away. She wasn't going to make love to Morgan with Friday in the room. She smiled. "I love you so much."

Morgan clutched the dog tag in her hand and murmured, "I feel like we can finally stop running. I feel like I'm already home."

Shaine wrapped her arms around Morgan. Her heart felt so full. They held each other tightly, nestled together under the heavy quilt, cocooned in the warmth of their love.

Bella Books, Inc.

Women. Books. Even Better Together.

P.O. Box 10543
Tallahassee, FL 32302

Phone: 800-729-4992
www.bellabooks.com